ESCAPE

Invasion of the Dead
Book 3

OWEN BAILLIE

ISBN: 1507540892
ISBN-13: 978-1507540893

Copyeditor: Monique Happy
Proofreader: Sara Jones
Cover design by Clarissa Yeo
www.yocladesigns.com

ACKNOWLEDGMENTS

Thank you to Kim Richardson for her brilliant insights, plot suggestions and thorough analysis of all story aspects. To Joe Barker once again for his keen eye and attention to detail. To Karen Dziegel for her prompt and precise feedback, especially about Blue Boy, and to DeLinda Giles for her excellent observations and reminding me about the importance of backstory with some outstanding examples. To the crew at Phalanx Guild Press, thanks for your support, advice, and motivation. Great to be on board with you guys and looking forward to more success all round.

Thank you to Monique Lewis Happy, my copyeditor at MHES, who turned this book around in record time during a difficult period. Thank you to Sara Jones for an amazing job proofing the story after further changes.

Once again, thank you to my wife, Donna, for her ongoing support and picking up the slack that allows me to spend more time writing. I simply could not do this without you. And to my three daughters for the chaotic fun you provide us.

And finally, thank you to all the wonderful readers who are still with this series. Knowing that you are engaged by the writing and story keeps me going every day. I hope this book is worth your time.

WARNING: Adults only. This book contain high-level violence and coarse language.

WAGGA WAGGA · YASS · CANBERRA

ALBURY

VICTORIA

· SEYMOUR

MELBOURNE

TASMANIA

3

ONE

CALLAN SAT SLUMPED in the seat with Blue Boy on his lap, one arm curled around the dog, staring out the window at the passing seas of yellow grass on either side of the scarred country road. A cold, contemplative silence had spread through the group. He had been here before, driving away from death, surviving somehow, by the thread of existence.

Most of them had endured. *Luck*. His grandfather, Jim—dead now—had once told him that luck was *everything*. People lived and died by luck. That's what it came down to really, didn't it? Whether any of them moved left or right amongst the gunshots, they were all so close to wearing a bullet in the head. The thought made him uneasy. *It's only a matter of time.*

Eric had run out of luck. Callan's gut tightened. Kristy and Evelyn had briefly described his death amongst the hundreds of zombies at the military facility. He left the campervan to investigate a noise and wound up facing a horde. What might have happened had he not warned the others? Callan wished he could have been there. He stuffed his knuckle into his mouth and bit down, welcoming the pain. It didn't work though. He'd never share another beer with the man; he would never again seek his counsel for guidance. They had only known each other for a short time, but Eric was impossible not to like. Even love, had time permitted. He missed him already. Even though their experience had been short, Eric had been one in a hundred, the kind of man that, in truth, Callan aspired to be: calm-headed, measured, and kind. Callan was gutted but knew Julie would be worse.

The campervan chugged along the winding road towards the main highway. Bodies littered the edges of the blacktop, their heads spread like jam through the wispy grass—probably shot by Steve and his crew. At least *they* were no more. The thought gave Callan some satisfaction. They weren't infected, and Callan hated that, but they had used all their luck. Zombies picked at the dead carcasses, chewing on severed limbs, their heads buried deep in organs. A week ago, Callan might have ordered Evelyn to pull over so they could shoot them. Not anymore. There were too many, and the last reserves of his strength had vanished in the climactic battle. Besides, to what point? Were they going to hunt down every zombie on the continent?

Part of him wanted that. The idealist. He recalled stopping with Dylan on Silvan Road, back in Albury, to kill the zombie who had been feeding on a cow. He swallowed a dry throat, suppressing the pain of the memory. Sherry had been alive then—Sherry, whom he had adored and idolized. She had been his girl for almost two years; he would have married her, and just before her death, she'd found out she was carrying his child. How he had wanted kids. That dream was dead now. Callan had told himself he didn't love her, that her treachery and the way she treated him didn't deserve it, but, in truth, he had loved her deeply, and his fall had been long and painful. He was probably still falling. Had it not been under such circumstances, had he found out about her affair with his best friend, Johnny, in the normal course of life, it might have taken him much longer to recover. Now though, with battles to fight and lives to save, he buried it in danger and necessity. But the root of pain would be there one day, for him to dig out and deal with, and the thought scared him more than the wretched monsters.

Blue stirred. Callan patted his head and the dog relaxed. Callan looked towards the front of the camper, to the stretch of dark, winding road beyond, and caught movement in the rearview mirror; Evelyn's eyes lingered on him for just a moment. It made him a little uncomfortable. What was it—admiration? Lust? Interest? He sensed all three, but his radar for such things had always been poor. It didn't matter. Even if there was a flicker of interest, he had no desire to fuel it. In another time and place, he might have chased the light, but nothing remained of him except a mass of numbness. She wasn't a girl he might normally notice, like Sherry, but there *was* something about her. She had joined them in unusual circumstances, after barely escaping the lunatic men at the Army base in Wagga Wagga. He admired her fight for survival and the way she cared for her son. She was pretty, too, in her own way—a woman who bloomed into a flower once you got to know her. *A nicer version of Sherry,* he thought.

They climbed another short peak and found a group of zombies wandering over the road ahead. Evelyn pulled the wheel left, swerving around the first stragglers, then wider and onto the shoulder, doing a good job of avoiding them. The last thing they needed was more damage to the van, or being forced to stop and engage in another confrontation.

Like a statue, the last feeder watched them pass. Callan lifted Blue off his lap and onto the floor, then stood, ignoring the physical and emotional pain. No doubt if he survived until tomorrow, the muscles he pulled and twisted today would cramp. His ears would hurt from the sound of gunshots. His heart would ache for an indefinable amount of time. Kristy and Sarah had patched his arm, reducing it to a dull throb. He supposed he was lucky to be alive.

Blue Boy arched his torso. Callan leaned over and rubbed his head, encouraging him to rest. The dog slumped back down, laying his head on the floor. Blue should have been dead. More than once. Callan recalled the dog's initial appearance in Albury, surviving alone on the streets until being adopted by Dylan's father before his death. Blue was tough and resourceful, although the possibility of infection

concerned Callan. What were the chances that dogs might be immune? He couldn't remember seeing an infected animal, and that gave him hope. He would do anything for the mutt. Was his ambush of Klaus too extreme? No. He had to be sure. He wouldn't risk it. The dog meant more to him than anyone, except Kristy.

Evelyn steered the camper around a long corner. Callan grabbed hold of the sink to steady himself, taking it all in; Dylan, Klaus, and Gallagher snuggled around the kitchen table, although only the latter two were in conversation. Jake and Sarah sat cross-legged on the top bunk, looking at books, trying to escape reality. Jesus, Sarah had almost died back at the Albury hospital. Now she had killed a man. There was no giggling or laughing as there had been. Kids were more adaptable than adults. Kristy sat in the passenger seat beside Evelyn, and Greg approached, balancing himself with ease from years of surfing. Dylan appeared to be most affected, aside from Julie, who remained in the bedroom with the curtains drawn.

Greg clamped a hand on his back. "Lucky. Very lucky."

They shook hands. "Nine lives, mate, nine lives." He nodded in Dylan's direction, and whispered, "How'd he go down there?"

"Great. I mean, we work well together. There was a moment though when…" Greg shook his head. "Never mind."

"What?"

"I thought… he was gone. I thought they had him. I went for the door and only turned around for a moment, and when I turned back, one of them had a hand around his leg and his mouth right there, so bloody close to Dylan, I thought *he's gone, get out of here.*"

Callan was frozen with anticipation. "What did you do?"

"I went back and grabbed him, of course."

"Did he get bitten?"

"Said he didn't."

"He doesn't seem too glad to be alive now."

"Maybe it's all caught up."

"Let me talk to him." Callan shuffled past Greg and slid onto the cushions beside Dylan. He lay back against the seat with his eyes closed, a forearm laid across his face. Klaus and Gallagher were scouring over a map of Victoria. "Hey, man. How you going?"

Dylan groaned but did not look up. "Alright."

"Sure? You seem quiet. I know this shit gets to me sometimes, too."

"Yeah."

"We survived again though, didn't we? We're still here."

Dylan removed his arm and sat up. His eyes were bloodshot, his expression slack. He looked beaten. "For how long, though? Chances are that one of us will be dead by the end of tomorrow. The odds are against us. Sooner or later, one of us has to die, right?"

Callan frowned. Dylan's self-composure was renowned. Even when his mother and father died, he'd maintained his self-control. Callan had admired that, adding to the growing respect for his former nemesis. What had tipped him over? Surely, it hadn't been the facility. Albury had been just as bad. Dylan seemed close to the edge. To stay alive, they needed him with a clear mind; what happened the next time they went into battle? He needed to know Dylan had their backs.

Callan glanced at Greg, who looked away. No help there. He had to be careful, here. Try and pry out what was bothering Dylan. He almost preferred the Dylan with whom he disagreed, the confident, measured man who had always been willing to argue a point.

"What is it, mate? I've never seen you this downcast."

"I'm just sick of it. Same thing every day. Will any of us even be alive tomorrow, or the day after? It's a waiting game. Who will be next?" Dylan lay back and closed his eyes.

Greg was staring at them. Callan wondered if there was more to it. Or perhaps it *was* just the same thing every day and it had finally caught up to Dylan. Callan had felt his own tenuous grip on life fracturing at times, but so far, he'd held on. His mother had often told him he was ignorant of the world, and that in times of stress, it would serve him well. Maybe this was one of those times.

Callan caught Gallagher's eye. He pushed himself out from behind the table and lurched towards the front of the van. Gallagher stood close.

"He's probably suffering a little PTSD. It was intense down there. None of you are trained for this. I'm surprised it hasn't affected you sooner."

"I guess."

"Things build up." Dylan hadn't moved. "Give him some time. He'll be alright." Callan hoped so. Dylan had been reliable. "We owe you," Gallagher said, tipping his head towards Klaus, who had moved to one of the bottom bunks. "Both of us. You may just have saved mankind today, or at least given them the best chance of beating this thing. You had any military training?"

"No. I could barely shoot a month ago. In fact, my father …" His thoughts trailed off. He hadn't thought about his mother or father for days. A pang of guilt surfaced. He'd been so adamant about checking their safety early on. Now, in their pursuit for life, they were almost forgotten. "My father always said I was a poor shot."

"Well, he'd have to change that opinion, I imagine."

Callan latched onto a seat as Evelyn swerved to miss another object. They rolled up and over the final incline, and the road ahead stretched on towards the horizon like a long, black carpet. They were edging closer to the main highway and would soon turn south towards Melbourne. Before that though, they wanted supplies—weapons and food—they barely had enough to last the night. They needed to find a town nearby that provided those things, but one that wasn't so overrun by feeders that they'd die trying.

Sobbing sounded from the back of the campervan. Julie pulled the curtains aside. She was crying, her eyes red and swollen. She kept wiping at them with a clumsy hand, trying to stop the tears. She reached the table and stopped. Nobody spoke.

Julie pointed at Callan. "You… you did this. It's your fault. If you hadn't convinced him to come on this damn adventure, we'd still be in Holbrook. I'll never forgive you for this."

Callan wanted to tell her that it wasn't he who convinced Eric to come along. It had been all Eric, searching for a way out. But he knew that such words would do nothing to appease her heartache. "I'm so sorry about Eric. He was a fine man and we will miss him immensely. I wish I could take it back. I really do." Julie pressed her trembling lips together. He felt her pain. He thought about comforting her, but her sobbing grew and she turned for the bedroom and drew the curtain across the doorway. Callan watched her leave. He felt the burden of leadership settle on his shoulders again. He did not enjoy it. He was no leader. He knew no more than anyone else. He made it up off the cuff as he went along, and he rarely got it right. People had been injured and died. His heart ached for all of them.

TWO

"SHOULD WE CHECK on her?" Kristy asked.

Evelyn shook her head. "No. Leave her be. There's nothing we can say right now that will make it any better. She just needs time."

Kristy knew that if anyone understood Julie's pain, it was Evelyn. Callan had mentioned that she lost her husband prior to the plague. "I'm worried about her though."

"I'll talk to her later."

"Are you right to drive?" Kristy asked. Evelyn nodded from behind the driver's seat. Kristy sat beside her. "I can take over at any time. Just let me know."

"Keep talking to me. I'm trying not to look at the bodies on the side of the road. Trying not to think about what we just went thorough. How are *you* going with that?"

"Better than I thought I would a week ago. We've been through so much now, I'm afraid to say, but it's almost become normal. You're lucky you missed most of it, being in the shelter. It's all coming strong at you right now, but you'll adapt. We all do."

Evelyn tightened her hands around the wheel. "I hope so. I hope I'm alive long enough to."

Kristy thought Evelyn had as good a chance as any of them. The woman didn't appreciate her own strength. There was a deep fortitude, a determination to survive. Had Evelyn saved Kristy's life during the battle? She thought she might have. Even before that though, Evelyn had saved herself and her son from certain doom in Wagga.

The heat shimmered over the blacktop. Kristy was glad for the air conditioning. They approached a heavy vehicle that had run off the side of the road. Feeders ate the former occupants of the truck that didn't look like zombies. Nobody asked to stop. Evelyn kept her foot down and the engine whirred, edging them closer towards town. The killers slowly disappeared in the mirror and the smell wafting in through the vents improved slightly.

While pleased to see cows and horses roaming the wide, yellow paddocks, Kristy wondered how long they would last without human intervention. They would die off eventually. At least they weren't sick yet. Even Blue Boy, who had probably come into contact with the virus before today, remained in apparent good health. It was something they couldn't know without proper blood work from a lab.

They reached the apex of the hill and she caught movement off to the right at a rickety farmhouse. It might have been a man or woman, but they disappeared. She thought of telling the others, but what then? Would they stop? Would they impose their group on somebody else? No. They had purpose now. With Klaus on board, they had a destination. Purpose.

A green sign appeared on the roadside as they approached an intersection. It read YASS. GOULBURN. MELBOURNE. The camper slowed, and Evelyn guided it through the left turn.

"Head for Yass," Callan said, standing behind Evelyn. "They'll have a small hunting store, and, if we're lucky, a store with groceries."

Evelyn took a hand from the wheel and flexed it. "You okay?" Callan asked. She nodded and wrapped her fingers back around it. He reached out and placed a hand on her shoulder, smiling gently. Kristy saw affection in the smile that went beyond the general care and consideration Callan had shown of late. "It's okay. We're okay, for now. This is what happens. We fight, we survive, and move on."

12

"I know. I'm learning as we go."

"You're doing great. We're lucky to have you."

Kristy said, "You were amazing. Beyond amazing. I'm sure you saved my life."

Evelyn waved them off. "Stop it. Both of you. I'll lose my shit."

"Okay," Callan said. "Kris, is Dylan okay?"

"I don't know. Something's bothering him. Did he say anything at the Army base?"

"No. What about when he returned?"

Dylan wasn't the most talkative person on earth, but when she'd spoken to him after they'd returned, he'd been quiet and unresponsive. If Callan had noticed too, maybe there was more in it. "He was subdued. More than normal."

Dylan sat at the table with the others, but he wasn't engaged in the conversation. He looked worried. Either something had happened at the Army base, or… a thought struck her, sudden and painful. What if he no longer had feelings for her? What if he realized he'd made a mistake? *He slept with you, now he wants out.* Not Dylan. She shook off the idea, burying the knowledge that he wouldn't have been the first man to do such a thing. She would talk to him soon. But the burden of worry slipped over her. Something wasn't right. And she had to find out what.

THREE

LAUREN STOOD AT the apartment window, looking down onto the mess of Franklin Street. The half-eaten remains of a young male grinned up at her from the gutter. Once, she would have looked away, but it was all the same now. She was desensitized to the gruesomeness of death and the undead.

The heat was all around, almost tropical after last night's rain. She pushed sticky hair back from her forehead. Beyond the body, the old market buildings stood abandoned, tempting with their treasures. She knew what else lay inside, urging them out of hiding. In the distance, up the road, which had only weeks ago been covered in afternoon traffic, they wandered. Not the smart, aggressive ones, but the passive, stupid kind, although there were enough of them to eat their way through the city, which she suspected at that very moment they were doing.

They were on the seventh floor of an apartment building on the corner of Queen and Franklin Street in the north section of Melbourne's central business district. Lauren and her friend, Claire, rented the place, but two had become eight, now, after an elderly couple had joined them from a lower level a day ago. In the apartment next door, the generator pumped on, providing valuable electricity. Setting it up had been the one good thing Todd had done since the plague had come. He'd even managed to get the ventilation right so they didn't poison themselves with fumes.

Laughter drifted in from the lounge room. Todd and Lenny had spent the remainder of their time drinking. With the bottle shop attached to the convenience store downstairs, they had ample supply to last months. She supposed the girls were there too, enticing the boys with their tight clothes and parted legs.

From the white crib in the corner, the baby squawked. Harvey's dummy had fallen out, and his puckered lips searched for it. She plucked it up and slipped it back in. The lines on his forehead relaxed, and he drifted back into comfort. She watched him, adjusting the light wrap lower on his chest to cool him down. She had him in a sleeveless top and a nappy, trying to provide some relief from the heat. It appeared to be working; his sleep was generally still, aside from the constant dummy sucking. Lauren had avoided giving it to him in the beginning, but following the outbreak, she had abandoned the idea when he wouldn't settle. He slept better with it.

Watching him still brought a sense of amazement. He was only six weeks old, but already he had changed her life. She was busier now, and thinking of herself was always the last option. But she wouldn't change his life for anything. Having a baby had always been a goal, but she had imagined it under entirely different circumstances. She should have been spending time with her mother, going to breastfeeding classes, and starting off at a mothers' group, where other woman with newborns shared their stories and learned from the teachers. Instead, she was hiding out in an apartment building with a group of dislodged people, scratching for food and waiting for the dead to eat up the rest of the city. How long would they last? The thought made her feel sick, if only because her son's welfare was at risk. His father, her boyfriend, was useless. He'd done just enough to keep himself alive, and mostly that was due to luck. Now, he couldn't spare the time to help Lauren and preferred wasting time with Lenny and the stupid girls from the apartment on the level above. It pained Lauren to admit it, but the relationship was over—had been over for months, if she was honest. Part of her was glad, but she wondered how she was going to keep Harvey alive. It didn't matter. Lauren knew she would. She would do whatever it took to survive—for Harvey's sake. *Whatever it took.* And she knew her words were not fluff to make her feel better.

She wondered briefly about her parents and her brother, Dylan. The last communication with her father had been weeks ago. According to him, Dylan was off camping somewhere. Maybe he was still alive. Lauren had convinced herself they were all dead, for the sake of being able to move on.

The sound of an engine drifted in through the side window leading to Franklin Street. Occasionally, a vehicle would meander its way down the road, looking for safe passage through the city. The group decided early on to stay concealed, and it had worked so far, keeping them out of trouble.

A white wagon moved through the clutter, swerving between piles of debris and broken-down vehicles. Several feeble zombies picking at litter stumbled towards the noise. The vehicle slowed as the rubbish narrowed the road, its engine whirring as it scraped aside cars. It caught the tip of a grey sedan and stopped. One of the zombies slapped a hand on the side window.

From the yellow painted front of a travel agency, four more dead hobbled out through an open doorway, suddenly interested. *This is how it went,* Lauren thought. The other zombies—two more of which had just arrived—lurched away as if they might catch something. These new ones were not the feeble zombies that plagued most of the city. This lot were part of the growing number of faster, more capable killers that terrified her.

Grimy windows rolled down on the white sedan; the muzzles of a rifle and two pistols poked out. The blasts made Lauren flinch as they echoed along the street and rolled across the city. Gunshots were not uncommon. Two of the zombies dropped, but the remaining pummelled their fists through the windows and tried to seize the people inside the car. Another gunshot cracked and a third leapt backwards and fell onto the road with half its head missing.

With only one faster zombie remaining, a dozen of the slower kind emerged from hiding spots and descended on the car. Sensing greater trouble, the vehicle jerked forward, smashing into the debris. But the last crazy wouldn't give in. It reached inside the driver's window and yanked the person out by the throat like a rag doll. They hit the ground and skidded over the bitumen. A man in orange overalls, like those of a prison inmate, fought back, swinging his fists, striking the side of the zombie's legs. It released him and dropped to its knees. He stuck his hands up, but the thing brushed them aside and buried its face in his chest. Movement flashed from inside the car as the others battered against the glass. The door came open; more gunfire sounded, but the throng of feeders worked their way into the opening, pulling a woman clear, and then Harvey cried out, and Lauren turned away, her stomach curling.

He'd lost his dummy again. She picked it up with a shaking hand and slipped it between his tiny lips. He resumed suckling, oblivious to the horrors of the world outside.

Claire appeared at the doorway and entered. "Those fucking assholes have almost drunk all the booze, again." A clatter and crash sounded from the street. Claire went to the window. "Oh God. More of them?" Lauren couldn't look. "We're almost out of rice, too." Lauren nodded. "What does *that* mean?"

"It means I know."

"What are we gonna do? There isn't enough for everyone."

She wanted to tell Claire that her useless boyfriend could miss out, along with his friends, and the two girls they had let in from the other apartment, but something stopped her. Perhaps it was that everyone and everything else was spiralling down into degradation. The world was in the final stages of complete chaos. Lauren wanted to maintain some semblance of decency, even if it meant feeding people she disliked.

"We'll make it go around. But we'll have to go out at some point, maybe later tonight." The idea sent an icy touch over her skin. She had the baby, and therefore it provided immunity to going out, but the guys were drinking more each day, and might soon be incapable. Besides, last time they had gathered little of value for the greater group.

"Who's going to go? Nobody has the guts anymore."

She put a hand on Claire's arm. "We'll work something out."

"How can you be so calm about it? Why can't you be bossy, tell everyone what to do, like normal?" Her voice grew frantic. "We're going to die here, I know it."

Lauren had given up on being bossy. It hadn't worked, and she imagined herself having a breakdown from the stress if she didn't try harder to remain calm amongst all the shit that was going on. "You've been saying that since the moment this thing happened. We're not dead yet."

"It's going to happen though. One day, I'll be right. You'll see."

Lauren clenched her jaw. She glanced over at the crib. "Not me. Not Harvey. I'm not leaving him alone in *this* fucking world."

"What about the food?"

Lauren left the room, curling her finger for Claire to follow. In the lounge, Todd and Lenny were sitting beside the two interloper girls on the couch. Empty beer bottles littered the floor—some standing, others on their sides, the dregs staining the carpet. Once, she would have freaked out.

Todd slipped onto the floor, doubled over, trying to keep his beer can upright. Lenny lay back on the couch, his face red and pinched in hysterical laughter. Drunk again. Something was obviously funny, and by the way they looked at her when she entered, Lauren thought it might be about her.

"You guys look like you're having fun."

Todd rolled over onto his knees, glanced at Lenny, and burst out laughing. "You should try it some time. It might help." Lenny roared.

She had to fight the urge to punch Todd in the face. A glaze had slipped over his eyes, and they were now more bloodshot than the last time she'd spoken to him an hour ago. Her resentment and frustration surged, threatening to explode, merged with her shame at ever sleeping with Todd, for giving him her time, and thinking for the three minutes it took to make Harvey, that he *might* be different. She wanted to blame Seth, her previous boyfriend, the one she should have been marrying and having children with, but in truth that failure was still her fault. Whatever it came down to, she had made the choices. Lauren still remembered her father's words from a time when she must have been fourteen.

"Remember this," he had said, sitting on the end of her bed after her boyfriend had gone home. Lauren was still buzzing. They had spent hours trading wet, over-zealous kisses, stopping every ten or so seconds in case one of her parents opened the door. "Only you can make choices for yourself. We can give you all the good advice in the world, but it will come down to you deciding in a moment what's to

19

be done. *Choices* determine our lives. Whether you get in the car with the drunk driver, or whether you… sleep with that boy who's pressuring you. Every action has a consequence—some you can't take back."

Jesus, he had been so right, she thought. Sleeping with Todd had been an impromptu action on the back of too many beers and the debacle that was Seth. She recalled thinking the moment before whether it was the right move. *Stupid woman.* It hadn't been, and she was paying the price. Choices had to be made now though. She could push Todd's behavior aside and deal with it all herself, or force him to pitch in and help. Make him accountable, as they had taught her in one of her management classes at university. Thinking about her father's sensibility had calmed her.

"Todd, I need you to cut the drinking for a bit and help get this place more organized. We're out of food and I only have a half a tin of baby formula left."

Todd frowned, surprise quelling his humor. "What? Out? But we—"

"There's none. I know it might come as a surprise, but there are ten adults living in this apartment now. Food doesn't go far when there are that many mouths to feed."

"You can't count the baby," he said in a whiny, slurred voice.

"I'm not counting the baby, dipshit," Lauren said, grinding her teeth.

More laughter squeezed out. Todd didn't bother trying to keep it in. He'd never taken life seriously. Most things were one big joke. He ran for the booze at the first sign of trouble. She found that out early. When she'd told him she was pregnant, he disappeared for two days. She got a call from the police station early one morning asking her to come and collect him. The truth was that they were better off without him. He offered no value to the group—he had no skill that someone else couldn't provide. The only thing keeping Lauren from kicking him out was the fact he was her baby's father.

She bit down on her emotions. "You have to go at some point, Todd."

Lenny screwed up his face. "We went last time."

Claire stepped forward. "But you didn't get enough food. You admitted that. You promised to go back out again and get more."

Lauren put a hand on her shoulder. "Feed the kids, and the oldest, first. Don't worry about me, or these two, if there's isn't enough." Claire appeared poised to protest, then nodded and left. Todd slunk back on the couch, rubbing his left leg. Lauren knew what was coming next. He was going to play the injury card. If he did that, she thought she might lose it.

"My leg's still sore," Todd said, grimacing. Lenny dropped his eyes. The two girls watched her, oblivious. "And there are zombies all over the place."

Lauren ground her teeth. His weakness had reached a low point. Her anger fled in the face of his attitude. But she had had enough. "The zombies will always be there. *We* went out while they were there. Get over it." He sneered at her. "If you can't go out and get some decent food for all of us, Todd, I want you out. You can take your friends and leave." He stared back at her, eyes wide, full of disbelief.

"You can't do that."

"It's my apartment."

He glanced at Lenny. "What if we don't want to go?"

This time, Lauren raised her eyebrows, almost inviting him to try. In truth, Todd and Lenny could overpower them, but he knew she would always get him back, somehow. She wasn't going to stand there and argue though. "You've got until dark to go out and get something." Then she turned and walked away, waiting for him to shoot a smart remark, but it never came.

FOUR

JACOB DROVE DOWN the Hume Highway with a mouth full of bitterness, choking the wheel as he relived the previous night in Campbelltown. The blazing eye fell slowly in the west, taking with it some of the heat that had suffocated them for much of the day. He wouldn't be sorry to see it disappear. The car had no air conditioning, and the hot wind did little to cool them.

It hadn't even been twenty-four hours and he was stuffing the memories deeper, trying to forget them, the way he had this entire business from the beginning. He thought back to life before the plague, when such heat would have driven him to finish another long day on the tools and seek the cool blue waters of their swimming pool. Jacob had run his own successful plumbing business, employing more than two dozen men on varying sized commercial sites around Sydney. He had built it from nothing, with a legendary work ethic, sacrificing earnings in the early years to form a reputation for value amongst a most competitive industry. It had come at a cost though. His first marriage had broken down, and he had lost a daughter in the process, although he had long since buried the burden and disappointment of that. Funny how things worked out though—without the plague, he might not have stumbled upon the chance to repair that disaster.

Jacob lowered the window a few more turns and closed his eyes to the heat. At least it would keep him awake. Rebecca had drifted off beside him. She had fought heavy lids for hours, staring off at the passing terrain. Their lack of conversation hadn't helped, but even after several weeks, she would not engage him in anything more than the necessary discussion. Even then, her questions and responses were terse.

So he drove on, waiting for the battered blue wagon they had to shit itself and just come to a stop on the side of the road. After the beating at Tarcutta, it had limped along at half pace. He didn't dare push it too hard, although it helped conserve fuel. They hadn't been able to find any, and it felt like they were on their last legs. He'd pegged Seymour, a sizeable town north of Melbourne, as the place to reach. Had to be *something* there—fuel, food, maybe even a comfortable place to rest; even another vehicle. They were plentiful, but most didn't have the keys, and nobody knew how to get them started without.

He kept glancing at Rebecca. Some of the others called her Bec, but she had not yet told him to call her that, as though he hadn't yet earned that right. He supposed that was fair. He loved the name Rebecca. After all, he had given it to her.

Her eyes opened and she frowned. "What?"

Jacob suppressed a smile. She reminded him of her mother. "Nothing."

It was true. He *was* just looking. Making up for lost time. All the years he'd spent away from his daughter had vanished in the sands of time. He could never get them back, and it filled him like a sickness. What he could do was make the most of every moment from here on, even if she still detested him. It was a miracle he had her back, sitting beside him now in a world gone to ruin as they drove towards an unfamiliar city and the wispy promise of help. She was all he had now, really. Monica, his second wife, had perished at Campbelltown. The memory ached his heart, and it took every bit of willpower to stop the image forming in his mind.

Jacob held his breath, willing the pain away, grinding his jaw until it ran up into the side of his head. He imagined taking the knowledge of his wife's death and wrapping it up in a bundle, shoving it inside a box, and closing the lid. It worked, as it always did, and the thought drifted. During his brief Army days, they said he was the most competent at compartmentalization. Monica had sometimes called him cold-hearted. That made him chuckle. He thought of Arty, and his insistence that there were facilities and people in Melbourne who could help fight the virus. After Campbelltown, Jacob had to make a decision about where to go. North was out—they had witnessed the destruction firsthand, although some of the others from the group had gone that way. South was their only option, and although he suspected Melbourne was going to be in a similar state to Sydney, they would stick to the outskirts and find their destination. Beyond that, Melbourne was springboard to Tasmania, and he had heard from a man in Yass that people were gathering there to make the crossing. Bass Strait was a treacherous body of water though, and whoever made the trip would require a competent person to skipper the boat. Jacob held little hope of finding someone, but that didn't deter him from the notion.

He looked into the side mirror for the tenth time just to make sure the battered four-wheel drive was still following. It was there, some distance behind, dusty red, cracked windscreen, two men peering at them through the glass. Four of them. *Four out of twenty-two.* They'd lost some of the finest people Jacob had ever known. Monica, Arty, Gary Edney, and of course, his good mate Samuel. The thought of the way he went out sent a shiver up Jacob's neck. Sure, some of them had to have survived, but who knew where they had gone. John and Sandy; their children, Greg and Amelia. Stuart, the butcher. He could go on, but knew it did no good. It just happened that the two that made it weren't what Jacob considered friends. They'd joined the group just south of

Sydney. His policy was always to let anybody who contributed tag along, and he hadn't turned folks away so far. But these men mostly kept to themselves, almost as if they were planning something. Samuel didn't trust them. It didn't seem fair. *Wasn't.* He wished he could change it, but what would he have done differently? Probably not stopped so close to the road. The service center had been enticing with its large awning and the shop, but the sentries had failed and it had cost them in the end. They all knew the risks though. Knew what this new life was like. Each day they ran the gauntlet of death by just staying alive. Sometimes he wondered how they would ever make a life for themselves again.

"How much further?" Rebecca asked, shifting into a more comfortable position. She was tinier than Jacob had expected given his large frame, although her mother had been petite. Rebecca had her curly blonde hair and narrow features, too, along with those blue, seductive eyes. What had she gotten from him? He would find out. *You need to spend time with a person to discover such things.*

"A while yet."

"We got anything else to eat?"

"Crackers. Staple diet of the new world."

She didn't smile. "Where we going?"

"Seymour."

"Never been there. You?"

"Long time ago. With your mother, actually." That silenced her.

She slumped, peering out the front window in thought. "Tell me about her. What you remember."

Despite all the time that had passed, he still remembered her vividly. Jennifer Jabowski was a beautiful woman—in Jacob's eyes, anyway, and that's all that mattered—attentive and obsequious. She was fearsome too, when unappreciated. Jacob had spent too much time trying to build his business

26

and not enough being a husband. That pushed Jennifer to look elsewhere for the love and attention that a woman required. Jacob put up little resistance, and *that* still burned away at him. But it wasn't Jennifer's fault. None at all. Still, he didn't feel like talking about it today.

"Maybe another time, okay?"

She settled back into the ripped leather seat in silence. Jacob thought about the potential towns they had passed in favor of Seymour. Wagga, Albury, Wangaratta. But there were reasons why he had foregone them all. They were more than lucky at Tarcutta, just south of the Wagga Wagga turnoff. The others wanted to stop at Wagga, and Jacob had almost taken the exit, but in the final moments, his foot gunned the accelerator past the intersection. It had almost cost them their lives. A blockade greeted them just beyond. What sort of people tried to take advantage of others in a situation like this? Men had lined the road with vehicles in an attempt to stop traffic and hijack people for whatever items of value they carried. They caught a gap in the corner of the blockade though; Rebecca had spied it. Jacob made for it and smashed through, metal screeching on metal, sparks flying. Following closely behind, the others penetrated a different section and drove with part of the front end missing. Remembering what the fellows from the other group said about Albury, Jacob kept driving. They added fuel at a service center and filled plastic bags from behind the counter with the last of the savory foods.

As Wangaratta approached, he had another bad feeling. Still, he left the Hume Highway and drove northwest along the Great Alpine Road towards the center of town. A long line of zombies trailed all the way back along the roadway and around a bend, beyond sight. They were a mix of fresh and old bodies, the withered skin and dark sunken eyes of the long undead, and the pale, unbroken flesh of the recently

27

turned. Jacob presumed they were migrating out of the town looking for fresh food.

"Please turn around," Rebecca said. Jacob thought that was a sensible idea. He braked, checking the rearview mirror to ensure that the others were doing the same, and pulled to the side. The red four-wheel drive did the same further back.

The closest zombie detected the vehicle and lurched at them. Jacob thrust the gear into reverse and drew back on the clutch, pressing the accelerator down simultaneously.

"Go," Rebecca said, eyes locked on the feeders. Two of them had closed in, and would be at the car in seconds. "Go!"

Braking again, Jacob guided the stick into drive and swung the wheel tight to the right. A *clunk* on the rear sounded their arrival. Body twisted, Rebecca leaned on the back of the seat, watching. Jacob caught them in the rearview mirror.

He slammed the pedal down, but the engine gurgled, and the car didn't respond. Terrified, he lifted his foot and repeated. This time the vehicle thrust forward, throwing them back. The two feeders fell forward where their support had been.

They scooted away and linked back onto the Hume Highway, vowing to keep to the main road for now.

On they drove as the afternoon sun drew towards the western horizon, their fuel diminishing, their stomachs calling for more than potato crisps and sweets. But Jacob dared not leave the main road again, despite protests from Phil and Tommy, the other two trailing in the vehicle behind. The choices were slim now—they needed to stop before Melbourne. That left Seymour, one of the bigger townships in the region, the last of decent size before hitting the outskirts of Melbourne. He wanted to ensure they had sufficient supplies and a belly full of food and drink. Who knew what they might face in the big city, even trying to remain on the outskirts. He decided then as they whirred along the blacktop, the tussock grass peering out from rock embankments at the base of gum trees, that they would stay the night in Seymour. He felt better having made the decision. They couldn't all be overrun, could they?

After Wangaratta, they zipped through Benalla and Violet Town. Rebecca piped up as they passed a hotel on their left and a string of dark shops on the right, separated from the main road by a line of trees. Smoke drifted in lazy columns from most of the buildings. Rotting bodies lay on the pavement. Another town gone to ruin. There didn't appear to be any zombies, but Jacob knew they were probably hiding nearby.

"Killing Heidi," she said, almost matter of fact.

"Huh? Killing who?" He drew himself away from the macabre thoughts.

"Killing Heidi. This is where Killing Heidi came from." Jacob's expression said he had no idea what she was talking about. "The rock band. Well, they've broken up now, but they had some killer songs. *Killer* songs."

"Oh." She liked music. *Rock* music. She had to get that from him. Not her mother. It was he who insisted on having the radio playing in the car, or belting out at home whenever they were plodding about. In truth, he loved all forms of music, had gathered an appreciation of it over the years— from his father, no doubt, but it was rock 'n' roll, that mesh of instruments and seething vocals that made his pulse pound more than anything else. Surely when God was up for a great time, he had the legends playing in Heaven. There was something about a catchy riff, thumping drums, a bass guitar, and a screeching voice—male or female—that got him going. And if Rebecca enjoyed it as much, if she'd acquired a love of music through his genes, then he was grateful for that, if nothing else.

"You like music?"

He cleared his throat. "No." She raised her eyebrows in mock. "I goddamn *love it*." Rebecca smiled—the first since Campbelltown—maybe the first for him in weeks, and that lit him up inside.

They chatted about it as Jacob drove the last winding leg towards Seymour; her love of nineties rock—Nirvana and Pearl Jam, Soundgarden and Rage Against the Machine. A little heavier than his favorite stuff, but he wasn't too old that he couldn't appreciate it. He asked if she knew of the Beatles—of course she did, but she hadn't heard a great deal of their music. He promised to track down a CD somewhere along the way for her to listen. *The White Album*, he suggested, which was his favorite, and he found himself describing the mix of styles and influences. She listened with wide eyes and rapt enthusiasm for *his* enthusiasm, and he realized they had found a similar passion.

And then they were there, pulling off the Hume Freeway and onto the Goulburn Valley Freeway, heading south towards the Seymour Township. In the distance on their right rested the faint lines of the train tracks, cutting their way between a cluster of trees and a sea of golden pasture where animals had once roamed. The road swung around and they crossed two thin tributaries off the Goulburn River and turned into Emily Street. The backyards of houses smirked at them in silence. No cars or people in sight. That was more worrying. Were they all herded up somewhere waiting for visitors?

Jacob saw the hospital in the distance and wondered whether they should go there, but recalled Callan's story about the one in Albury and decided to pass.

As they approached the first section of shops, worry stirred in his gut. The buildings on either side of the road had their windows smashed. Glass lay in a spattering on the pavement outside, and a wispy trail of smoke swirled from one. He spied movement inside what looked like some sort of hotel and slowed the car.

Rebecca sat up. "What are you doing?"

"I just wanna—"

And there they were, scratching about the rubble inside the building, pushing past each other in pursuit of some unseen food. Tables and chairs had been smashed up and overturned. Bodies lay at irregular angles. Something caught Jacob's attention on the left, and he saw a similar scene in another building. And then another and another. It was as though someone had pushed a button and let them all out of their cage. He gave up after that.

"Can we turn around?"

What would they find beyond here, though? Every other town was going to be in a similar state. Supplies and weapons were what they needed. But Seymour contained everything they needed amongst its zombie population. If they left now, there would be nothing between here and Melbourne. They had no choice.

"A bit further. There'll be a safe place here. We just have to find it."

Jacob guided the car to avoid the same old abandoned stuff on the road—vehicles, rubbish, even bodies. In the mirror, he saw that feeders had wandered onto the street beyond the other car, drawn by the sound of automotive engines. More appeared from shop fronts.

They approached the intersection of Emily Street and the Goulburn Valley Highway. On the right lay a smoking pile of rubble, a blue sign poking up through the bricks like the arm of a zombie. POLICE. Jacob followed the road around the corner, peering into the debris, looking for signs of life. He knew there would be none.

Jacob moved slowly. Behind them, the four-wheel beeped its horn. Phil stuck a finger up from behind the front window. Jacob supressed a curse. They were idiots, he decided.

They followed the street around the corner to the left. On their right, the shady umbrellas of a dozen oak trees spread across the scruffy lawn of a sizeable park.

They took the corner and almost slammed into a vehicle stuck in the middle of the road. Zombies surrounded it, attempting to get at something through the passenger door. Jacob braked and swivelled around, looking behind, looking for a way back. But the red four-wheel drive had pulled in close behind them and there was no way out.

FIVE

DYLAN SAT AT the kitchen table watching them talking about him. Listening to their whispers and accusations. Maybe they already knew. Maybe they were plotting against him. Why didn't they come and talk to him? They were staying away. Greg refused to look at him. He knew what he'd done. He'd left Dylan to die, turning his back on him.

The bite on his neck. The wound throbbed. He needed to have it washed and cleaned. More importantly, he was infected with the zombie virus and needed treatment. Dylan knew the outcome of *no* treatment as well as anyone else. At that moment, the virus worked its way through his blood, changing his cells, changing *him*. His skin was hot and itchy. He wanted to scratch it away, but didn't dare look too obvious to the others.

Kristy was already suspicious. He didn't want her to find out yet; he wasn't prepared to face the fact she knew he was going to die. He needed to talk to Klaus, the scientist. He'd know what to do. Once it was out though, he worried they would all know. Klaus and the admiral were dealing with the same situation and they had managed to keep functioning. *Toughen up,* Dylan told himself. The buzz though. The buzz in his blood, the buzz in his head. He could feel it. Johnny all over. It had driven him mad. He killed himself in the end, unable to handle the thought of becoming one of them. Dylan closed his eyes. If he didn't get a grip, they'd work it out soon. Greg probably suspected and was telling Callan now. Two days. That's all he had. Two days and he'd end up like Johnny. He should check on the bite and at least make sure it was clean so it didn't get infected. *Infected.* You are, fool.

He sat pondering his short future, feeling as though he was gradually going mad. Eventually, the van slowed and pulled over to the roadside at the top of a hill where a corrugated tin shed doubled as a toilet block. They were near Yass, and soon they would be battling their way into another town. They would need him, and he wouldn't be able to avoid that. The others began leaving the vehicle. Kristy looked his way and signaled with a nod of her head. *Get moving.* He waited for the kids to go, then slid out from behind the table and followed.

"You okay?" Kristy asked, taking him by the hand.

Maybe she didn't know. Her concern was heartbreaking. Part of him wanted to tell her, but the words stuck in his throat. It would kill everything they managed to forge over the last weeks. He would rather suffer the knowledge of his imminent death for a day or two longer than have her look at him with pity. "Dylan?"

He cleared his throat. "Yeah. I'm fine. Just a little tired. And I've got a headache."

Kristy rubbed a hand on the back of his neck and he stiffened. She noticed it and pulled it away as though touching a hot stove. "You're warm. How long have you been feeling like that?"

"Couple of days," he lied.

"I'll get some paracetamol."

"Okay. But I gotta pee first." He walked quickly towards the toilets.

"Come and see me when you're done."

The door opened with a squeal and he slipped inside, feeling safe again. He slipped off his shirt and tried to assess the bite, twisting and turning. It was impossible to examine from any angle, and there were no mirrors. His fingers touched the wound, and when he pulled them away, sticky blood covered the tips. Dylan shuddered.

He emptied his bladder, left the cubicle, and headed towards the others standing on a gravel mound at the edge of the clearing. Kristy stood beside Greg with her arms folded. Dylan recalled the incident back at the base that would eventually cost his life. Had Greg deliberately left him to die? Had his act caused Dylan to get bitten? They were questions to which answers, at this point, were impossible. Dylan's gut told him there was something in it, but when he considered all Greg had done for them, saving their lives on multiple occasions, it didn't make sense. It was difficult, though, to shrug off the image of Greg's face as he turned for the door, leaving Dylan to die.

But he came back.

He reached the group and stood amongst the long weeds beside Callan. They were looking down at a panoramic view of the Yass Township. The structure of the settlement was spread across several miles, dotted by trees, and flanked by a golf course in the distance. The Yass River cut through like a python, its body thick on the outskirts of town and thinning to a narrow tail beyond the spillway as it wound its way through the center of town. Smoky columns rose from several buildings. The occasional crash or boom floated to them. There was no movement of cars or people. The main street wasn't visible, but there were plenty of stalled vehicles on the outskirts. The most obvious thing was the smell, the slow decay of the dead and rotting food almost unbearable.

"Seems quiet," Greg said.

Callan shuffled. "Yeah. But the bastards are down there." He looked up at the sky. "I still think we can make it in and out before dark."

"No," Kristy said. "Not tonight. We have one torch. If we get stuck …"

"I'm with Kristy," Evelyn said. "I think we stay here and go in the morning. We've got enough to get us through the night. Who has the energy to do anymore today?"

Callan considered this. "I suppose."

Sarah called out from the van. Kristy left and Dylan relaxed, as though she couldn't discover his secret. A day ago, he'd have never dreamed of such a thing. The notion stung him with sadness, and he doubted keeping it from her. Holding onto secrets was poison. Eventually, it caught up to you. He learned that with Johnny and Sherry, who had betrayed Callan with their affair in the most deceitful way. The truth had been revealed in the end, and to what good? As he moved away, leaving the others to continue their discussion, a voice stopped him.

"Hold up." Klaus approached, adjusting his glasses. "I've been watching you since we left the facility. Is everything okay? You don't seem your usual self."

Dylan started to respond. Did the scientist know something? Were the symptoms that obvious? Maybe he was changing quicker than Johnny did. Perhaps he should tell Klaus. He could help. He'd keep the secret. He needed to be alone, to collect his thoughts, and decide what to do next. He turned for the camper. "I'm fine."

Klaus jogged after him. Dylan stopped, and Klaus pulled in close. "No you're not. Agitation. Reticence. Irritability. They're all sym—"

"There's nothing wrong with me," Dylan snapped. Klaus raised his eyebrows. Dylan cursed himself for endorsing Klaus' suggestion.

Klaus reached out and took Dylan's hand. "Your capillaries are enlarged." Dylan pulled away. "Tell me what happened before it's too late."

That was it. He knew. Somehow, he knew. Dylan glanced around to make sure the others weren't watching. "I've been bitten."

A shriek sounded from the van. A zombie, its skin paper-thin and gaping with sores, shuffled out of the bushes, hooked hands clawing at the air. Jake was closest, standing by the doorway. He didn't make a sound, but bumbled backwards and fell onto the gravel. The thing staggered forward to within a few feet. Blue ran at it, barking. Dylan moved, catching Callan and Greg from the corner of his eye with the same intention. They were too far away though. Kristy leapt out of the van and landed near it, a kitchen knife in her hand.

There was no hesitation. She swiped the blade at the zombie's neck, opening a wound that sprayed blood over the gravel. It made a desperate lunge at her, not quite finished, and hooked its fingers onto her black leathers, drawing her close. Kristy hesitated—or waited, Dylan thought, then swung the knife in a roundhouse arc and jammed it into the side of its head. Blood jetted out. Its hand fell away, and it slumped to the dusty earth with a thud. Kristy helped Jake up, then walked over to a clump of grass and wiped the blade clean. The others stood back, watching. Kristy disappeared inside the van with Jake.

"Let's sweep the area to make sure there are no more," Callan said. Gallagher dragged the zombie off into the bushes.

Dylan wanted to finish the conversation with Klaus, but the scientist followed Kristy inside, and Callan seconded Dylan for the scout. The discussion would have to wait, although he was worried now because Klaus knew his secret.

Callan led Greg, Dylan, and Gallagher through a wall of brush at the edge of the parking area with hand weapons and one of the gunman's discarded pistols from the defense facility. The land dipped and rose; shallow gullies filled with bushy saplings and monstrous logs covered in moss, leading into rough, rocky ridges. They spread out and weaved between gum trees and eucalyptus, through tangled brush, until they hit the highway again. Gallagher suggested the zombie had probably wandered from town, so they doubled back beyond the camp, checking to make sure no others had stopped for a visit, and cleared an area of equal size on the west side, too. They scared a wombat and two kangaroos, but saw no zombies. Blue disappeared for a time in chase, but reappeared shortly after, panting. Satisfied, Callan led them back, Dylan eager to find Klaus, hopeful the scientist had thought of a way to help.

Dylan found him sorting through supplies in a storage compartment at the back of the camper. "What can I do?" he asked, startling Klaus.

For a moment, he thought Klaus was going to say nothing. "Are you sure about the bite?"

Dylan leaned his head forward. Klaus pulled the collar of his jacket down. "Is it bad?"

He let the jacket go and stepped around to face Dylan. "It's a bite. Similar to mine. Telling me earlier would have been more helpful. What were you thinking back at the defense facility? If you'd spoken up when Callan was arguing for the dog, you might have been better off. We can't reverse the degeneration, only halt it."

It did seem irrational now, and Dylan struggled to explain it. His emotions were turbo-charged, rolling on a wave of sentiment. In the moment, it had made sense, but now he saw Klaus' logic. Dylan shook his head. "It just felt like the right thing to do at the time."

"How do you feel? I've noticed contrasting moods."

"Yeah. I feel okay at the moment. Was feeling crazy before though. I couldn't concentrate when Callan was arguing about the dog."

"There are varying symptoms—the admiral said he initially felt like he was going mad, and that his skin itched as though his blood was burning."

Going mad. Maybe that's what was happening to him. "I haven't had that yet. Just a bit… strange."

Klaus nodded. "What's done is done. I need to get you some of that serum."

"Is there enough? I mean…"

"There's some. We're not out yet, but one more person will reduce the quantity for the others."

"I don't want—"

"You have no *choice*, if you want to live. I can't believe Kristy is let—"

"She doesn't know." Klaus raised his eyebrows. "I haven't found the right time, and I'm worried she'll …"

"You're risking trouble there."

"I know. I'll deal with that later. How long have we got if there's four of us using it?" Callan appeared outside the camper, talking through the entrance. He glanced their way and headed towards them. Dylan thought of Johnny, and the pity they had all had for him. "I don't want anybody else to know yet."

Klaus considered the answer. "Don't worry about it. That's my problem."

"How do we do this then?"

Callan had almost reached them. "I'll get the serum. If you're adamant you don't want the others to know, then we need to find a quiet spot. I only need a moment."

"Let's go."

SIX

A STRING OF zombies pushed in around their vehicle. Others lurched towards Phil and Tommy's car. "What the fuck are they doing?" Jacob hissed, sticking the shift into reverse. He could see it all turning pear-shaped in a matter of seconds. Tommy was bent over the wheel trying to get the vehicle restarted. Had he said something about a dodgy starter motor? Beside him, Phil made silent screams.

What did he do? He had a rifle with half a dozen rounds. He could shoot some of them, but the bullets would quickly run out. Did they have any weapons? Only the ax, and he didn't fancy taking them on with that yet.

Forward was the only way. The idiots had driven too close to him. They could fight for themselves. Jacob stuck the gearstick into drive and gunned the accelerator, but the car didn't respond. He tried again, and this time the engine roared, propelling them forward. "Hold on." Rebecca grabbed for the door handle and the center console.

He drove up onto the curb, clipping a pole that held up the awning of a store. It collapsed, part of the roof crashing down behind them onto the zombies. The noise was deafening. He pulled the vehicle back towards the center of the street, clipping several more zombies, causing them to fall under the car with a series of thumps.

From the corner of his eye, he saw more coming from a BWS liquor store, a shambling line of the most gruesome zombies. Their skin had withered to the point that it almost looked like transparent paper; the flesh on their faces had lost chunks, revealing dark holes. They walked with broken feet and bent legs; several had lost their arms; one had lost them both. But they all had teeth and could adequately inflict a bite, which would end with their death.

Jacob lined up half a dozen more and drove hard when engine cut out, the power fleeing under his foot. "Shit! SHIT!" He pumped the pedal furiously. They rolled to a stop as zombies reached them, clapping on the windows.

"Grab the ax." Rebecca swivelled towards the back seat and yanked the weapon out.

The mirror told him the other car was overcome, like a beehive engulfed by drones. They had two doors open, zombies fighting to get at the fresh meat.

Fists beat against their vehicle. Jacob knew he had to forget about the others and worry about himself and Rebecca.

She screamed at them, furious. "Get away!" If it came down to it, she would take a few out, he was sure.

But zombies covered Rebecca's side of the car. Jacob twisted again, looking for another way. They were everywhere at the rear, fighting for position against the paint. Only three scrambled along his side and he figured that was their best shot. "Follow me."

He snatched the ax from her and unclipped the door, pushing rearwards with his backside facing them. Their hands groped at his shoulders and neck. Jacob swung an elbow and felt the hard point connect with a jaw. Bone cracked and one of them fell away. He spun, bringing the ax up into position, and swung in a tight arc to suit their proximity. The blade cut into the throat, jetting blood onto his shirt, sending the second one down like a falling curtain. The third zombie crawled for him, but Rebecca wasn't yet out of the vehicle, as though she was tied to the seat by some invisible force. Jacob leaned in, reached across the seat, and grabbed a fistful of her shirt. She flew out of the car screeching, clunking her head on the door. In one motion, he swung the ax and struck the third zombie in the cheek, sending a spray of crimson juice. The

41

others, in their bumbling, tattered bulk, were almost there. Burning anger rushed through him, tempting him to stick around and fight.

"*Run.*"

They did, abandoning their vehicle and remaining possessions, their shoes smacking the roadway as they ran down the middle of the street. *Rebecca. Rebecca. Rebecca.* Jacob kept repeating to himself.

They ran on, hearing the groans and grunts of the feeders chasing, Jacob refusing to turn back. Rebecca had fallen slightly behind. "Keep going," he said between heavy breaths. The last month or so had conditioned him, but he was still a slightly overweight middle-aged man.

As they sprinted along Station Street, more shops greeted them on their right. Zombies filled the doorways and beyond, in the shadows of the stores, fumbling between aisles and around counters. There was a fish and chip shop, a bakery, a jewelry shop; even a sports store, where Jacob wished they could search for weapons. The Australia Post shop stared back, forever silent, no longer a deliverer of messages and parcels as it had been for so long.

Panting, Jacob stopped. Rebecca stood with her hands on her knees. This was nuts; fifteen minutes before, they were safe in the car, driving towards Melbourne. They had opened a surprising gap, and had about thirty seconds before the line of zombies caught up. They had to get off the road. On their right, a bushy garden area covered an ornate brick square that led to the railway line. The lines ran parallel to the street. Further ahead, a long V/Line train was stuck in the middle of the tracks, and beside it, one of those old handcars.

"Follow me," Jacob said. They hurried across the road towards the trees, disappearing from view. He knew the zombies would track them if they didn't get far enough away.

He thought about going back and trying to find a car with some keys and fuel, but discounted the likelihood.

They reached a break in the trees. In the fading light, Jacob spied the train station in the distance—a small building on their side of the tracks, a larger one on the other. Lengths of chain fencing ran parallel to the lines. They might have a chance if they reached the other side of it.

He peered back through the scrub and around low-hanging branches. For a moment, he thought they were clear, and then he saw one pushing through the undergrowth towards them. "Quickly."

They ran, more panting, stumbling, and cursing. Finally, Jacob reached the fence and leapt up at it, lobbing the ax over the top. The chain link rattled, and the weapon hit the dirt with a *thump* on the other side. Rebecca followed up the barrier, although she was much smaller, her hands clawing at the links below Jacob's feet.

"Climb."

The zombies were close. Twigs and sticks cracked and popped, their slobbering and shuffling and moaning and grunting audible. They were the slow, uncoordinated type, but in a moment, the chasers would be upon the fence. If they weren't over it by then, it might be the end. Jacob thought momentarily about dropping back down and kicking them away, but the element of risk kept him attached to the fence and he continued on, swinging his leg over.

"Come on," he said down to Rebecca, and she started to climb.

One of them reached the fence. It raised a flapping, broken arm, bone protruding from the shoulder, and slapped its hand against the wire. Rebecca glanced down, but still she did not scream. She was almost out of reach, but fear stole her movement. Jacob sat with one leg over the top, poised to drop down the other side.

43

Instinct took over. He swung his leg back over and lowered himself, fence shaking under his weight, until he was in line with Rebecca's head. He struck out, the heel of his boot hitting the zombie in the face with a dense thud. It fell away like loose bark from a tree.

Jacob reached out and gave Rebecca a lift. She scrambled up and he followed, using his arms to pull himself skyward, and then they were at the top, throwing their legs over and scaling down the other side. Jacob dropped halfway down and called for Rebecca to do the same; he would catch her, and she did, and he thought her trust *had* to grow after this. He grabbed the ax and they staggered away from the fence towards the building as others reached the barrier, poking their bony fingers and decomposing hands through the wire.

Jacob looked back and saw the faces peering in at them and wondered if Phil and Tommy were amongst them.

SEVEN

EVELYN ROLLED THE van to the back edge of the clearing, beneath the shaggy cover of gum trees, out of sight from the road. Beneath the stony rise, the town stretched out before them, dark houses and the occasional plume of dirty black smoke. She still found it odd that she had become the driver, although she didn't mind; it was an important purpose that suited her, and with it, she was making a small contribution to the group. That was the most important thing, and held with the values her parents had taught her at a young age. She couldn't sit back and let these people carry her and Jake. She needed to support their existence, feel like she was contributing.

At fifteen, her father had driven her to the local shopping center to explain the value of work ethic and contribution. "Time for you to get a job," he said, pulling up outside the entrance. "'I'll be back at closing time. You should have two offers by then." She'd waited for him to break out in a smile. "You're old enough to learn a few valuable lessons. Working in the real world will be good for you. My parents never made me do it, and I suffered for some years trying to acclimatize myself to life." Still didn't respond. His expression softened. "You'll be fine. Smile. Talk with confidence, and tell them you're capable of anything."

She had gone in as a timid, sceptical teenager. At lunchtime, she called her father and asked him to come and pick her up.

"How many offers did you get?"

"Seven," she said with an uncommon pride.

He was silent for a time. "You're a good girl. You do

everything we ask and you never back down."

They made her pay boarding, too—sixty dollars a week. She had thought that a bit steep, but again, it was about the value of contribution. On her twenty-first birthday, they gave her a term deposit statement for a little over thirty-eight thousand dollars. She cried uncontrollably for ten minutes.

"That's all the money we took from you as boarding. We added the same amount you saved, and the rest is interest from the investment. Spend some if you like—a new car, or even a holiday." She hugged them and pledged her eternal love.

Tears spilled down her cheeks at the memory. What wonderful parents they had been. She was upholding those values by working hard for the group and maintaining her contribution. Driving was a big part of that.

She joined the others in the back of the camper, wiping her eyes.

"There's a farmhouse nearby," Callan said. "It looks empty, but we're gonna check it out. Might be some supplies. I'm going with Greg." She gave him a mocking look. "Anybody else want to come?"

"I'd like to," Evelyn said.

"Me too," Jake added.

Evelyn pulled Jake to her. "Is it safe, though?"

"We'll be fine," Callan said. "We won't be long, anyway. Bring some bags though."

They walked a crooked, ascending path through stout trees that prodded them with spiky leaves. The men held the branches aside when the trail became too tight. Darkness blocked out much of the light, and Evelyn pushed her eyes wide, looking into all the corners. Blue Boy ran ahead before circling back, ears pricked. He was their early warning system.

A chook house greeted them first, no more than loose wire fencing with a square box and a roof, patched together from old fence palings and housing boards. The chooks sauntered around the outskirts, cooing and clucking, picking at invisible scraps in the dirt. Callan opened the gate with a screech. The animals fled like the escapees they were. Greg glanced at Callan, then Jake, and Evelyn read the question in his narrowed eyes. Do we kill them? Blue thought so. He chased them around the yard. Callan had to call him off, and he slunk away full of disappointment.

"Later," Callan said, and pushed on towards the house. "Check for eggs, big guy." He looked at Jake. Seven perfect eggs went into a bag. Evelyn's stomach awakened in anticipation.

The rickety old farmhouse stood atop another hill no more than a minute's walk along a rutted dirt road with tall timothy grass down the middle. It was cut from lengths of timber that had faded to grey stone under years of summer sun. All manner of accessories hung from hooks around a porch that ran the length. A John Deere tractor sat huddled in the grass with weeds growing up through the engine. A beaten up, pale blue Toyota four-wheel drive with dark patches of bare metal on the body sat parked beneath a handmade lean-to. The keys were inside, and after Greg wrenched the creaky door open and climbed up behind the wheel, it started with a tired groan. In a paddock nearby, several sheep ate from a buffet of long grass. Callan talked quietly with Greg about killing one of them for meat, but didn't know how, and decided he would check with Gallagher. From an apple tree close to the house, they picked a bagful of the ripe fruits, each biting into one as they patrolled the exterior, looking for more opportunities.

There was little more of use, so Callan and Greg entered the house, clearing each room before calling Evelyn and Jake inside. In the kitchen cupboards they found some tinned food—spaghetti, baked beans, tuna—a giant bag of dog

47

food—and some packets of pasta that would last a few more weeks, but beyond that, everything had spoiled.

Outside, they strolled down to a lazy creek behind the house where Callan asked Jake to help him fill plastic containers they had discovered in the pantry. Evelyn stood back with Greg, watching them. Callan assisted Jake down to the edge of the creek, holding his elbow. Callan unscrewed the container, handed it to Jake, and instructed him on the best way to fill it. Jake laughed. Callan laughed. Blue barked. A flash of delight rushed through Evelyn. Jake filled the can, and when he was done, Callan held up his hand and they made a high five. He was a good man, Callan; fiery and opinionated, but he was passionate and caring.

"What was Callan's girlfriend like? The one that died?"

Greg only paused for a second, watching the boys. "Horrible, mostly. Why do you ask?"

"I just wondered. He seems like a nice man."

Greg considered his response. Evelyn thought he might not answer. "He is. He has his faults of course, but he's got a good heart. He'll pretty much always do the right thing. Sherry never appreciated what she had. Maybe she understood in the end, but she never got best out of Callan."

With the weighty containers of clean spring water, Callan and Jake climbed the stepped bank from the edge of the waterway. Jake reached the top first, but tottered and overbalanced. Evelyn saw in her mind's eye that he was going to fall backwards into the water. She cried out, but Callan, still holding the container, shot a hand forward and steadied the boy.

"Oh my God," Evelyn said. Greg laughed.

"Trust me. There's nobody better to look out for your kid than him."

Callan gave Jake a gentle nudge, allowing him to gain

traction on the treacherous edge, and then he was up, smiling, laughing, offering a hand to help Callan with the water. Blue Boy yapped. Evelyn smiled. They walked back towards them laughing aloud. There had been a number of suitors after Cameron's death, but she hadn't quite been ready to consider them, and she'd used Jake as an excuse, sizing up each of the men as a suitable proxy for his father. None had given her the feeling Callan had just now, and she knew that if anything did ever develop between them, Callan would have ticked the first and most important box.

"What's funny?" she asked as they returned. Jake was almost hysterical.

"Men's talk," Callan said, winking. Evelyn nodded and tousled Jake's hair. She couldn't recall such laughter from him. He hadn't looked so happy since before the plague.

As they walked back up the slope to the house under a growing darkness, Evelyn thought of what she and Jake had gone through to be there now; so many close calls, standing at the door of death, almost giving up back in Wagga as the zombies chased them along the street. The thought made her feel ill. She was grateful she hadn't surrendered; grateful Jake had urged her on, and Alex had picked them up on the street, even for what they had gone through at the barracks. These people—Callan, Kristy, Dylan, Greg, Sarah, Julie—even the new men from the Army base—they were good people, and they were lucky to have found them. But as she drew closer, she realized her exposure to pain and loss—Eric, for example—increased. It reminded her of losing her father all over again, biting deep into her heart, stirring emotions she thought were long buried.

Callan wanted to drive the Toyota back to the campervan. They found some usable diesel fuel in Gerry cans underneath the porch and stacked it in the rear of the four-wheel drive with the water and food.

They reached the camper to find the others setting up for a basic evening meal. The sun had dropped low in the west, casting the sky in an orange hue. The meal would be simple, but none of them would starve. For now, they were free of zombies and the immorality of those humans who would seek to thwart their struggle for survival.

"Can you do me a favor?" Kristy asked. Evelyn nodded. "Speak to Julie. Find out if she's okay. I know she won't be, but she needs to know we haven't forgotten about her. That we care."

"Have you—"

"No. I thought you could do it. You've got the ..."

"Experience." Kristy nodded, eyes downcast. Evelyn touched a hand to her arm. "It's okay."

Evelyn approached the rear bedroom and pulled the drape aside, her heartbeat growing more rapid. Why was she worried? Because she understood that people touched by recent profound loss are unpredictable. Some feel they have nothing left to lose. Julie had been with Eric for many years. Evelyn lost Cameron after eleven, and she knew the devastation it caused. It was the first time in her life she had considered the idea of not being around.

She sat on the end of the bed, considering her words. Julie's earlier outburst had been full of anger, blaming them for Eric's death, as though they had been the ones to push him out the door towards the carnage. It wasn't fair, but she knew to look beneath the facade to the underlying emotion; Julie needed someone to blame.

How did she begin? Would Julie scream her out of the room? It might even get physical. Evelyn had struck her mother across the face after a particularly raw comment. She couldn't recall what it was now, but it had burned deeply.

Evelyn sat on the bed. The other woman didn't move. The blanket had curled back. Evelyn folded it forward, covering Julie's back. She watched her breathing, wondering what she might say that would offer comfort and hope. There was nothing. Perhaps it had been a silly idea to try. Julie needed time; that was the only thing that had ever helped Evelyn. Minutes. Hours. Nights. Days. Weeks. One after the other, until every tenth day was bearable.

She was about to leave when Julie stirred. A leg at first, then her left arm, and finally she lifted her head and their eyes met. Julie's were puffy and red. Evelyn hadn't seen anyone cry with such profound despair since... since she had done so with Cameron.

"Thank you." Julie's voice hitched, full of tears.

Then she lay back down. Evelyn waited for her to say more, but she buried her head in the pillow. What did she say? Evelyn took herself back to when Cameron died, and the days afterwards. Although his death hadn't been unexpected, it had been until that point in her life the most challenging thing. As she thought about it though, it dawned on her that comparing experiences wasn't going to work now. It wasn't what Julie needed or wanted from her.

"We're all so sorry for your loss, Julie. We loved Eric. He was a caring, wonderful man." She started to cry. "You're still here though, and we need you, the way you need us. The way the world is now... we're here for you, when you're ready. We're your family now. I know Eric would want that. Take your time. We'll be waiting."

She found the others eating outside on a plastic foldout table and chairs that someone had discovered in a storage compartment of the camper. The sun had finished its final descent, a picturesque view, reminding Evelyn of another time and place. Callan and Jake were joking around again, and this time Evelyn watched the older man without restriction on her feelings.

Kristy set aside a plate for Julie, doubtful she would eat.

When someone suggested they turn on the outside light on the camper, Gallagher insisted they move inside, which they did, reluctantly. For just a moment, life had been normal again.

Shortly after, the curtains to the back section moved, and Julie appeared. The conversation ceased. She had dry, puffy eyes, and a red nose. She was still hitching, but had stopped crying. "I'm sorry."

Callan put the map down, rose, and put up a hand. "Nothing to be sorry for."

Julie pressed her lips together and nodded, fighting back tears again. An overwhelming sadness filled Evelyn. She fought the urge to go to Julie and throw her arms around the older woman. How she must be feeling. Thoughts of Eric returned. Pressure filled Evelyn's eyes. He'd been such a decent man. The pain reflected in Julie told them more; how she had loved him, and it reminded her of what she'd had with Cameron.

Evelyn ignored her doubt, stood, and opened her arms to Julie, who fell into them, sobbing.

"I'm okay," Julie said, almost wailing. "I'll be okay."

Nobody spoke for a long time. Finally, Julie pulled away. Gallagher handed her tissues and she dabbed at her inflamed eyes.

"Thank you. And I'm sorry for my outburst before. It was… uncalled for. I know it's nobody's fault. Except them."

Callan stood near the door with a soft, understanding expression. "Really, it's fine."

"No, it's not." She squeezed into the seat on the end of the table. "My mother died when I was seven, and my father was incapable of looking after me—I mean, it wasn't that he didn't care, but he was in his early fifties and that generation was far less capable than it is today. I was the youngest child, and both my sisters were teenagers. I got shipped off to live with an aunt and uncle. First in Hawthorn, then Diamond Creek, but nobody wanted me." Evelyn leaned across the table and put a hand over Julie's. She gave an appreciative smile. "It wasn't until I met Eric that I found someone that wanted me." She gathered herself, before continuing. "And I've had him ever since. To lose that now… it feels like I'm seven years old again and nobody wants me."

"No," Evelyn said. "That's not true. We want you. You're part of our family now." There was a chorus of agreement.

"That's right," Kristy said. "Don't forget that. Ever."

Julie accepted their support with more tears. She picked at the food as the children crawled into their beds and the others each found a sleeping place. But it took Evelyn a time to fall asleep; the image of Callan stealing glances at her stuck in her mind's eye well into her dreams.

EIGHT

KRISTY WOKE TO strips of grey light beneath the blinds, bumping into Dylan as she rolled over with pins and needles in one arm. She slipped out of bed, added clothes, and went outside, stepping over bodies lying on the floor of the camper.

Hard morning sunlight greeted her, promising another hot day. A light wind tickled threads of her hair, and on it, she smelled the slow decay of the town below. They would go there soon, and that thought filled her with dread. On the road and the outskirts of townships, they were mostly safe. Heading into the more populated areas, they faced great risk. *Necessary risk.* They were far from their destination and wouldn't make it there without guns and more supplies.

She wandered about the camp, looking over the four-wheel drive and thinking about Dylan. She put an arm around him last night, chasing a little comfort, but he rolled over, disinterested. What was happening? Had he lost interest after sleeping with her? It had happened to her before, early in her relationship career, but with Dylan, a man she had known for so long, and with honesty she had never encountered, it seemed implausible.

The others rose soon after, stretching, sluggish, slipping through the camper door so as not to wake those still asleep. Kristy went back inside to check if Dylan was awake, and found Julie standing at the kitchen sink, clearing away clutter and assembling the remaining food in a pile.

"Good morning," Kristy whispered with a smile. Julie returned the greeting, and Kristy admired the woman's spirit to keep moving on. Kristy tried to wrangle breakfast duties off her, but she insisted on it. Kristy supposed it took her mind off other things. She even managed a smile as Sarah and Jake sat at the table waiting for boiled eggs.

Kristy kept thinking about the change in Dylan. He had gone outside, so she decided to confront him, draw it out in the open, and ask questions from which he couldn't hide. She found him conversing with Callan and Greg by the farm vehicle.

"Can I talk to you for a moment?" He followed her to the edge of the clearing with an expression of annoyed expectance. "What's wrong?" But as she waited for an answer, it came to her with a pang of worry. "Are you sick?"

His face twisted into an expression of disbelief. "What?"

"Your eyes are red. Your nose, too." She put a hand up to his forehead, but he stepped away.

"What are you doing?"

"Dylan, you look—"

"I'm fine." He circled and headed back towards the others. "Stop doting over me. You're not my mother."

She was incapable of a response. Greg wandered over, his soft smile holding her feet still. "He's not himself at the moment. It was pretty bad down there yesterday. Just give him a day or two, he'll come around."

"I hope you're right. He looks sick." She wondered whether he had somehow contracted the virus. What if he'd taken in a splash of blood or a scratch had gotten dirty? The possibilities were endless. Was irritability a symptom? Part of her wanted to chase after him, thrash out the issue, but mostly she was scared it would become worse.

"Could just be something he picked up along the way. We're all running on empty at the moment."

Greg had a point. Kristy lacked energy. She could do with a day or two of sleep.

Back in the van, Julie had prepared a basic breakfast of eggs and fruit. Sarah, Jake, and Evelyn all sat at the table eating in silence. Julie held up the frying pan and offered Kristy one of the soft fried yolks. She took one and snavelled it down, her stomach grateful. Evelyn began making a list of things they would need. Kristy contributed a couple of items, but her mind was elsewhere.

She tried to find Dylan before they left, but he had disappeared. She fought a battle of leaving him be, as Greg had suggested, or insisting upon a discussion about whatever was bothering him. The thought of him somehow being infected preyed on her mind. And if he didn't want to be with her anymore, she wanted to know that, too. But after sweeping the clearing, she still couldn't find him...

Callan insisted on using the grimy blue Toyota four-wheel drive they had found at the farmhouse. It wouldn't break any land-speed records, but it had a bull bar on the front, reinforced sides, and heavy-duty tires. Their range of weapons was limited to two tire irons, the biggest knives from Julie's kitchen, and a hammer Greg had found under the sink.

Kristy waited as the others climbed aboard the van, and Callan and Greg into the Toyota. They were set to drive away when Dylan finally returned. Kristy watched as he went directly for the four-wheel drive, feeling her hopes sink. She jogged across the clearing to him.

"You're not coming with us?"

"I wanna discuss strategy with Callan and Greg." He kissed her softly on the lips, but Kristy felt anything but romantic as he climbed into the car. She walked back to the van and slumped in the front, peering out the window, feeling her loose grip on their relationship slipping away. She considered asking Evelyn for advice, but raising it with another person in any sort of depth would only make it more real. For now, she had to sit tight.

Evelyn led them in slow, cautious progress through the outskirts of Yass, the smell growing worse as the farmland and scrub became a sketchy line in the rearview mirror. As they entered the fringes of the township, the first abandoned cars greeted them. The van drove on over broken glass and bloodstains on the roads, even up on the curb where the occasional traffic accident blocked the way. There were no packs of feeders, but they saw more than two dozen wandering about before they hit Main Street. Several approached the van as it drove past, one close enough to thump on the side, but after what they had witnessed in the last week nobody flinched, and the energy they had once possessed to kill every zombie they saw was now sensibly conserved.

Evelyn circled the streets looking for the hunting store, passing another selection of shops where the supermarket sat silent. Kristy watched Evelyn navigate the van, wondering how she had ended up in the driver's seat again. She supposed it was fitting; Kristy felt safe with her behind the wheel. Her concentration was impeccable, and she handled the camper as though she had been driving one for years. Kristy had no doubt that Evelyn's work at the Army facility had saved lives.

"I drove my grandfather's tractor when I was a girl, and all through my teenage years," she said when Kristy queried it. "Used to ride up and down the paddocks slashing grass. Even though he could have done it himself, I think he wanted to make a farmer out of me."

"I know you think you got the better deal of this," Kristy waved a hand around, indicating the van and the people, "but we did pretty well too."

Evelyn laughed. "Trust me, I still owe you guys."

Kristy felt comfortable talking to Evelyn, as though the two had been friends for years. She listened well and had a wise head on her shoulders for such a young age. It was her chance to get Evelyn's take on Dylan's behavior, and asking a question was easy. "Have you noticed anything strange about Dylan since yesterday?"

"Since the Army base?" Kristy nodded. "Nothing stranger than anybody else has been." She looked away in thought. "He's been a little quiet, but … why?"

"Something's not right. I can just sense it."

"What did he say?"

"Nothing. That's the way men are, isn't it?"

Evelyn smiled. "He's probably still a little rattled from yesterday. Based on what Greg said, they had some pretty scary moments down there. I'm sure he'll be good soon."

They hadn't even talked about what had gone on underground. Maybe that was the problem—Dylan needed to talk about it. If Kristy knew what had happened, she might be able to help. Still, she wasn't sure which way to go from there.

The men had taken the lead in the four-wheel drive, and now stopped at the curb outside a shop with a sign that read YASS OUTDOOR SPORTS AND CAMPING STORE. It was a tiny shopfront with two large windows and a glass door that might once have been a house. On the right was KING CHARCOAL CHICKEN, on the left, the AUSTRALIAN HOTEL, a wide, two-story building that would fit three or four normal size stores.

"Doesn't look like much," Kristy said. "I hope it's got guns." If they didn't find a decent stash of weapons here, their chances of gathering enough supplies in Yass were limited. With the irons and knives, they could probably scratch out enough to keep them going until the next town.

Greg pulled the glass door open, and they all disappeared inside the shop. A cold feeling washed over Kristy, as though it might be the last time she saw them, but she ignored it.

Every day—hell, every *hour* they were up against this sort of stuff.

They soon returned, Callan with an armload of guns, and Greg lumbering behind carrying a brown cardboard box. They split the loads between the Toyota and the campervan, and in two more trips, they had enough ammunition to last weeks. Kristy picked through the pile inside the doorway of the camper, enjoying the feel of the rifles and pistols.

"We're back in business," Greg said as he placed the last box of ammo at the foot of the pile amongst flashlights, ropes, and a plethora of camping equipment.

"It might look like a lot," Gallagher said, peering up from a folded map laid out on the table, "but we will burn through that pretty quickly."

Greg smiled at her. Kristy tried to return it, but she knew it wasn't becoming of her. Greg frowned and put a hand on her arm. "You okay?"

She tipped her head from side to side. Greg was the last person with whom she could discuss Dylan, but she was grateful for his sentiment. "I'll be okay." This time she did smile, and in it was her appreciation of his friendship, that he had been able to get past her relationship with Dylan, and not outwardly portray any bitterness towards her. Kristy knew from experience that was a difficult thing to do in such a situation. Greg hadn't been drinking, either, and she wondered whether he had turned his own corner. "How's your leg?" He nodded, indicating it was much better. "Did you finish all the antibiotics?"

He smirked. "Yes, Doc. No grog either. Have you noticed?"

This time her smile was radiant, and the response in his features warmed her. He drew back, beaming. "I did. You've been quite amazing, you know." But she was cautious not to overplay her position and mislead him. "Keep up the good work and you'll be the healthiest of us lot in no time." He stepped from the van with the last lot of ammunition for the four-wheel drive. Things between her and Greg were returning to normal, and she was thankful for that at least.

NINE

CALLAN LED THEM through a thin gap in the sliding doors of the Ritchie's supermarket. He'd thought about bringing Blue, but decided the dog was safer in the campervan. Unlike the stores they had visited in Albury, this one was almost untouched. Its location—on a side road off the main street of Yass—kept it from the bulk of traffic. The Woolworths supermarket closer towards the center of town had probably received far more attention. Callan didn't care—as far as he was concerned, they had struck gold.

Greg, Gallagher, and Evelyn—who had, using Kristy's influence, convinced them to let her join—followed Callan into the store. He was glad to have Evelyn along. By Kristy's report, she had fought superbly at the defense facility, although it meant he no longer had only himself to worry about. Whilst he would always look out for Greg and Gallagher, they were more conditioned to fighting. Evelyn was not. And if he was honest, he had developed a soft spot for her, and her kid, which meant he really had two people to consider.

In pale light from the outside, they ran hunkered through the cash registers and into the main body of the store, where shadows lurked and who knew what else. Callan had the 9mm pistol cocked and ready. Greg broke several trolleys away from a long stack just beyond the registers and swung one each towards the others. Staying together, they rolled their rattly trolleys towards one end of the store.

"Stay alert," Gallagher said.

The aisles were clear and the shelves patchy, although it would be more than enough for their requirements. Callan guessed that whoever had run the store had insisted on keeping some stock right up until the death knock. Thankfully, given its location off the main street, few people had discovered it yet.

The smell was horrendous, and despite having dealt with it every day, it made him nauseated. The thick scent of moldy food struck as they strolled into the former fresh food section. Callan and Evelyn both covered their noses. With the lights off, dark corners loomed, and nearby something scurried away. Callan raised his pistol and followed the moving shadow, but it was only a rat feeding on the wheel of a watermelon scarred by a thick layer of dark green mold.

At the edge of a pallet of green oranges, Gallagher almost tripped over a feeder hiding underneath a flap of waste cardboard. Callan thought it was dead, but it kicked like a giant crayfish and rolled over onto all fours, hissing and grunting. Greg stepped forward and placed the barrel of his rifle against its head.

"Wait!" Callan shouted. The gun boomed, shattering the silence. "Jesus, man, we don't want to draw any more of them."

Greg kicked the zombie over with his foot. It wore a brown shirt and black slacks—the supermarket uniform. Dark, thinning hair led back from a crusty face, with large, bulging eyes that would never close. "Sorry."

"Alright. Let's do this quickly. Non-perishables and all the processed food we can get our hands on. Two per aisle, we leapfrog one aisle at a time. Evelyn and I will take number one."

Callan didn't know why he had chosen to partner her. Perhaps it was that he thought she probably felt most comfortable with him. He glanced her way as he led her into the first aisle, the pistol locked in his right hand. Her soft eyes and high cheekbones cut pretty angles. Had he thought that about her before? He didn't know. The shadow of Sherry's presence clouded most of this thought. It was nice to move beyond that, if only fleeting, but he knew his head should be on the job. *Focus.*

Evelyn laid her rifle into the trolley and pushed it into the bakery aisle. Beyond, in the next row, the sound of movement drifted to them above the silence. *Just Greg and Gallagher,* Callan told himself. But images of his time with Dylan back in Albury had burned terrifying memories into his mind.

The bakery aisle contained flour and other useful ingredients. They managed a handful of packages each, and rounded the corner into the next aisle where pasta, sauces, and other items filled most of the shelves. The place was silent. That made him uncomfortable.

Callan jerked his trolley to a stop as he spied the type three. Evelyn almost crashed into him. He placed a finger on his lips and she bit down a response. It hadn't noticed them yet. It stood with its back pressed against the wall near the rack of fridges full of curdled milk and spoiled cream. Something had its attention in one of the other aisles. Callan stepped backwards, rolling the trolley away, until they were out of sight.

"Jesus," Evelyn said, scooping her rifle out of the trolley.

"I have to kill it."

"We need to leave."

"*No.* We're not finished. Wait here."

Callan pressed himself against the rack and tiptoed towards the end of the aisle. At the corner, he clicked the safety off and raised the weapon. Before it reached position though, a rabid growl greeted him, and then it was on him, the stained blue overalls, the smell of rot and death knocking him to the floor.

Evelyn screamed.

Callan fell backwards, searching for the zombie's stomach with the gun, but the thing outweighed him by thirty pounds. He hit the tiles with a thud, the breath exploding from his lungs, and the gun discharged, blowing a hole in the rear wall.

The zombie took hold of his throat. He pried a hand at one bony arm and brought the weapon around, aiming for its head, but it swatted the gun away like a cardboard prop. His free hand grabbed for the arms, but its strength surprised him. His breath slowly dissolved and he knew it wouldn't be long before he choked to death.

Gunfire roared, disintegrating the zombie's head. Callan turned away as blood spread across the floor and shelves, covering pasta sauce with dark muck. He rolled away, coughing for air, and scrambled to his feet.

Evelyn maintained the rifle on the feeder, gun smoke drifting around her thick brown hair. She looked cooler than he would ever be, her face stern, uncompromising, ready to do it all again if needed. In that moment, she was a kick-ass woman and he thought she had never looked better. The thing had caught him off guard, but she had saved him. Perhaps he wasn't as capable as he thought. "Thanks. I owe you one."

She managed a smile, but her hands were shaking. "No. Now we're even."

Gallagher and Greg arrived, their trolleys half-full of stock, and they all agreed to finish as quickly as possible. They parted again, moving down the next lane stacking water and potato chips into gaps in their loot. They entered the confectionary aisle, the shadowy loading bay doors at the end of the aisle peering back at them. Callan paused at a stack of colored sweets, his mouth watering. He split open a pack and shoved a handful at Evelyn. They chewed, smiling like children.

Movement near the doorway caught his attention. "What's that?" He let go of the trolley and cocked the pistol. Evelyn's brow furrowed, eyes on the space ahead.

"Where? I can't see anything."

Callan pointed. "There, beside the doorway."

"It looks like a… man."

Callan approached, pistol cocked. "Greg! Gallagher! Here!"

The man lay up against the wall beside a pallet of empty cardboard boxes, camouflaged in his brown uniform. Callan stepped in front of Evelyn, conscious she didn't get too close, and stopped about ten feet from the man. He stirred, moving one leg, rotating his head towards them slightly as though he were waking from sleep. Callan knew immediately that he was more advanced than both the man who had killed himself returning from the lake, and the one driving his family in the back of the truck to Melbourne. A tingle of apprehension touched the skin on his arms.

The skin on the man's face had washed out of color except for the blotchy red marks where sores had appeared. His hair was thinning, showing a pink, cracked scalp underneath. He was frail, as though coming off a bad illness, and a red wound on his shoulder that was probably a bite glared at them. But mostly, he reminded Callan of Eric— same age, similar look, except for the advancement of the disease. The memory of their good friend stung.

Greg and Gallagher arrived. "He's sick," Callan said. Gallagher crouched before the man, placing his rifle on the floor nearby. "Don't get too close."

"I've already got the virus."

Callan had forgotten that. Gallagher was taking the serum Klaus had formulated. But it was too late for this man. The man made a noise as he tried to face Gallagher. Callan edged closer. "He's trying to say something."

At first, the words were soft and unintelligible, his mouth and tongue dry. Gallagher went to one of the trolleys and removed a bottle of water, cracked the top and put it to the man's lips, then helped him sit more upright against the wall. His words were surprisingly clear after the water. He peered around at them all, his blue eyes lucid, as though the virus hadn't yet touched them with its poison.

"You killed the other one, didn't ya? I felt it." Nobody spoke for a long moment. Gallagher, squatting beside the man, glanced up at them. "They call me, you know? The crazy ones. They got some kind a power of the mind. The other ones too, they feel it. They're scared of 'em." He launched into a coughing tirade, and Callan imagined his ribs rattling. It lasted half a minute.

"What do you mean they call you?" Callan asked in a slow, incredulous voice.

"I hear their thoughts. They talk to me. With their mind." He blinked, rubbing his eyes. "Sounds crazy, I know, but this whole thing is goddamn crazy, isn't it?" He sat up, and Gallagher gave him some more water. He took three long gulps. "Never mind if you believe me or not. But let me tell you this: they're planning somethin', the crazies. Tryin' to turn everyone like them so they can take over. They've been working on that since the beginnin'. They take the weaker infected and make 'em stronger." He looked up at them. "They'll win, you know. They won't stop until there are no humans left." He looked at Gallagher's rifle on the floor, then up towards Callan. "Can you people do me a favor?" He lay back against the wall.

Nobody spoke. It was probably the right thing to do. Callan would do it if nobody else wanted the job, but he hoped Gallagher or even Greg might volunteer. This man reminded him too much of Eric. He had killed plenty, and would kill again, but every context was different and sometimes it was harder.

"I'll do it, sir," Gallagher said, collecting the rifle. He stood, nodding for the others to leave.

They pushed their trolleys back down the remaining aisles together. Evelyn jumped when the shot rocked the store. "Don't think I'll ever get used to that sound."

Greg loaded his trolley with several boxes of matches. "You will."

TEN

KLAUS SAT QUIETLY in the campervan watching the storefront through the window, waiting for the zombies to appear. He knew they weren't far away. He could feel them in his... where? In his mind? In his blood? He wasn't actually sure. For perhaps the first time in his life, he faced a question to which he had no plausible answer.

Since he had injected Dylan with the serum, Klaus had not administered himself any more. There wasn't enough. With Dylan, Gallagher, and the dog receiving treatment, they wouldn't last two days. And despite heading towards Melbourne, there might be nothing waiting for them. They might not even make it in two days. At least this way, he reasoned, two or three of them would still be in a reasonable state. If it came to it, he would cease treatment of the dog and administer a placebo. The others couldn't find out. They would argue that *he* needed to stay alive, but it went against his core beliefs. He wouldn't take the drug whilst others required it, including the dog. He had promised Callan. And if it got near the end for him, he would write down the formula so they had a record for someone else to use.

Still, he hadn't thought it would affect him immediately following his decision. He was wrong. He woke up feeling nauseated, full of sinus pain and congestion. He'd considered speaking to Dylan or Gallagher about his symptoms, but he was paranoid about alerting them to his change. He wondered how long he would last without treatment. A small part of his decision was that he could monitor himself, but without proper blood work, he was just guessing. That was another priority. He should have been documenting data and results on the virus' behavior. If they could just get to the facility, he wouldn't have to worry about such a possibility.

A long white building sat beside the hunting store—once a hotel—and he imagined the folk who would patronize it coming and going on such a warm summer day, aching for a beer or wine to quench their first, maybe a soft drink for the kids. Klaus wasn't a drinking man himself, but he would have given much to be back there now in the old world where such a thing might take place.

He counted the cars parked along the main street. Maybe a dozen. Where had the people gone? Why had they just left their vehicles and never returned? Were they shop owners? Employees who had come in sick and been unable to return to their cars? Most likely they had been attacked along the way and either killed or changed. It was a sad thought, knowing how many similar stories probably existed in the world. He knew they were out there because of the smell. It told him that death was prevalent, undeniable, and overwhelming. It clung to them like a mist, scratching inside their nostrils, hanging onto their clothes. Klaus had acclimatized to it but was infrequently reminded of its putridity. How he wished to smell a rose or nice flower, just once.

He hated waiting. The children sat at the table drawing on paper with colored pencils Julie had taken from a plastic box full of knickknacks. The dog lay curled at their feet. Kristy was rearranging cupboard space to take the load of groceries they were about to receive. Julie had managed a little better. She was a strong woman, but didn't quite realize the depth of her strength. She reminded Klaus of his mother. Dylan paced outside the van with one of the shotguns as though on guard duty. Klaus supposed he was. He had picked up a little since Klaus had administered the injection of serum, but if they didn't acquire some more soon, he would be back to where

69

he had been. They had to reach the facility in Melbourne as quickly as possible, for all their sakes. But which location? The Commonwealth Serum Laboratories had two sites: one in Broadmeadows, the other in Scoresby. Klaus knew little about the production capabilities of either. He would have to make a best guess. He was leaning towards the Broadmeadows site though. If he recalled correctly, the Maygar Army barracks sat on the same road, conveniently located off the Hume Highway, which ran all the way from Sydney to Melbourne.

Movement drew Klaus from thought. He glanced out the window and along the street, thinking one of the others had exited the hunting store. The thing walking in slow, steady movements underneath the awning of the YASS BAKERY did not resemble anybody Klaus had come to know in the past twenty-four hours. He studied the mutation, noting its movements: neither slow and clumsy, nor fast and aggressive. He had not seen many of what Harris had called the 'in betweens.'

Dylan climbed back into the van, a thin line of sweat on his brow. "Hot out there."

Klaus waited for him to mention the zombie, but he hadn't noticed. "We have a problem out there." Dylan raised his eyebrows. Klaus pointed. Kristy followed his finger, too. "Only one so far."

"It's a type two," Kristy said.

"A what?"

"They can handle a basic weapon, have more perceptive senses than the type ones, but are nowhere near a type three."

"Harris talked about them. You've come across these before?"

"Yes." Kristy pressed her face against the window. "They possess more faculties: basic understanding, comprehension, and limited problem solving. If we just wait, it might disappear."

Dylan snapped open the chamber of the gun. "Let me kill the fucker. I'll go out there and blow its head off."

"No." Kristy put a hand on his arm. "Don't. Let's wait and see."

"And give it the chance to get hold of one of us?" Dylan made for the door with the shotgun raised.

"You shoot that and we'll have company. They have an acute sense of hearing and smell. The shot will draw them, and the dead body."

Dylan screwed up his face. "What do you suggest then?"

"Don't engage yet. Just leave it like Kristy said."

The kids were kneeling on the seats and leaning against the curtains at the wide window running along the length of the kitchen table. Julie remained at the sink washing dishes, but she kept glancing over her shoulder. Klaus read the anxiousness in her posture and expression. The zombie's presence made her uncomfortable. He felt for her. She had lost her husband to these things—all she had cherished in the world, all that she had known for so long. Klaus had a similar reaction when someone mentioned the word cancer, the disease that had taken his mother.

Klaus stood, went to Julie, and placed a hand on her shoulder. She flinched. "We'll be okay. It's outside, and we're in here."

She nodded, wiping over the sink. "I know, but... I just *hate* them. I hate them all. I'd kill every last one of them if I could." Her bottom lip trembled. He had not met her late husband, but knew from the way she had adored him, and by the accounts of the others, that he had been a special person. "I'm sorry. I can't imagine what you're going through."

"They're vermin. I'd run them all over if I thought it would help."

71

Whilst he understood her hatred and sympathized with Julie, Klaus saw another side to the affliction, and wanted her to see that, too. He was sick too; as was Dylan. Would she be so quick to kill him, or Dylan, knowing what they might turn into? Had she thought about her husband and what had become of him? What if he had turned, too?

"It's not their fault." She stiffened. "They were all children, or mothers, wives or sisters, at some point. We need to keep that in mind. I agree, they're best all killed, but don't hate them for what they've become. None of them asked for it."

The fire in her eyes softened. She unclenched her fist and laid it on the sink. "I know that. Believe me, I ask myself every day what happened to Eric. Did he turn into one of them?" She fought her emotion. "I hope not. But it's difficult to see past what they look like."

"That's the challenge in life, isn't it? Seeing past people's physical appearance or actions brought on by things out of their control. The disabled person. Somebody who looks different. The crime of someone who has faced sufferance via their victim. I'm not saying we treat these things any different, but just don't hate the people they were, the things they've become."

The edges of Julie's mouth curved up slightly. "You're right. Thank you, Klaus. I hope you find whatever you're looking for in this world. I'll take the kids into the bedroom. Keep them away from it." She threw an arm around each of them, kissing the top of Jake's head, and they disappeared behind the curtain.

Klaus went to the window. The zombie stood on the curb, nose in the air, looking from the shop front to the van. "Its sense of smell is far more acute than that of a dog," Klaus said with admiration.

They watched it for several minutes before it started for the van. Dylan stiffened. Kristy went to the sink and removed a long blade knife from the block.

"Just wait a moment," Klaus said. He was still worried about drawing others. "It may—"

"More," Kristy said. "Down the street."

She was right. Klaus counted eight wandering in a broken line along the curb beneath the store awnings. One gnawed on an arm.

"Oh shit," Dylan said. "We'll need more guns."

Kristy bent to a bag near the door and removed a 9mm handgun. Klaus knew she had been an emergency doctor in the previous life, but now she looked Army-trained. He wished he'd been able to adapt like that.

The first zombie closed in on the van. Blue Boy began to growl. Dylan squatted beside him and curled an arm around his neck. The feeder reached the driver's side and stood sniffing the air. Klaus noticed the window had been left down. The zombie put its hands on the glass and stuck its head through the opening.

Dylan squatted and crept forward, pointing the gun towards the window. The zombie's legs slapped against the side of the van as it tried to climb in.

A gunshot sounded from inside the supermarket.

The zombie fell backwards out of the window and took off across the curb towards the sliding doors. Nearby, the other group closed in on the campervan.

ELEVEN

EVELYN SUSPECTED THAT the situation was about to intensify. They drove their trollies down the aisles, collecting the remaining goods on their list. Underlying, she felt the rush of killing the zombie and saving Callan, but it was slowly fading with the reality of what the infected man said.

"This way," Callan said, spinning his trolley in a circle as they added tins of pineapple juice to the unsteady pile. Evelyn followed as they joined Gallagher and Greg from the other direction. She thought they were lucky not to have found another zombie in the store, although, in her short experience, where there was one, there were always more.

As they approached the cash registers, another feeder had managed to pry the entrance open and shuffle into the store. Beyond, a group of them reached the van, clubbing at the windows and door. She hoped Jake was safe in the van. Cold fear tightened around Evelyn's belly. It was the facility all over again. The distraction lost her control of the trolley and it skewed towards the zombie. As she wrenched it back, she rammed it at the thing, knocking it backwards and sending it tumbling over a plastic Labrador waiting for coins to be slotted into its head for guide dog research.

"Hold tight," Gallagher said. He hurried forward with the pistol in a two-handed grip and fired twice into its head.

"Leave the groceries," Callan said, his trolley smashing against the wall in the corner. "They'll need help outside."

As much as Evelyn had fought bravely at the defense facility, a sickening fear seeped into her gut. She tried to recall what she had done in the last escape. It had been instinct, split-second decisions without thought of the risk to her. *Be strong.* She took the rifle in both hands and locked it in place.

Callan led them through the narrow opening to the wide concrete area underneath the supermarket awning. The zombies, hovering along the length of the camper, slapping their bloody, crusted hands against the side, turned immediately and came for them, their interest in the secured contents of the vehicle forgotten.

Evelyn stayed back, unable to gain a clear shot, as the others ran forward, firing into the group. Callan turned in a small circle, firing the handgun, altering his aim and firing again, blood and muck showering the air. Each shot was an episode in precision—no wasted movement or time, as though he had been doing it all his life. She realized his movement had a pattern, his body shielding her from the front.

The other two men did the same; Greg with the rifle, Gallagher with a handgun. In short time, they had laid the posse flat, a dread of gruesome bodies with the pavement and campervan painted in a layer of red, grimy fluid.

The door swung open. Armed with a handgun and a rifle, Dylan and Kristy spilled from the step, followed by Klaus, and Blue Boy, who ran straight for Callan.

"Jake?" Evelyn asked, running towards them.

"Fine. He's fine," Kristy said.

"We need to move," Gallagher said. "There will be others here soon. They're drawn by the smell of the dead and the sound of gunfire. You'll have two dozen feeding on this lot within five minutes."

"There's a chemist just up the road," Kristy said. "I need to get some more supplies."

Gallagher wiped a forearm across his perspiring brow. "You'd better hurry."

Kristy and Dylan left. "Can you go with them?" Callan asked Greg. He nodded and followed.

Evelyn, Gallagher, and Callan retrieved the trolleys from inside the store and parked them in a line outside the van. They had managed to find most of the essentials—flour, long-life milk, crackers, and plenty of pasta. Evelyn joined Julie as Callan and Gallagher handed stock from the trolleys in to them. As they worked, Julie spoke in a croaky voice. "I want to thank you. For not pushing me too hard last night."

Evelyn placed a gentle hand on her arm. "Of course. I've been where you are. Good days and bad." Julie nodded, pressing her lips into a line. "We need you, Julie. You're a part of this group, an important part. We all look to you for something, especially Jake and Sarah."

"I have to keep telling myself that, reminding myself that even though Eric and my kids are gone, I still have relevance in the world." Tears spilled as she spoke. She wiped both eyes with the palm of one hand. "I know Eric forced me to come along with you all. Who knows what would have happened if we didn't? At first, I blamed Callan for it, but Eric decided. He thought it was the best thing for us, and I trusted his judgment for many years."

"Things happen. Bad things. My husband died of cancer before any of this. He smoked cigarettes for years and I told him to stop, but he knew better."

Julie tilted her head. "You poor thing."

"Yeah. Both of us."

They embraced, a mother and daughter kind of hug, and it felt *good*. Evelyn missed the affection of her loved ones; she needed the physical aspect. It was part of her. It annoyed Jake, and Cameron had only displayed affection knowing she needed it. Lately, there had been little about. As her arms tightened around Evelyn, she sensed Julie was the same, the squeeze just right. She had not expected much from Julie in the beginning; she had probably written her off, if she was honest, but Evelyn had a sense that there was more to this woman than they had seen. Eric was a wise, wonderful man, and she didn't think he'd have stayed with Julie so long if she hadn't possessed endearing qualities.

The remaining supplies wouldn't all fit. They stacked four trolleys of groceries, and despite Julie and Evelyn piling them into the cupboards, they ran out of space. Callan and Evelyn drove the rest to the battered Toyota and loaded them into the rear.

"Thank you," Callan said after stacking the last tins of fruit juice. "Back in the store. You helped out."

"Saved your ass, you mean?"

Callan chuckled. "Oh, I'm gonna have that one hanging over me forever, aren't I?"

"Yeah. I'll milk it." He made a mocking face. "I suppose you might have done the same once or twice though. Let's call it even."

For the first time, Callan smiled—really smiled—and the delight washed over Evelyn like the sun on a cold day. She found herself momentarily lost for words, and a thought struck her hard—but she squashed it, leaving it for later consideration, when the intensity of the moment—the situation of survival, had passed.

He frowned. "You okay?"

"Yeah. It's... nothing." She turned away. "Let's get moving. I don't like hanging around here."

They hurried back to the camper where warmth and acceptance awaited. With incredible luck, she and Jake had found their place. They had taken them in with her faults and mistakes. She was contributing now and that made her relax. Perhaps most of all though, she thought Cameron would approve. He would have liked Callan and Kristy, Julie and

Greg, and the others. He would tell her to stay close to these people. With them, she and Jake had a chance to survive.

Stocked with medicine and food, armed with ammunition, and all still alive, they would push on. They had come a long way in twenty-four hours, but she knew there was a long way to go.

TWELVE

DARKNESS CAME AND went, followed by the blackness of a hot, moonless night, and a cool early morning. Still, Todd and Lenny hadn't left the apartment to find food. They spent the evening and most of the night getting more bombed out of their minds, talking trash and cavorting with the girls from the apartment above. Following a sparing dinner, Lauren asked Todd to go out, and he promised they would after dark. They made excuses, as Lauren expected they would. They also made noise for most of the night—thankfully, Harvey hadn't woken—and by the early morning hours, the group had fallen asleep. Lauren followed soon after, certain that Todd had cheated on her. But it bothered her little. She found all that remained of her feelings towards Todd were those afforded to any human being—simple decency. She would do nothing beyond that.

By mid-morning however, when they were still sprawled in a twisted mass beneath blankets and sheets and pillows in one corner of the lounge, Lauren decided it was time to break up the slumber party and start getting things into order. She knew they wouldn't go out of their own volition; she had to force them, which meant another confrontation, and that would no doubt bring its own issues.

She fed Harvey, changed his nappy, and wrapped him tight in two light muslin cloths. He loved to squirm, and she found if she didn't do the double wrap, he would wriggle free, and wake often. She slipped in his dummy and wrapped up the bag with the dirty nappy just as Claire entered.

"Breakfast is done. The last of the crackers."

"Did you eat?" Claire looked away. "Claire?"

"What? Did you?"

Lauren hadn't eaten for almost twenty-four hours. The hunger pangs had passed and she still had energy. If it went on for too long though, she'd feel lethargic.

"I have to make these guys go out and find us some food."

"You know they were shagging last night?"

She stared at her friend. Claire was the most tactless person she had ever known, but at least you got the truth in one punch. "I didn't. I suspected, but…"

Claire laid a gentle hand on her arm. There was a warmth in her eyes that unsettled Lauren. "He's a fucking asshole. Forget about him."

"I'll get them up. We need food."

"Good luck."

Lauren walked out through the sitting room and into the kitchen. A sudden thought locked hold of her mind. It was crazy, but she knew if he got physical, nobody could stop him. She needed back up. From a wooden block on the bench, Lauren removed a carving knife and slipped it into the back pocket of her jean shorts.

In the lounge, bodies were heaped under the covers in a lumpy pile. She had no idea who was who. She peeled one of them back, hoping it was Todd, but instead found the blonde girl wearing only a pair of panties. She bit down her anger. *Another time.* She dropped the covers back over the girl's breasts and lifted another section. Todd lay at an odd angle, his mouth open, chest moving slowly. A small pile of orange vomit surrounded his head. *Disgusting. What the fuck had she ever seen in this guy?* She poked him with her foot. "Todd?" Nothing. She did it again, feeling her anger spinning out of control. "Todd." Stony. This time, she bent her leg back and rammed her sneaker into his shoulder.

He came awake suddenly, eyes wide and goofy. "Owwww." He gawked around and found her looking at him.

"What?" The dickhead probably still hadn't realized she had kicked him, so she did it again. "Stop that!" Todd scrambled to his feet, baring teeth, and stood before her.

His short, wiry brown hair lay flat on his head. He hadn't shaved for a week and now had a scruffy beard like a Neanderthal. She hated beards. His eyes were red, his skin blotchy. Her vision fell on a love bite halfway along his neck. Lauren swallowed, fighting the urge to pull out the knife and slice off his nuts. Instead, she pointed a finger at him.

"You two are going out to find some food and you're not coming back without some."

The sleepiness washed out of Todd's eyes. Suddenly he was awake, standing before her. "Don't you *fucking* tell me what to do. Those days are over. Why don't *you* go out and get the food?"

Lauren stood there for a long moment stupefied by what he said. She kept repeating it, trying to understand *how* he said such things. All the time she had defended him to *her* friends and sometimes even his. All the things she had done for him: paid his study fees, fed and housed him, even clothed him when he ran out of cash. What a fool she was. The rage boiled up in her, jaw grinding, fists clenched. She heard Claire say something from behind, but it didn't register. Her mind had separated—one part pained by what he said, the other infused with an uncontrollable rage. Before she knew it, the knife was out, pointed at him, blade thick and glistening.

Todd stepped back, his features taut and terrified. Lenny and the girls had woken and now stood off to the side, watching her with wide eyes. Blondie slipped a green t-shirt over her head.

"Hey, come on Lauren," Lenny said. He was wearing only underpants. "What are you doing?"

A voice in her head *did* ask what the hell she was doing. A knife, pointed at her boyfriend (ex) and her baby's father? She lowered it, hand falling to her side.

"Okay. No stabbings today." Todd's shoulders dropped. "Unless you don't pull your weight and find some food."

Todd snarled. "What?"

"Until last night, *Todd*, we were partners—girlfriend and boyfriend, the parents of that little baby boy in the other room. But I've come to the realization that it's no longer going to work."

"Why?"

"*Fucking her*," she pointed the knife at the blonde girl, not even sure which one he'd been with, "might have something to do with it." Both Todd and the blonde girl looked down. "Added to your lazy-ass efforts around here since this thing happened. Okay, you went out to find food *once*. Eighty percent of what you brought back was alcohol. I've asked you repeatedly to do things. All you've managed to do is find these girls from upstairs and eat most of the food we *did* have for everyone else." She shrugged. "We're all sick of it. *I'm* sick of it. Either you start helping—by getting food, firstly—or you get out. That's the deal."

Todd considered this. He looked to the others for support, but nobody met his gaze. To Lauren, he said, "Or what, you'll stab us all?"

"No, Todd. Just you. While you're sleeping."

It felt good saying that. She wouldn't do it, but at that moment, he didn't know if she was serious.

"Fine," he said, gathering up his shirt. "We'll go."

"*I'm not going*," Brunette snapped. Todd snarled.

"You need to go across the road to the market," Lauren said. "They'll have rice, flour, and staples—get as much of that as you can." The idea that they might not return flashed through her mind, but if that's what it came to, Lauren was prepared for it.

"What about the other places?" Todd asked. "Anywhere else we can go?"

"The 7-Eleven on the corner of Elizabeth Street and Franklin."

She tried to think of something inspiring to say, to bridge the conflict, bring them back together as a group, but she was empty. Her mother or father would have found the right words. They had a knack of knowing what to say in the moment. Maybe it came to a person after they had kids.

They left soon after. Todd didn't even look back.

THIRTEEN

JACOB CLIMBED DOWN from the seat at the edge of the wall and sat, watching Rebecca. It was a small room in the railway station building, connected to a larger waiting area via a door. Jacob had deemed the smaller section more prudent to their needs because it had steel gates on both sides and two access points. They might still find themselves trapped, but it was the best of a bad situation.

"Still there?"

He nodded. The zombies had amassed at the fence on the opposite side of the tracks. Jacob couldn't believe they hadn't worked out that if they wandered further along the railway line they'd find a crossing. He had not intended, when they climbed the fence, for the train station to become their place of safety, even for the night. On arrival, they had absolutely nothing besides the ax. No vehicle, food, or clothes. He had sat almost three hours, waiting for the feeders to break down the wire barrier and find them. They should have kept going, but Jacob had decided it was time to stop and think it out.

Later, under cover of darkness, and without any light to guide him, Jacob fumbled his way further up the line away from the gathering, and cut across the tracks. Rebecca lapsed into silence when he told her his plan. Jacob was reluctant to leave her, but he scouted the area to make sure it was clear, and left her with the ax. He made it through the shrubbery, and snuck across the road to a small, noiseless supermarket nestled amongst a row of other stores. He ended up hitting gold, including what he considered the most remarkable thing: a revolver. It even had five rounds. There was enough food to necessitate several trips. He went back and forth, hands full of plastic bags and kids' backpacks into which canned goods, matches, batteries, and water were stuffed. There were various zombie activities during the supermarket runs, and Jacob decided to hang tight during the night and wait for the safety of daylight.

They still had the zombies beyond the wire fences to consider. Even if they managed to sneak past the barricades, there were too many of them in the town—they couldn't win on foot. If he was alone, he might risk it, but Rebecca's life was too valuable to put in such a situation

Silence had settled over them for a time, when Rebecca asked Jacob to talk about her mother. He did, finding himself falling easily into the recollection. As much as he had loved his second wife, Monica, Jennifer had been the love of his life. He had built his hopes and dreams around her. They traveled together, made plans for building their dream home, and Jennifer was planning a return to study. They laughed endlessly in the early days, before Jacob stripped away the joys of their lives with his absence. How he regretted it all these years past. Sometimes things didn't work out as expected.

"Sounds like you loved her."

"Oh, I do. I've never stopped."

She did not ask any more after that, lapsing into another long silence. He'd thought the music discussion might have given him some credibility and lured her out of her shell. He wasn't giving up though.

The small building grew hotter as the sun rose past its zenith. They drank the water without care, and picked at a tasty Italian oil tuna in a can, which they spread on crackers. The remaining supplies stayed in the backpacks and plastic bags in case they needed to leave in a hurry.

When Jacob checked through the high window of the building again, he found the fence had collapsed in one place.

"Shit."

"What is it?"

"They've broken through. Get your backpack on. Grab the ax."

Jacob ran to the front gate and pulled the bolt from the hole with a resistant screech. It appeared they were coming from the northern side, which meant they'd have to go south. But when he finally drew the gate open, the zombies were everywhere, covering all available exits. Jacob turned around to call for Rebecca, when she ran into him.

"You got a pack?" She nodded, holding up the ax in her right hand. The left contained multiple plastic bags chocked with supermarket items. "Good. Don't move." He raced back into the small room and scooped up a half-dozen plastic bags with one hand and two backpacks with his right, slinging them in a sloppy fit over his shoulder. *The gun. Get the gun.* There was a moment of terror when he was certain it wouldn't be where he had stashed it. He was wrong though, and he dropped the chamber out, ensuring there were still five rounds.

Rebecca snuck back in behind the gate as feeders wandered about the railway yard. Jacob stood motionless on the platform as he tried to locate a visual pathway through the horde. Male and female zombies of every age and size stumbled over the tracks. Somehow, they hadn't spotted them yet, but he knew it was coming. Their only advantage was the platform sitting four feet above the tracks. Jacob doubted any of them could climb up onto it, but if the zombies wandered further down the station, they would find a ramp by which they would eventually reach the pair. They had to move.

After careful examination, Jacob thought he had spied a way out. The feeders struggled walking over the railway line.

Many had fallen, and most failed to negotiate the steel tracks with any proficiency.

"South," Jacob said. "Straight down the center of the tracks. No stopping, okay?"

Rebecca nodded, her voice trembling. "Okay."

Jacob leaned down and kissed the top of her head. "You swing that ax if any get too close, alright? But don't worry. I *will not* let anything happen to you." She managed a faint smile. "Walk down the platform then we jump off the end."

Rebecca led them, feet moving faster than Jacob had imagined, bags slapping against her legs. He was proud of her courage, thankful she was finally doing what he asked. Jacob hung back a step, watching the feeders. At first, they didn't notice, wandering in circles and bumping into each other. He thought they might have caught a lucky break. But then a large woman wearing a flowery dress and a huge swell of breast spied Rebecca. She grunted, alerting others, and then they were stumbling after them, eyes locked on his daughter.

Rebecca hesitated. "Keep going," Jacob said. She did, hurrying away from the edge of the platform. Jacob fought the urge to shoot the fat woman for blowing their cover, but she didn't pose a threat yet and he refused to waste twenty percent of their ammo on her.

As they approached the end, Jacob took the lead, glancing back along the tracks. He had hoped they might have gained a head start, but the fat woman led a pack of a dozen or so, as though she had spied them first and they would be her kill. Jacob had to decide whether they should abandon the plan or make a run for it. If they returned to the train station building, the feeders would eventually find their way in. Of that, he was sure. But where would they run? How far down the tracks would they make it?

In the distance, Jacob saw the V/Line train they had passed the previous day. There was another machine beside it, along with a collection of items stacked to the side of the tracks. At worst, he supposed, they could climb up into the train and hide there.

Jacob took over the lead and slipped down off the platform, losing half the bags in the process. By the time he picked several up off the rocky tracks and slung a backpack over each shoulder, the lead zombie was almost upon them. "Quick."

Rebecca hesitated, eyeing the oncoming threat. "No, I want to stay. It's too dangerous."

He didn't think this was her being difficult, but terror at the prospect of being caught. "Now, Rebecca. Jump. I'll catch you."

She wasn't going to do it. Jacob thought about shooting the closest feeders, but what happened after five rounds? He would be out of ammo, and whilst the ax might take a few more down, they'd be quickly overcome. Rebecca wasn't going anywhere. He reached out and grabbed her hand, yanking her forward. She tumbled off the platform, cursing him.

She hit him in the stomach with her knee on her way down, knocking the wind from him. Gasping, Jacob wheeled, facing the fat woman who had closed the gap to ten feet. Beyond her, they were lining up like ticketholders at a Black Eyed Peas concert. *The gun*. Even then, he wouldn't have it out in time. Rebecca was on one knee, fumbling with the bags. They had to go. Jacob took her hand and pulled, moving along the tracks. She cried out, dragging one leg over the sharp stones. This was not looking after her, keeping her safe, as he had promised. This was taking her to the edge, risking her life. She couldn't find her feet. Jacob lifted, feeling the muscles in his left shoulder twinge, but she came off the ground, her shoes circling. When he lowered her, she found them, and then she was running beside him, crunching over the packed stones.

Jacob twisted around, expecting to find them on their heels, mouths open, poised to take chunks of flesh from their backs. But the gap was decent, at least ten, maybe fifteen yards, and the throng had thinned—no less numbers—but they were spread out further.

"Look out!" Rebecca shouted.

Only yards ahead, a man in slacks and a checked shirt waited. The skin of his wretched face was almost the color of his pale, wispy hair. Flesh hung in flaps from his bicep and forearms. Jacob knew instantly that other feeders had taken chunks from him, and he would take chunks from them. There was no time to pull out the gun or the ax; Jacob did all he could think to do. He smashed directly into the zombie like a rugby player, tucking his shoulder low to hit the thing directly in the chest. The lack of weight surprised him. The feeder fell back against the tracks with a crunch and they ran right over him.

"Keep going," Jacob hissed. He was almost out of breath. His lungs burned, and a pain in the lower left section of his belly spoke of too much time sitting at his desk. But he would move until his heart stopped or his lungs collapsed. There was no other choice. Their one advantage was ground speed. They quickly moved away from the chasing horde, opening up a gap of fifteen yards. That was the break they were after.

They were still coming as they reached the V/Line train, but the distance had opened up and he now had time to make decisions. Other zombies flitted about on either side of the track in pursuit.

They staggered along the rocks and walked around the side of the train, heading towards the front. Some of the carriages were for freight, empty now, as though goods were to be loaded. Further on, other items had been assembled beside the tracks, and a picture of what had been going on formed in Jacob's mind. The stuff was old, almost antique, but some of it had been cleaned up and painted. It was as though all the equipment was being sent somewhere for an exhibition, but the loading process had been abandoned halfway through. There was a small hand-powered railcar, a number of old railway signs, three signal boxes, part of a gate, and various other items that Jacob couldn't identify. None of it helped them though. They walked further along the line, conscious that the feeders were now gaining on them.

They reached the end of the collection where a larger railway handcar sat on one set of tracks, and the V/Line driver carriage on the other. This is what they had spotted from the other side of the fence the day before. An idea struck Jacob. He had been planning on using the main train for safety, but the truth was, he couldn't move it anywhere. If they stayed in the train, they'd be stuck there until the zombies decided they were of no value or someone came to rescue them. Either option might mean never.

He stood in the stones at the edge of the tracks, deep in thought, Rebecca beside him, glancing back at their oncoming attackers. "We have about thirty seconds," she said. "And there's more coming from the other side."

Jacob thought he might have a way out. Whilst the wheels on the handcar possessed flecks of rust, the body and chassis had been repainted. It might work. How far did the tracks go? V/Line trains always linked to major cities so he assumed these tracks would lead to Melbourne. Sure, there might be other trains in the way at some point, but for now, they had a clear run. He couldn't think of a better idea, and the thought of being stuck in the V/Line without going anywhere was claustrophobic.

"Up on this," he said, stepping towards the handcar. He swung the bags onto the platform, the backpacks, and then the ax, keeping it at close hand in case.

"This?" Rebecca asked in disbelief. "Where are we going on this?"

"Out of here. Move. They'll be here in a moment." Jacob was confident now they were going to be okay, that he would keep Rebecca safe, as promised. He had lost all the others, but not her, his daughter, the last one.

He took the bags off Rebecca and helped her up onto the handcar. The feeders were close—he had to give them credit for their unwavering persistence. He supposed they would chase them all the way to Melbourne if nothing else of greater value appeared along the way. Jacob swung a leg up onto the platform and pushed himself on.

He had never used one before. A post stood in the center about thigh height. From it, a long bar sat horizontal with two handles on each end. Jacob supposed they could stand on either side and both pump—one down, the other up, and vice versa—but he believed one person could probably drive it. He shifted his position, trying not to knock any of their supplies off the edge; floor space was limited. He took the handle and pushed down about ten inches, feeling the resistance of time and inactivity. He pulled upwards, his arms straining, and the other side of the handlebar lifted. A rod connected underneath followed the bar upwards. Jacob trailed the connector rod down and saw it moving in a slow circle. At the base of the machine, a crank began to turn a large gear.

"Hurry." The handcar moved several inches. "Yes!" Rebecca shouted. "Keep going. They're here."

The number of feeders chasing had doubled. It was as though they had put a call out to each other. The first hands clubbed the side of the handcar. A face appeared near his feet and he kicked out, striking it in the nose. It tumbled away, but others took its place.

He pumped the handlebar again, pushing harder, realizing it was going to take maximum effort to get the thing moving. But it was *moving,* although the feeders clutching at the sides were starting to quell their momentum. Their slobbering noises grew loud, and the smell of their decaying flesh and rotted aftermath of feeding stirred the thin semblance of food in Jacob's stomach.

"Get the ax and knock them away." Rebecca bent over and picked it up. It suddenly looked far too big for her. "But don't get too close." She began swatting at them, missing the first two times and whacking one on the third try.

Jacob peered back towards the station again. *Head down, ass up. Stop looking.* But something caught his eye near the platform. It was moving fast—too fast for a standard zombie. It was either a person, or…

Terror drove him. He pushed and pulled the handlebar with every ounce of remaining strength. The resistance was enormous—mostly now the feeders attached to the edges, trying in their incompetent way to climb on board. He didn't think they were capable, but they thwarted the escape, and the thing running towards them from the platform would have no trouble accessing their flesh.

"There's two of them," Rebecca said. "The runners. They're coming fast."

Two of them. Jacob staggered, as though all the strength had run free. Maybe it was over. Maybe their luck had run out. But they had been so close, so very close to freedom.

He couldn't let that happen. He snatched the ax from Rebecca's stagnant hands. "Step back." Using the flat end of the blade like a thin sledgehammer, Jacob swung the weapon. It struck the first feeder square between the eyes and it fell back, gurgling. Another came for its place and Jacob repeated the action, opening a gash in its head that squirted blood across its comrades. The thing tumbled to the rocky tracks, and this time none replaced it. He belted several more in the head, removing two, and began to get on top of them. He gave the ax back to Rebecca. "Try that." Jacob took the handlebar again and pumped. The car edged slowly away.

As he pushed and lifted, the things running towards them drew closer. It was going to get messy. Several zombies fell away, unable to keep pace. One caught an arm on the platform and managed to hang on. Rebecca made a small swing with the ax and clobbered it in the side of the head, but it didn't fall. Jacob stretched his leg around the center pylon and kicked it in the face. It dropped to the rocks with a crunch.

Only two feeders remained. They had almost passed into the outskirts of Seymour. If they escaped this lot, they would reach endless paddocks that filled most of the space to Melbourne. There would be no zombies there.

Jacob glanced up and saw a third crazy running through a field from the main road like a ferocious animal. Long hair trailed behind. *Female.* It was as if they were calling each other to the cause.

"There," Rebecca said in a cold voice. "Straight ahead."

"What? What is it?" Jacob turned around to face their intended direction and found it.

A *thing*, once human, but no longer, stood on the railway line wearing only a pair of brown pants. Its muscles rippled with sweat as though it had just completed a weights session in the gym. Purple blemishes ringed its neck and mouth. Short black hair. Dark, shadowy eyes. *Four crazies.* Either way, he had to get rid of them.

"Pump," Jacob said, holding the bar still for Rebecca to grab. It took her a second, but she understood, laying down the ax and stepping over the bags to stand at the pylon. They had gathered some momentum, and now the muscles in her forearms rippled and she had to stand on her tiptoes to push the bar down. "Give it everything you've got," Jacob said, and with that, he faced the zombie standing on the tracks.

He took out the revolver and checked the chamber once again, just to be sure. It was in his nature to double and triple check things. Long ago, when Rebecca was a toddler and they all lived in the one house, Jacob had always done a final check of the doors before bed. Just to be sure.

Five rounds. There were four crazies. He could do this.

He lifted the revolver and took aim. The car ran smooth over the tracks, quicker than ever. The zombie didn't move. Jacob took sight—its long forehead—and held it, waiting for the thing to move. Was it anticipating him? They were fast, but *that fast?* The car drew closer. Still, it didn't move. Fifteen yards. Jacob pulled the trigger.

The bullet made a neat, bloody hole in its forehead, and the zombie collapsed. It tumbled off the tracks, but its legs remained over the left rail. They would need more speed to run through it.

Jacob grabbed the handlebar on his side and pumped. The car sped up. Rebecca's red face peered back at him, full of strain and discomfort. *How much longer could she last?* Jacob gave three more pumps as the car's thick steel wheels hit the zombie's leg with a crunch. The car jumped a little, bucking them, but kept moving. The mangled leg flipped off the track and lay at an odd angle on the rocky beach.

The entire episode had drawn his attention away from the other pursuers though. They closed in, only yards away, all within easy reach of the car. Jacob released the handlebar and took aim at the closest. *Jesus, these things can run.* It grabbed onto the edge of the platform, sprinting beside them. Jacob supposed an elite athlete could manage the task, but it was still impressive. The muscles in its arms and legs flexed with each movement. Lesions covered its face and neck, the expression was flat and indifferent. Its dark, soulless eyes regarded Jacob though. In them, he saw a cunning and perseverance that chilled his skin.

He couldn't find a clear shot with Rebecca on the bars. He stepped around her and drew the gun to within two feet. The thing hissed at him, baring sharp, stained teeth. From behind, one of the others barked an unintelligible word. The feeder pulled itself forward with muscly arms and swiped at the gun, knocking it from Jacob's hand. He grabbed for it, fumbling, but it fell into a bag of tinned food.

The car slowed. Jacob swirled and found Rebecca had let go of the handlebar. She was bending over, fiddling with something on the platform. *What the fuck was she doing?* Pressure filled his chest; they tottered on the brink of losing it all. It had been under control. His simple plan was going to work. He searched for the revolver and found it between two plastic bags. From the corner of his eye, he saw the zombie climbing up onto the car.

Jacob dove for the gun. His fingers curled around the handle and he drew it out of the tight spot, rolling onto his back amongst the stuff he had gathered from the supermarket. His finger touched the trigger, but as he pulled his aim around, he watched Rebecca pull the ax into a high backswing.

She swung it forward, screaming, and connected with the zombie's face creating a sound like splitting timber. It fell back with the ax lodged in its face, pulling the handle from Rebecca's hands. She shrieked and tottered backwards. But the thing hadn't fallen off. It reached a strong hand around and removed the ax, tossing it aside.

Jacob crawled forward over the bags and tins as the zombie drew itself up onto the platform again. This time though, Jacob was waiting, and shot it between the eyes. Its head exploded and it sailed into the grass.

The other two were on the edge of the almost stationary car. Jacob pointed the gun at the closest, a burly man with a long, orange beard, and fired. The shot missed. The thing growled, snapping teeth, and swung a meaty fist that caught air. Jacob fired again. The shot blew the side of its head off and it tumbled onto the tracks with a crunch. Rebecca was back pumping the handlebar, utilizing the last of the car's movement. She understood the rhythm now, and the car quickly picked up speed. Jacob twisted around. One shot remained. He focused in on the thing's forehead again. If he missed, they were probably dead. The ax was somewhere further back and all they had beyond that were bags of tinned food.

Before Jacob pulled the trigger though, the fourth feeder slipped off the back. The car rolled away as the zombie came to a stop and stood, watching them. Jacob considered firing, but who knew when they might need the bullet. He dropped the gun onto the platform, took the other side of the handlebar, and began to pump.

FOURTEEN

THEY STOPPED AT a picnic area with toilets and coin-operated barbecues around midday, forty-five minutes after they'd left Yass. Callan and Greg had driven the battered four-wheel drive. Nobody thought it would make the trip all the way to Melbourne. They had the opportunity to swap it at a number of small roadside stops, but Callan said that if it broke down, they'd just return to the van.

Kristy tried to catch a moment with Dylan, but she couldn't find the right time amongst eating and weapons inspections. Callan had him loading rifles and handguns, placing them in certain locations through the four-wheel drive and the campervan; storing ammunition for ease of access at a later stage. Kristy decided to wait. She wanted to sit with him and find out how he was doing—the simple stuff they had missed since before the defense facility. It was as though they couldn't find time to be alone any more.

The food they collected at the supermarket came out in various forms to be fried, boiled, and toasted. Gallagher suggested they not go too crazy—yes, they were all hungry, but they were training their stomachs to take small portions and overeating would destroy the conditioning. The kids had tinned spaghetti on gluten-free bread—remarkably, it was sealed in a vacuum pack and still within the expiry date. It wasn't the same as the normal wheat flour kind, but nobody complained. Blue Boy lay outside at the foot of the stairs eating a mix of dry and wet dog food from a shiny steel bowl. He looked like he was grinning as he licked his lips. After they'd eaten and cleaned up and were ready to move on, Klaus raised the incident in the store.

Sitting at the table, Callan spoke of it with a stern, serious expression. "He said they could communicate with their minds."

Klaus chortled. "*I knew it.* Amazing."

"You say it as though you almost admire them," Greg said.

"Oh, I do, Greg, I do. I admire the nature of the *virus.* I hate them all and want nothing more than to kill them, but for the science of the virus and what it has done to them, one can't help but admire its capabilities." He adjusted his glasses. "The thing is—we suspected some aspect of mind connection. We had infected people at the defense facility that claimed the threes were talking to them."

Kristy's face went slack. "*What?*"

"We generally put it down to delusions or nightmares, but I always had my suspicions that there was more to it." There was a moment of silence as Klaus remembered. "I recall the threes standing to the side of the door and just staring at the wall. We thought they might have been in some sort of trance. It wasn't until later that we realized those infected in earlier stages were screaming."

"What… does that mean?" Kristy asked.

Klaus sipped from a can of soft drink, considering. "I think at the very least, they can communicate using their minds—call each other for help, and even cause pain. The type threes, anyway—you said the man in the store was bitten by a type three?"

"He didn't say, but there was a type three *in there* with him."

"I think we have to assume the threes have incredible intelligence. We had one at the defense facility that would systematically test our protocols. It got to the point where we had to change our pathology routines *every day* just to get blood samples."

Callan frowned. "What do you think they're doing?"

Klaus looked around at them. "They're growing an army—killing off the weak and turning those with characteristics they think they can use *into* threes. The ones and twos live to eat, surviving on flesh—sometimes even their own. They wander around easily distracted, moving from one body to the next. While the twos have simple comprehension, the threes are always searching for more of their kind, thinking about expanding their numbers. They sometimes kill the ones and twos. One day, there will only be type threes with which to contend."

That was a thought Kristy didn't want to consider.

Callan laid the map out on the kitchen table as they prepared to leave and traced a line with a bright colored marker all the way down to Melbourne.

"We have to go through Albury again?" Dylan asked.

Callan shook his head. "We don't have to pass through any town. The Hume Highway bypasses everything. We just stay on it and sail all the way into Melbourne."

"Even better," Klaus said, "is that the facility we need to reach is about a three minute drive *from* the highway. It's called a different name by then—Sydney Road—but it's just the same."

"So we stick to one road pretty much all the way there?" Evelyn asked with a hopeful expression.

"Yep," Callan said, and tapped the map. "If we want."

"And how long until we get there?"

Gallagher leant in, tracing his finger over the lines and measuring the scale with his eye. "About six or seven hours, depending on stops."

"Will we make that tonight?"

"No," Callan said. "I think we should stay somewhere tonight—somewhere quiet and safe, off the track and away from any sort of population. Head into Melbourne tomorrow morning." They all agreed.

When it came time to pull out, Callan decided he wanted to ride in the camper. That left Greg to drive alone. Dylan volunteered to join him. Kristy pulled him aside, unable to stand their separation any longer.

"Why don't you let someone else ride with Greg? We haven't spent any time together since... the other night." Dylan glanced at the birds in the trees, a hand over his eyes to shade them from the sun. "Dylan?"

"We will. I promise. There's just some... stuff I need to sort out with Greg."

"Stuff?"

"Nothing you need to worry about at the moment."

She shook her head. "But that's just going to make me worry. You can't say that and not elaborate."

He raised his eyebrows in a touch of defiance and walked away. "I can."

And so she trudged back to the camper, glancing over her shoulder. *They never look back.* He pulled the door of the Toyota shut, engaged with Greg, a rifle already in his hands. Kristy slumped into a seat behind the driver—Callan, it appeared, would take the wheel for a time, leaving Evelyn by his side in the passenger seat. Callan noticed her gloom.

"What's up, babe?"

"Dylan. He's still acting strange."

Callan studied her. She disliked him looking at her that way because he was able to gauge her thinking, and she didn't want him knowing what had transpired between her and Dylan. Although, that was childish—surely he'd have worked it out by now. He had accepted that she and Dylan were going to be together, when, in the beginning, he had been against the idea. How things change, she thought, on both fronts.

"Give him time. He'll come around."

Did she have time? Did any of them? Each day might be their last, and if anything happened, Dylan would regret the wasted opportunities.

The Hume Highway rolled on, a flat, smooth motorway flanked by galvanized railing on the long, sweeping corners, endless white posts with their silver reflectors, and the constant yellow and green bushland of the southern New South Wales Riverina. The cows and horses had been replaced by pods of kangaroos bounding their way across the wide paddocks and undulating hills. Klaus reinforced their thinking that animals did not suffer or were not exposed to the virus. Callan said nothing of this. Blue Boy was playful and energetic in patches, spending most of their driving time lying behind or below whichever seat in which Callan was sitting. The roads were empty, and each time they rounded a bend or passed over a rise, the three of them peered into the distance for signs of other vehicles. They passed through small towns—Jugiong, a turnoff to Coolac, the Dog on the Tuckerbox just before Gundagai, and then the town of the same name, where they peered out off the highway down into a strip of rustic old buildings and shops, looking for signs of movement—people, or feeders. There were none.

"How far do you think we'll make it by dark?"

"Maybe Seymour."

"And tomorrow we'll make it into Melbourne." Callan nodded. "And then what?" Kristy had thought about this. Maybe that was why Dylan was so uptight. His sister had been in Melbourne.

"We head to Klaus' facility. Get what he needs. Decide from there."

"You know Dylan is going to want to try and find his sister."

Callan shrugged. "I know. We'll just have to assess it when we get there. If it's too crazy, we won't be able to go. Sometimes we don't get to do what we want if it's not for the good of the group. I found that out."

"Yeah, but isn't this different?"

"Why?"

"Because he's already lost his mother and father. What if she's alive?"

Callan's expression softened. "Let's just wait and see what condition Melbourne is in before we make any decisions."

"Well, I think he needs to look for her. He's been strange of late, and I can't help but think maybe going to Melbourne and wanting to find his sister has something to do with it."

"Dylan's always been strange." Kristy glared at him, but his tone was light. "The group decides. That's the way it has to be. No exceptions."

Dylan had changed for the worse, but Greg had gotten better. He was no longer walking around with a bottle in his hand. Kristy didn't know if it was the bleakness of the situation, losing his grandparents, or the admiral's influence. He had struck up a friendship with Gallagher, the military man, whom Kristy had kept a close eye on after learning of his alcohol problem. Perhaps it was that they had a more common enemy. Either way, neither of them seemed to have taken another drink.

Kristy offered to relieve Callan from driving for a while and was surprised when he accepted. She knew he couldn't sit still for long—had been that way since he was a boy, constantly finding trouble in the classroom for disrupting the other children. He set the van to cruise control and they swapped over. She suffered as a passenger. Part of it was the sameness, the feeling that they weren't really getting anywhere. Driving was different. It required concentration, and of that, she had bucket loads.

Cool air blasted onto her face as she wrapped her hands around the wheel. It was a more comfortable seat, too. She slipped her Dolce Gabbana glasses down over her eyes and settled in. It was the control, her mother's voice said. Kristy understood that was a big part of it. She liked the control—a boyfriend had once told her she was a control freak, and that's why she became a doctor. It gave her more control of her life, and the lives of others. She had never disagreed. It felt good to be driving, to have all these people's lives in her hands. She wouldn't let them down.

The tiny town of Tumblong came and went, empty, like the others, and then a sign appeared for Wagga Wagga, and Evelyn bristled in her seat, remembering the chaos they had faced, almost certain death.

"What's the next town?" Kristy asked, watching the approaching turnoff.

Callan leaned forward. "Tarcutta. Straight through."

The highway continued its long arc, moving alongside the gentle flow of a feeder creek that wound its way to the Murrumbidgee River. It was pleasant driving, easy, and Kristy thought she could do it all day, if nobody else wanted the gig. Following Dylan and Greg in the four-wheel drive was almost calming, although they seemed to have picked up speed. Kristy pushed harder on the accelerator. But as the road inclined slightly, taking them up over a rise and concealing the road ahead, Kristy thought she was probably moving too fast. She applied the brake just as Greg did the same, but they still rushed over the other side, and what awaited them made her grip the steering wheel tight.

Ahead, at the end of another sweeping curve, the smoking wreck of a vehicle lay in the middle of the roadway. There was another behind it, and at their side, a pile of bags and

103

boxes. Beyond them, a throng of cars and a small Army truck sat parked across the highway, covering almost the entire blacktop all the way to the edge. Two vehicles were moving around, repositioning themselves to avoid any gaps in oncoming traffic. In the mix were sedans and several four-wheel drives. Kristy estimated they had about thirty seconds.

"It's a road block," Evelyn said. "One of those cars has been blown up."

Kristy stayed in tight behind Greg and Dylan. Callan appeared at her side. "Don't stop. Is there somewhere we can sneak through?"

Kristy slowed the camper, scanning the roadway in the distance. "No. There's nothing. They've blocked the entire road."

"Slow down. Follow Greg. He might try and pass around the edge."

"How?" Kristy doubted that was possible. Doubted it a great deal. The four-wheel drive might squeeze past, but the camper was wide and cumbersome. Despite this, she followed the four-wheel drive.

"It's *them*." Evelyn whispered. "From the barracks."

Callan peered ahead. "Are you sure?"

She nodded. "Same car Alex picked us up in."

"Who's Alex?"

Evelyn raised her eyebrows. "Never mind. They're crazy, Callan. I'm sure they killed Alex. If they find it's me, or you lot, because you saved me, they'll kill us all."

Gallagher and Greg appeared with rifles. Callan glanced at them. "We don't want a gunfight if we can help it. Who knows what sort of firepower they've got."

Kristy braked harder as they approached, expecting to hear gunshots. Greg and Dylan pulled away.

"Don't lose them!" Callan said. "We don't want to get separated." Ahead, as they rounded the last, long curve,

Dylan pulled the Toyota four-wheel drive towards the left shoulder. "He's going off the road. Everyone grab onto something."

A sudden dread overcame Kristy. In the back of her mind, she knew she had saved lives, survived herself, and kicked a whole lot of ass over the last few weeks, but at that moment, her metal slipped away. Maybe it was the seed of doubt planted by Dylan's absent love. She'd been running on the strength of that until yesterday. His detachment since the defense facility incident had affected her, translating into a sudden lack of self-belief.

"Oh God, it *is* him," Evelyn said. "Rick. The one who tried to take me."

Several men with guns came into view. They had another group of people surrounded. Probably the ones from the smoking cars, Kristy thought. The van slowed, and the four-wheel drive began to pull away, edging closer to the side of the road. Greg took the four-wheel drive to the shoulder and the wheels ripped over the rocky edge, sending up dust.

Ahead, one of the roadblock cars veered towards the shoulder, trying to block Dylan and Greg as they approached.

It was down to her, though. She had wanted the control and now she had it. She lifted her chin and gritted her teeth. "Hold on," Kristy said.

FIFTEEN

THERE HAD BEEN long periods of silence after they had taken off from Yass. Dylan had done the right thing by offering to travel with Greg when Callan had chosen the van, intent on quizzing Greg over the defense facility incident. A few days ago, they'd have found a way to make small talk. Now, silence filled the time. Dylan stole the occasional glance, but Greg remained focused on the road ahead, occasionally glancing up in the mirror to ensure the campervan was following.

Dylan had run it though his head a thousand times, but still he couldn't be sure either way. It burned at him, wanting to know. *Needing* to know. He thought about asking Greg outright. *Did you leave me to die?* But forevermore things wouldn't be the same, and that might affect the group beyond the two of them.

If he broke it down though, everything pointed to Greg leaving him for the zombies. The man had opened the door and hesitated returning. What had gone through his mind in that moment, Dylan wondered. Had he hoped the delay would be enough for Dylan to die? Or had he genuinely thought Dylan was gone? Either way, as a result of that action Dylan was bitten, and now he carried the burden of a death sentence, even if the serum could keep him alive.

"I need to know why you hesitated back at the Army base. You thought about leaving me, didn't you? You wanted me to die."

"What?" Greg's eyes widened and his mouth fell open. "What do you mean? Of course not—"

"Don't fucking lie to me, Greg. I saw it. You were through. You were gone. You hesitated. That hesitation …"
He couldn't tell him the rest.

"I came back, mate. Not only did I come back, but I saved you."

Sincerity. Greg was not a person known for lying. Dylan scrutinized the lines of his face, looked into his eyes, searching for the truth. It was hard to fault. Dylan wanted to believe him; wanted to think he had developed a friendship with Greg that would guarantee either of them being there when the other needed it. But Greg had done that countless times. Dylan remembered those moments—at the gate of his parent's property, and other times at the Army facility. But something inside him, some inner voice told him on this occasion Greg had left him to die. Dylan wanted an admission to that. Maybe it was because of Kristy. He could handle that. Love was a powerful motivator, and he knew that Greg loved Kristy. Maybe he thought getting rid of Dylan would make a happy ending to that plot. Dylan scratched at the insides of his forearms. His skin itched everywhere. The serum had only relieved it a little.

"I'm sorry man, but I don't believe you."

"I promise you, mate. The only reason I hesitated was because at first I thought you were gone. I had to get the door open, check it *could* be opened. As soon as I did that, I came back for you."

"I got bitten." He watched the road unfold between low-sketched mountains in the distance. He waited for Greg to speak. Would he tell the others? No. He was tight-lipped, if nothing else.

"Tell me you're fucking around." Dylan shook his head. He gritted his teeth, hating Greg and himself, hating the entire world for their situation. "And... it happened right then? As I went for the door?"

Dylan nodded. "Yeah. Right then." He wanted Greg to feel his pain. Even if he had always meant to come back, Greg had contributed to it. Deep down he knew it was the wrong thing to do, but he didn't care.

Greg closed his eyes for a moment in disbelief. "Shit. *Shit.*"

It seemed like he cared, but Dylan wouldn't be fooled. "So you're saying you did not leave me—you did not hesitate in hope I would be killed?"

"Do you know how fucking mental that sounds? What's wrong with you? I saved your ass half a dozen times before that. I could have just shot you and left you for the feeders a hundred times running around that fucking place."

That made sense. "I don't think you wanted to kill me or for me to be killed, I just think the opportunity presented itself and you took it. Or nearly took it. And that *nearly* cost me my life. And will in the end."

Greg's face hardened, eyes narrowed. "I fucking hope you're joking."

They were speeding now. Greg's agitation had transferred through the pedal and they were going too fast as they came up over a rise. The vehicle floated up over the top and dropped down with a bang. Dylan instinctively reached and grabbed the door handle, checking they weren't going to crash. Chaos ahead. "What's that?"

"An accident? Maybe a roadblock. That car looks like they've been—"

"Blown up. There's an Army truck." Dylan studied the scene and all at once, it made sense. "I bet you these are the bastards from the barracks. They're stopping cars and stealing supplies from people." Greg decelerated, and the old Toyota's brakes squealed. "I need to turn around."

"No!" Dylan shot out a hand towards the wheel. "Don't stop. Can you get through?"

There was no space on the right side, but to the left, the earth sloped down into a tangled gully of tall grass. Their four-wheel drive would handle it without pause, but the camper might have problems. They hit the gravel on the left shoulder. A scene came into view; there was a group of men holding guns, surrounding five or six people.

Dylan pointed. "There. We can make that gap."

"We won't make it!"

"We've got no choice. Drive down into the grass if you have to."

Greg slowed the Toyota as they approached the narrow gap. Gunfire cracked and the heavy clunk of metal sounded deafening. Both men jumped.

"Shit!" Dylan said. Another shot, and the side window in the rear compartment exploded, showering glass on the supplies. Greg swerved further to the left and almost took them off the road. A third shot boomed and more shots on metal. They were going to get killed. Dylan thought about returning fire, but he was misplaced for a clear shot. "Faster man. We can't stop now."

The narrow pass between the last vehicle and the edge of the road rushed towards them. Dylan hoped the campervan was close behind, but even then, he didn't know if they would make it. Greg's face was tight, jaw clenched, two sets of white knuckles around the steering wheel.

"We're not gonna make it," Greg said again, twisting the wheel.

"Do it, man. Don't you fucking stop." In the side mirror, the van had fallen behind. What were they doing? He sized up the width of the camper, certain the gap wouldn't be broad enough. A thought occurred. "Can you nudge the last car aside?"

Another gunshot zinged off the road. "What?"

"Make the gap wider. Ram it aside so the van can get through." Greg considered this. "If they have to go down the embankment, they might not get back up."

Greg shook his head though. "If we do anything more than clip that thing, we'll bounce off it. I've had my share of car crashes, believe me. They'll have to take their chances." Greg gripped the wheel tighter. Dylan reached a hand out for the dashboard. "Hold the fuck on."

They hit the shoulder at a pace; the vehicle slid sideways, then straightened. They clipped the edge of a black sedan, metal clashing like swords. Tires grumbled over the rocky shoulder as the left wheels skirted the edge of the highway. It dropped, and the four-wheel drive dipped on an angle, Dylan tipping. He thought: *We're going over*. He leaned the other way and Greg did the same. Gunfire barked, followed by the clamorous sound of bullets punching metal. The Toyota hit a pothole, propelling both boys off their seats. They drifted towards the edge of the embankment. Greg yanked hard towards the right and the tail end skidded out. *Gone. We're gone this time.* But the thick, right-side tires caught the bitumen, and they skidded back onto the highway. On their right, several men were in squat positions firing at them with rifles. Dylan ducked as more bullets clinked. Another side window shattered. More shots rocked the sky. And then they were past, racing along the roadway beyond.

SIXTEEN

CALLAN PULLED THE belt across his stomach and clipped the buckle. Kristy looked unsettled, but he was confident in her steady touch. She had changed immensely over the last few weeks. Her courage and surety had inspired them all, made him confront his fears daily. Her efforts—along with Evelyn's—at the Army facility had saved all their lives.

Julie had gathered the kids down off the bunk and strapped them into the seat around the table. Callan caught her eye and nodded. Gallagher, Klaus, and Evelyn had also buckled themselves in. Gallagher had Blue on the seat with an arm around him.

Well ahead, the four-wheel drive approached the blockade amidst gunshots. They took the narrow shoulder, skidded sideways momentarily, then caught hold of the blacktop and snuck back onto the roadway. But as they approached, he saw it was too narrow for the camper. They would have to drive down the embankment.

"Grab on," Kristy said. "I'm going down the embankment. If we try to get around that edge, we might flip."

She was right. They'd roll down the side and end up on their roof. It was just too narrow. And stopping wasn't an option. There were too many of them. They'd be shot to death.

Callan spotted a rough old track that led down into the grassy gully below. He had no idea how steep or clear the ground might be. If it was too rough, they would get stuck, and he couldn't imagine they'd be able to reverse out of there.

111

He remembered seeing plenty of clear sections along the length of the highway—some of which were driveable.

"You're right," Callan said. She threw him a smile. "You like this shit?"

"It's another chance for me to prove I'm a better driver than you. Just like the trail down the mountain from Lake Eucumbene, remember?" There was mock in her expression. "You couldn't handle the Jeep and the boat." Callan smiled, but beneath her sureness, he detected the underlying fear in her voice.

The edge of the roadway approached. The first gunshots punched the side of the van. One of the kids screamed. Callan instinctively ducked. And then it was on them. Kristy braked at the last moment, turning the camper fractionally right to line up with the faded wheel lines in the grass. The van rumbled over rough ground, shaking like a carnival ride. More screams. It bumped and bobbed down the rough track, the wheel slipping and jiving between Kristy's hands. "Hold on!" Callan yelled. She did, grimacing, feathering the brake, trying to keep control without losing momentum. Finally, they hit the bottom with a crunch, the fender scraping over the ground. Callan thought the ground might be okay. Through foot-high grass, the rough outline of twin trails continued.

The rough earth vibrated up through the wheel and seats. The embankment sped past on their right as he searched for the trail back to the highway. Somewhere, gunshots cracked, rolling across the sky. They were safe for the moment, the gully keeping them below the line of fire.

"Everybody stay down!" Ahead, the faint tracks climbed sharply to the right. "Follow that," Callan said.

Kristy pulled the wheel, hitting the hill with a mighty thump. Cutlery flew out of the drawers. Callan lifted off his seat, the belt yanking him back down, his teeth making an audible click.

The wheels spun on loose rocks, then caught and thrust them upwards through shorter grass and onto the rocky roadside. Shots peppered the van, shattering the glass over the kitchen sink and clunking into the sidewall. Callan held his breath. Just a moment longer. Kristy held on with a grim, desperate expression.

When they hit the bitumen, Callan pumped his fist. Kristy gunned the engine on as more gunfire cracked, whizzing past the moving van.

"Bloody nice work," he said to Kristy. "That was close."

"I didn't think we were going to make that."

"You did real good."

When the blockade was a tiny form in the mirror, they reached Greg and Dylan in the four-wheel drive, Kristy pulling in beside them as she lowered her window.

"No idea how we got through that," Dylan said.

"Can't believe we made it," she said.

"Let's move," Greg said. "We took a shot underneath the hood. Should be okay for now."

Callan checked the back window. The blockade was disassembling. One of the vehicles circled towards them. It wasn't over yet. "Oh fuck. They're coming. Go." The campervan wouldn't outrun any of the sedans, and it wouldn't be long before the old Toyota got caught, too. "Just go as fast as you can. Don't stop." He put a hand on her shoulder as he slid past. "You've done great, sis."

"Need some help?" Gallagher asked.

"Sure. Back window."

Callan picked a rifle from the cupboard and crept towards the back of the van. They entered the rear bedroom where Julie had cried herself to sleep after Eric's death and slid alongside the bed to the back window. Gallagher stood on

113

one edge, moving a side table to gain access, and peeled back one corner of the curtains. Callan climbed onto the mattress and rose to his knees, peering through the gap in the middle.

A big Ford utility chased, not much more than a bucket of rusty metal. Every panel was dented, and Callan decided it could well do with a bit more. Two men leered out the front window holding shotguns, and a third sat behind them. He glanced at Gallagher and nodded. They could handle this.

Callan reached down and unwound the window. He was thankful the fly screen had been removed. The wind whistled in, the smell of country and warm air filling his ears and nose, a pleasant change from the gruesome scents in the towns.

"Shoot to kill?" he asked in a whisper, not taking his eyes off the enemy. He saw fury in their expressions; they hungered for their victims' harm. It angered him. They'd had a difficult enough time with the undead, and now another group of stupid men wanted to fight? It was probably more than that, if they remembered the campervan, but there was no place in the new world for bruised egos. He remembered Steve Palmer and the others; they had returned after two freebies. *That* would not happen again.

"Yes," Gallagher said. "If they get hold of us we won't have to worry about where to sleep tonight."

Callan squatted beneath the window and poked the gun out through the middle. Gallagher did the same in the corner. He had to unwind it further to gain the angles they wanted. *The killing angle,* he thought. The Ford closed to within fifty yards, despite the camper's slow progression to top speed. An arm holding a handgun appeared from the back window and fired three times, the sound like rolling thunder, though all shots missed them.

Callan sighted the man behind the wheel. "Driver." Gallagher took aim for the passenger.

The men still hadn't spotted them. Callan drew the driver into his sights as more random shots exploded from the pursuit car, clunking into the back of the van. Gallagher made a whistling noise. Callan had been about to pull the trigger. He realized that the men were likely drunk, middle-aged, and probably couldn't make out the back of the van, let alone hit it.

"Count of three. One, two…"

Callan pressed the trigger. Shots smashed through the front window. The vehicle jerked sideways. He saw the driver's face fill with surprise. It skidded and flipped, sailing through the air for a handful of seconds before hitting the road with a thunderous bang, glass shattering over the road. It rolled down the highway with a screech and cry of twisted metal.

"Shit," Callan said with an incredulous chuckle. The camper sped on, his heart thumping. He thought about taking another shot for good measure and blowing up the car, but they had stopped their pursuers. Gallagher held out his knuckles and Callan touched them with his own.

"Nice work," the admiral said. "You're getting good at this."

SEVENTEEN

EVELYN TOOK THE wheel from Kristy and moved away from the blockade with her foot pressed to the floor. Driving away from another precarious situation had become a daily occurrence. She'd watched the action from the side mirror in the passenger's seat, hearing the bullets clunk into the van, watching Callan and the admiral take positions at the back window. She hated to admit it, but when the other car crashed, she felt a huge amount of relief. The explosion several minutes later lit up the sky. Although men had died, there was no remorse for their deaths, only a growing admiration for Callan.

As she drove on, the others rearranged things in the back of the van. Kristy disappeared with Sarah. Callan and Gallagher were hanging around the gun cupboard. Jake visited her briefly, checking in, which was all he seemed to do of late. It was as though he was gaining more independence every day. Aside from her, he spent most of his time with Sarah and Julie; Evelyn was grateful for their company. Julie was a substitute for his grandmother and Sarah the sister he never had. She thought about them all, including the sick men, Klaus and Gallagher. Each had a skill the group would draw on at different times. Mostly though, she thought about Callan. How he continued to lead them through difficult situations. In addition to her admiration, she found her fondness for him growing daily.

She hadn't been with a man since Cameron, and he was her first. But she was getting ahead of herself. She doubted he considered her in such a manner. Sure, they had a connection, but she'd had a number of close male friends back in Wagga, even when Cameron was alive. Just because they got along well didn't mean he desired her. Evelyn knew she wasn't pretty the way the others had described his fiancée. She was still overweight—although the current diet was taking care of that, but mostly she felt awkward, and almost dorky. A close friend had once described her in that way, although he had followed it up by saying it was an endearing quality. She had been mortified, heightening her self-consciousness, and had never forgotten the comment. Still, it was all too soon for him, even if she could overcome the other obstacles. What she could be sure about was that he liked Jake. They got along well. Jake adored him, even in the short time they had been part of the group. He seemed to sense the similarities with his father.

The sun retreated to the west, filling the sky in soft, ginger light. The temperature had been milder, but still not cool enough to leave the air conditioning off. They were burning fuel with it on. Once, she tried to turn it off, but the children complained about the heat, and she reneged.

She'd been driving alone for almost twenty minutes when Callan dropped into the passenger's seat. She smiled. Blue Boy fell at his feet, never far from his master. "You're our go-to driver now. Miss Reliable. I meant to ask earlier if you've always been like that?"

Evelyn shook her head. "No. When my husband was around, I didn't really take over anything. I mean, I organized Jake when he was young, but Cam took care of everything else."

"Sounds like he was one of the good guys."

"He was. I think you'd have liked him. I know he would have liked you."

His mouth curled up. Such a friendly smile. It changed his face from pleasant to handsome. *Stop.* "How long before our next break?"

117

"Seymour is about four hours, maybe a touch over."

"Do we have to get to Melbourne tomorrow though?"

"Klaus seems to think it's a matter of urgency to get more of the serum. We're guided by him."

Callan sat back in the seat as the last light of the day vanished. They learned much about each other—where they went to school, their childhood ambitions. Callan spoke of Sherry, and this time he did so with less pain in his voice, and more reflection of a woman who sounded like she hadn't treated him well. Callan spoke of his parents, Evelyn of hers, and for both of them, it was cathartic. She talked about Cameron, of his death prior to the plague, and when her voice cracked describing his final days, Callan reached out and squeezed her hand. She didn't know why, but talking to him was easy, and comforting, and she hadn't felt that way in forever. Six months after her husband died, Evelyn had gone on several dates. There had been no connections, no spark of any kind. She'd only accepted because her parents had pushed her to do it, to get back on the horse from which she had fallen very, very hard. No horses for me yet, Evelyn had thought at the time. Maybe ever. But sitting there with Callan, she smelled the distant stables.

They followed the long, slow arc of the Hume Highway towards Melbourne. They passed thorough Holbrook, and Callan told her the story of his mate, Johnny, and his treachery, but how Johnny had redeemed himself in the end. The place was devoid of zombies though. In the rear-view mirror, she saw Julie pause at the sink and put a hand over her face, stifling tears. She had been strong until then.

Albury was next, although they stuck to the Hume, bypassing the town center. Evelyn slowed the camper, weaving between the shells of vehicles, following the route set by Dylan and Greg in the four-wheel drive. On the other side of Albury-Wodonga, Callan offered to swap, but Evelyn was still comfortable.

At a service center about twenty minutes outside of Wangaratta, they stopped for fuel, refilling their cans and stretching their legs. The place was empty, and although the shop was still in reasonable condition, much of the supplies had been taken. Still, there were enough chocolate bars to cause her a minor breakdown and order Jake to brush his teeth twice. They stayed longer than they should have, prolonging the inevitable.

Bypassing Wangaratta, they went around Glenrowan, a place made famous by Australia's most notorious criminal, the bushranger, Ned Kelly. Benalla, Violet Town, and Euroa all passed by in darkness and silence.

Approaching Seymour, Callan decided—after consultation with the others—that this was the place they should stay the night. He had Evelyn signal Greg and Dylan by flashing the headlights, and they pulled over soon after. They found a place well out from the town center and off the main highway so that if any more of the crew from Kapooka had decided to give chase, they were well concealed. They parked under the low-hanging branches of a gum tree, where the soft breeze would scrape leaves over the roof of the camper all night, but nobody minded.

Evelyn should have been exhausted, but her discussions with Callan—learning about each other, had energized her. As they exited the camper to stretch their legs, she found herself glancing in his direction, looking for a reciprocal gesture, but it didn't happen. She dismissed her silliness, pushed the thought aside and gave Jake a hug. He had attached himself to Sarah, slightly older, who was charged with learning about medical treatment from Kristy. She worried he wasn't get enough of her attention, but Jake rejected her concern. Kids were resilient, she knew, although for how long he would be affected by the situation she didn't know.

While some of the men disappeared, sweeping the area for feeders, the van filled with smells they hadn't experienced in weeks. Julie had managed to bake a small loaf of fresh bread, and they ate it topped with the last sliver of butter, onions, and thick Green's gravy. Their silence spoke of its taste.

Afterwards, Callan drew the map out of a compartment over the sink and unfolded it on the table.

"Victoria." He spread it, folding down the edges. "We're here." Evelyn leaned in from the side and saw the name SEYMOUR. Callan drew his finger downward along a bumpy line to Melbourne. "About an hour or two and we'll be in the city."

"Where exactly are we going?" Evelyn asked.

Klaus reached out and pointed to the northwest— Broadmeadows—then followed a short line running west from Sydney Road, a continuation of the Hume Highway on which they had done most of their travel south. "The Commonwealth Serum Laboratories." He coughed as though trying to clear his throat, but it turned into something more, as if he was choking. Callan put a hand on his back.

"You all right?"

"Fine," he managed. Evelyn passed him a glass of water. He sipped and continued. "They make vaccines and test all sorts of medicinal supplements for viruses. They should have the ingredients to make the serum *and* the technology to mix them."

"Are you sure?" Kristy asked. "They have another site, don't they?"

"Yes, but this one is closest to us. When the world was the way it was before, they did all the things we need. Now, who knows? We'll find out."

"Broadmeadows was a rough place when I lived in Melbourne," Julie said. "High crime rates. Tough people. You didn't hang around there if you wanted to keep your head on your shoulders."

"Well, let's hope it's changed."

Evelyn had a question. She had been wondering where they were going *after* Broadmeadows, once they had acquired more serum. But Callan beat her to asking it.

"While we're here, why don't we talk about the plan after we get the serum."

"I need to go the city," Dylan said, "I have to find out if my sister's still alive."

"We've all got family we want to check on," Callan said. "But we—"

"I know that. But I'm going there whether you guys are with me or not."

"What?" Kristy said. "You'd leave us all behind?"

"You wanna drag everyone through hell to get there?" Callan asked.

Dylan stared at Kristy. "Fuck you both." Kristy recoiled in horror. "She's my sister. I know you both have each other, but some of us don't have anyone."

Evelyn watched Dylan's expression. His tight eyes and flexing jaw said he wasn't going to change his mind about this. He was different, of late. Something had changed in him. He had gone underground with a far more steady temperament, more buoyant, engaging. Now he was quieter, but at other times, impatient, aggressive.

"We can make that choice later. We're on the same goddamn side here." Gallagher stood and walked between them to the door. "What else can you tell us about Melbourne?

Julie looked sheepish as she spoke. "I was born there." She handed Jake a glass of water. The light had almost disappeared now. She pressed one of the switches and pulled the curtain above the sink shut. They waited for her to continue. "Lived there until I was eighteen. Met Eric, and we moved to Holbrook. He drove trucks for a long time."

"Where in Melbourne?"

"Northcote. Almost inner city. Older area, but still a lovely place."

"Is your family still there?"

Her face softened. "No. As I said before, my mother died when I was young and my father when I was much older. All my aunties and uncles have passed. Both of my sisters live in Queensland now. We don't talk much."

How sad, Evelyn thought. She had nothing to complain about her childhood.

"So you know Melbourne well?"

"Oh, yes. I knew those streets as well as anybody. Spent my days on them until I was a teenager. Things were different then. Kids played outside without fear of adult interference. We'd create our own trouble. You caught a tram into the city to explore and spent your day wandering around. It was a wonderful time." She blinked away the memories and took on a more serious expression. "Melbourne is different to Sydney in that the streets of the CBD are set up in a square, north to south, creating a rectangle pattern. The street names are arranged in some order, from west to east—Spencer, King, William, Queen, Elizabeth, and so on. It's easy to find your way around. A number of main arterials run right into the city—several join up to High Street, which runs directly through Northcote. And the Hume Highway, which we've been on since the beginning, turns into Sydney Road and runs right through Carlton and to the north of the city."

"Okay, then," Greg began, rubbing his stubbly beard, "say we find Lauren and manage to survive. What happens after that?"

Dylan had listened in stiff, irritable silence. Now he unfurled like a sleeping animal. "Tasmania, of course." Callan laughed. "It's a good idea. Smart. Safe."

"We don't know what's in Tasmania. It might be more infected than the mainland."

"I doubt it," Klaus said. "Melbourne will be hell. Tasmania has the best chance of being least affected."

Callan asked, "How do you know?"

Klaus raised his eyebrows. "Last reports we received were that they had far less infected than the mainland. They also have a research facility. It was one of the last with which we had contact. We lost *our* signal. They might still be operational."

"Who's going to fly us there?"

"We're not going to fly," Dylan said with a knowing look, as though he had been waiting for this moment. "We're going to find a boat at Station Pier and the admiral is going to drive us."

EIGHTEEN

DARKNESS HAD COME again. Lauren sat in Harvey's room watching him sleep. It was a place she came to think, usually to get away from Todd, but now he wasn't around to get away from. Part of her wished he and Lenny, even the girls from the apartment above, were still there. What were their names? Denise… and Sherryn or Sharon? She couldn't recall. Their introduction had been amidst some emergency or another. But they had gone out that morning on her insistence to find some more food, and hadn't returned. She supposed they might have run away, deciding the apartment, and her demands, were no longer worth it. More likely though, they'd been killed. She shouldn't have cared. Part of her didn't. But it meant Harvey would grow up without a father—as pathetic as Todd was—and that made her sad for him.

Decision time was upon Lauren again. Same old problem—still no food. Whilst it was everyone's problem, she felt obligated because it was her apartment. And she had Harvey. He was down to the last bottle of baby formula. Why couldn't she have persisted with breast-feeding? God knows she had tried. She had taken advice from everyone, but in the end, Harvey hadn't wanted it.

The options were limited. Lauren would have to go. Claire was determined, but incapable of the physical duress a trip to the streets might entail. Lauren loved her dearly, but she was a city girl, raised with a silver spoon in her mouth, and only just starting to gain her independence after several years living out of her parents' home. Furthermore, she could only leave Harvey behind with Claire. If anything happened to Lauren, she needed someone to take care of her son. That thought caused a sickly feeling in her stomach. That only left the elderly couple. Steve might be some help, but they would have to leave his wife, Lorraine, behind. Lauren didn't know if they would separate.

Where to go? Not the markets. Especially not in the dark. The 7-Eleven? She had suggested that to Todd. In daylight, it was plausible, but now it was a fully-fledged mission. They had no weapons beyond kitchen knives. It really only left them with the convenience store downstairs. It was a long shot. Todd and Lenny had last checked it, returning with a torn carton filled with several half-bottles of wine. Lauren had not been down there for almost a week, and then the choices had been narrowed to basic sweet biscuits and salsa dip. There weren't even any crackers. Lauren called Claire into the bedroom soon after, and explained her plan.

"You're fucking crazy," Claire said.

"Do we need food?"

"Yes."

"Who else is capable of going out there?"

Claire looked away, biting down a response. "Steve?"

"He can go with me, but he can't go alone." She had no comeback to that. "But I need you to do me a favor… if I don't make it back."

"Fuck off, Lauren. Don't say that shit." She bit her fingernails. "This is where people are stupid. They do stupid stuff. If you see a zombie, run. Simple. Don't be a hero."

"Listen." Claire almost swallowed her fingers. "I won't do anything stupid, but *if* I don't make it back, you need to take care of Harvey for me." Claire's face pinched into disbelief. Lauren stuck up her hand. "You're the only one I trust, babe. His father is dead, or gone. For good. If I disappear, he'll have nobody but you." Claire's face relaxed, eyes wide, lips a straight line. All the bravado had fled. "I hate to put it on you, but life's not fair now."

With two hands, Claire took Lauren by the scruff of her collar and pulled her forward. Her lips trembled, and in her right eye, tears welled. "I will look after Harvey if anything ever happens. But tonight, you are *not* going to die. Understand?"

Lauren threw her arms around her friend and hugged her tight. "I won't. I promise." After a long moment, she tried to pull away, but Claire wouldn't let her.

Afterwards, Lauren dressed in the heaviest clothing she owned. A leather jacket she hadn't worn for some years that wouldn't fit anymore. She still had a little baby weight, but at least her arms were covered. She slipped on a couple of tattered, indoor leather gloves that one of her previous housemates had left, and a set of horse riding boots she had brought from Albury but never used. Steve wore a pair of jeans and a shirt. Lauren felt guilty.

They climbed down the stairs without incident. Hopefully the front door was still locked. It had kept the zombies and potential intruders out. Technically, they had to leave the building to enter the store. Just a dozen or so steps along the pavement, but once they stepped outside, the protection was gone. Lauren peered out the door into the darkness, waiting for her eyes to adjust, searching for shadowy movement. Steve stood behind her, his heavy breathing grating on her nerves. Why were older people always like that? Her father had been the same, although thinking of him filled her with sadness. She'd have accepted all his annoying habits and faults just to have him there now. Lauren wondered if he was dead. She thought so. And she wasn't just saying that to set her mind at ease. In her heart, she believed it.

The darkness was still. "Let's go." Lauren pried the door open, holding the big kitchen knife in front of her. It was much cooler outside, heat from weeks of closed doors and no air-conditioning trapped inside the building. Steve placed the door shut. Lauren couldn't lock it and risk fumbling for a key if they needed to get back inside quickly.

They hurried along the pavement until they reached the corner, pausing outside the convenience store. She thought about all the times she had come here to grab a drink or bite to eat on the way to university. The times they had run out of milk or toilet paper and she had to rush downstairs, and Mrs Yin, the owner would chuckle at her. She thought about the Yins—Mr and Mrs, who owned the shop—a late middle-aged couple whose sons were grown up. They were lovely, and looked after Lauren and Claire like their own. Mrs Yin was a mad Collingwood supporter, and during football season would deck the shop in black and white colors. Lauren smiled at the memory, despite the sadness of it.

She pulled the flashlight from her pocket in preparation. The door was partially open, enough for them to slip through, but still Lauren hesitated. These might be her last few moments. What if they met their death and she never saw Harvey again? *Stop it.* She closed her eyes and imagined an easy passage through the store, where they discovered a source of edible food, and left without issue. The strong, sensible part of her mind kicked back. She cleared away the negative thoughts and tried to focus. She activated the flashlight and stepped through the doorway with the knife in one hand and the flashlight in the other.

The stink of spoiled milk hit her first. She screwed up her nose, placing the back of her hand to it. She almost tripped over something, but caught her feet. "Shit." She stood, casting the light over the floor, Steve at her side. All the shelving had been tossed, scattering wasted food and broken containers in a thick layer. A glass cabinet lay in shattered pieces. Lauren poked the beam around, revealing more mess

127

near the counter and the fridges, but there were no signs of zombies. A narrower section of the shop ran further back along Franklin Street where they kept wine and beer in fridges. No doubt, Todd and Lenny had filched their stash from them.

They picked their way through the rubble, kicking over rotten food stained with blood. She went directly to her stash of baby formula and was relieved to find the two tins. Beyond that though, there were plenty of empty packets and cardboard boxes with nothing but fresh air. Lauren took a large step to miss a bloody mess, when the heel of her boot slid across the floor.

Steve caught her by the elbow. "Steady on."

"Thanks." Her heart pounded. She kept expecting something to happen. And what if it did? She had seen plenty of zombies, but hadn't actually had to kill one. Could she do it? Lauren flexed the knife in her hand, imagining driving the blade into a person's flesh. She shivered. But these weren't people, she reminded herself. And they would tear her face off in a moment. *Will* tear her face off, if she let them. A noise sounded from somewhere inside the shop. Lauren froze. Steve bumped into her. "What is it?" he whispered.

"You didn't hear that?"

"I'm deaf in one ear."

"There's something in here." Lauren held the knife out further. Her mouth was dry. Suddenly she didn't want to be there. She wanted Todd and Lenny back. This was something they should be doing.

Another noise broke the silence at her feet. Lauren shrieked. Something flashed past, leapt up at them. A cat appeared, arching its back. It rubbed its flank against one of the big water cooler bottles that had fallen on the floor. Lauren turned to Steve, who was smiling. The cat drifted over to them, purring. It was a chocolate color, still plump. Lauren squatted and scratched behind its ears. "Someone's still eating enough. You scared me, Mister." She didn't know if it was male or female, but it sounded like a good name. The cat stuck its neck out, still purring. How nice it would be to take you home, she thought.

They pushed on towards the back of the shop, checking every conceivable hiding spot where a forgotten box of crackers or biscuits might be hiding. They found plenty of empty wrappers and some evidence of food that had been squashed to pulp, but nothing they could return with to the apartment.

Following the third sweep, Steve suggested they try another shop—maybe the 7-Eleven Lauren had mentioned, or one of the other smaller marts deeper into the city. She felt deflated, knowing they had failed the first step and wasted their time. Now they would either starve, or she and Steve would have to risk their lives on a greater scale by going elsewhere.

She glanced around again, searching for that missing place that everybody else had forgotten. Her eyes rested on the refrigeration units. There wasn't much left in them now. Most of the beer and wine had been taken—only the cheapest stuff remained, and without power, it had long ago warmed. Lauren crossed to them. She'd been there several times already, but only offered passing interest. Now she stood before the wide glass doors and stared. Lacking their regular contents, the racks were exposed. Lauren saw they angled up towards the back of the units. These were common in supermarkets. Items were stacked from the rear, sliding down towards the front, so that as patrons took a product, another would replace it. She shone the torch up towards the back and the light fell on several cardboard boxes stacked near the edge of the racking.

They propped the doors open with a broken piece of shelving. There were four large boxes in all, and Steve reached inside to draw them out. Lauren was ecstatic. They were placed too carefully for them not to be important. Somebody probably couldn't carry all the stuff and had stashed it with the intent to return later.

Inside each box was a backpack containing several large bags of rice, packets of flour, cartons of eggs, and almost two dozen cans of tinned food. Tears of relief threatened. All the doubt fled. They would be able to eat for a while longer yet, and she hadn't failed the others. There was enough in the stash to last them a week, if not longer. A thought struck her as she handed the first pack to Steve. Did they need it all? The question seemed absurd, but the goods had clearly been hidden from view. What if the people who had done it were like them, hungry and desperate? What if they'd scrapped and fought to find it?

"We should leave some of it behind," Lauren said, and explained to Steve. He gave her a long, thoughtful look. She thought he might argue the point, but in the end, he just nodded and placed two of the packs into the racking.

Finally, armed with two stashes of gold, they started back for the doorway. Lauren felt light of burden for the first time in days. They didn't need Todd and Lenny. She would rally the troops and find a way to get it done without them.

It was tough with the heavy pack on her back, but she was able to maintain the torch beam ahead and grip the knife in her other hand. They cleared the rear section with its broken bottles of wine and beer fridges, but as Lauren stepped into the main section, another noise sounded from near the doorway. *The cat.*

"Here, kitty kitty," she called in a soft voice. She waited for a response, perhaps a *meow*, or its idling purr, but the silence stretched out.

"Maybe it wasn't the cat," Steve said.

"What else could it—"

The crash of glass sounded from the front of the store. Lauren screamed. The torch beam wavered and her grip on the knife loosened. Steve shouted something, but she couldn't hear it over the remnants of the noise and her sideways movement. He stepped around her and placed himself in front, waiting for the attack.

It came at them from their right, out of the depths of the counter and the remaining empty racks once filled with magazines and baseball caps. The shadows rolled, mixing and merging as one, before Lauren swung the flashlight around. By the time she had it pointed in its direction, the thing was on them, grunting and slobbering and calling for their flesh. She poked the beam into its eyes. Steve tried to knock it out of the way, but he fell aside, losing his footing on the cluttered floor. Lauren slashed at its throat with the knife and missed. It lunged for her; she couldn't make out if it was a woman or man. It knocked the knife away with a meaty hand and then all she had left was the torch. They were going to die, she thought in a flash. She had battled through it all over the last few weeks; keeping the group fed, dealing with Todd and Harvey, the loss of her parents and Dylan, only for it to end like this.

A silhouette appeared in the doorway. It might have been another one of them, come to join the feast. But the shape moved quickly, skating over the rubble towards the zombie. A blade flashed, and blood sprayed outwards from the zombie's neck. It slumped to the floor. The man—she saw him, now, cloaked in a hooded jacket, his baby face and pale eyes staring back at her from above average height. He tossed the body aside, then put out a hand for Steve and lifted the older man to his feet.

"We have to leave," the stranger said. "Now."

131

He led them out of the store and stopped on the pavement, glancing in the opposite direction from the way they had come, as though he was expecting to find somebody.

"This way," Lauren said, not waiting for him to follow. She was grateful for his rescue, but they had to get back to the apartment.

She pushed on the glass entrance and stepped inside, holding it open for Steve, and it appeared, the stranger. After he passed her, she swung the heavy door shut with a thud and locked it, unable to believe they were safe.

NINETEEN

THEY BEGAN THEIR trek as the morning sun cast its orange light from the eastern horizon, pulling out onto the wide rolling flats of the Hume Highway. The morning was clear, bright, and promised another long day of scorching heat that would further desiccate the thirsty ground of the northeast region of the state.

Dylan had suffered through the night beside Kristy. Their contact had been minimal, and despite the heat, he had worn a t-shirt with a collar, afraid that if he was naked, she might see the patch with which Klaus had dressed the bite. Twice she had put an arm over him, a potential precursor to more, but he ignored it. She rolled over in a huff, and Dylan cursed himself, sure tomorrow would be the day that he died—or worse, something happened to her; he would rue himself forever for wasting precious moments.

The serum had calmed his agitation, but not his paranoia about the bite and its consequences. He was still reluctant for her to know, despite understanding somewhere, deep in his increasingly paranoid mind, that it hurt her. He was changing too, serum, or not. It was as though the virus dulled certain feelings and intensified others.

They were cordial in the morning, hugging briefly, but the hurt on her face—the soft shadow of her dark eyes that told him she had barely slept—broke his heart. She probably thought his feelings had changed. A deep part of him knew he should say something, but he couldn't bring himself to do it.

"Are we good?" she asked in a hopeful voice.

He nodded. "Yeah." But they went no further. It was as though a wall had suddenly gone up between them, and they had nothing left to discuss. Others stirred from sleep. Kristy left the camper and Dylan despised himself for not chasing.

The group prepared to leave quickly, packing and eating without much word. Klaus signaled Dylan and he made for the scrub, away from the rest. Klaus checked Dylan's bite and administered more serum.

"Is this stuff working?" Dylan asked.

"You tell me," Klaus said. "I can't be sure without blood work. Your symptoms don't seem to be getting any worse. How do you feel?"

"Different, I suppose. I bit calmer, but I still feel like I might lose it at any time."

Klaus wiped a sleeve across his nose. His voice sounded odd, as if he was congested. "That's probably normal. I'd like to be able to give you more, but we don't have much left, and besides, there may still be some side effects. Each of you will process the virus and the serum differently. Just keep me abreast of any significant changes." Klaus broke into a coughing fit, his face turning a fierce red, spittle flying from his lips.

"Geez, mate, that doesn't sound too good." Klaus waved him away. "You sure you're getting enough of that serum?"

"Forget about that," Klaus snapped. "Let me worry about the medicine."

Dylan bit down on a response as Klaus walked away. It was most unlike the scientist to respond in such an aggressive manner, and he wondered whether the pressure of it all was beginning to take its toll.

Blue Boy sat near his feet as they took their places in the van. Greg and Gallagher agreed to drive in the Toyota. The admiral was a good influence on Greg. Dylan hadn't seen either of them take a drink in days. He was laughing more, and clearer of mind.

Dylan tried to be optimistic as they drove out from underneath the low hanging gum trees. Two kangaroos bounded past and he hoped it was a positive omen. They had still not observed one sick animal.

Two things sat at the horizon of the day—the extra serum they needed, and his sister. Whatever happened after their first stop, Dylan was going to the city, even if he went alone. He couldn't shake the feeling that Lauren was still alive.

The Hume Highway continued in long, straight runs through lightly scrubbed bushland. As they approached the northern towns of Beveridge and Broadford just beyond Melbourne's outskirts, the chatter died down. They were closing in on a broader urban area comprising four million people, and nobody knew what to expect.

Craigieburn arrived, the tip of Melbourne's north, and on their right side, they watched silent houses spreading away from the highway against the backdrop of a low hill. When they hit Somerton, an industrial suburb full of caravan manufacturers, transport companies, and a multitude of large warehouses, more vehicles began to appear on the opposite road going north. Most were abandoned. Occasionally, they saw a lifeless corpse sitting behind the wheel.

It only got a little worse. Cars had stalled going towards the city, and many more heading north in the opposite bearing. As they approached the major intersection with Camp Road, dozens of cars were scattered about the roadway, pointing in every direction. On their left, vehicles littered the parking area outside the K-Mart store. Zombies floated about the lot at their slow, bumbling speed. Bodies lay on the ground, some alone, others being feasted on by their brothers and sisters. And like the large shopping complexes in Albury, a smoke column reached high into the blue morning sky.

Evelyn guided the car into the right turning lane, following the folded map Callan had set before her on the dashboard. Ahead, further down Sydney Road towards the city, the route was a parking lot. When the time came to go further south, he would have to find another pathway to find Lauren.

They crept along Camp Road, crossing a train line, the boom gates ripped from their posts and shattered into countless pieces.

"It's just up ahead," Klaus said as the van climbed a slight rise. On their right, a green lake sat nestled between various small warehouses. A sign pointed north suggesting *Saturday Night Greyhound Racing.*

They drove over the slope and onto a flatter section of road. On the right, a series of wide squat buildings peered out at them from behind a high fence topped with barbed wire. Rolling green lawns in need of mowing surrounded the structure. A cannon, once used in some distant war, sat in the middle of the lawn.

"Maygar Army Barracks," Gallagher said. "No good."

Evelyn slowed the van. Gallagher pointed them out in the dark windows, standing behind the glass, stumbling around. It wasn't a place they might stop and get help.

They left the barracks behind. Three hundred yards ahead, behind another fence and a row of tall conifer trees, they saw the top of a large building with the words CSL in red letters.

"Pull up," Callan said. Evelyn did, braking hard and pulling in behind a small truck parked up on the curb. Abandoned road works signs lay flat in the curbside grass. Another hundred yards along, a group of five or six people stood at a set of traffic lights outside what appeared to be the entrance, dressed in Army clothing and holding machine guns. He didn't like it. He had expected they would simply drive up, enter the building, and collect what they needed.

The others joined them in the camper, and Gallagher stood behind the driver with a rifle and scope at his eye. "They're guarding the facility," he said. "Waiting for people to approach the gate. But I don't think they're military."

Klaus stood beside him. "Under such circumstances where a virus has affected the population, this sort of facility becomes very valuable. In all likelihood, they have taken over the facility."

"What sort of value?" Evelyn asked.

"Vaccines. Antibiotics. It doesn't matter. Men always find the tradable currency, and this—a place that manufactured medicine in a world where such no longer exists—has a high currency. I'm surprised the government didn't try to lock it down." Klaus turned away and sneezed twice. He groaned. "Summer cold."

"So does that mean we won't be able to get in?" Dylan was already thinking ahead.

"I wouldn't say that," Klaus said in an unconvincing tone. "It will just be more difficult."

Evelyn turned off the campervan and they sat watching the men outside the entrance, careful not to show excessive movement, although Gallagher was certain they were hidden behind the abandoned truck.

Shortly, a man appeared out of the bushes behind the fence. He was medium height, with a Middle Eastern complexion. He wore jeans, runners, and plain green t-shirt. He had short black hair, and a scruffy beard. Gallagher pointed the rifle. The man put up his hands.

"Who the hell is that?" Callan asked.

Kristy went to the window. "He looks friendly. Maybe we should talk to him. He might know something about the facility."

"What if he's one of them?"

Gallagher said, "I don't think so."

Callan led them in a bent-over sprint across the footpath to the fence protected by the road works equipment.

The man greeted them with a friendly tone. He'd been returning home after scouting for supplies, walking through the hedge at the edge of the site. He wasn't part of the group. He lived on the other side of the facility. All of his friends and relatives had died, except for his wife, who was back at the house. Mobs of people patrolled the area, fighting for control of the facility. Each day he went out alone checking houses, looking for supplies and things that might have been left behind.

Dylan said, "We're trying to get into that building."

The man shook his head. "You can't. I've been trying for a week. Those men have taken it over, and they kill anyone who tries to get in."

Gallagher crept up behind the tip truck and peered along the street through the scope of the rifle.

Callan hooked fingers into the chain link fence. "Have you tried talking to them?" The man raised his t-shirt and revealed a bandage over his right shoulder. "They shot you?"

He nodded, smiling. "They've taken many shots at me. I've found a way in, but I'm afraid if I go in there alone, I'll get caught, and die. There was another man who lives nearby that I was working with, but I haven't seen him lately."

Dylan wasn't sure he liked the man, but he couldn't put his finger on why.

"Why do *you* want to get inside?" Kristy asked.

For a long moment, Dylan thought he wasn't going to answer. "To find some medicine." The smile faltered for the first time. "My wife is sick."

"The virus?" Kristy asked. The man nodded. "What happened? Was she bitten?"

"I don't know. She came down with a head cold. She was acting peculiar—kept saying we were going to get killed, very paranoid, and angry all the time. It was most unlike her."

Dylan looked away. *Sounded familiar.* He wondered whether Kristy would put two and two together. He glanced up to check she was looking at him. She was, and his face filled with heat.

"We need to get into that building," Kristy said. "Can you help us?"

Callan said, "We might be able to help her. *If* we can get inside and find what we need."

The man's eyes widened. "Really? I can get you in." He pointed back along the road. "There's a small cut in the fence in the next property. You crawl through there, and then do the same again into this facility. They've been there for years."

"But how do we get inside the building?"

"I'll show you. Do you have weapons?"

"Yes," Callan said. "Enough to put up a fight. What's your name?"

"Ahmed."

Callan asked, "Who's going with Ahmed?"

"Me," Dylan said. Kristy shot him an icy glare. He frowned back at her, and she turned away.

"I'll go, too," Gallagher said.

"Klaus," Callan said. "Nobody else knows what they're looking for." Callan put a hand over his eyes to shield the sunlight, and waved Klaus from the camper.

"We need to distract them," Ahmed said. "Whoever is coming into the facility will need to follow me. The rest will need to drive the van further up to the gate as if you're trying to get in. They will engage you. Tell them you're looking for help. Medicine. They won't hurt you but will tell you to leave. That will take their focus away."

"Are you sure?" Kristy asked.

"I've seen it done before several times."

Klaus stepped gingerly from the van and shuffled across the curb to the fence. He wasn't moving well, Dylan thought. Something wasn't right with the scientist. Blue Boy followed. Dylan wondered whether the dog would growl at the man, but he sat patiently on his haunches beside Callan, who explained the plan, guiding them away from Ahmed. "What do you think, Klaus? We're placing a lot of trust in this man."

"Yes, we are, but I don't see we have a choice. Without him, our chances of getting in are minimal."

Dylan shielded his eyes from the sun. "Couldn't we approach the gate and ask them to let us inside?"

"He told us to do that, so I guess we'll find out if it works or not."

"How much serum is left?" Dylan asked.

"Not much. We need to get in that building."

"But if we're careful with the ser—"

"No!" Klaus said. Dylan stepped back. "There won't be *enough*. There isn't enough now." He massaged his temples. "We need to get in that facility or those of us infected won't be going much further."

"I think that makes it pretty clear," Callan said.

In the end, after a little more gentle persuasion, they all agreed that Gallagher and Dylan would accompany Klaus and Ahmed.

"We need to move," Ahmed said. "Drive up to the gate and ask to be let in. After they reject you, keep driving along this road and take the left turn. The street runs along the fence line of the facility. We'll meet you there."

"How long do you think it will take?" Callan asked.

Klaus scratched his head. "I have no idea. Could be thirty minutes. Could be four hours."

It felt like déjà vu to Dylan, as so much of their lives had lately. He didn't want a grand goodbye with Kristy. It was as though the sentimental part of him had been supressed by the virus. But she probably didn't understand why he had requested to go into the facility. He didn't want to hang around this place too long. He would keep them moving and hurry their progress towards the city. He had a fleeting thought of telling Kristy all of this, but decided dropping that on her and running off wouldn't be fair. He would do it immediately upon his return.

Her eyes were glassy as he they hugged. "Be careful," she said.

"You too." He kissed her softly on the mouth, lingering a moment. He knew he should say more; tell her how much he still loved her, but instead, he turned away and considered what lay ahead.

Inside the perimeter, Ahmed walked parallel to them as they followed the footpath away from the campervan. Dylan turned back once. Callan stood at the door, squatting beside Blue Boy, a hand around his neck. Kristy had disappeared inside the van. They passed another fence and came to an overgrown block where snarling weeds and blackberries covered the fence line. Ahmed could go no further. Another chain-link fence ran at right angles from the road. "There's a cut in the wire up a little way. Go through it, and then walk diagonally to this fence."

They found the inconspicuous opening in the weeds and wriggled through it, Klaus catching his shirt on the sharp wire ends. Dylan couldn't shake the feeling that they were walking into danger, and as they crossed the heavy undergrowth, he posed the question to the others. Klaus couldn't keep pace though. Dylan slowed, waiting for the scientist. Sweat ran down his face with the exertion under the hot sun.

"What choice do we have?" Klaus asked, still agitated.

They reached Ahmed and he pulled the flap back to allow them easier pass, then led the three of them through a tangle of brush, ducking behind an old shed. Was this crazy? Who was this guy and why did they trust him so quickly? Through the fence, they watched as the campervan and Toyota drove off towards the gate.

"We wait here a moment," Ahmed said, peering around the corner of the shed. Dylan stood behind.

Fifty yards away, near the entrance, several men patrolled with machine guns. If Ahmed had wanted, he could call out to the men and they would probably be shot. Suddenly Dylan didn't want to be there, regardless of whether he was getting serum or not. He considered returning to the street and waiting for the campervan. He stepped out from behind the shed. A hand grabbed his shoulder and yanked him back.

"What are you doing?" Ahmed's brows angled down sharply.

"I—"

"They'll *kill* you if they find you in here."

A noise sounded from the gatehouse. Another vehicle had pulled up in front of the gates. The men patrolling the grounds hurried towards the entrance, leaving them unobserved.

"Now," Ahmed said. They ran.

TWENTY

AS THEY PULLED away from the curb, a black BMW turned into the entrance of the facility from the other direction. The men standing outside the gates flocked to it, guns drawn.

"Keep going," Callan said, standing beside Evelyn. "Drive slowly. And be ready to speed off."

Evelyn feathered the accelerator, watching with a cautious eye. Her stomach fluttered, but not in the way she would have liked. Men and guns were not her favorite thing of late. They were driving into a potential situation, and the group had split. They all mattered to her now. Each of them had contributed to her and Jake's survival in some way. "How close?"

"Just pull into the turning lane, but don't drive up to the entrance."

She glanced back to make sure Jake was seated, and saw Greg standing behind Callan with a rifle. She guided the camper left into the turning lane and pulled up. Ahead, the black sedan was parked at right angles in front of the gatehouse. Six men, some wearing bandanas, others ponytails, stood around it, holding machine guns and pistols. Two were close to the sedan, talking to the occupants. Despite the strong feeling, Evelyn resisted driving away. "I don't like this."

Greg stepped closer to the front window. "Yeah, me neither."

"Hold on," Callan said. "Let's see what happens. Based on what Ahmed said, they should turn the BMW away."

One of the gunmen noticed them and started towards the campervan. He said something to the others, and laughed. The driver of the black sedan became vocal. The door opened and a man climbed out of the passenger side. A ponytailed gunman barked a command at him. The man kept coming. Ponytail raised his pistol and shot the passenger. Blood exploded from the back of his head and he crumpled to the ground.

"Go. Go!" Callan screamed.

Evelyn released the brakes and chirped rubber as they leapt away from the curb, pulling back out onto Camp Road. As they passed the gatehouse, gunfire chattered, clunking into the van. Sarah screamed. Evelyn screamed. The men dropped.

"GET DOWN, JAKE!"

Evelyn couldn't get down. She wanted to; she felt her limbs and body pulling at her to drop, but she held tight to the wheel. The thud of bullets and the sound of ripping metal echoed through the inside. She should have been protecting her son. She risked a glance back; Julie had both Jake and Sarah lying down on the seats, her ample body covering them. A feeling of deep gratitude washed over Evelyn.

She slowed the camper as they approached the first left turn, crunching the curb with the rear wheel. Instinct told her to keep going, to drive straight on, but Dylan and the others were inside, and the man had said to meet them down the side—

"There's a man chasing us," Kristy called out. She stood at the back window.

Evelyn took the first street, running parallel with the boundary of the CSL site. Trees lined the road, providing shade from the incessant sun. "Goodie or baddie?" Evelyn asked.

"I don't know. I think it was one of the men from the sedan."

"Where do I go?" Evelyn asked.

Callan dropped into the front seat. "Keep going for a bit."

"Are you okay, Jake?" she called out.

"Yes, Mom." Julie still had both the kids under one arm.

On their left, heavy foliage filled the inside perimeter of the facility grounds, towering above the barbed wire fence. On the right, the snarling gardens of abandoned houses peered at them. They reached a bend in the road, away from the CSL grounds and deeper into the suburban folds. Evelyn didn't think they wanted to go that way, and Callan confirmed her thinking.

"Pull up here," Callan said. "At the corner."

Evelyn climbed the gutter and parked on the grassy curbside behind a red sedan with weeds growing around flat tires, a relic of the street's former inhabitants. Armed with rifles, Callan and Greg moved towards the back of the van, checking the view from each window. In the distance, gunfire popped and cracked.

Kristy stood at the side window. "I don't think it's safe to wait here."

Callan rubbed his temples. "Let me think." He started pacing.

Evelyn had never witnessed him so stressed. Usually, his calm demeanor prevailed. She supposed this was different though. He couldn't influence the outcome. He had to wait, dependant on the others.

"He's coming," Kristy said. "The man who was chasing us."

Callan opened the side door and stepped out, followed by Greg and Kristy. Evelyn left the driver's seat and went to Jake, who hugged her tightly around the waist. He was okay. That was her number one concern. Through the back

145

window, Evelyn saw man approach the van. Greg and Callan were walking towards him with their rifles pointed, Kristy trailing just behind.

In a loud screech, the black car that had been parked at the gate rounded the corner and drove directly at them. The others halted. The man kept running, screaming words Evelyn couldn't understand. She fought the urge to start the engine, drive them away, and return later for Dylan and the others. Her instinct burned like a bad tummy ache. Whilst zombies were their main enemy, people were just as dangerous. Greed and brutality seemed to have infused the psyche of those who remained. It reinforced the luck she and Jake had in finding this group. She pulled Jake closer.

The man had almost reached them. Callan put up a hand, signaling for him to stop. Greg held his aim tight, looking down the line of the gun. Beyond, the car slowed, pulling into the curb.

The man reached Callan and slumped over, hands on knees. His big stomach drooped, and his wrinkled face was flushed with exertion. He stood up and brushed his thinning blonde hair askew. They began an exchange that Evelyn couldn't hear. The black sedan stopped, and two men leapt out—one tall in a t-shirt and jeans, the other shorter, in similar attire, brandishing a gun. Evelyn had a fleeting moment of panic when she thought the gunman might start trouble, but he put a hand on the running man's shoulder as if to check his condition.

Shouts sounded from the other side of the fence. Gunfire exploded. Bullets clunked into metal. And then everybody was running.

TWENTY-ONE

DYLAN AND the others reached the closest building in a fifty-yard run by following Ahmed in a squat line. They fell against the wall and peered out at the grounds, expecting gunmen to be on their tails. Klaus stood bent over, hands on his knees, coughing and spluttering as though he had just run the fastest mile of his life.

Gallagher put a hand on his shoulder. "Klaus, what's the matter?"

The scientist shrugged off the hand. "Nothing. I'm just not used to it." He stood tall, adjusting his glasses. "Let's go."

Ahmed signaled for them to follow and they rounded a corner into a rectangular cove with three sides. A number of large, aluminium shafts covered by grates exited the building horizontally. Dylan searched for a door, or some other opening, but the walls were vertical, towering above them two or three stories high into the cloudless blue sky. "Tell me we're not going into them," he said.

Ahmed looked apologetic. "There used to be a door on the western side they sometimes left open, but it's locked today. I already checked earlier, on the way past." He took hold of a grate attached to the front of one shaft and yanked it off.

"You've done this before?" Dylan asked.

"I've crawled around in them for a little way, but that's all."

Dylan didn't like confined spaces himself, and thought about whether he absolutely had to be here. Perhaps he could wait outside for the others to return. He imagined being stuck out there for hours. He was there to keep them on schedule.

147

"You don't know where the shafts lead?"

"Everywhere. It's a maze. There's an entry point into most rooms though. I've looked down into a few. I was too scared to try anything else. But I did see one of the gunmen poking around."

Gallagher approached the shaft, holding the pistol. Klaus still wasn't armed, refusing to hold a weapon. Dylan slotted the handgun into his waistband and double-checked the extra cartridges in his pockets. Ahmed moved aside, holding the grate. "Are you coming with us?" Dylan asked.

"No."

"Why not?"

"I'll meet your friends on the other side. I'll keep them concealed until you return. Just follow the perimeter of this building south," he pointed, "and I'll be waiting at the fence."

Dylan studied Ahmed, wondering what it was about the Middle Eastern man he didn't like. Was it his appearance? No. He'd had friends over the years from all different backgrounds. Ahmed was too convenient. He was *too* helpful, too keen to get them inside the facility. It was almost as if he'd been waiting for them. Dylan wondered if he even had a wife. Ahmed returned his gaze.

"I've dealt with that sort of scrutiny all my life. You don't trust me. I understand. But you still have a choice. Find your own way into the facility. See how far you get."

"If you're lying and we survive this, I'll kill you myself."

Ahmed's hard expression softened. "There won't be any need for that, I promise."

After they had piled into the air-conditioning shaft, Ahmed resecured the grate, filling the space with shadow. "Good luck."

They worked their way forward at slow pace. None of them had any idea where they were going, but Klaus had a sixth sense for directions. But he appeared to be sicker, coughing regularly into his arm to stifle the sound. Dylan was certain somebody would hear them. The darkness between rooms made them move faster, but light from the ceiling openings guided them, and they were able to study the contents of each area from high above.

The first time Klaus suggested they might try and drop down, Gallagher had removed the ceiling grate before he realized there was a gunman in the room. Dylan couldn't see, but he watched Gallagher's head disappear into a hole in the shaft floor. Moments later, he shot back up. Somehow, he managed to refit the grate without alerting the man. They waited another ten minutes for him to leave before moving on.

Three rooms and a lot of crawling later, they gave it another shot. This time they made it down onto a desk before a man entered. He looked strikingly similar to Klaus—average height, white lab coat, glasses—although he was mostly bald. He stumbled back against the wall, dropping his clipboard when Gallagher levelled a gun at him.

"Who... are you?" the man asked, his face twisted into a look of terror.

"Shhh," Gallagher said, dropping onto the tiles. He approached, keeping the gun trained on the man. "Help us find what we're looking for, and you won't get hurt."

His voice quivered. "Are you part of the men out front?"

"No. We've come a long way. We're looking for some medicine." Gallagher closed the door. "Who are you?"

The man explained that he was a lab assistant who had worked for CSL, and had initially been tasked with compiling information about the virus from sources around the world. He lived near the facility, but as the pandemic progressed he did not bother going home, sleeping in the first aid room and eating from the cafeteria. He'd kept to himself, working at night mostly, following social media and using electronic communications to gather information. Slowly, people stopped coming to the facility, until eventually, he was the last. He'd begun tampering with influenza vaccines in hope of creating an inoculation, but he didn't have the training or expertise, and mostly just wasted samples. When he finished speaking, Klaus explained the results of his research, and the man became animated.

"We have supplies of interferons here. They're used in the treatment of MS, leukaemia, hepatitis, and autoimmune disorder."

"You have stock?" Klaus asked. Dylan read the eagerness in his face. *No*, it was more than eagerness. It was desperation. A sudden, shocking thought entered Dylan's mind. He didn't know whether he had guessed or if his instinct was somehow more receptive. He backtracked, reflecting on Klaus' behavior of the last few days. It all made sense.

"You haven't been taking the serum," Dylan cut in.

Klaus' face went blank. He searched for a response. In the end, his shoulders sagged. "So what?"

Gallagher said, "Holy shit, Klaus, have you lost your senses?"

"Yes. I certainly have."

"How long since you took any?" Dylan asked.

Klaus closed his eyes, exhaling a long breath, as if gathering control of his aggravations. Then he shifted his glasses and rubbed the bridge of his nose.

"I stopped taking it when I started administering it to you."

"He's bitten, too?" Gallagher asked.

"At the defense facility," Dylan said. He supposed it no longer mattered who knew about his infection. He would tell Kristy when they returned.

"There wouldn't have been enough. I've had to reduce both of your dosages. In fact I doubt whether it's doing much good at all."

Dylan and Gallagher passed a look. *That* made sense, Dylan thought. He had begun to feel better yesterday, but the feeling had diminished overnight. His paranoia and angst had returned.

"That's noble, Klaus, but a little short-sighted," Gallagher said. "If you die, we'll never produce any more of the serum."

"I thought I'd be capable enough to make more before that happened."

Dylan understood. The virus clouded your judgment and created delusions. Despite knowing this, though, Dylan was powerless to stop his own destructive reactions.

"We have inventory," the lab assistant said.

"There is a particular type I need. Not the standard variants used to treat the illnesses you mentioned. These are special. I'll need to see the stock."

"I can take you there."

"What about the militia?" Gallagher asked. "I'm surprised they've kept you alive."

"Thankfully, they leave me alone. Probably because there's nobody else to provide them basic medicines when they need it. And…" He gave a false smile. "I told them I was close to making a vaccine. I think they believe they can sell it off to the highest bidder."

Gallagher circled the room, picking through various items atop the benches. "What about zombies? Any inside the facility?"

"No. The militia killed them all off. We never had many to begin with. The facility held well."

Klaus said, "Take me to the stock."

The man, whose name was Mitchell, led them quietly along the corridors, pausing at corners, opening doors that seemed to appear from nowhere. It reminded Dylan of the defense facility, only without the zombies. They covered long hallways with darkened rooms full of benches, cupboards, and unused apparatus. Several sets of stairs at the end of hallways went both up and down. Dylan recalled the detail of the base in Canberra. He was glad Greg wasn't there; otherwise, his paranoia would have been through the roof. Mitchell explained that this section of the building housed the laboratory and testing areas, and further back, towards the rear of the facility, were the manufacturing and blending services.

"There are a couple of other small ingredients I'll need to blend with the interferons," Klaus said as they passed through another door. "They're not unique, but they increase the longevity of the interferons when the mix is dosed correctly."

They reached a set of stairs. Mitchell stopped at the bottom. "Actually, I don't think it's a good idea you come with me to the stores."

Klaus adjusted his glasses. "Why?"

"Because if the men catch us they'll shoot us all dead on the spot. They don't get down here much, but up there…" He let the thought sink in. "Me, alone? They won't say much. They'll let me go about my business. They know I'm working for them—I mean, working on something for them. They won't interfere."

Klaus ground his jaw in thought. He studied the man's face. *I'm working for them.* Had that been a slip of the tongue? Either way, a nagging suspicion surfaced. He couldn't pinpoint it—all Mitchell's actions so far had been positive, but it was too easy. They found the one man in the whole facility that could take them directly to the drugs they required. Dylan didn't like it.

"It makes sense," Gallagher said. "How far is it from here?"

"Not far," Mitchell said. "I—"

"But how will you know what to bring back?" Klaus asked.

"Write them down." Gallagher turned to Mitchell. "You got a pen and a piece of paper?"

"Great idea." He slipped a ballpoint and a small spiral notepad from his top pocket and handed them to Klaus.

"Hold on," the scientist said. "Can I talk to you two for a moment?" The three of them huddled off to the side.

"Don't take too long," Mitchell said. "I detest being out in the open like this. I like to keep moving. I normally just get my stuff and hurry back to the lab."

"You're agreeing with everything he's saying," Klaus said to Gallagher. "Why?"

"Because he's bullshitting. But how else are we going to get the ingredients?"

Klaus' brow twisted in thought. Dylan saw the cogs in his mind working at rapid speed. Sweat still beaded on his scalp. He removed his glasses and wiped his face with the back of his forearm. "We leave him now, or disengage him from the current course, and we don't get the interferons. We let him go, he comes back with it. They need the serum blended and produced as much as we do."

Gallagher nodded. "He tries any funny stuff and we'll deal with that."

Dylan supposed it made sense. He was almost certain Mitchell wasn't telling them the truth. Just how that played out was yet to be seen.

TWENTY-TWO

CRAZY SHIT began to happen, and Callan had no idea what was going on or how they were going to survive this time. The man who had run down the street after them was infected—early stages, he said, like the passenger shot at the gate; they had come to the facility looking for help. He fled the black sedan and ran for his life, whilst the other man, who drove the car away from the gate, shot one of the militia and wrestled the car back into possession before fleeing. The gunmen had come hunting though, and now it appeared Callan and the group were caught in the crossfire.

One of the BMW men fired at the fence line. The tall driver ran to the back of the sedan and popped the trunk. Callan didn't wait around to find out what was next. He ran towards the campervan and saw Kristy disappear around the back of it on the street side. Greg fired at the bushes. The dark shapes of the gunmen were everywhere, darting out from behind trees and running towards them across the grass clearing beyond. Some were even squatting at the fence, firing at them. Gunshots filled the air. Windows shattered in nearby houses. One of the militia fell down as the side of his head exploded.

"Don't fucking shoot," Callan yelled at Greg. "They'll think we're with the others." But his voice was lost amongst the crack and pop of discharging weapons. A man standing at the fence lifted his gun and took aim. Callan decided against his own advice. It was too late for diplomatic talks. He snapped his rifle into line and fired twice, hitting the man in the throat.

It was like a fireworks show. Evelyn banged on the driver's window, chasing his attention. The van lurched forwards off the curb. She was leaving. *Great move*, Callan thought. But as she tried to steer it back onto the road, the van clipped the rear of the red sedan parked in front. The crunching, screeching sound of metal on metal filled the air. The camper halted, then moved backwards in fitful starts.

More shouts came from the other side of the fence. A man slowed near the barrier, holding some sort of large-barrelled gun. Callan took a moment to focus on the weapon and realized it was a grenade launcher. "MOVE!" he screamed at Greg. "GRENADES!"

He didn't know if Evelyn had observed it too, but the campervan burst off the curb and onto the road with a jarring crunch. Callan ran after it, grabbing a fistful of Greg's collar as he passed. "Run for fuck's sake!"

More gunfire cracked from the street side of the fence. Callan wished the BMW men good luck. He sprinted after the campervan alongside Greg. They could make it. Evelyn would slow down once they escaped the immediate gunfire. They reached the side of the camper when an explosion ripped the air apart and shook the ground. "Keep running!"

But he couldn't resist a look over his shoulder. The fence line was full of militia from the facility. They peppered the last two men standing from the black sedan; the tall man who had been driving the car lay on the ground in a bloody mess. The red sedan behind which the campervan had been parked was aflame, orange licks rising from the hood and the trunk. What shocked Callan though was that it had moved five or six yards along the side of the road. They had just made it.

Seventy yards from the scene, Callan banged on the side of the camper, and it slowed. Julie swung the side door open and they leapt up into it on the run. She yanked it shut with a crunch.

Evelyn took off. Callan lost his balance and reached for the sink, sick, dizzy, and breathless. He needed to sit. He stumbled to one of the seats at the table and hung his head between his knees. When he looked up, he was surprised Greg was doing the same. Jake and Sarah were strapped into the passenger seats near the front. Julie lurched forward and dropped in beside Evelyn. A sudden spear of terror struck Callan. He stood, whirling, searching the van, choking on the question.

"Where's Kristy?"

His eyes met Evelyn's in the mirror. The van stopped, throwing Callan forward. He threw out a hand and latched onto a cupboard, feeling nausea take over.

Evelyn swung around. "*What?* I thought she was with you."

Callan bolted through the main bedroom to the rear window. All three men from the black sedan lay on the road. Orange flames covered the red vehicle. Men dressed in rugged clothing wandered around the area with their guns pointed. Cold fear spread through him. Where was his sister?

Evelyn reached the back, Greg following. "Where did you last see her?"

Callan tried to think. He resisted rushing out to look, knowing he'd draw the militia immediately. Where had she gone? "She ran towards the front of the van, while you were still parked. You didn't see her?"

"Yes," Evelyn said, dropping her gaze. "But I was... too busy trying to get the van away. She was huddled by the red sedan. I thought she was waiting for you."

The thought struck Callan like a slap across the face. He peered out at the burning car. If that was the case, then she was dead. He tried to swallow, but a lump stuck in his throat. Greg and Evelyn were staring. He was their leader, but he couldn't think of anything to say.

Gunfire sounded. Several men with machine guns walked down the road towards them. Evelyn scurried away toward the front. Callan watched them, unmoving. They had to go. But his sister... they could circle, and come back looking for her. *If there's anything left.* The thought made him sick. If he lost Kristy too, he'd never forgive himself. She was the last link to his old life, to his family, to his dead parents.

"We'll have to come back," Greg said, his blank expression telling Callan he feared the worst too.

The van lurched away. "Zombies," Evelyn said. But there were only a few, and they watched the van pass with almost disinterest.

Callan sat and tried to think it through, his mind clouded by uncertainty. What if Kristy was lying exposed in the street and the militia had found her? He imagined what all those men would do to a pretty girl like her. Callan closed his eyes and shuddered at the thought. They needed to get back to the area and search.

He headed for the front of the van to join Greg and Evelyn. Sarah lay on the bed, sobbing, Julie at her side stroking her hair. The older woman gave Callan a grim expression.

"Where am I going?" Evelyn asked.

"Left, just here. We'll pull over up ahead and wait a bit. Make those guys think we've left. Then head back around and look for Kristy."

Evelyn found a spot in the gutter between several cars. Houses in need of painting and repair lined the street on both sides, their front yards scraggly and overgrown. The smell drifted in through the pores of the van, thicker and stronger than before, as though this section of Broadmeadows contained more dead bodies than elsewhere.

Callan slammed a fist against the cupboard. What could they do but wait? The others watched him, their faces stiff and uncertain as he stood in the doorway looking out at the silent street. He analyzed his options. If he went back now, he ran the risk of getting killed, and perhaps for nothing if she'd been close to the blast. If she had, it wouldn't matter how long they took. If she managed to get away, hopefully she was hiding nearby. That was her best chance, but as far as hope went, he couldn't imagine a less optimistic circumstance.

"What do you want me to do?" Evelyn asked. She kept looking from the rear window back to Callan.

"I don't know."

"We can go out there and have a look," Greg said, holding a rifle.

"Not yet," Callan said, shaking his head. "Need to let it settle. They'll give up soon and go back to the base. It's too risky."

"What about Ahmed and the others?"

Callan had forgotten about them. Ahmed had said to meet them at the fence line on the road where all the crazy shit had just happened. He hoped the man was smart enough for his own sake not to return there yet. "They'll just have to wait for us."

Callan had another sudden, uneasy feeling. He stood and whirled, searching the floor of the van. Blue Boy... "Where's Blue?" Jake dropped off the top bunk and looked underneath the table, where he sometimes curled up at people's feet. "Has anyone seen him?"

"Not since he followed you out," Greg said.

TWENTY-THREE

HOLD ON, Klaus told himself. *Just a bit longer.* He'd never imagined the virus would have affected him so badly. It was like a head cold and fever all rolled into one, his muscles and bones aching with a unified chorus. Worst of all was the itch under his skin that couldn't be scratched. Through his blood, it coursed, sending him closer to the edge. The others had told of their friend, Johnny, who had suffered the same way. He killed himself. Klaus held slim hope that he could manufacture the serum before he turned, but beyond that, his outlook was grim. The medication couldn't reverse the affliction. There was no going back.

Instead of climbing the stairs, Mitchell took them a short distance to another laboratory. It held similarities to the one from the defense facility, including a small compounding chamber off the back they could access through a sliding glass panel and air-lock. Klaus wondered if the structure was based on a national protocol for such facilities. Mitchell left them after estimating he'd be gone for twenty minutes.

Klaus gathered himself as he took in the machinery. He wanted nothing more than to sit down and rest, but now that he had the equipment he'd been seeking, he could put it to use. He buried his pain, the voice of his mother ringing in his mind, telling him to fight on.

"I want to take samples of your blood. Test the progression of the virus." Dylan looked at him sceptically. "Don't worry just yet. I need to check the markers and it will help estimate the dosage going forward."

Klaus found a stash of hypodermic needles and vials. He started one of the analysis machines and sat them down at a

159

bench. After applying a tourniquet to the upper arm of each man, he withdrew three vials of blood from the inside of their elbows. It took all his will to hold the needle still. When he had finished though, the strength had fled his body, leaving him exhausted. He sat for a moment pretending he was inspecting a redundant piece of equipment.

When he had gathered himself, Klaus left the others in the front room and entered the rear chamber. Getting the machines running and the blood prepared took him longer than he expected. His hands trembled and his vison filled with white spots. Sweat ran down his forehead. He didn't like it and wanted to quit several times, take some water and rest for a while, but such surrender was beyond him. A deep indefinable knowledge that he *must* push ahead kept him moving, his feet shuffling across the floor, his shaky hands working the equipment.

A short time later he returned, avoiding eye contact, unwilling to give away their condition through the disappointment in his expression.

The virus in Dylan's blood was the least aggressive of the three. Klaus suspected it had slowed even more following the initial dose, but with the reduction Klaus had administered yesterday afternoon and earlier that morning, activity levels showed signs of increasing again.

"You might feel strange for the next ten hours, but beyond that, assuming we increase the dosage, you'll start to feel better again." Dylan tapped his foot and bit his fingernails. Klaus imagined it burning away inside him. He would battle through until the medicine began to work its magic again.

Klaus turned to Gallagher. "I'm afraid it hasn't worked so well for you." Gallagher didn't flinch. "We'll up your dose, and see what it does. Unfortunately, once we leave this facility, we won't be able to check your blood again. How do you feel?"

Gallagher tilted his head from side to side. "Not too bad."

"What about you?" Dylan asked.

Klaus tottered. He reached out for a bench and missed. His vision turned spotty. Dylan leapt forward and caught him before he fell. "Just need to sit for a moment." Gallagher found him a chair and filled a plastic cup with water. "I'm all right," Klaus said after several minutes. But he wasn't, and he saw the knowledge in the worry on their faces. "As soon as I get some more serum into me, I'll be fine."

Gallagher and Dylan hunkered around him. He took three more glasses of water, unaware of his thirst. "We each cope better or worse, suffer the effects to varying degrees," Klaus said between mouthfuls. "We'll change your course to morning and night, Admiral, same as mine. Dylan will stick to a daily dose."

Mitchell returned soon after with a trolley full of plastic containers. Cold mist rose off them. He explained their storage in a refrigeration unit on the upper level. He had also brought a number of portable chillers to transport the finished product in vials.

"How are you going to do this?" Gallagher asked Klaus. "You can barely stand."

Klaus motioned towards Mitchell. "He'll have to help me."

Mitchell and Klaus dressed in special coveralls; Klaus had to sit to get his on. They wheeled the supplies through the glass airlock and into the chamber beyond. Klaus wavered in and out of focus, fighting to keep his feet and what remained of his senses. The fever bit hard, but at least it was cooler in there. He had Mitchell write the recipe out on a piece of paper, noting the amounts of each ingredient and the compounding process. It was much faster than the batch he'd formulated back at the defense facility. He had refined the original process, but mostly he thought it was because he no longer had time.

Dylan was pacing when the doors to the glass airlock finally opened. Gallagher sat on one of the benches with a frown of concern. Mitchell and Klaus exited the other room. Klaus tried to smile, but his face ached.

"Twenty-eight vials," Mitchell said. "The cooler containers take ten each." He loaded the containers up and handed one each to Dylan and Gallagher.

"How long will all of this last?" Gallagher asked.

"Depends." Klaus took another sip of water. "Months I would think. Although, if we start giving this stuff out to others, it will of course run out sooner."

"Are we done?" Dylan asked. "I need to get back."

"Yes," Klaus said, turning to Mitchell. "All done."

"Let me just switch off the gear in the other room and we can go." Mitchell disappeared back into the airlock room.

Klaus reached into his pocket and pulled out a piece of paper. He handed it to Gallagher. "Just in case, this is the formula for the serum. If we ever get separated or, heaven forbid, worse, you could, in theory, use this to formulate another batch." Gallagher stuffed it tightly into his own pocket.

"Let's go," Dylan said. "We've got the stuff. I have to tell Kristy what's happened. And Lauren. I need to find Lauren."

"All right," Gallagher said. "We'll get there soon enough."

"We've been in here for hours …"

The voices drifted. Klaus found himself looking for Mitchell, who had disappeared. He was in the other room peering back at them. A noise sounded from the front of the room. A man holding a machine gun entered. He was dressed in washed-out Army gear and a headband, followed by a second man carrying similar gear.

Klaus got a bad sense the moment he spotted them. Gallagher and Dylan turned, raising their guns.

"Don't you fucking move," the front man said, jabbing his weapon forward. He had a large head, a dark shade of beard, and intense green eyes.

Oh, shit, Klaus thought. They were going to spot the serum and take it, leaving them with nothing. He'd keep suffering. The goddamn virus would get him after all. Klaus held out a hand. "Please, we don't want any—"

The man smiled, but the dirty teeth he bared chilled Klaus' skin. "I told you not to fucking move."

A sudden, terrible thought overcame Klaus. Losing the serum wasn't going to be the worst of his troubles. He could read the intent in the man's body language. Klaus knew, the way he knew the virus would get him in the end, that he was about to die.

The man fired. Klaus felt heat and pressure in his chest, as though someone had reached into the cavity and pushed from the inside. He flew backwards into a table and the last thing he thought was, at least he hadn't failed.

TWENTY-FOUR

GALLAGHER SHOT the first gunman in the forehead. Bloody pulp exploded from the top of his skull, and the man crumpled to the ground. The second turned his gun on the admiral and Dylan thought he would hit Gallagher before he could fire, but either Navy training made you move like Flash Gordon, or Gallagher was freakishly fast. The second gunman joined the first in a dead heap.

Dylan ran to the scientist. Klaus lay on his side, a dirty red wound over his heart, blood pooling underneath his body. His spectacles had cracked and fallen away. Glassy blue eyes stared ahead. "Fucking assholes." He walked over and laid a boot into the first man's ribs. He did the same for the second. He turned back to Klaus, feeling no better.

"Poor bastard," Gallagher said, standing over Klaus. "He deserved better."

He had not connected with the scientist in the beginning, but Klaus' silence in keeping Dylan's secret and his willingness to administer the serum had probably saved Dylan's life. In Klaus, Dylan saw a commitment to others, a desire to help. Klaus stopped taking the serum for them. He was their great hope; was going to save them all. He did, at least for a time, Dylan thought.

"There's nothing more we can do for him. We need to leave," Dylan said.

Gallagher nodded. "What about him?" Mitchell paced the chamber room.

Dylan said nothing for a long moment. "You know this was all a ploy. He probably alerted them when he went to get the drugs." His hand flexed around the pistol. "Bastard deserves to die." He started for the chamber room.

"Just leave him. He's worse off working for them."

Dylan stopped at the glass, looking in at Mitchell. He knew part of it was the virus talking, imbuing him with rage. It was difficult to fight, especially when one of their friends had died.

"Come on," Gallagher said. Dylan eventually turned away. Gallagher squatted and reached out with his thumb and forefinger, closing Klaus' eyes. He sat for a moment, watching. They had been the last two survivors on the base. "We'd be dead without him." *So true,* Dylan thought. "I doubt there's another serum in the world at this moment. He created it. I cursed him once. Hated him, even. But he redeemed himself. No question about that." He crossed himself. "Rest in peace, sir."

Mitchell banged on the window. His muted voice barely heard. "Can you leave me one of the cases of serum?"

Gallagher sneered. Dylan started towards the door, holding two of the cold packs. Gallagher had the other. "Do you remember the way back?"

"Yeah. Won't take long. Stay behind me though. Good chance we'll see the enemy."

Gallagher was able to retrace their passage like a man who is trained in such things. Had it been left to Dylan, he would have been wandering the hallways for hours. Directions were not his strength.

As they moved along the corridors past more silent rooms and dark corridors, Dylan thought more about what Klaus' death meant for the group. They had lost another strong, logical mind. Klaus wasn't the first person in every conversation, but when he spoke, they all listened and valued his judgement. They had excellent stocks of the serum, but in the longer term, they would run out. He had given Gallagher a formula, but who knew whether they would ever find someone capable of using it?

Dylan's focus turned to Kristy. He would try to make amends with her over their minor argument, but if she sided with Callan again, he would part company with them. He hated the idea, but he had to find out if his sister was still alive.

They located the room without interference. Gallagher pulled the air-conditioning vent free from the roof and tossed it on the floor. He placed a chair underneath, and then climbed up and slid the cases of serum and weapons through the hole. Dylan did the same, and heaved himself up into the shaft with a clunk.

At the grate leading out into the grounds, Gallagher paused, listening for activity. Dylan heard nothing. Gallagher pushed the screen out and they both slid to freedom. It felt good to be out in the open air again, though the bright light stung their eyes. The shaft had been hot; sweat dripped from their foreheads and in the nooks of their bodies, but now the sun burned, and Dylan found the heat stifling in his Kevlar clothing. He had a distant memory of wearing shorts and a singlet top on such days in summers past, swimming in the lake or in the pool at home. A deep part of him ached for that again, but he knew that was a life long gone.

Gunfire popped in the distance like firecrackers on New Year's Eve. Gallagher stepped forward with his gun raised and assessed the situation. Ahead stood the boundary where they had entered the facility, defined by a high fence topped with rolling barbed wire. Beyond, trees and bushes dotted the earth, leading to houses from where Ahmed had apparently come.

"Follow me," Gallagher said.

They ran hard up against the building, sprinting from one object to the next, looking for the best cover. The contour of the structure provided further protection; boxed sections jutted out from the main body, along with several lengths that cut off any view further ahead. Gallagher had an innate sense of where to go and when to stop. Dylan watched him, following his actions and style, trying to predict his next move. They passed a section of earth that had been dug up, silent machinery parked off to one side, as though some kind of construction had been taking place. Finally, they reached the last corner and headed north towards the front of the facility. By Dylan's calculations, if they were to continue straight ahead, they would reach the street where Ahmed had suggested they meet. However, between the edge of the building and fence line was a grassed area of more than fifty yards over which they must cross, exposing themselves to whoever might be watching. They stood behind an excavator, surveying the area for signs of the enemy or the campervan.

"That fence," Gallagher said. "We run for it. Cross there, where it's the narrowest section of open ground."

Suicide, Dylan thought. He had survived everything else, just to die here? That was the risk they took every day with almost every action. He needed to find Kristy and after that, answers to Lauren. He should expect more of the same.

Gallagher sprung away. Dylan ran, every step weighted with the expectation of a bullet, the crack of a rifle, or worse, an intense burst of machine gun fire. He pushed himself to keep up with Gallagher, the middle-aged military man much fitter than he had expected. They reached the edge, panting and ran along the fence line towards the southern corner where a cluster of bushes and shaggy trees covered the yellow grass. Dylan searched beyond the barrier for sign of Ahmed or the campervan. It was empty, just a normal suburban street filled with flaking weatherboard houses, their front porches cracked and bordered by flimsy steel railing. Dylan stopped when he saw flames coming from a red car where the street swung around a corner ahead.

"Where's the opening?" Dylan hissed.

Gallagher ran along the fence line hunched over, peering between the long grass. "Here."

Then the gunfire started. The man was situated on the other side of the fence—the side to which they must cross—on the street towards the main road. The rifle cracked off shots. Had it been a fully automatic machine gun, Dylan suspected they would be dead. Gallagher dropped onto one knee—Dylan thought it was the coolest gunfire pose he'd ever seen—and began firing back through the chain link. Bullets whizzed through the air, chewing up grass and pinging off the fence posts.

"Go," Gallagher shouted. "Get through. I'll cover you."

Dylan hurried towards the fence. He pulled the flap back and slipped his leg through, catching the scuffed fabric of his dirty, smelly Kevlar clothing on a loose wire. *Shit.* Just what he needed. He fell short again; the asshole would shoot him dead with his jacket stuck on a fence. That would be it. But then he pulled hard and the jacket tore free. He came up from a squat and found cover behind a stout tree trunk, firing on the man standing in the middle of the street. "Go!" he screamed. Gallagher finally broke, racing for the opening as chunks of earth danced around him. Dylan stuck an arm around the trunk, clenching his teeth as he fired, willing the bullets to find their mark. His fourth shot hit the man in the chest. He fell back with a thud and the gun clattered onto the road.

"This way, Gallagher said, leading them to a bend in the road past the wreckage of a red sedan. The smell of burned metal and scorched fuel stung Dylan's nostrils. Another gunman wandered out of a nearby property. He spied them, lifted his gun, and fired.

Gallagher put him down with a single shot. He dropped the empty cartridge and snapped another into the pistol. Dylan gave a crazy laugh. He'd never have guessed Gallagher was so proficient.

He didn't know if they were going the right way but trusted Gallagher's judgement. They ran at a pace, weaving between abandoned vehicles and across messy front lawns, following the curve of the street through suburbia. There were no more men, but several zombies lingering in overgrown front yards had taken up slow pursuit.

They rounded another corner that led all the way to the main road. Halfway along the street, the campervan pulled out of another side road, heading away from them. *What the fuck were they doing?*

Both men ran ahead, screaming and waving their arms. The van braked suddenly. The red reverse lights glowed, and then it began to move backwards towards them. Dylan supressed his anger, sure they had reason.

The side door of the camper opened and Callan leapt out. The moment Dylan saw him, he knew something was wrong. His face was creased with worry, his shoulders stiff, hands clenched at his sides. Callan was intense by nature, but this was different. Dylan read fear in him.

"What is it?"

"Kristy's missing. Did you see her on the way here?"

"Kristy?"

"No," Gallagher said.

Dylan didn't understand. "Missing?"

"Blue Boy too." Callan looked from Dylan to Gallagher and back again. "Where's Klaus?"

"Where's *Kristy?* What the fuck do you mean she's missing?"

"We can't find her. We haven't seen her since… there was a big gunfight. That other car we saw at the gate and lots of the men from the facility. It was crazy. Total chaos."

Dylan staggered. All his anger fled. The world became surreal. He heard the others talking, Callan saying something, but the words no longer registered. She was missing? Was she dead? He sat on the road. It was all he could think to do besides faint. Callan ran through an explanation of what had happened. Dylan listened, trying to make sense of it.

"Evelyn saw her last by that red car?"

Gallagher squinted. "The red car? Up around the corner, near the fence?" Callan nodded. Gallagher stiffened. "Bloody hell, if she was near that… there won't be much left of her, I'm afraid."

Exploded. Kristy exploded. A thought struck him then: life without Kristy. He imagined it. An existence of such terrible thought that he began to gag. He would be sick. His breakfast rose up his throat. He bent forward on all fours, swallowing it back down. He took deep breaths until it passed, then turned to Callan, his own grim face a reflection of Dylan's. "Do you think she's dead?" Callan said nothing. *Yes.* What did he do? Go back and look for her. There were gunmen still around. They'd shoot him dead. Maybe he was better off that way.

On cue, shots sounded from further along the street. Three men walked down the center of the road armed with machine guns. Callan and Gallagher ran for the van. Dylan didn't move. Gallagher jogged back to Dylan and grabbed him by the collar, lifting him off his feet.

"Come on. We're not done yet." Dylan stumbled after him.

The van drove towards the main road. Dylan sat by the window with his head between his legs and his hands shaking. His entire body was numb. He'd always thought the saying was stupid, but now he understood. It was as though his body had shut down all his senses to stop it hurting so much. This had been the last thing he expected to find. He could have handled anything, but Kristy.

"Where are we going?" he asked.

"We're going back to collect the four-wheel drive."

"And then what?"

Callan said, "I'm going back to find Blue Boy."

Evelyn looked up at the mirror, her eyes wide, face taut. "Out into that? With those men floating around? You're crazy. You'll die, like—" She cut herself off, but her lips trembled. Tears filled her eyes.

"I can't leave him *out there*."

Dylan didn't want to ask the next question, but he forced himself, knowing it would shape his decision going forward. "Does anybody think Kristy is still alive?"

For a long time, nobody spoke. Evelyn took them north past the main road and into another section of Broadmeadows. The streets narrowed, the houses even worse in this area with crumbling couches on the porches behind broken railings. She kept making right turns, trying to get them back past the main entrance to the facility where they had left the four-wheel drive.

Callan's face had lost all color. "Not if she was hiding behind that red car. Nobody saw the bastard with the grenade launcher until the last moment. There's no way Kristy would have seen him from there." He swallowed, forcing himself to go on. "That thing took a direct hit from a grenade. It was thrown five yards. There's no way she survived that."

"It was a mess," Gallagher said gently. "Having some familiarity with hand grenades, I agree with Callan."

Slow comprehension dawned on Dylan as Evelyn turned south. If there was no chance Kristy was still alive, there was only one option for him. He had promised himself he'd look for Lauren and that nobody would stop him; he'd go alone, if that was what it took. *Now's your chance.* The truth was he never thought it would actually happen. He had always thought at the very least, Kristy would be with him.

Ahead, the main road sat waiting for them. When they reached the intersection, Dylan saw the tip truck parked on the roadside up ahead. Behind it, the blue four-wheel drive they had discovered on the farm just out of Yass twinkled in the sunlight. Was his decision made? Did he have anything left to debate? Evelyn took off and pulled in behind it, concealed from the entrance to the facility. If she was gone, what was keeping him alive? *Lauren.* He wanted to cry; he felt the build-up of tears from the depths of his soul, but like with his mother and father, he pushed them deeper, to a place where he hoped they might never return.

"I'm going to the city, then," Dylan said. "To find my sister. To see if she's still alive." He waited for them to argue, prepared for a quarrel. In truth, he needed the four-wheel drive or the camper.

"I'll take the four-wheel drive to find Blue Boy," Callan said. "You take the camper, and everybody else."

Evelyn fought back more tears. "You can't go out there alone."

Greg said, "I'll go—"

"No." Callan put up a hand. "I'm doing this on my own. He's... my dog and I know it's a risk. I'm not going to jeopardize anyone else."

"Come on. Don't be stupid."

"Save it, Greg. You've done enough. Look after these people. Go with Dylan to find his sister. *Nobody* is coming with me."

Callan stood and fed rounds into his pockets. He loaded the rifle, and from a bag near the sink took a handgun and several magazines. He went to the door and put a hand on it, then turned and looked at them all: from Gallagher, to Julie, to Greg, to Dylan, Jake and Sarah sitting on the bunk, and finally to Evelyn. "Take care of yourselves. I mean that." Sarah leapt off the bunk and ran to him. She threw her arms around his waist and hugged him tight. He rested a hand on the girl's shoulders. "I'll be back," he whispered. She wouldn't let go. "Hey," Callan said, squatting, lifting her chin with the tip of his finger. "You have to take care of them okay? You're the only one with medical training now. Doctor Sarah. They all need you."

"But I don't know anything."

"Yes you do. Kristy... Kristy wasn't stupid. She picked you because you're smart and capable. She knew you could handle it." Sarah nodded. "Remember what you learned. Hopefully you won't need it." Sarah managed a half-smile. Callan kissed her on the forehead, and stood.

In the driver's seat, Evelyn sobbed. Julie's face was tight, grim. Sarah stepped away and Callan opened the door.

"Wait," Greg said. Callan paused, halfway out the door. "Where will we meet you?"

"You're going to find Dylan's sister? What's the address?"

"410 Queen Street. At the top, near the Queen Victoria Market."

"And what if she's not there?"

"Station Pier," Gallagher said. "I'll be trying to find a ship to take us across Bass Strait."

Callan nodded, and then disappeared out the door.

TWENTY-FIVE

KRISTY'S EYES came open with a start. She coughed, searching for her breath, and sat up, pain filling her head in dizzying waves. In her dream, she had died, drowning in a wave of blood and bodies, her friends and brother included. Now, realizing what it had been, relief washed over her, pacifying the ache in the rest of her body.

She was lying on a soft bed in a house. Faint light seeped in from around the corners of curtains. A small room with the door closed. She tried to swing her legs off the bed, but nausea drowned her and she fell back down onto the pillow and closed her eyes. What had happened? She lay there summoning the thoughts. The gunfight. Running. Hiding behind the red sedan. Seeing the man with the big gun, and then running some more towards the house with the brick fence... a big explosion. After that, it was blank. She must have been knocked unconscious.

She eventually made it back to sitting up, listening for voices, noises, any indication about where she might be or who had taken her there. The only thing she heard was the distant chatter of gunfire. That meant she was probably close to the facility. It also meant it probably wasn't long since it had happened. Where were the others?

She swung her feet off the bed, her ripened socks touching carpet. She stood, swaying, and put a hand out for balance. *Keep moving. You'll be all right.* Slow steps took her to the doorway, where she paused, pulling it open a crack. There was the chance a crazy person had captured her and that they wouldn't let her leave, or that they might try to harm her. That sounded fairly implausible though, as her hands and legs weren't bound, and the door wasn't locked. Still, she should be cautious.

She left the room and entered a hallway. The smell of old food and something unfamiliar reached her. She crept ahead, towards sunlight, passing several closed doors on her right, until she reached another room. In the center sat a table, with four chairs. On it lay a woman wearing a hijab, the conservative dress of a Muslim female. Her eyes were closed and she had the same look Kristy had observed many times in the ER. The hairs on her neck stood. She couldn't move. *You're used to this,* she told herself. These were strange circumstances though.

She considered examining the body to decide how long the woman had been dead. Had she been sick? Was she infected? She decided to ignore it for now and work on finding out who had brought her there.

She walked across the small kitchen and passed through a door. She stopped inside the next room when she saw a man on his knees praying in the corner.

She knew who it was at once. It was the man who had taken Dylan and the others into the facility. *Ahmed.* He made a soft, crooning noise. There might have been a sob, too. Kristy stepped back out of the room, and waited.

It was a strange moment, being stuck between a person in prayer and a dead body. Kristy herself wasn't religious, but she understood the value of religion to others, and respected their choice to decide and follow whatever faith they chose. Their mother had been Christian, and occasionally went to church, but had never imposed the religion on her or Callan. Their father had been a proud atheist.

She kept glancing over at the body, expecting it to come alive. The next time she looked back into the lounge, Ahmed had finished and was standing before her. There were tears on his cheeks. He was smiling, but there was a deep pain in

175

the curl of his lips, and his sagging eyes were filled with heartbreak.

"I'm glad you're alright," he said.

She tried to smile back, but his grief was infectious. She imagined the roles reversed, if it were Callan, or perhaps worse now, Dylan. "Is… that your wife?" He nodded. "I'm so sorry." He wiped his eyes with the back of his hand, smearing tears over his face. "How long?"

He shook his head, unable to say more. Kristy waited. He gathered himself, smearing more tears, before removing a handkerchief from his pocket to blow his nose. "She followed me out. Or must have been worried that I'd taken too long. She wouldn't accept she was sick. I told her…" He clenched his jaw, shook his head. "I wish I had taught her how to ride my motorbike. At least then, she'd have been faster. After I found you, I had to carry you home. I saw her at a distance in another street, but didn't dare call out. There were gunmen nearby, and she was hiding. I thought she'd be safe. I rushed home with you, and came back, but she'd been shot. I found her lying in the gutter. She was… dead already."

Kristy tried to breathe. "Oh… God… no…" She fell back against the wall. The pressure in her chest was unprecedented. Suffocating. The air wouldn't come. Had she heard right? Instinctively, she put a hand out and rested it on his shoulder. She tried to say something but her eyes filled with tears. She mumbled the words sorry, all the fairness in life ripped away in that moment.

Ahmed went into the kitchen. Kristy followed feeling faint again, fighting to gain control. Had it really happened like that? He had left his wife to die because of her? Guilt settled around her. Why did it always have to be so unfair?

In a soft voice, she asked, "What happened to me?"

"I was coming to find you guys. I worked my way around the back of the building to where I said I would meet you all, but the gunmen were everywhere. I took a different route and came out on the street after the explosion. I had to wait in the bushes until they were gone. I didn't notice you lying less than six feet from me. You must have been near the car when it exploded. I found you in somebody's front garden on the other side of a brick fence. I carried you home from there. I think if I had left you though, they would have found you, because by the time I reached the end of the street they were all over the place where you had been."

"Thank you. I can't begin to say how grateful I am to you for saving me, and how," she glanced at his wife, "sorry I am for your loss."

"I knew she was sick and so part of me... but I didn't expect it so soon. I wasn't prepared. The men who want to take control of the world are horrible and have no respect for life. This is what is left after the plague. My religion talks about a great event coming to mankind because we did not treat the world with respect."

A noise sounded from outside the house. Ahmed hurried back into the lounge room and peeked out from behind a curtain. Kristy followed and did the same from another.

Men walked the streets, wielding machine guns. Several stood outside a house across the road. One kicked in the front door. Another man threw a rock through a window. What were they doing? Hunting down people, or zombies? Either way, it scared her. These men would not see reason.

"There," Ahmed said. "Do you see that?" Kristy drew the curtain wider, searching the street. Besides the men, she saw nothing unusual. "Look again." She did, and caught him further along than she had been looking. Her stomach dropped, twisting into knots. It was Blue Boy, with his nose pinned to the ground. One of the men had noticed him, and was walking in his direction.

TWENTY-SIX

DYLAN FOUGHT guilt as he watched his friend jog away from the campervan. Any other time over the last week, he'd have gone with Callan. Things were different now, though. He thought of Kristy, and his stomach climbed into his throat. He swallowed it down and shoved the thought away. No. *No.* He wouldn't deal with that yet. Couldn't. But the guilt seeped in through the cracks. Guilt for the time he had spent away from her, for the way he had treated her over the last few days. It had been the virus, for sure. Part of him wondered whether going for Lauren was crazy, another move brought on by its effects, but it was the only way he knew how to deal with Kristy's death. Find something else on which to concentrate. And he had promised himself that he would check her apartment, find out if she was still alive. That was his focus now.

Dylan explained to the others how he had been bitten at the defense facility. There were questions about why he hadn't told them and he answered them honestly. Afterwards, he and Gallagher both took a fresh injection of serum.

Dylan fell into the passenger seat beside the driver. "Let's go." Evelyn's cheeks glistened. She started the van and they lumbered off, turning in a circle and returning the way they had last come to avoid the facility perimeter. "You okay?"

She nodded, but there was little surety in it. "You?"

"No."

The van drove back over the hill and down towards the train tracks. Dylan recalled the blockage of cars on Sydney Road. They would have to go a different way. Julie would know.

She was sitting at the table with a fleshy arm around Sarah. The younger girl had red, glassy eyes. The first two people she had met in the group were now gone. There was heartache and loss all around. Only a day ago, Julie had lost her husband, and she had battled through every minute since. It was a lesson for Dylan. He needed to be strong—for himself, as much as the others. He slid in beside the older woman.

"You said you know Melbourne well. What's the best way to get to the Queen Victoria Market?"

"Sydney Road. It's the most direct route. Takes us almost right to it."

"It was jammed. I don't think we can get through."

"High Street runs all the way to Collingwood and into the east of the city. But we'd have to cut back to the west if we went that way."

"I guess we'll try Sydney Road first."

But the continuation of the road on which they had driven all the way from Sydney was congested; trucks with double trailers and a multitude of other vehicles closed off any pathway through the thoroughfare. As they paused at the intersection of Camp Road, Dylan saw zombies moving between the cars in a long, broken trail all the way to the horizon.

"They're everywhere," Evelyn said with sick distaste.

"We can't go that way."

The road east was straight, before turning in a long, sweeping bend. A freeway ran underneath in both directions, upon which sat hundreds of cars in an unprecedented traffic jam. Evelyn had the window down, and on the breeze came a smell as bad as anything they had encountered, even in Albury. More zombies, moving between vehicles, others with their upper bodies buried in windows, or feeding on rotting

179

flesh they had dragged from the wreckage. Dylan was grateful they passed over the graveyard quickly.

"What do you think the city will be like?" Dylan asked Gallagher

"Klaus always said Melbourne—any capital city for that matter—would be overrun. It won't be fun, that's for sure."

"What about the chances of finding a boat at Station Pier?"

Gallagher scratched the back of his neck. Dylan had noticed him doing it regularly and wondered if it was the virus. He'd been feeling an incessant itch on his skin for a couple of days. "I've commanded ships before. It's unlikely we'll find any of that size, but if we're lucky, something smaller might be docked."

Evelyn turned right onto High Street, which paralleled the train line. "This runs all the way to the city," Julie said, leaning on the back of Evelyn's seat. Dark circles shadowed her red eyes. She had handled Eric's death well, and now seemed strengthened by their needs; as if she had made it her mission to care for them all, especially the kids. Purpose, Dylan realized. She had found a purpose.

Dylan tried to take strength from Julie, but the pain was too fresh. He tried to think of something else—Albury, the city, Lauren, even Tasmania, but he couldn't escape the fact that he would never see Kristy again. He had spent his last night with her, beside her, in her presence. Perhaps that single night of making love was all he was ever supposed to have. It filled him with a deep sadness, different to losing his parents. As an adult, they'd had less contact. Dylan was preparing to move out of home at some point. But Kristy... Dylan had envisioned her as a growing part of him, someone with whom he should spend *his* future, for as many days as he had left. In a way, she was the one whom he had chosen—as she had chosen him—to spend their final weeks or months together.

He let the thought drift. His head ached. The pounding wouldn't let up.

High Street took them south in a relatively straight line, running through the outer Melbourne suburbs towards the inner city. They passed strips of shops, where looters had pulled items out through broken front windows, littering the streets with debris. Cars sat abandoned in the middle of the road, on the curb, and the odd one rammed through the front of a store. Should they stop and try to filch something of worth? Probably just cause them more trouble. Besides, Dylan was on the way to find Lauren, and he didn't want to derail that.

He noticed Greg sitting in the back alone. The big guy was feeling it too. He had probably loved Kristy as much as Dylan had. It made him feel sick to think of it. They met eyes, and Dylan offered a knowing look of despair. After the incident at the Army facility, and then their discussion on the way down to Melbourne, he wasn't sure things would ever be the same between them. Dylan had accused Greg of an unforgivable act, and even if Greg hadn't done it, the mistrust would always be there. And as much as Dylan wanted to believe, he would always be cautious.

The road was relatively clear. Side streets led off the central trunk, filled with parked cars and the occasional smash. There were zombies, but fewer than the outer suburbs, as though they had left for more gruesome pastures. One of them spied the campervan approaching in the distance and shuffled from the pavement out onto the road. Evelyn didn't slow. She ran it down like a weed under the mower. The body thumped into the front of the vehicle and splattered over the road.

They followed the train line on their left for a time before leaving it and picking up the tramline as they passed through Reservoir and into Northcote, where dark houses and

181

storefronts grinned at them, promising deadly delights. More vehicles and a growing number of zombies wandered along the lines. A burnt-out tram carriage sat like a dead relic. In the distance, tall city buildings sketched themselves against the changing color of the sky.

It had been bright and hot an hour ago. Dylan knew from Lauren's accounts that Melbourne's weather was prone to rapid change, and now as a breeze pulled clouds across the sky, the first signs of such appeared. Summer storms were common, but of late, there had been more, as though a portentous meaning existed.

"I don't like this," Julie said, as more zombies appeared along the road. "Their numbers are growing."

She was right, but as Klaus had said earlier, cities were full of people, many of whom had become zombies. It was going to get worse. Dylan thought of Klaus again, the man who had essentially saved his life—Gallagher's too—and felt a pang of sadness for another lost amongst the many. Who would be next? Callan? Evelyn? Gallagher? Himself. He'd come so close many times. Now his life hung on the thread of medicine. Was that any way to live? He saw Sarah though, and supposed she was no different with her insulin, relying on it daily for survival. Maybe one day, if the world ever returned to normality, the virus from which Dylan suffered would also be considered a chronic illness.

Evelyn drove on in silence, hands clenched around the wheel, her face grim, eyes focused on the ever-changing road. She had become a skillful driver, maneuvering between obstacles, even avoiding wandering feeders when they unknowingly staggered in their way. Twice she broke away from the road and drove directly down the tramline until an abandoned carriage blocked her way.

They reached the end of St. Georges Road, where Julie pointed off to the left. "That way. It meets up with High Street and then runs into the top of the city."

Evelyn guided the camper around a long bend. On the right, bushes concealed what the sign referred to as the MERRI CREEK. Dylan saw pale fleshy figures moving in the scrub.

They reached a set of traffic lights at the intersection of High Street. Evelyn steered right and drove into a crowd of zombies congregated in the middle of the road. She slammed on the brakes, and Dylan found himself flying forward towards the dashboard. He struck his forehead on the panel and crumpled to the floor.

Evelyn stood from the seat, looking frantic. "Sorry."

He climbed into the passenger's chair, feeling wetness above his left eyebrow. He touched the place and found a spot of blood. Behind him, others had toppled over, including Julie. Dylan and Gallagher both reached out to help her up, and sat her on another seat.

"That's why they invented seat belts," Julie said, rubbing her elbow.

"More of them," Greg said.

Evelyn put the gearstick into reverse. "Hold on," Dylan said. "Where are we gonna go?"

Gallagher adjusted his rifle. "Is there another way around?"

"There is," Julie said, "but it'll take time. Maybe another hour or two, depending on the traffic." She made a silly face. "Well, you know what I mean."

"It's worth a thought," Gallagher said.

"No," Dylan said. "We might not even make it all the way around. It might be worse. We've been lucky getting here." Nobody spoke. "Besides, we've been through worse.

Remember the throng of them on the hill on the way to the army base?"

The campervan stood idling as the first drops of rain fell onto the windshield. The group watched the zombies milling around a crash scene. They were groping at the doors, trying to pry one of them open. Dylan suspected there were bodies inside. The rain fell harder, beating against the windscreen as a gust of wind blew it sideways. Soon the zombies' clothes stuck to their fleshy bodies, strands of hair matted against bony skulls. Dylan scanned the group for type threes. He remembered them in Holbrook, with Callan, watching them tear through the type ones, converting them into their own kind.

"I don't like it," Evelyn said. "There's too many. We should—"

Dylan shook his head. "Anywhere we go, we're going to face this sort of thing. We could drive two hours east and it will be no different. We got through at the defense facility. We can do this."

"He's right," Greg said. "We're just avoiding the inevitable if we try and go another way. And it might be worse."

Dylan wondered if he was being selfish. Lauren might only be a handful of miles away and he didn't want to waste any more time trying to reach her. Was he willing to risk the others to find out if his sister was alive? Yes. He was. She might be all he had left. "I know we can get through this. We just have to be strong. If we divert at every sign of feeders, we'll be diverting for the rest of our lives. We need to take a chance. It's the quickest way. Julie, what do you think?"

After a long moment, Julie sighed. "I suppose so."

Evelyn swivelled around to the front, crunched the gearstick into drive, and took off.

"Fast," Dylan said. "Go as fast as you can."

TWENTY-SEVEN

CALLAN RETRACED the path Evelyn had taken in the campervan until he was near to where they had found Dylan and Gallagher. He wanted to maintain a distance in case any of the men from the base were still searching the neighborhood. He left the blue Toyota in an empty driveway, giving the impression it was just another abandoned car in a street full of them. He loaded a 9mm pistol and stuffed it into his waistband, then filled his pockets with extra cartridges and rounds for the rifle he would carry. Finally, he took an old shirt Kristy had worn camping and tied it around his wrist.

Blue was smart. He'd survived weeks in Albury on his own before they had taken him in. He was more than capable of surviving alone. And if he left the group, he must have had a reason. If he could find the dog, Callan would use his sense of smell and Kristy's clothing to locate her.

He saw the first militia from a distance shortly after leaving the four-wheel drive. Thankfully, he encountered none up close, allowing him to alter his course where necessary, although he could have killed them all at least once. They were not trained militia; hell, he wasn't trained, and he was more competent than them.

Despite this, he made quick progress along the streets, moving in and out of tangled front yards, running for the cover of trees and bushes. He thought of them all as he made his way back to the red sedan—Sherry, Bob, Howard, Eric, Klaus, and… no, he would not put her in that same group yet. Although he had indicated to the others that he thought Kristy was dead, he didn't truly believe it. Not yet. Part of it was getting them to leave. Going back into the area was too

185

risky for all of them, and if they thought she might still be alive, they wouldn't have left. At least now, they were safe, and if anything happened to Callan, they would continue on.

He jogged around a corner, staying hard against an overhanging tree whose leaves had covered the pavement. It was Blue he was after first, Blue who had the best chance of survival. He hoped the dog hadn't gone far. He wondered why he had left the van. A part of him wondered whether Blue might have had enough of them. He had been a loner before they found him, wandering the streets and surviving on his own. Perhaps he had decided to just leave. It had irritated him at the time, but now, as he spotted the dog standing beside a power pole about half a dozen houses ahead, all such feelings vanished.

The grass was scruffy, yellowing in parts, and Blue had found a scent at the base of the pole. He cocked his leg and urinated, then sniffed the grass, working his way towards the next house. Callan ran.

On the opposite side of the road, a man dressed in Army gear appeared from a dilapidated house. He had a machine gun slung over his shoulder and dark glasses. Callan stopped, his muscles tense. The man wandered in a circle as if waiting for somebody. Blue had also stopped. Callan clicked his fingers, calling for the dog, but he was too far away.

The man had seen Blue; he whistled, and Blue's ears pressed back against his head, tail stiff as lead pipe. A cold shiver touched the back of Callan's neck. He had to do something. Who knew what the man would do to a wild dog? He considered running up the street and defending Blue, but he knew other militia were about. He hoped Blue had the sense to stay back.

Callan stepped in behind a low bush on the nearby lawn and readied the rifle. He lost sight of the dog. The man whistled again, and walked across the road. Callan found a clearer line of sight and came around to the side of the bush, abandoning his cover. He squatted on one knee and brought the Remington bolt action up to his eye.

The man held out his hand, calling the dog by some unfamiliar name. Further along the street, a second man appeared and drew his gun into position to make a shot at the dog.

Callan looked down the line of site at the new militia. Who did he shoot first? The first man still hadn't crossed the road, hadn't even taken aim yet. But as soon as Callan fired, he would draw their shots. It would put Blue in further danger, but what choice did he have?

Blue noticed the second gunman and began to move backwards. The man fell onto one knee, tightening his aim. That was it. Callan levered the bolt of the Remington and placed his finger on the trigger. His heart raced, thudding in his chest. He was comfortable with this gun, had shot it a hundred times and rarely missed now.

The shot cracked and the Remington bucked. The man toppled forward and fell into the yellow grass by the gutter. The first man abandoned Blue Boy and swung his machine gun around. Callan shifted slightly to the left, drew the man into his sight, and fired. The man's head exploded. He fell onto the road and sprayed blood across the blacktop.

Blue spun in a circle, barking. Callan sprinted towards the dog; afraid he'd bolt again.

"Blue! Blue! Here, boy, come to me." The dog stopped, confused, as another voice entered the equation. Beyond where the first man had appeared, a third brandished another machine gun, and fired at Callan.

He ran forward, sizing up the man's position, and stood behind a power pole. The machine gun chattered, carving up bushes and chopping light branches from surrounding trees. The pole vibrated under the thud of several rounds.

In his mind's eye, Callan saw the man walking slowly down the driveway with the machine gun blaring. Callan steadied his breathing, thinking about how far he had come. Did this man know the people they had shot, the dozens and dozens of zombies he had killed, mostly taken in the heat of battle, without a moment's thought? He had done it all and more and no longer considered missing. He imagined controlling the shot so that it always ended up at the target in his mind's eye. He had built a cool self-belief into his actions supported by the endless repetition of practice.

The machine gun fire stopped. Callan stepped out from behind the pole, the Remington at his eye, and knocked the careless man down with a shot in the face.

He met Blue Boy on his knees; the dog wagging its tail, ears pushed back, whimpering with delight. "You scared me, boy," he said, wrapping an arm around his neck. "*Scared me. Don't do that again, okay?*" Callan kissed him on the head. Blue pressed his ears down and jumped back into position, poised to run. Callan reached out to him, but the dog scooted away.

Behind them, from a street or two away, shouts floated to his ear. The gunfire had drawn men. They had to leave quickly.

Blue took off along the street. He stopped outside a neat house with shorter lawns and a weedless garden. Callan jogged to it, met by a redbrick building topped with orange tiles. It stood out amongst the raggedy front porches and snarling gardens in the other properties.

Callan slowed his jog. "What is it, Blue?" The dog ran forward again, racing towards the house. "Blue! Get back—"

A gunshot cracked. Several men ran along the street. Callan chased the dog.

TWENTY-EIGHT

AHMED RETURNED from one of the bedrooms with a shotgun in his hand.

"Where did you get that?" Kristy asked.

He looked guilty. "I found it on a dead man the other day. I don't really know how to use it—I mean I do, but I've never fired one before. I thought it would be good to have."

"It was a good idea. I've had lots of experience. Do you want me to show you?"

He shook his head and lifted his chin. "No. I should do it." *Chivalry wasn't dead,* she thought. "We should move away from the front windows though. In case they spot us."

"Okay." Kristy followed him into the kitchen. "Do you have any more weapons?"

From a wooden block on the bench, Ahmed took a long carving knife and handed it to her. It was heavier than a normal knife. She turned it over in her hand, light glinting off the wide steel blade. Perfect. She had killed zombies with a knife before, but not men, although, there was a first time for everything.

When the gunmen had passed, she would have to try and get back to the others. They'd be worried. The last she knew, Dylan was still inside the facility. How long ago had that been? "Is there a back way off the property?"

"Yes," Ahmed said. "I can show you where to go but I can't protect you once you leave this property."

"What do you mean? You can come with me. We have a group and we're heading to Melbourne and then on to—"

His face folded with disbelief. "I'm not going anywhere. I need to bury my wife."

"Oh… of course. I'm sorry."

His frown folded. "It's okay. I have to follow the Muslim custom. It was important to her and it's important to me."

It surprised Kristy. She had thought most people would abandon religion under such circumstances. Kristy believed that something guided them all, but she wasn't sure exactly what. As a doctor, her life depended—or had—on science and fact, and she clung to such in most circumstances. Although she felt belief was a personal choice, and the most important thing was the humanity and decency of every person.

"How long does the burial process take?"

Ahmed considered this. "It's long." He took his time, as if confirming what lay ahead. "I must bathe her, soon, within several hours of her death. Normally, other Muslim women would do it, but… given the circumstances, some things are not possible. She must then be wrapped in the *kafan*—a plain white cloth. Normally she would stay like that for several hours, while well-wishers visited to pay their respects and offer condolences to the family." He paused, gathering himself.

"You don't have to explain anymore," Kristy said.

"No, I want to. To make sure I remember it correctly, as much as to explain why I can't come with you. After that, I will say a prayer and then I will go out into our small backyard and dig a grave. I will bury her, and mark it, and decide what to do next."

A thought struck her though. "Are there any circumstances where this process can be forgiven? Say if, your life depended on it?"

He shook his head. "No. If the process is not followed, the person won't be accepted into Heaven. I couldn't live with myself if that happened."

"I understand."

He smiled. "Thank you. Religion is *everything* to a practicing Muslim. We live and die by the principles—the true principles, which are often quite different to those in the media."

A noise sounded from the back of the house. Ahmed clasped the shotgun in position, looking awkward, and stepped forward. Kristy followed, feeling her heart rate kick up a gear. She held the knife tight, knowing she had passed many tests in combat and was capable of the same again.

They left the kitchen and entered a short hallway that led to the back door. On either side sat several bedrooms where all the curtains were drawn. A clatter sounded from beyond. Ahmed stopped at the entrance, listening. After a moment, he said in a whisper, "Somebody is outside. If we wait, they might leave."

"Is it locked?"

He nodded.

The short horizontal handle moved down slowly. There was a push against the wood, but the thing didn't budge. Whoever was out there tried again. The timber creaked, but still it didn't open. Then something struck the door, and the house shook. Ahmed jumped back. It came again, and Kristy thought it was probably someone's foot trying to kick it in.

Ahmed lifted the shotgun. Kristy raised the knife. She didn't think a zombie had the capability of such action—it was more likely one of the militia that had attacked them at the facility.

From the kitchen, a moan sounded. Kristy's skin goose-fleshed. She glanced at Ahmed. His face had gone slack.

"What was that?"

Kristy made a tight little shake of her head, but in truth, she knew. It meant only one thing. Ahmed's wife might have been shot dead, but if it wasn't in the right place, she would rise again. Ahmed's mouth fell open. "Is … is that …"

Kristy gulped a dry throat. A zombie. No doubt about it. She thought about having to kill Ahmed's wife. He wouldn't be able to do it. The back door banged again.

Ahmed said, "They're trying to kick it in." He edged forward, poking the shotgun out. "I'll shoot them if they come in here. I will."

Kristy wondered if Ahmed knew the specifics of using a shotgun. "Get close," she said, gathering her courage. In the kitchen, the table scraped over the floor. Ahmed mumbled something in a foreign tongue.

"Take it easy," Kristy said. "Just be ready to shoot." But the real threat was in the kitchen. Whilst the door was locked, they should deal with her first. "Ahmed?" She signaled him, and finally he turned and followed.

Ahmed's wife stood beside the table, arms by her side, staring towards the front of the house. She made a low, unintelligible slobbering noise that turned Kristy's stomach. Tears streamed down Ahmed's face.

She knew he wouldn't be able to do it. Dylan had not been able to kill his mother. Kristy wondered if he would be able to kill her, if it came to this. But Ahmed surprised her. He raised the shotgun up to his shoulder.

"You'll have to move closer," Kristy whispered.

The zombie turned and wobbled towards Ahmed. His eyes widened and the gun fell away. The thing's mouth opened and closed as if trying to speak. Ahmed sobbed and raised the gun, taking sight. He stepped towards her as she reached for him.

"Shoot," Kristy said. But Ahmed hesitated. The zombie fell forward, reaching for Ahmed's throat. "SHOOT IT!" It took Ahmed by the neck, pulling him closer. Kristy raced forward and pulled at the thing's shoulder, trying to spin it around. She raised the knife and picked a spot on the side of its head.

"No!" Ahmed screamed. He yanked his wife away from Kristy and they crashed into the kitchen sink. The zombie groped, clawing at his skin, and Kristy thought *He'll die with her*. Maybe that was better—they'd be together, wherever that might be.

Ahmed used the shotgun to hold her back, but the hands were strong, the eyes burning with a desire Kristy had witnessed too many times before.

Kristy picked another spot on the side of its head and held the knife up, but in their struggle, Ahmed pushed his wife away and she lost the opportunity.

Thunderous gunfire exploded from the back of the house, the sound of splintering wood and shrapnel. The intruders had blown the door down. Kristy saw them in her mind's eye before it happened, a bunch of militia, with guns and grenades, ready to lynch them to a post and burn them alive. Almost worse than the zombies. Ahmed dropped the shotgun and Kristy scooped it up. She swung around to face the back door, her finger on the cold metal trigger.

The tip of a rifle appeared in the doorway, followed by a big, shadowy body. By the time she recognized Callan's face, it was too late; her finger had reacted. The gun roared, but at the last millisecond, she pulled the shot left. The wall exploded as Callan turned away, falling back through the door. Blue Boy raced in, growling and barking at the zombie.

Callan sprung to his feet amidst the plaster dust. "Jesus Christ, it's me!"

"I'm sorry!" Kristy said.

Callan spied the zombie. His reaction time was fast, brushing past Kristy with the rifle pointed. It had Ahmed by the throat, poised above him, and by some fluke, it had still not taken a bite from his neck. It was as though he could fend it off but didn't have the strength to finish her. Callan kicked her aside with his size thirteen boot. The zombie went sprawling over the floor among Ahmed's shouts. Callan lifted the rifle and fired into her face.

The noise was deafening. Ringing filled Kristy's ears, and she covered them, backing away, wondering if this time she would finally rupture an eardrum. Ahmed dragged himself over the floor, repeating a silent word in Arabic. He flung himself over her body, sobbing.

They stood watching him as he cradled the body of his dead wife in his arms. Finally, Callan went to Kristy and pulled her to him in a strong hug. "I thought you were dead." His voice croaked and he squashed her to his big chest. "I thought for sure you were gone this time."

"So did I." Kristy gave a brief explanation of what had happened. "Where is everyone else?"

Callan made a strained face. "We all thought you were killed in the explosion. Evelyn said she saw you sitting by the red sedan. It was a mess. We were attacked by gunmen on one side and zombies on the other. I'm sorry; I should have tried harder to find you."

"You did. You found me." It could have been much worse, Kristy realized. Luck played a huge part in survival, and she had plenty of it. "So why didn't you leave?"

"Blue Boy disappeared. I came looking for him. He led me here. To this house."

The dog sat on his haunches looking up at them, tongue hanging out. He might have been smiling. Kristy squatted, reaching out, and he came to her. She rubbed his neck and cuddled him, kissing the stop of his head. He had been an astounding dog. There was pressure behind her eyes. "Thank you, Blue. Thank you for not giving up on me."

Ahmed was talking in a low voice, crooning as he cuddled his dead wife.

"So Dylan left too?"

Callan nodded. "Yeah. He thought you were dead. He's gone to find out if his sister is still alive." Kristy understood, but it hurt her to think Dylan had given up on her so easily. She wondered what she would do if the roles were reversed. "Don't blame him though. I'll be honest, sis, I didn't really come looking for you. We thought you were dead."

She touched a hand to his arm. "It's okay."

"But we have to leave," Callan said. He disappeared towards the front of the house.

Kristy squatted beside Ahmed. "You can come with us, if you like. We have a group of people." Ahmed didn't move. He was still cuddling his wife's body. "Ahmed?"

"There are more men on the street," Callan said, returning. "We have to move, now."

Kristy put a hand on his arm. "Ahmed, please?"

Callan squatted nearby. "We're going to the city. We have a ship captain and we're going to find a boat to take us to Tasmania. Station Pier. That's where we'll be."

Finally, Ahmed pulled himself away, sobbing. His eyes were red-rimmed and glassy. "Get out."

"What?" Kristy said. She shrunk back from, as though struck. "What—"

"*Get out of my house.*"

"Ahmed—" He began to cry harder. "Ahmed, please, come with us. Those men will find you soon, and they'll—"

He climbed to his feet, stumbling, hands balled into fists at his side. "Good! Maybe that's what I want. You killed her. She's gone, because of you." He started forward. Blue growled.

Callan stepped between Ahmed and Kristy. "Come on. Let's go."

"*No*," Kristy said. "Ahmed, please." Callan herded her towards the back entrance. Ahmed had stopped. The tears came in a rush, and he broke down, glancing back at his dead wife. Kristy's heart ached. Callan guided her towards the back door with tears in her eyes. Then they were away, Ahmed's sobs disappearing as new sounds filled her ears, just as bad.

TWENTY-NINE

THUNDER GRUMBLED in the distance. The darkness of the clouds suggested it was later in the day, but it couldn't have been later than four or five. Rain lashed the windscreen, and Evelyn switched the wipers to full speed, peering through the crowd of zombies before them. Dylan had told her to drive fast, but after the Army facility in Canberra, Evelyn had sworn she'd never drive into such madness again. And while this wasn't the same, the circumstances were still terrifying and risky. *That's life now*, she supposed. *You're cool in a crisis.* This was going to be a challenge though. It wasn't that there were so many of them, but the road was only so wide, and full of barriers and tramlines. There were only so many places through which she could pass.

And she couldn't find a clear route. There was a car in the middle amongst the sea of dead. She decided to go straight for the horde, roll over them like pins. They'd get some damage to the van, but they could make it. *Drive fast,* as Dylan had said. Ram the car out of the way, if she had to. She turned around to tell them all to be seated, to have their belts on, but they knew the rules now. Everybody was secure in place.

Evelyn punched the accelerator. She hit the first few, and they spun aside with a heavy thud. Others stood in her path, confused, unsure which way to go, and she mowed them down, splitting them apart like rotten fruit. Blood sprayed up the windscreen. She barrelled on, but slammed into something unseen with a crunch and a bang. The van jumped sideways. She didn't stop though, urging the vehicle forward amidst the scrape of steel.

197

"There's a motorbike," Greg yelled from the side window. "It's stuck."

It had jagged itself underneath the camper and screeched an unbearable noise as they dragged it along the road. The engine revved, but it would go no further.

"Keep going," Dylan shouted.

"I'm trying!"

Zombies thumped the side. Sarah screamed. Evelyn gave another thrust, but it lurched once, and revved high again. She pulled the wheel left and drove forward; the bike slid loose, allowing some movement, but they bounced over a low concrete barrier. A steel railing used to protect tram passengers blocked further passage, and the camper came to a sudden halt, tossing them all forward. Zombies attacked the bloody windscreen.

"Reverse," Gallagher yelled. "Throw it in reverse."

Yes. Reverse. Why hadn't she thought of that? She slammed the stick back and thumped the pedal. The van jerked backwards, throwing them all again, and drove over feeders standing at the rear, jiving and jumping. When she was clear, she braked, peering forward for a pathway.

A mass of zombies, the broken-down car, the motorbike, and a narrow road lay before them. She searched for another way out, feeling the claws of desperation sink into her thumping heart. It all came down to her.

Their best chance was slightly left, down a side street off the main road. A median strip lay in between. Beyond sat a big bluestone church, a large blue box with high windows and a tiny door. Zombies couldn't get into *that*. Something caught her eye. One of the church doors was open. An arm reached out and closed it.

Rain swept in on a strong gust of wind, shaking the camper, the wipers almost irrelevant. A zombie got hold of one of the moving arms and tore it free with a cheap snap.

198

The remaining swung across the glass, but the visibility was terrible, water teeming over the damaged limb. More feeders crowded in, drawn to the van and its contents like flies to old meat. There was no other choice but to take the side road and make the safety of the church.

Evelyn accelerated, jamming the front tires into the curb. The engine screamed; they weren't going to make it. *She would have to reverse*—then the wheels leapt up over the edge, bouncing the van, clawing their way over the strip.

"What are you doing?" Dylan yelled. Zombies were still coming, the road ahead filled with wandering stragglers. "We need to go the other way."

"We won't make it. I'm going for the church."

"No! You can't—"

"I saw someone. There are people inside. They have to let us in!"

"Good thinking," Gallagher said. "Head for the back entrance."

Dylan's protest was drowned in tire squeals and the clunk of feeders bouncing off the van. Evelyn's body felt like it had been drawn out, tight and stiff. Her knuckles were white around the wheel, her jaw hurting with tension. She wanted to hand the driving over and let someone else worry about them getting there safely, but it was too late to renege on her obligations.

The service road was clear of feeders, but the rear-view mirror told a different story. Evelyn rammed the camper off the curb and onto the street, running at right angles to the main road. Ahead, the street swept up and over a short rise and on their right sat a driveway entrance into the back of the church. There were two faint parking spaces marked by small rocks and a flat timber sleeper. She swung the vehicle in and parked diagonally across both spaces.

Gallagher was already standing near the door. "Wait here. I'll get them to let us in."

"You'd better hope somebody's home," Dylan said.

Gallagher opened the door and hung off the step. "Greg, come with me. Dylan, stand here and guard the van. Evelyn, keep it running and get ready to drive away fast." He paused in thought. "No, turn it around so we're ready to go in the other direction."

Evelyn preferred having someone tell her what to do. With Callan gone, she worried they would lack leadership, but Gallagher was stepping up. Dylan stood in the doorway with a rifle and Greg was halfway between the van and the church. Gallagher jogged to a heavy wooden door and thumped on it with the back of his fist.

"Open up!"

A dozen or more zombies shambled their way up the road towards the van. They were no different from the ones in Wagga, and Yass, and at the defense facility in Canberra. Old people, young, even children, all pale skin and ropey hair. Their eyes boggled, their clothes were torn, and their grey tongues lolled from their mouths like giant slugs. They all wanted one thing: human flesh, preferably from those who were living; however, if it came to a pinch, they'd eat the dead. She knew they had once been people—sons and daughters, fathers and mothers, brothers and sisters—but she wanted to kill them all, and would have sacrificed a lot to make it happen. No doubt in her mind, they would reach the van and engage to the death yet again.

"Open up! Please!" Gallagher screamed. He pulled on the door handle repeatedly, but it wouldn't budge.

The rain pelted the windscreen in thick drops. Somewhere over the city, thunder cracked, and two or three seconds later, lightning flashed. *Close.* Her father had taught her to count the seconds. Dylan set himself on the gravel outside the doorway and fired at the oncoming crowd. One took a shot in the throat and slumped to its knees, then fell face down onto the road. The others shuffled on. Evelyn thought it was lucky there were no type threes, although she knew they were never far away. Greg fired into the group too, taking several down. He and Dylan had enough time to reload. Evelyn considered driving through them.

Gallagher had run around to the side of the building, searching for an entrance, but there was nothing besides a small window cut roughly at a height of about twelve feet. Evelyn expected him to come back and try to kick the door in, but instead he disappeared towards the front of the church. A handful of zombies drew away from the line after him.

"He's leaving us," Evelyn said, pointing. "He's gone."

Dylan said, "He won't leave."

Greg and Dylan finished reloading and began firing on the remaining feeders, shooting those closest with deadly accuracy. The blood and killing had drawn others though. Beyond, a broken line stretched on down the side street to the main road.

A zombie reached the driver's side of the van and stretched for the slightly open window. Evelyn jumped back, scouting for a weapon. The silvery blade of a knife they had taken from Yass glinted at her from the top of a sports bag. She leapt off the seat and pulled it out. The zombie had two hands over the top of the glass, trying to climb in. Evelyn reached forward and jabbed the blade deep into a pale eye. It fell back into a thin puddle with a splat. She fumbled for the button and raised the window.

Half a dozen bodies lay on the road. The men had worked their way back to the van but were out of ammo again. Both were saturated, hair plastered to their heads, water dripping down their faces, their clothes wet and heavy. They were poised to re-enter the van again when Gallagher appeared at the rear entrance to the church.

"This way," the admiral shouted. He stood in the shadow of the door, holding it open.

Other feeders had climbed the slope, splitting their attention between the van and the church. Greg jumped up onto the step and stuck his head through the doorway. "Let's go."

"We need to move," Evelyn said in her calmest voice. She scooped up a large bag as Julie ushered Jake and Sarah towards the door. Greg called them out from the middle ground between the van and the church. He'd ceased shooting, waving Julie through the door. Dylan stood a few steps behind him and helped them towards Gallagher.

They were going to make it, Evelyn thought, closing the van door. She followed Julie and the children with the bag of guns, glancing towards the main road as she splashed through puddles on the stony earth. Bodies lay at awkward angles in clumps where Greg and Dylan had shot them dead. Further back, others wandered towards them, but they were slow and distracted, and then she was there, taking Gallagher's hand as he pulled her into the darkness of the church and slammed the door shut behind them.

THIRTY

AFTER LEAVING SEYMOUR, Jacob and Rebecca had pumped their way the roughly fifteen miles to Broadford when Jacob called it quits for the night. It was well past dark, but light from the part moon showed them flashes of the landscape around the modest train station: trees on a high bank, power lines running parallel to the tracks. The bats were calling, the mosquitoes sucking their blood at every opportunity, and the last heat of the day hung around with the promise of an imminent storm.

Jacob's arms ached. He'd borne most of the work, refusing to let Rebecca do more than ten minutes at a time, and he knew he'd suffer the following day. She was a trooper though; he had to give her that, even if she was barely talking to him. She could distinguish between normal life and the need for survival. Her mother would have been complaining the whole time, crawling to a corner of the car and curling up into a ball the moment it got tough.

Still, he couldn't believe they were still alive. He kept replaying their escape from the Seymour station over and over in his mind, goose bumps chilling his skin at the thought of the zombies getting hold of Rebecca. He had promised to keep her safe, but for how long? He had promised to keep all of them safe over the course of the last few weeks, and only she remained. He had failed, and it burned at his soul like poison.

The station at Broadford was nothing like Seymour. The car slowed to a stop outside the sixty-four square-foot box cut into an embankment about halfway down the platform. Double tracks led in both directions. Jacob thought they might face a track change at some point ahead. He leapt off the car onto the hard platform and climbed over a guardrail, keeping the torch beam low to the ground. He walked a few paces then climbed a set of stairs and tried the door. Locked. He flicked the torch back towards the car where Rebecca sat, head slumped forward. Exhausted. They both needed rest and sleep.

They had lost the ax back at Seymour; otherwise, he could have broken the door in with the blunt end. One bullet remained in the revolver, but he didn't want to waste that on a lock when he might need it to save a life. He would have to kick the door in, but was paranoid about the noise it would make. He swept the yellow beam through the darkness around the station building, searching for the flash of eyes, or other movement. The bushes and trees were still, the gravel pathway leading to a car park, which he assumed was empty. He considered searching for a vehicle but decided the risk wasn't worth it. He might spend hours trying to find one with keys *and* fuel, all the while avoiding zombies. For now, the rail car was working, despite the physical demands, and he would take that to avoid risk any day of the week.

Jacob circled the tiny building, peering through the windows, using the torch as much as his paranoia would allow. He had to be sure there were no feeders inside, although until they entered he couldn't be certain. He would have to take the risk.

Two more completed laps and a quick check to make sure Rebecca was still unharmed and he stood before the door, testing it for weak points. He decided the lock was old and flimsy. It buckled and banged under the pressure of his first kick, but did not open. He peered around, waiting for zombies from the shadows beyond the torchlight. The night remained stifling and silent. On the third try, the door crashed open under his heel, and again he waited, expecting for certain that this time they would be drawn to the noise. Nothing. He touched the door with the tip of the revolver and it swung open with a rusty creak. He winced, wondering if he could possibly make any more noise. He stepped inside, poking the torch beam through the darkness, digging it into the shadowy corners and behind the green-painted desk. A four-legged chair, open-mouth dustbin, and several dented filing cabinets sat silent. A plain blind had been pulled down over a wide window. There was enough floor space for the both of them. Hope beckoned.

In short work, they had their packs and remaining supplies inside the station building, the door bolted from the inside using a secondary lock. In darkness, Jacob pressed his face against the glass, searching the silence outside for movement.

They did their best to close the gap in the blind, and then lit a pink candle from the IGA supermarket and placed it on the desk. Rebecca ate uncooked two-minute noodles, while Jacob chewed half a pack of Savoy crackers for the thousandth time.

The silence grew, making him uncomfortable. This was his daughter, for God's sake, his flesh and blood. Surely, they could find something to discuss? But he was afraid of saying the wrong thing again, of pushing the wrong button and sending her into further silence. He understood her reluctance to accept him, but after this long, and all they had battled, she should have been coming around. Perhaps it was his unwillingness to discuss the issues, to explain his motivations for leaving when she was a child. He wanted to; he wanted to tell her that he had thought about her every day since walking out with his three bags of clothes and bootload of junk that he'd never taken out again, except to toss into the rubbish bin. He wanted to tell her that he'd tried to build the business for her, to make a name for himself so that one day she might be proud of what he'd done, so that if she saw how hard he had worked she might understand the *why*. But it hadn't eventuated. Everything he'd worked for had been destroyed along with the rest of the world. What did he have left? Nothing. Nothing but the wisdom of his failures and pain of things he couldn't change. *You have a daughter.* He did, and his gratitude for that went beyond words, but he didn't know how to handle her. To Jacob, she was akin to a bag of snakes.

Fatigue and exhaustion pulled at him. He tried to keep his eyes open, tried to think of an opening line to start the conversation, but he had never been good with such around Rebecca. He drifted, sleep taking him with a sweet, lustful cloud.

He woke later and found her cross-legged, watching him with a sad expression. The candle burned on. It was still dark outside. "Why did you leave?"

"Wha?" He tried to sit up, but his aching, aging body wouldn't allow it. Did he hear right? He knew he should wake up and talk to her, but his eyelids were heavy. They fell closed. He was so tired. *So tired …*

When he next woke, spears of light had broken through the edges of the blind. Morning. This time when he tried to move, it was easier. He rolled onto his side and pushed up with his elbow. On all fours, he saw Rebecca had fallen asleep against one of the packs. She looked so vulnerable lying there. Nothing like the difficulty she could be. He crawled aside and sat watching her sleep, the slow, gentle rhythm of her chest rising and falling. How many times had he missed watching the same when she was four, or seven, or twelve? It burned his gut like acid. It had all been for nothing, and he had missed everything. What could he do though, keep beating himself up? He had promised he would repay her, somehow. He couldn't change the past, but he pledged again that he would make her future better.

He was outside when Rebecca woke. On his return to the station building, she had a can of tomato soup open and was drinking from it as though it was a soft drink.

"Careful you don't cut yourself on the edge."

She kept drinking. When she was done, she placed the can in the rubbish bin and collected up several more scraps from the carpet and did the same again. He noticed the candle, torches, matches, and spare batteries had been packed, stacked neatly in one corner. She was anal about that sort of thing. This pleased Jacob.

Still, she said nothing, but he caught her glaring at him as they backed out of the station building and headed towards the rail car. He wanted to ask, but if she was anything like her mother—and in this way, he suspected she was—she would eventually talk. He had learned over a long period before their separation to give Jennifer space and not force discussion about what was bothering her.

Clouds rested like a squadron of fighters in the west. Jacob smelt imminent rain and wondered whether they might get a soaking later in the day. He didn't know where they were going, only that the tracks led all the way into Melbourne. Others he had spoken with in their travels suggested they would head there, and it was *somewhere*; at that point, he had no better ideas. How long would it take? A full day, maybe longer, he thought. They had traveled almost a quarter of the way the previous afternoon, but today would be the killer, if they could survive.

Jacob began the pumping motion, expecting his muscles to tighten with resistance. Surprisingly, they only gave a dull ache as his blood flow increased. The handlebar kept coming loose, but he tightened the bolts with his fingers, which helped. Rebecca faced forward, her back to him, the wind in her face, as they gathered speed. Her blonde, silky curls trailed behind, and he thought it was one of her nicest features.

They took turns at pumping as they passed through more stations—Kilmore East, Wandong, Heathcote Junction, Wallan, and Donnybrook—each with their small weatherboard buildings, discarded and disused; none of which were places Jacob wanted to stop. But they needed rest, and after Rebecca's shift, Jacob felt the twinge of overworked muscles in his arms and shoulders. He let them drift to a stop in the middle of an open field with the widest view to anything that might attack. None did though, for there was nothing out there. After a silent drink, they pushed on.

Approaching Craigieburn Station, they had reached the outer limits of Melbourne. That meant more feeders. It was inevitable they would face them soon, although he held hopes that the train tracks would offer some protection. There were zombies at the station. Rebecca watched them as they passed the platform, wandering down the road on the town center side. Several were caught in the twisted carnage of a fence that had been smashed down by a rampant motor vehicle with all its glass broken.

At the lower end of the station, there was a choice of two tracks. One sign read BROADMEADOWS LINE, the other UPFIELD LINE. They sailed through, taking the pre-selected track, which was the Upfield line, Jacob unsure if it was right or wrong, but knowing they should both eventually lead them into Melbourne.

It was Rebecca's shift when the rain first came, pounding the open car with large drops. Jacob urged her to stop, but she shrugged him off. He silently admired her resolve. Sooty grey clouds covered most of the city sky. He had known rain was on the way, but this was going to be more than they might weather. He wondered about the next station and decided they would stop there if it fell any heavier.

The first zombies appeared as the tracks, still running parallel to the Hume Highway, meandered their way along the backside of an industrial area—warehouses, large blocks of retail outlet shops, and the odd manufacturing site. On the right, scruffy paddocks eventually met houses and the suburb of Broadmeadows.

They were still about a hundred yards away when Jacob noticed something on the railway line. He knew it had to happen sooner or later; they had sailed all the way from Seymour without a problem. He motioned for Rebecca to slow down, and she did, noticing the concern on his face as he drew the revolver from his waistband. As they approached, he spied feeders standing off to the side in the shadows of several buildings. These were not the stupid ones that had mostly attacked in Seymour, but neither were they the crazies that had chased them on the tracks. *Somewhere in between.*

As they approached, Jacob recognized the obstacles as large rocks, and that he would have to climb down and remove them. He scanned the long grass at their side as they rolled along, searching for a weapon, but it was empty. He had a single round left in the revolver, but beyond that, only his fists.

The feeders stirred from their hiding places. What fascinated him in a distant way was their ability to think beyond the necessity for blood and flesh. They had planned the maneuver, but how had they known to do so?

The rail car had almost stopped. Jacob pumped several times, urging them forward. The handlebar rattled again, the nuts working their way loose from the bolts. An idea struck him. He fiddled for the bolts underneath, and this time, instead of tightening them, he spun the nuts the other way.

The bar fell out of its holder and rattled onto the floor of the car. Jacob picked it up and tightened his hands around the weapon.

THIRTY-ONE

"DO WE just leave him there?" Kristy asked as Callan closed the back door of Ahmed's house. The darkening sky grumbled overhead. Blue Boy trotted at their heels, now eager to leave the property.

"I don't think anything will move him right now. He's grieving."

"But that's horrible."

"You can't force him."

They reached the timber fence surrounding the back yard. Callan peered over the top for the militia. Somewhere, gunfire popped and cracked.

Kristy stopped. "We can't, Callan. We can't leave him here."

She didn't understand. *Lucky her.* She hadn't really had to face intimate death, not up close, like he had with Sherry. Callan understood what Ahmed was going through. He'd be numb now, except for the burning in his stomach. Unable to breathe. No focus. Nothing in the world would make sense. He'd wonder how he was going to make it to tomorrow, and the next day. Callan wished he could tell him that it did get better, if only a little at a time.

"Let him go."

Voices reached them from the other side of the paling fence. They both ducked. Callan took Blue under his arm and the dog's tail wagged. They waited in silence as the voices faded down the street.

"Please," Kristy whispered. "He saved me. I don't want to leave him behind."

"You can't make a person do what they don't want to do. He can only deal with one thing at the moment, Kris. Let him go."

Callan climbed up on the fence railing and swung a leg over. "Pass the dog up to me." Kristy did, struggling to lift him up to the height Callan required. Eventually they managed it, and Callan dropped Blue from a safe level onto the pavement below. Kristy followed, and he helped her down. They jogged across the road to the opposite path, Callan perusing for more men. He slowed his pace to match Kristy's struggle. "You okay?" She said she was, but Callan stayed beside her.

It didn't take long for them to locate the blue Toyota four-wheel drive.

"You parked it in somebody's driveway?" Kristy asked, as they stepped over loose trash from a bin pressed up against the garage door.

"Yeah. One of my more clever moves."

There was a moment when Callan thought the car might not start, but eventually the old engine turned over, rumbling and groaning to life. How long before it gave out though? He thought they had done well for it to last this long. He just hoped it didn't drop dead on them in a moment of crisis.

"Fuel is getting low. We'll need to find some soon. All the extra stuff is with the campervan."

Callan backed it out onto the road under a rough idle and accelerated down the street. Blue grinned at them and collapsed across the seat, tongue hanging out. Callan followed the street around the block and out onto Camp Road, taking the same back streets they had used to bypass the entrance earlier.

Rain fell as they reached the main road, well past the entrance to the facility. Callan paused, glancing towards the opening, then turned left and drove on, checking the rear-view mirror as the old Toyota shook its way to top speed.

The wind howled through the window as raindrops splattered Callan. The ancient wipers screeched over the window, smearing dirt and water and making visibility worse. Callan pressed the water spray and, surprisingly, it shot a jet out onto the glass. Atop a short rise, they saw bands of rain hanging from low, dark clouds over the city.

At the bottom of a long, gradual slope, they approached the railway crossing. Before the world had moved on, Callan was paranoid about them, and now he looked both ways out of habit. On the far left, about a hundred yards away, a vehicle sat in the middle of the tracks. He slowed the four-wheel drive and drew it to a stop about fifty yards before the gates. A rough dirt road speared off to the left.

"Are they… people?"

They were two of them, standing on top of something that looked like an old carriage or train platform, waving their weapons at a mob of zombies hovering around the edges, groping at their feet.

"They need help."

Instinct took over. Callan steered the vehicle onto the loose rocks and took off fast. The wheels spun on the gravel, snaking the car from side to side. He gathered control before it ended up in the tall grass pushing in on both sides, and then slammed into a pothole. The vehicle shuddered, chassis and joints squeaking.

As they approached, the two people grew clearer. One was a middle-aged man brandishing a piece of pipe, the other a younger woman using a shorter weapon.

"Oh my God, that's Jacob," Kristy said.

Callan narrowed his gaze. The man was dishevelled, with a tall, sturdy frame and thick grey hair. "I think you're right. And that must be Bec." They were still twenty yards away.

"Grab the pump action off the floor in the back. It's already loaded." Kristy reached around and came back with a trusty Remington .308. "You right for this?" She nodded.

He hurried the vehicle forward and rammed the front end into a spread of zombies crowded in close to the platform. The vehicle bounced off the railway tracks and the feeders went sprawling. The platform shook slightly; Jacob and Bec clung to the center column.

Callan swung the door open and leapt out. Kristy followed. "Leave Blue inside." The dog leapt against the back window, barking.

Numerous zombies left the side of the rail car and came at them. Callan put the rifle barrel to the first pasty forehead and blew its head off. It fell back against the side, knocking another to the stony tracks. He shot that one too, spreading its brains over one of the big rail car wheels. Gunfire sounded from the other direction; he heard the pump of the barrel reloading and felt a swell of pride for his sister.

Others came for them, sensing the sweet scent of fresh food, but they left full of disappointment. The two newcomers were capable, their skills borne from situation after situation of fighting, often under more duress and against greater odds. They used their hands and feet with speed and dexterity, their weapons with an eerie competence. Shots cracked, more zombies fell, and they each did it with a precision and efficiency at which Callan would later marvel. Jacob and Bec continued to use their limited weapons and were able to finish the last of the feeders off until, finally, a pile of bloody, mutilated corpses lay around them. Callan eyed the scene, breathing hard. Kristy bent over, hands on knees.

"Better than any aerobics class at the gym?"

She nodded, grimacing.

Jacob stood atop the car with his hands on his hips, puffing. Bec slumped to the floor of the railcar and dropped her legs over the side. "Boy, are we glad to see you," Jacob said.

Callan gave him the thumbs up sign. "Talk about luck. You guys must have it in bucket loads."

"We've had our share of both," Jacob said.

"Where are you headed?"

"The city."

"So are we. Pile in."

Jacob suggested they stick to the railway lines. The route was slow and bumpy as Callan guided the four-wheel drive through weeds that tickled the bottoms of the doors and the underside of the carriage. Still, it was far better than the roads, and there were no more zombies yet. They passed rising smoke trails from the suburbs on both sides of the track, and once, they saw a car driving along a deserted road heading away from the railway line.

Jacob told their story of the decimation at Campbelltown, gazing out the window as he spoke. Only four of them had escaped from the service center that he was certain of, though he suspected some might have gone north. Bec was silent as she listened to the names of the dead and what they'd done for the group.

Sadness filled Callan. He had met a number of them, had shared food and drink with, back at Campbelltown. They had taken him and the others in, provided them shelter and other essentials during the storm. Now, most of them were dead. Monica, Jacob's wife, was among them. Callan imagined what he would be feeling. It was a sad fact of their new life, and a stark reminder that at any moment, their lives might end. They drove for a way in silence, watching the dirty clouds split apart and regroup.

"What's the plan now?" Jacob asked after they passed Fawkner Station.

"The others have gone into the city. Dylan had a sister living near the Queen Victoria market and he wants to check it out. We're meeting at Station Pier after that. Tasmania is the end goal."

"Tasmania. How?"

"Boat. We have an ex-Navy guy—was an admiral, and claims he can steer a ship across Bass Strait."

"That's a long way. The seas don't come much rougher."

"We don't have another choice. Nobody can fly a plane. Otherwise we're stuck on the mainland, and I can't imagine too many places will be safe."

"Melbourne is going to be terrible. We barely went into Sydney and it was bad enough. Tasmania makes a lot of sense, but getting there is going to be tough."

They passed through another station, and on the horizon, the hazy outline of city skyscrapers appeared above the rough inner-city rooftops. A rain belt swept in through dark, bubbling clouds, sucking the light from the sky, and in short work, mid-afternoon grew dim and ominous. The wipers scraped and moaned across the windscreen, doing little to prevent the deluge. Callan slowed the vehicle as the rugged track began to fill with water. He didn't want to drive on such a poor trail in the rain. When he got the chance, he would pull over and stop. At one point, the tire footprints became overgrown, and Callan steered them with difficulty through the tall weeds and soggy earth. They hit a deep pothole that tossed them up and down in their seats. Lightning flashed nearby, and the crack of thunder made Bec and Kristy jump.

They drew close to another station—Coburg, according to the signage on the buildings backing onto the railway line—and soon the familiar fence and platforms appeared. It was an older style red brick structure with enclosed rooms, a veranda, and a toilet block. It appeared clean and unattended, but as they pushed closer to the station, it appeared their track along the edge of the line had finished. Ahead, snarling overgrown scrub, heavy with trees, barred their way. Callan pulled the four-wheel drive out of the weeds and up onto the rocky tracks. He stopped at the edge of the platform, the engine idling. "Looks a good place to pull in for now."

"We're not going any further on this line, anyway," Jacob said.

At the end of the platform sat a train barring their way.

THIRTY-TWO

THE SHADOWY church was cool and inviting. An old man in black plants and a white shirt led them through a series of back rooms and a long, twisting passageway away from the beating hands of the dead on the weighty wooden door. "Oh, don't worry about them. They can't get in."

They followed him until they reached the gap between the chancel and the nave where rows of seats were split by a pathway down the center leading towards the front doors. A dozen candles sat around the walls and upon several tables on the chancel. The place had a warm, gentle feeling despite the battering rain and wailing winds outside.

"Come, come," the man said, motioning with his hand. "I'm the minister of this church and everybody is welcome here." Other people sat in the pews. They all glanced up as the group entered.

"Thank you, Reverend," Gallagher said respectfully.

"Harlan. Call me Harlan. I'm far too old for all that 'reverend' or 'minister' business. And I've never really subscribed to it. I was baptised Harlan. I like that."

He put out a hand indicating they should sit in the front row, which they did, and he stood before them as he probably had so many times before, leading mass.

"Just a few rules, if you don't mind. Not too much noise. Be respectful of others. You're welcome to stay here the night, or two, or three, or whatever suits you. We have a little food—we were scheduled to have a celebration the week this all happened, so we were stocked up—but it will run out eventually. Still, you're welcome to it if you need it."

Dylan took the lead. He was frustrated they had gotten so much closer to where his sister might be, but thankful for the hospitality. "Thank you, Harlan. We won't stay long. Just until the storm passes and the… attackers move away."

Harlan's eyes widened and he chuckled. "Move away? You might be waiting a long time. They've been banging on my doors for weeks. A team of men spent two days cleaning up the area around the church for me. The creatures came back though. Just be glad it wasn't the clever ones. They come and go and when they're around, the others aren't."

"Regardless, we'll need to move on as soon as possible. My sister is in the city. I need to find out if she's still alive."

Harlan nodded. "Well, I'll leave you to it. I'll just be poking about if you need me. We'll serve some dinner soon, and if you need to sleep in here, find a place and get comfortable."

When they were alone, Julie organized the group with a quiet, methodical influence, setting them up into areas and getting Sarah started on the treatment of Gallagher's latest injury. She disappeared briefly to talk to Harlan about meals and blankets. In the beginning, she had voiced her resentment at being part of the group, and Dylan had dismissed her standing, but slowly she was proving him wrong. Whilst at times, her grief was visible, Dylan thought she was managing the loss of her life partner incredibly well. She kept busy, organizing them, contributing to discussions about their destination, and doting after the children. They had warmed to her, sensing her maternal instinct, and she to them. Losing Kristy, he took strength from Julie, knowing if she was able to get by, then he must too.

Part of him wondered whether Kristy might be still alive. It was different than Eric—he had walked out into a horde of zombies. Nobody had seen Kristy die. Evelyn said she had been near the explosion, but what if she had somehow made it safely clear? Perhaps that was why he hadn't fully grieved yet. Maybe he didn't believe. He couldn't process the loss until he knew for sure.

But why had he left then? If he wasn't convinced Kristy was dead, he should have stayed with Callan, at least to look after him. They had forged a tight bond over the last few weeks. Dylan's actions were not in the spirit of the friendship though.

His head ached. Too much thought. Reasoning his actions had been difficult lately. He knew the virus had messed him up. Most of what had happened after the Army base in Canberra was a blur. His behavior towards Kristy now seemed strange, and he couldn't believe he still hadn't told her. It was as though his head was finally clearing and he was observing the world with a more logical perspective.

"Are you all right?" Evelyn asked, sitting beside him.

"I don't know, to be honest. I've had so many crazy thoughts lately. I don't know what to believe."

"Yeah, I know what you mean. We'll get to your sister's apartment. Tomorrow maybe, after we get some rest. I think we all need it."

Sarah did a good job on Gallagher's arm, cleaning the wound and patching it with a roll of gauze. Kristy would have been proud. Dylan worried about her illness though; he knew nothing of it and wasn't sure anyone else did, either. What if she took a turn, or needed real medical attention? He supposed there were always going to be medical complications. He and Gallagher were fighting their own battle. Without Klaus, they were flying blind, and even Kristy would have been able to provide some guidance, or check if the symptoms had progressed. Klaus said Gallagher's blood work had shown signs the virus was getting worse. Dylan tried to clear his mind and not consider the long-term implications of the illness, or the general survival of the group. It would all take care of itself.

They ate from the church stores while seated in the front pews, promising Harlan they would replenish his food from their own they had collected from the IGA store in Yass. Biscuits—almost their staple food now—topped with dried fruit, and apple juice. It was hardly out of a cookbook, but it sufficed. Harlan explained how he had been preparing for a celebration of the church's anniversary and had stocked up on "party food" for the group. Nobody had ever showed up.

"Have you heard anything about the government or military from people passing through?" Gallagher asked.

"A guy who stopped by here a few days ago had a radio—Army band—but he said not much was happening. The airwaves have been mostly silent since the third week of January`."

"You were part of the military," Dylan said to Gallagher. "What happened?"

The admiral shook his head. "I can't say much beyond the initial stages when things started to go bad. I was… a little incoherent."

"I was following it closely," Harlan said. "As soon as I heard the first reports of a global virus, I began to prepare. They called me a little crazy. *'The old bugger has finally lost it,'* some said. But we've been on the edge of a pandemic for some years. The bird flu in 2009 was the first stage. It's talked about in the Bible. I won't preach, but I can tell you that for us, it's not a surprise."

"How do you explain the dead people coming back to life?" Gallagher asked. "I don't recall such discussion in the Bible."

The minister considered this. Dylan watched his face closely, the wrinkles and sunspots, the fuzzy eyebrows, the wispy grey hair retreating from his forehead. "Men."

221

"Men?"

"This reanimation was an act of men; of that I have no doubt. I can't provide you undeniable evidence, but I feel it in my bones. I know I'm right."

Gallagher said nothing. The other people were all walk-ins: a father and his son, similar in age to Jake, a woman in her thirties, a man in his fifties, and a couple of teenage boys who had been there for a week. They all smiled politely, but kept to themselves.

After dark, Greg and Dylan poked their heads out the rear door through which they had entered. The campervan was still there and appeared to still have inflated tires and an intact body. The rocky ground was saturated; rain continued whipping against the bluestone walls and the doors. The boys copped a faceful, but, armed with guns, they swept the parking area in cautious silence, expecting a gruesome figure to lurch from the shadows at any moment. It was clear. The van had dents on the front and sides, a broken indicator light, and the remaining windscreen wiper was bent beyond repair. They took blankets, cushions, and pillows, deciding it was still too risky to sleep out in the camper. Dylan wondered whether it was the right time to move. If the feeders were elsewhere, they might get a clear run into the city.

"We can't leave tonight," Greg said, armed with a box of food. "I know what you're thinking. I want to get to your sister, too, but driving through the city in the dark is too risky." He knew Greg was right, but still, it was difficult to accept.

Julie arranged their bedding as Harlan doused some of the candles. It was warm and cozy though, and as they lay in their beds and listened to the renewed rain whip against the high windows, Dylan remembered something he had said to Kristy so long ago. *I'll marry you some day.* Had she been there, they might have done so. They were in a church, with a minister.

He sobbed as he lay awake in the faint light thinking of his failed promise, wishing she were there beside him.

THIRTY-THREE

CALLAN AWOKE in the middle of the night from a dream about Klaus. They were back in the defense facility in Canberra, and the scientist was trying to tell him something, but Callan couldn't make out the words. He kept moving down a long tunnel. Klaus wouldn't follow, despite Callan calling out for him. Afterwards, he lay there for a long time, searching for sleep again. He called Blue Boy close and found comfort in the dog's warmth.

After a time, he sat up. They were in the largest room of the station, with a high ceiling and strong, concrete walls. The main door leading out on the street had been bolted shut. Candles sat in all corners and on benches once utilized by people waiting for trains to transport them about their daily lives. Callan stood, stepped over the others on the floor, and went outside into the darkness, Blue at his heel. Rain still fell in heavy sheets, pounding on the tin awning. Callan strolled along the platform and tried to distinguish the outline of the vehicle. It was still there. He peered along the tracks in both directions, looking for signs of movement, but there were none. Should they post a sentry? After what had happened at Campbelltown, it might be an idea, but Blue was there, and he tended to sense things early. Besides, what could the four of them do against an Army like that? He wondered when their time would be up. How long would they survive by the skin of their teeth? They needed a place to go where they could barricade themselves in, like a prison.

It would do for tonight, but tomorrow they would need to move again. He had a rough idea where Dylan and the others were going and beyond that, they had agreed to meet at

Station Pier. Whilst their latest rest had been recuperating, he felt guilty for not pushing on. What were the others doing? Were they in trouble, or worse, dead? There was a high chance, he supposed, and that left him with a feeling of underlying dread. Every day was another in risk to all their lives. Callan wondered if Dylan could handle any more loss. At the moment, he thought Kristy was dead. If his sister had passed, too, it might tip him over the edge.

He had thought Kristy was gone. If it hadn't been for Blue Boy, he might never have found her. Callan reached out and scratched Blue's neck. He squinted with pleasure, his pink tongue hanging out. He'd disappeared for a little bit earlier, probably off scavenging. All the dog food they'd collected at Yass was in the camper. Callan hadn't thought of that, but he hadn't thought he'd find Blue, either. He had to admit they were in a better position now, if they were able to regroup. Blue hadn't shown any symptoms, and even if Klaus was right and the dog was immune, Callan would feel better if he had a shot.

Callan thought of Klaus, the plucky little scientist. What a man to have come up with medicine to halt the destructive virus. One day, if any of them survived this, he would ensure Klaus' name was known in recognition for all he had done. Klaus had saved Dylan's life. He might have ended up like Johnny. He thought of Ahmed, the Muslim man who had essentially saved Kristy. He owed the man a life debt. Ahmed was the first Muslim he had ever met—Christianity was the major religion in Albury, although religion on the whole was dying. Callan had been baptized as a child at his mother's insistence, but beyond that, he had never attended church outside a wedding or funeral. Had leaving Ahmed behind been the best option? He couldn't have forced him to come. Grief was powerful, and not to be challenged. Callan didn't hold much hope for Ahmed, though. He was stuck in the middle of an area full of zombies and men who wanted to kill everyone they found.

The shadows moved, and he recognized the pale color of his sister's hair in the darkness. She sat beside him. "Can't sleep?"

"Nah. You too?"

"I didn't really thank you for coming after me." She squeezed his shoulder.

"To be honest, I thought you'd been killed. Blue though, he knew. He ran off and led me to you. He's a smart dog." Kristy put her face to his nose and rubbed his neck, making soft cooing noises. "Imagine where we'd be without him? He's saved us all at least once."

"I wonder where he came from? I don't recall ever seeing him in town."

"Doesn't matter. He's one of us now. He's our dog."

"He's *your* dog, Callan. He lives for you. He does what you ask."

Callan laughed. "Unless you're missing. Then he won't obey me."

Kristy was right though. He'd loved his other dogs, but in only a week or so, this dog had wriggled its way into his heart like no other. From his courage, to his charm, it was impossible not to love him. It made Callan vulnerable though. Such vulnerability was a worry in a world like this. What if Blue didn't make it? The thought struck ice into Callan's heart. He wouldn't let that happen.

The rain eased, and they returned to the station room soon after. This time Callan found sleep easier, and there were no more dreams.

THIRTY-FOUR

LAUREN WOKE on top of her bed in the clothes she had worn outside the previous night. Bright light bled in around the edges of the curtains, but most of the room was still in shadow. She guessed it must have been around nine. Harvey was gone, but her panic fled when she heard his cry from the kitchen. *Claire.* She couldn't recall waking once in the night to tend him. Had her friend taken care of her son while she slept? She had been tired. It was as though weeks of sleep deprivation from all the anxiety about Todd and Lenny and about not having sufficient food to feed the group had caught up to her. Now they had enough to last a little longer. She and Steve and... the mystery man who had saved them, had done what Todd and Lenny could not.

She slid off the bed and passed water, then went out into the kitchen where the others were standing at the bench and gazing out the window. Her corner apartment had never been more important, providing multiple views out onto the street.

"Morning," she said, putting her arms out to Harvey, whose tiny face peered back at her. Claire smiled, passing him over. "You're a darl. Thank you. Did he wake in the night?"

"Yeah. You were snoring."

Lauren made an apologetic face. "What are we looking at?"

"There's a group of men wandering about down there," Steve said, holding a mug of steaming coffee. "Want a brew?" She said she did. *Thank God for the generator,* Lauren thought. Finding diesel fuel to power it had been a stroke of luck. "Alexander says they've been following him around the city for two days."

Alexander. The tall, underfed man—barely—that had saved her and Steve the previous night. Now, minus the hoodie, his long blonde fringe fell over his face, and she recognized the misfortune in the sharp angles of his features. He hadn't spoken much since arriving—not that Lauren had heard, anyway. But she might just owe him her life, so she wasn't going to rush into judgment or make it difficult for him just yet.

"Sorry. If I hadn't shacked up with you lot last night, I reckon they might have found me."

"Who are they?"

Alexander shrugged. "I don't know. Probably just a bunch of assholes that get their kicks out of killing people—and zombies—and taking whatever they can for themselves." Lauren followed his gaze out onto the street. On the opposite side, a man with a ponytail and a sleeveless shirt poked a pile of refuse with the tip of his gun. Dark tattoos snaked down both arms. He had a beard and wore dark sunglasses. "I tracked them a week ago. They generally stay closer to Punt Road and pick about Richmond and Collingwood. I reckon they're only this far west because of me."

Lauren shifted Harvey to her other arm. Steve handed her a coffee and she sipped, savoring the smell. "What do they want with you?"

"I sort of found a stash of food. Apparently, they considered it theirs. It might have been, but I didn't know." He brushed the fringe from his face, revealing eyes as blue as the Caribbean. "I thought they'd leave me alone if I came over this way."

"How bad are they?" Steve asked.

"Bad. I've seen them kill men in cold blood, cut their throats, or shoot them at point blank range. If you've got something of value, they'll take it."

Claire said, "The city's a big place. Maybe they won't hang around long."

Alexander shook his head. "They don't go further into the city." There was a quiver in his voice. "Nobody does."

"Why?"

"That's where the bad ones are."

Lauren had a terrible feeling she knew what he meant. "The smart ones?"

"Yeah. They're smart. And fast. And they're building an army, changing all the slow and stupid ones into whatever it is they are."

"I don't like the sound of that." The man disappeared from view and the group dispersed from the window.

Lauren fed Harvey, changed his nappy, and put him down for a sleep. She led a tidy up of the apartment, and Steve took Alexander to refill the fuel drum for the generator from the supplies room on the level below. While they were gone, Lauren locked the door and checked the street from the window for signs of the men. A single zombie wandered along the road picking through the rubbish.

She sorted the packs of supplies into meals, rationing the quantity by weight. Steve and Alexander reappeared with fuel, batteries, and nappies. Lauren found herself drifting past the window often, looking down onto the street. Their existence frightened her. Zombies were one thing, but humans causing trouble were more unpredictable.

By late afternoon, the men had returned, meeting in a group at the intersection of Queen and Franklin Street. There were six of them, all wielding long barrelled weapons, firing them into the sky like firecrackers. The people in the apartment crowded around the window, but when one of the men looked up towards them, they fled from view.

Lauren wouldn't let anybody approach for another ten minutes. She crawled to it on her hands and knees, peeking over the skirting board. The group had disbanded, but she saw two groups of two walking down the street searching each building. She knew it was only a matter of time before they reached her apartment block. After that, the countdown would be on and she was helpless to stop it.

THIRTY-FIVE

JULIE WOKE to light coming in through the high windows of the church. At first, before the fog had cleared from her mind, she forgot where they were; she even forgot that Eric was dead and that her life had been completely destroyed. She lay there staring up at the high roof of the nave, ignoring the hard wooden floor biting into her hip, and waited. She had followed a similar process each morning since Eric's death. The tears would come and she would lie there a while longer and let them. It was cathartic. But on this morning, there were no tears. She lingered, thinking of her day ahead without him, but still she did not cry. Confused, Julie slipped out from under the blankets.

She left the nave and followed the small passageway towards the back of the church. The clatter of movement sounded from the kitchen. She found Harlan, the minister, pottering about, assembling supplies on a small table. There were several bags of flour and a carton of eggs. Maybe she could make pancakes for the children; they always seemed to cheer them up.

"Good morning," she said, greeting him in a soft whisper.

"Morning." Harlan offered a toothy smile. "How are you feeling after a nice rest?"

"Better."

"The rain has passed. There's no sunshine, but it's warming up again."

"It'll be hot soon."

"Yes," he chuckled. "I suppose it will. Although this building keeps quite cool." He rearranged the stash of food, adding salt and a packet of teddy bear biscuits. "Would you like a tea, or some coffee?"

"I'd love a tea, please."

"We still have bottled gas."

He filled the kettle and ignited the gas hot plate. The tin began to whir. Harlan washed two mugs, glancing at her from time to time with a smile, as if reading her posture and expression. Julie tried to remain impassive. She thought about her inability to cry, and wondered what it meant. Of course the lump of sickly lead in her stomach was still there, but it was as though she had run out of tears. She felt a stirring of guilt and tried to push the thoughts away.

"Are you alright?" Harlan asked as the water warmed.

No, she thought, *I'm not.* Was she ready to have this discussion? He would pry it all out of her, no doubt. She supposed he was better than any of her traveling companions. She had been more religious as a child, attending services each week, but it had drifted with her marriage and children. Eric had never been one for faith. Julie supposed that if she were truthful, she didn't know if she still believed. But Harlan had a kind, gentle way about him, and before she debated her action any longer, the words rolled off her tongue. "My husband died a few days ago. I'm still ... struggling with it all."

"Oh." His eyes averted, his lips pouted. "I am sorry." He put two tea bags into the mugs decorated with fading flowers. "Do you find strength in God?"

"Once. A long time ago." She waited for him to show scorn, but he did not look up. Did she go further and tell him how she really felt? She wanted to hold it in, but she had in truth been seeking such a discussion with somebody of an older vintage. "I'm not sure I believe anymore."

This time he would yell and order her from the church. He took the lid off the sugar bowl and scooped two spoons into his own mug then raised his eyebrows to Julie. She nodded. "One please." She waited for him to finish, still expecting his wrath. When he didn't speak, she said, "You're not going to say anything to that?"

He smiled. "Our beliefs as an individual are our most important right. Nobody should tell another what to believe in. No religion enforces this. You've seen things, experienced them, and consequently, they have altered your belief. My job is not to make a believer out of you, but to put your circumstances in the light of God and let you make your own decision."

She was taken aback by his acceptance and logic. "Why do you think he died?"

"Sometimes there is randomness in the world. People's actions create circumstances. Their decisions. We can say God did this to punish us, or to test us, or any of that, but the truth is, I don't know why He did it. I can't always find an explanation. But that doesn't mean I don't believe in Him. Maybe there was a reason your husband died. Maybe you just don't know it yet."

Harlan continued. "My view is that God, and through his son, Jesus Christ, has provided us a set of beliefs and values to which we can uphold ourselves. If everybody did that, the world would be a much better place. People don't though. They have their own moral compasses and from this they make decisions and take actions, and as a result of these, there are consequences for all of us."

Julie thought that was a fair and reasonable way to put it. God was not responsible for everybody's actions. He set an expectation and it was up to people to live to that. She wanted to tell him about the way she had been feeling and what it all meant. He had put in her in a comfortable space because he had not forced his religion on her. He accepted her beliefs as her own, and she knew he would not judge her now. She could tell him the rest. They sat, sipping at the steaming brown liquid. He was patient, as though he knew her pain was coming.

"I've been thinking about killing myself. Since Eric died, I've wondered about the point of going on. My life has always revolved around him. What will become of me? What will I do?"

"What has stopped you carrying out these thoughts?" The question shocked her. She stared at him. "It's a fair question. It must be something important. Your grief is palpable—from the moment I saw you, I knew you had recently lost someone close. Part of you aches to leave this world, but there are reasons keeping you here."

Julie felt dumbstruck. "I don't know."

"Are you still considering it?"

"Not as strongly."

"Why?"

She lacked the emotional stability to consider this before, and knew it was only with Harlan's presence and support that she could do so. If she loved and missed her husband so much, what was keeping her alive?

Harlan went on. "Suicide is never the answer. I believe we all have a part to play, and sometimes it takes us a while to understand it. You've found your place in the group."

"It's my camper—Eric's and mine—perhaps they are keeping me around for it."

"I'll warrant that's not it. You don't notice it because you're too humble, and you've done the same thing all your life. I'll argue that Eric relied on you more than you him, and I'll go further and say these people rely heavily on you, too, and will more so in the future." Julie blew air as if he was making it up. "We all need leaders—every one of us—and leaders come in different forms. Some are physical; others are emotional. Leadership is not always about standing at the

234

front with a gun and shooting dead your enemies. Leadership is about *stability* and *direction*. You feed them, you organize them, and you comfort them. They drive the van, but you decide where they go."

A sharp thought struck Julie. She couldn't recall when, but at some point yesterday, she thought they might have asked for her approval to do something. "I think the suicidal thoughts have passed. You're finding your place in this world and you are *essential* to the ongoing survival of this group. You just need to understand your purpose and hone in on that." Harlan lifted the cup of tea to his lips. "It will get easier. You'll never get over it, but eventually you'll learn to live with it."

THIRTY-SIX

THE FIRST thing Dylan thought of when he woke was Kristy. He lay there thinking of her absence and how it would impact his life. It was a different kind of sadness to that of his mother and father. He had only gotten to really know her over the last seven or eight weeks. They had always been friends, but their intimacy since returning from the lake had forged a special place in his heart. He would miss her desperately. But he still had Lauren to consider. He was banking on her still being alive, and it kept him going, able to keep the demons of Kristy's death behind the gates. Physically and emotionally, he had improved. The increased dosage of serum was clearing his mind and making him more sensitive to the world. That was both good and bad.

After breakfast, he and Greg slipped out the back doorway of the church as the first light of dawn raised its face in the eastern sky. The rain had passed. The camper was still intact. Further to the damage of the previous night, remnants of bloody smears covered the side doors and back window, the rest washed away by the rain. They swept the rear of the church and found no sign of feeders, although they saw a dozen or more wandering near the main road, consistent with them moving vast distances in packs, leaving little trace of their previous existence.

They replaced the food they had eaten from Harlan's stores with some of their own and returned the blankets and pillows to the campervan. They would leave soon, and Dylan looked forward to that. As Greg crossed to the campervan from the church with a box load of food, a man appeared holding a length of pipe. Dylan spotted him as he reached the vehicle and thought he probably had come from the side street.

"Give it to me," the man said, holding the bar up poised to swing. His clothes were dirty and ragged on his skinny frame, his face gaunt and chiselled.

"This?" Greg asked, holding out the box. The man nodded.

Dylan grit his teeth. Was there no respite in their existence? Zombies, men, weather, lack of food; it was all working against them. He felt like pulling the gun from his waistband and shooting the man dead. He could do it in seconds, but he got a sense that although armed, he didn't pose a real threat. The man continued watching the box of food. Hunger dripped from his expression. It was hard to feel hatred for that. They were desperate, just trying to survive. Dylan and the group had food today, but what about tomorrow? They might be in the same situation.

"Look, mate, you don't need to steal our food. We can give you a little, but that's it. We have people here. Young children who need it more than you or I."

A second man appeared out of the bushes holding a pinch bar. He tightened his grip and it moved like he knew how to use it. In his mind's eye, Dylan imagined pulling the 9mm out and killing them both. A third and fourth man jogged down the road, one clutching a baseball bat, the other a metal bar that would kill a man with a single blow. *Hold off,* another voice reasoned. One of the men rifled through the box Greg had left beside the camper door.

He looked up at Dylan. "You think we wanna do this?"

"We all have a choice."

"That's right. The choice to live or die. The time for being nice has passed."

"I don't buy that. I've witnessed more humanity of late than ever before. You want to take from us, fine, go ahead.

We'll think of something to tell the kids when they're crying from hunger."

The third man tightened his hands around the baseball bat. "We're sorry, but only the strong will survive in this world. Only—"

Greg made a face of disgust. "Ah, fuck off, man. You sound like something out of a movie. That's *bullshit*. Maybe the strong will survive and everyone else will die, but you lot will be alone and eating shit from cans every day, scrounging around the dumps for leftovers, until what? You run out of clean water and edible food? You'll die too, because there won't be anyone else to work with to help you fix it all up again. Is your head that far up your ass?" The man did not respond. "Where is all of this going? *If* we win the battle against those things, the only hope we've got is joining up with others and *rebuilding*. Growing fresh food, making clean drinking water." He shook his head. "The sad fact is that we've almost had more run-ins with people than the zombies. Can you believe that? We're killing each other when our enemy is much stronger. They'll wipe us out before we even realize what's happening."

Dylan was speechless. He'd never heard Greg talk like that before. His timing was superb. He wanted to slap him on the back and tell him he was brilliant. Instead, he gathered himself and tried to carry on the momentum. "There's a priest inside that church who is giving up his own food and offering shelter to anyone who needs it. He's running out of supplies, and when he's done, he'll probably die. He's too old to go and get it himself, but he still gives it over freely, without thought of himself. You don't need to steal it from him or us. We help where we can. Jesus, we've picked up enough people along the way. Others have given us food and shelter too. If we have any hopes of getting back to where we once were, it has to work like that. You get it?"

The men were silent. Their weapons had fallen by their sides, and two of them refused eye contact. As he had suspected, these men were desperate, not violent.

"We need antibiotics," one of the men said. He signaled another. "Dennis had an accident." Dennis lifted his shirt, revealing an angry red cut about six inches long on his belly.

Greg glanced at Dylan, who nodded. If it were antibiotics they wanted, it would be a small price to pay for a safe resolution. "We've got some antibiotics." Greg pointed towards the church. "I can get some."

The first man nodded. "We'd be grateful. And… any food you can spare."

Greg disappeared inside the church. Dylan still hadn't taken out his gun, but if they tried any moves, he was poised to do so. "You could join up with us," Dylan said. "We've come a long way. We sort of know what we're doing." After he said that, he thought of his parents, Johnny, Sherry, Howard, Eric, and… Kristy. They hadn't known what they were doing then.

"Where are you headed?" Dennis asked.

"The city. My sister was staying there before all of this happened. I need to find out if she's alive. Either way."

Greg reappeared with two small boxes of antibiotics. He walked up to Dennis and held them out. "These will do the trick. I used them myself a week or so ago. Got a nasty gash on my leg that got badly infected."

Dennis reached out for the boxes and took them. "Thank you." He slid the plastic shells out and popped a pill, then swallowed it.

"What about after the city?" the first man asked.

"Tasmania, we think. We've got a guy inside who can drive a boat. That's the plan, anyway. As I said, you're welcome to tag along. The more we have, the stronger we get."

The men passed glances between each other. "Thanks. But we've got unfinished business here," the first man said. He considered his next words. "Be careful in the city. Not only are there zombies running around, but there's another group of men who will kill you on sight, no questions."

Greg gave thanks, then reached down and picked up the small box of food. He walked over to the first man. "Here. We've got enough."

"You're good people. True to your word. I thought you were full of shit. Most are." He nodded to the others. "Good luck." And then they were gone.

THIRTY-SEVEN

IT WAS the heat that finally woke Ahmed. Although the curtains were drawn, the warmth of the room told Ahmed it was late morning. No air-conditioning in the afterlife, he thought. It wasn't the afterlife, but it might as well have been. Maryam was dead. He felt empty; as though he'd spilled his insides with all the tears he'd shed for his dead wife. He still couldn't fathom that she was gone, despite having completed her burial according to Muslim custom late the previous night with gunfire and explosions sounding around the streets of Broadmeadows. It had been the most difficult thing he'd ever had to do, especially after her changing.

Ahmed thought about what his father would say. *Weak. Crying like a woman.* But if he was so weak, why had he survived? It was not unacceptable for a man to cry over the loss of his wife. And besides, he didn't care. His father was dead, and he had endured.

But what to do now? He swung his legs off the side of the bed and sat up. He didn't want to stay. There were too many memories. He'd see Maryam around every corner and catch her scent in every room. They had lived and laughed too much in the house. Without her, it was really only walls and a roof. Besides, he was running low on food and supplies, and the last time he'd ventured into the store, it had been overrun by the dead.

He thought of the woman he had saved, and her brother. Part of him wanted to blame her—after all, it had been the pursuit of her safety that had ended in Maryam's death. Had he been alone, he could have helped her. *But then what?* Perhaps Ahmed would have been killed too. *Better off.* If he was honest. Though Maryam had already been sick, and she had made the mistake of leaving. He had told her to stay in the house, but for reasons he would never know, she had left.

Part of him had wanted to go with the woman and her brother. He knew that by staying, he risked his own survival, but he couldn't leave without following the custom of his religion. His wife's state for the next phase of her existence was of the utmost importance. They had not understood that. He saw the incredulous looks on their faces, watching a man who put religion before his own life. Or maybe they had. The woman had seemed full of empathy, and grateful for his intercession in saving her life.

Finally, he hobbled from the bed and relieved himself, then washed at the basin with cold water. He dressed in shorts and a t-shirt. From the pantry, Ahmed made porridge with powdered long-life milk, and ate at the kitchen table, where Maryam's body had lain less than twenty-four hours before.

Chewing on the gluggy muck, he weighed up his future. He imagined staying put, tending the house, scouting the area—full of crazy people and the dead—for supplies. Following this plan, he would at least be safe most of the time, behind four walls and a door, but for how long? How long before he crossed paths with the men from the facility, or one of the dead who randomly picked his house to search? The alternative was to ride away in search of the woman and her brother. Join with their group and flee across the sea to Tasmania. He'd always wanted to go there. Maryam and he had talked about a touring holiday in a campervan, exploring the national parks and the rugged terrain of the west coast. What else did he have? Even if he didn't manage to find them, he could always return home.

He knew where they were going. Station Pier in Port Melbourne. He and Maryam had ridden their motorbikes down there a number of times. They would glide along the freeway in the sun and finish by Port Phillip Bay, eating hot chips and drinking cold Cokes by the pier, topping it off with some of that vanilla bean ice cream at the store where you had to line up for twenty minutes. Maryam used to get so excited. The memory burned. He pushed it away and went to get a sports bag from the cupboard.

Ahmed packed clothes, toilet paper, soap, and deodorant. He filled the remaining space with food from the pantry—crackers, tinned pasta, noodles, and chocolate. He dressed in his leather motorbike gear—it would be hot, but he had once ridden in shorts and crashed, taking half the skin off his legs.

In the cool garage, he secured the sports bag to the back of his bike and filled the tank with spare fuel. He fastened his helmet then peered around the room a final time, wondering if there was anything else he should take. He had thought about some kind of weapon, but decided against it. He didn't think he could kill one of them, no matter what they tried to do, but now, as he stood beside his wife's motorbike and heard the distant boom of more gunshots, he supposed it would be sensible. He didn't have to use it. From the shelf, he took a long, yellow-handled screwdriver about ten inches long and slid it beneath the outer strapping of his pack. Then Ahmed wheeled his motorbike out the door and started for Station Pier.

THIRTY-EIGHT

THE GROUP said goodbye to Harlan and his small band before nine. They replenished the supplies and offered them passage in the campervan, but Harlan insisted on staying behind at the church. He said others would come and they would need his food and hospitality, and that if he died doing such, it would be in service of the Lord, which pleased him. Evelyn found a certain comfort in the man. It was hard to imagine he had ever made a bad decision or adversely affected anyone in his life. Was this what the service of religion did for you? If so, she thought it was a good thing. Harlan seemed at peace; content with his place in the world. Evelyn decided she would use that for perspective when she needed it.

Julie gave the old minister a long embrace. They said little, but exchanged knowing smiles and nods, as if they had shared some secret. Perhaps it was the age, or maybe Harlan had lost somebody close to him, too. Her demeanor continued to improve. It was hard to believe that Eric had been gone a couple of days, but Evelyn supposed the circumstances didn't allow for much deliberation. If Callan and Kristy *had* died, she would fight to be as strong.

Evelyn took driving duties again. She didn't mind. It gave her focus, and stole the chance for her to despair over Callan and Kristy. She'd spent much of yesterday afternoon and last night thinking about them. Was it Callan's departure or Kristy's likely death that saddened her the most?

Kristy had been a loyal friend since meeting. Evelyn would miss their chatter, sometimes about nothing—things that had once seemed important but no longer mattered. It had been nice to have another woman of similar age. What hurt the most about Callan splitting from the group was that he had not considered her at all. Evelyn knew she was being silly, but couldn't avoid the thoughts.

Zombies clawed at the van the moment they left the camouflage of the parking and re-joined the main road. They thumped the sides as she guided them back into the maze of carnage. She went around the car and motorbike that had so thwarted their attempts the previous day and, without the torrential rain and horde of attacking zombies, snuck through the mess and onto a clearer section of road ahead.

Stragglers stood about, picking through the empty carcasses in a garbage truck transporting a load of dead bodies. The smell was horrendous. Evelyn shoved a hand over her mouth as the morning's breakfast threatened to fly. Damaged buildings watched them pass. Broken glass covered the pavement, stock torn from stores left to waste away on the street. The heat radiated off the windscreen, the smell sneaking in through the vents. It was getting worse. Evelyn wondered how many dead would be in the city, how many feeders, and how much rotten food. The thought made her feel nauseated. How quickly the world went to ruin, she thought.

They drove on through the mess that was once Melbourne, a surprisingly easy run-down Hoddle Street through the northeastern side of the city. It was as though a single-lane path had been cleared. The roads were still full of battered vehicles, but they had been pushed aside, even piled up in some cases. As they drew closer, the numbers grew; endless zombies wandered about, milling over the grassy middle of the roadway, huddled in packs feeding on the fallen. Evelyn grew more concerned as they edged their way deeper into the haven of buildings. Luckily, most appeared disinterested in the speedy van.

245

Distant shots rang out as they drove further down Hoddle Street. At one point, as Evelyn tried to nudge aside a small Toyota Prius, a faraway noise grumbled across the sky.

"You hear that?" she asked Dylan, sitting in the passenger seat. "What do you think it is?"

He lowered the window. "Not sure. Sounded like an explosion. Maybe a bomb."

"Turn right up here," Julie said as they approached a large intersection. The group had been quiet, taking in the changing scenery as they progressed from tight, inner city housing to the wider spaces on the fringe of the CBD with its tramlines, Victorian-era buildings, and concentration of hospitals. It was a pretty area, nestled with towering oak trees and cheerful green parks amongst the structures. "Victoria Parade. We follow this all the way along to Franklin Street."

The new direction took them up a slight rise where, again, the street had been cleared. As they topped the slope and stared down the hill towards a sea of buildings, crowds of zombies loitered across the roadways and amongst the trees; far more than when they'd entered the fringes of the city. Amongst them sat an Army truck. Several troops stood around firing into the crowd, knocking feeders down with single shots.

They rolled on until a man with a rifle stuck under one arm spotted the van and jogged towards them. He held up his palm and moved around to the window. Evelyn rolled it down, glancing back at the others for support. Gallagher and Greg stood behind her.

"Ma'am, this area is restricted. Where is your intended destination?" The soldier glanced around, keeping track of the zombies. They were everywhere—fighting, eating, and shuffling their way in all directions. One appeared from the overturned carcass of a shiny blue sedan. The soldier turned around and took several steps towards it, then fired his rifle.

Brains and skull splattered the road, and the thing collapsed in a heap.

"Top of Queen Street," Dylan said, leaning over Evelyn.

"I don't think so, sir. We've got breakouts all over the city. You need to stay out of there."

"I have to find my sister."

The soldier adjusted his helmet and scanned the area again. No immediate threat. "I'm sorry to break it to you, but there's not many people left alive."

"I know. But we have to find out."

"If you go in there, we cannot help you."

"We've come through a bit already," Dylan said.

"Nothing like this."

"Admiral James T. Gallagher, Corporal. What's your operational plan?"

The man shook his head. "Limited, sir. We were sent in two days ago to evacuate any survivors. Seven teams of five men assigned to this section of Victoria." He glanced at the truck. "We are the last group still alive."

"What about Command?"

"Overrun. Everybody just kept getting sick. They couldn't stop it. We got deployed then, along with all the others. Most of the reserves are gone. There's just not enough of us. And the government... is no more. At least what we knew it as. I heard from one of the officers that there's a group of ministers stashed away somewhere working on getting this thing fixed." He scoffed. "But I don't believe it. You'd best get out while you can. We're waiting on two men and then we're gone too."

"What about the virus? Any word on its origin?"

"I heard it was a biological terrorist attack that went wrong. Something about the virus mutating and creating the more aggressive infected. If that's true...," A siren sounded. The man looked up sharply. "I have to go." He tapped the side of the camper window and said, "Get outta here while you can."

As the man ran back to the truck, numerous zombies lurched towards him. Without stopping, he shot three through the head and they slumped to the road. He leapt up into the backseat and swung the door shut. The truck rolled forward, squashing a zombie under the front wheel, then circled and took off.

"Go on," Dylan said. "We can't stop now. We're so close." Evelyn looked from one face to the other. Logic told her to circle back, that one person wasn't worth risking the group. She hated the way that sounded, despite the sense. *This is what we do,* she thought. They did crazy stuff that defied the laws of self-preservation. Sometimes they saved lives, other times they were lost. "Please," Dylan said.

Evelyn eased her foot off the brake and onto the accelerator. The van took off, crunching over broken glass and plastic fragments. Zombies stood aside watching. They weren't as aggressive as others, as if distracted; waiting for something. One scratched at the side of the vehicle. She sped up, and it fell away onto the road.

They battled on through the growing horde standing in congregation on every street corner. Following the dip of the road through another set of traffic lights, Julie advised Evelyn to take the next left into Franklin Street. Just out of the bend, the road sloped down again, four lanes wide, separated two and two by parking in the center. Sporadic cars filled the spaces at right angles. High brick buildings sat on either side, leading to a swathe of zombies at the intersection, moving in jagged step between piles of vehicles—cars, trucks, even a bus on its rooftop. Beyond, as the hill gently sloped upwards, the zombies were sparser, having broken away from the main mob. It was difficult, perhaps impossible, to find a path ahead through the chaos.

"I can't drive through that," Evelyn said in a thin voice. "You heard what the Army man said. We shouldn't even be here."

"We have to," Dylan said. "We're so close." He stood and pointed. "I can see the edge of the building."

"Which way do I go?" Evelyn asked. She tried to keep a top on her anger, fueled by fear that he would make her risk it. "Show me a way through that won't get us killed."

"She's right," Gallagher said. "It's too dangerous. There's enough of them to tip this thing over if they get aggressive. I can't see a clear way through."

"You can drop me off then," Dylan said, rifling through a pack filled with pistols and ammunition. "Right here."

Evelyn yanked the handbrake on. "Don't be stupid."

"My sister might still be alive. And from what that Army guy said, there *are* people left in the city. They're hiding out. Surviving."

"That's bloody optimistic, Dylan. The way he sounded, I don't think he thought there were too many people left."

"I don't care. I'm not giving up this close."

"I'll go with you," Greg said.

Dylan looked up at Greg as though considering the offer. "Okay. Thanks." He handed Greg two 9mm pistols and several cartridges.

A zombie crouched on the footpath, gorging on a dead body. Evelyn wanted to tell them that they *were* crazy, that one person wasn't worth it, that they wouldn't survive. Anything to stop them leaving, to stop more of the original group from dying. It would do no good though. Afraid she might doom them, she bit down the portentous words.

"We'll circle back and try to find another way around," Gallagher said. "We'll meet you at the top of Queen Street. Somehow, we'll get there. If you don't find... what you're looking for, wait on the street."

Dylan nodded. "Good luck."

Evelyn couldn't help thinking once again that it would be the last time she saw both men. They stepped out of the camper and Gallagher closed the door. She released the handbrake and stuck the shift into reverse as the boys jogged along the street together.

Gallagher slumped down in the front seat. Evelyn waited for directions. For the first time, she noticed the dark rings beneath his eyes and the red blotches under his nose. *He's getting sicker*, she thought. "Back the way we came," he said.

Evelyn turned the wheel hard to the right and circled.

THIRTY-NINE

CALLAN WOKE to a cloudless sky and the promise of more stifling heat. He knew Melbourne summers were incredibly hot—he'd visited several times during January to watch the Australian Open tennis tournament, burning under the incessant sun on the outer courts following the up and coming players around. Now such heat would bake the corpses, producing worse odors. Initially, the smell had clung to them like a shadow, but they had slowly accepted the suffocating stench.

He walked along the platform where he and Kristy had spoken during the night, checking to make sure the four-wheel drive was still there. Blue trotted after him. Bright morning sunlight forced his hand over his eyes, and he made a mental note to find a pair of sunglasses or he'd finish the day with a splitting headache from squinting into the sun. The street running alongside the railway station was empty. Numerous cars sat parked at the curb, but it might have been an early Sunday morning, people seeking that extra hour or two of sleep. So far, there were no zombies, and although that was a good thing, it worried him. As he reached the end of the platform, a metallic popping noise sounded in the distant sky.

A helicopter. Callan shielded his eyes, feeling a streak of excitement. He wanted to run back and wake the others, but didn't want to miss it. Where was it going? He found it eventually, in the distance, above the shadow of tall buildings poking high into the blue. Maybe it was the military, scouting for survivors.

He woke the others. Kristy looked peaceful, but he knew the news would energize her.

"We have to leave. I saw a helicopter flying over the city."

"Who was it?" Kristy asked, rubbing sleep from her eyes.

"I don't know. It was too far. It's hovering around the CBD."

They packed their gear into the Toyota and reversed along the tracks until they hit the blacktop for the first time in twenty-four hours. Callan was concerned at leaving the railway line. Few zombies had bothered them, and all agreed the tracks were safer than the roads. Bec told of another line that ran all the way into the city. She had lived in Melbourne for several years and used the line regularly.

They took Bell Street running east, an eight-lane road separated by a median strip of grass and trees. It was mostly clear, but Callan took the four-wheel drive at a pace to allow for any surprises, weaving between minor crashes and one giant pile-up that consisted of more than a dozen vehicles. As they came down off a hill, the train tracks glinted in the sunlight, but a train had come off the line and lay on its side, covering most of the level crossing and any access to the tracks.

Callan slowed as they approached the scene, twisting the wheel left and right, passing over broken glass and pieces of the wooden boom gates.

Jacob leaned forward on the seat. "Try down there. That way."

The way Jacob suggested meant going through a garden bed. Callan decided he had no choice. The vehicle jigged and bobbed as he rammed shrubs and plants and bashed across rocks. Finally, they hit the side of the tracks, spewing stones from beneath the spinning wheels, and found the faint dirt pathway through the weeds.

But the pathway ended as land on either side of the track narrowed. Callan was forced to take the four-wheel drive up the rocky bank onto the railway line, where it bumped along as he guided one wheel between the two rails and the other on the outside.

Things were going well until they came to a narrow point in the tracks where the derelict walls of old buildings drew close to them on both sides. Wire fences separated the structures, preventing vehicle access along the edges. It stayed like this for a time, narrowing further, before they saw boulders had been placed across their path ahead. Jacob recounted the issue that had almost cost their lives last time.

"We either move them, or go back," Callan said.

Jacob opened the door. "Let's go. Be quick."

Callan took hold of his rifle and snapped the handle open. "Sit behind the wheel, can you?" Kristy shuffled across the seat. Blue Boy leapt into the front as if to chase Callan, but Kristy wrapped an arm around his neck, holding him back.

The men hurried over the stony fill to the obstacles. Neither man had said it, but rocks on the track meant only one thing—people wanted to stop whoever was traveling on it. This made Callan think that others might have been using the railway line.

He lugged the first boulder off to the side where it rolled into a ditch and stopped. Jacob stood nearby with the rifle in position, scanning their surrounds. Callan bent to pick up the second when the flat crack of a gun echoed between the warehouses. A bullet clanged off metal on the truck. Somebody in the car cried out. Jacob spun, pointing the Remington, searching for the attackers. He fired several shots towards a grey-walled building, and they heard the distant clang of metal striking metal.

"Show yourselves!" Jacob screamed. He walked up and down the line, poised to shoot.

253

Callan waited, then bent for the second boulder, digging his hands underneath the hard rock, lifting with his thigh muscles. He shuffled off the tracks and dropped it over the edge. It rolled into the first with a weighty clunk. He circled back and bent for the final rock, jamming his fingertips into the sharp stones beneath. Another shot broke the silence, striking the Toyota again. Grunting, Callan fumbled the rock towards the outer rail where it clipped the top and rolled off the track. He spun and saw Jacob stagger alongside the vehicle, clutching his right rib cage. Blue barked. Jacob fell to one knee.

"Jacob?" Bec said.

Callan ran to him, boots crunching over the bluestone rocks. Kristy swung the door open and leapt out of the driver's seat, reaching Jacob as he slumped to the ground. The older man writhed, one bloody hand pressed to his ribs. He was taking short breaths through gritted teeth, trying not to cry out. On her knees, Kristy pulled his hand away. "Let me see."

Callan scooped up Jacob's gun and faced the attackers, pumping and firing, searching between the high walls of the buildings for movement. Return gunfire sounded.

He backtracked towards Kristy and yanked the door open. "In the car. Now. Bec, you're driving." He tossed the rifle into the front seat and bent, sliding his hands underneath Jacob's shoulders as he had done with the big rocks. "Grab his feet."

Somehow, they managed to lift him into the back seat, bumping his head on the door. Bullets whizzed and pinged around them. Callan expected at any moment to hear the hiss of a sprung tire. That would finish them. Jacob groaned. Blood smeared his t-shirt. Kristy slid in beside him, holding his head. Callan fired twice then leapt into the passenger seat as more bullets clunked into the chassis, the noise deafening in the small cabin.

"Reverse. Punch it."

Crying, Bec jammed the gearstick into R and floored the accelerator. The force jerked them all forwards as the car sped in reverse, the tires popping and crunching over the rocks. Callan spied a rusty old car behind a pile of garbage. A gun popped up from behind it, barking its tune. It looked like a .22 rifle. If so, Jacob had a chance.

The front window of the four-wheel drive blew out, spraying Callan and Bec with glass shrapnel. She screamed but somehow held onto the wheel, maintaining her backward course until Callan noticed a thin gap between the warehouses and called for her to stop. He slammed the gearstick into drive for her, and she hit the pedal without a word. They took off, leaving the tracks and jiving their way across a gap of dusty earth filled with more rusty machinery. They hit the street with a crunch, distant gunfire chasing them, Bec swerving to avoid the carcass of a steel trailer.

It appeared their attackers weren't done yet. A retro brown Ford sedan grumbled out from beneath a roller doorway in a nearby factory, tires chirping and blowing smoke. It straightened up, its big engine thundering, and narrowed the gap with a roar like a dinosaur.

Bec glanced up in the mirror. "They're catching us."

"No," Callan said. "Stay focused on the road and just drive." He unclipped his seatbelt, a red flag rising in his mind, and leaned out the window. He dropped two rounds into the Remington and tipped further through the opening, gathering his focus as he took aim. The wind blew into his eyes and the vehicle jumped all over the place. He fired, chewing a hole in the top left section of the hood just below the driver. The hillbilly screamed something at him and pulled closer. Callan pumped once and pulled the trigger again, striking the windshield. Glass exploded. The sedan cut right and came to a stop with a screech of tires, smoke floating from the back wheels.

Callan dropped back into the seat. "They've stopped. Keep going. Turn right here."

Jacob's eyes were slits, his breathing sharp, the pain written across his face in weary creases. Kristy kneeled over him, applying pressure to the upper right quadrant of his ribcage with a piece of fabric she had torn from the blouse under her Kevlar.

"How bad is it?" Callan asked.

"I don't know. I need to know if it came out the other side—" She cut herself off there and glanced at Callan. He suspected she was going to say if the bullet was stuck inside, he was in deep shit.

Bec had steered them back onto a course parallel with the railway line, but they were now on the opposite side from which they had originally come. Callan thought that was lucky—the roadway and train tracks were filling with zombies, and the carnage on the road would have prevented their progress. Still, they had their share of busted up vehicles. Bec sped along—almost too fast for Callan's liking—sitting forward in the seat to ensure her full weight reached the pedals of the big vehicle. She lacked the finesse of Kristy, jerking on the wheel to go left or right, braking hard and accelerating unevenly. It was like being on the Mad Mouse ride at a carnival.

She'd taken them up onto the curb to get around a three-way smash hogging the roadway when the engine began to falter.

Oh, fuck, Callan thought, glancing towards the fuel gauge. He recalled telling Kristy that they needed fuel, but when had that been, yesterday?

The engine gasped and spluttered. Bec read the instrument panel. "Oh shit. We're out of fuel."

FORTY

THE MEN PASSED by the apartment building several times throughout the day, via car and on foot, but they never stopped again until almost three-thirty. Lauren had expected it since they had started checking surrounding buildings in the morning. She had drawn the curtains closed for most of the day.

She tried to keep busy, cleaning out rubbish that Todd and Lenny had left behind, going through the baby's clothes again, tossing stuff he'd already outgrown. They moved garbage to the apartment two doors down. They had several fans running off the generator to keep the air circulating—it wasn't the usual air-conditioning, but it beat the suffocating heat in the other apartment.

It was a poor life, if this was to be it, Lauren thought. For the remaining people—Steve and his wife, and the others, there was nothing to do but sit and rest and talk and wait. For what, she didn't know. Help to come? Lauren doubted it would ever happen. It had been almost a month since the outbreak and weeks since the last television broadcast. Where was the government? She held no hope for their fortunes to improve anytime soon.

Changing Harvey, she had spent time alone letting him clasp her pinkie finger. He had a strong grip for a baby. She had nothing to compare against really, but it made her feel better. She wondered what would become of him. Would they survive in the long term, the world returning to the way it had been, or would he grow up in a place where lasting another day was an achievement? The thought of her son not making adulthood upset her. Lauren resolved to fight harder to ensure it happened.

Excitement rippled through them at the sound of a helicopter earlier. Steve considered going out into the street to flag it down. Alexander wanted to climb to the rooftop. Lauren argued that they would never notice either of them no matter where they stood, and that if it was the Army or the police, they should sit tight until help arrived. On a clock radio in the bedroom, Steve tried to locate a transmission, but all he found was static.

And then the men returned. Some argued they should flee—Steve and his wife and the others. Lauren told them she wasn't going anywhere, but they were welcome to leave if they wanted.

The group assembled on the grassy roundabout at the intersection of Queen and Franklin Streets. Lauren leaned against the window, Steve on the other side, peering out through a gap at the edge of the curtains. A stocky man with a shaved head stood in the center, talking to the group with exaggerated hand signals. He kept pointing to the building, and, occasionally, the other men would look in their direction.

A deep terror crept over Lauren. She somehow knew the men were going to come to her building and search the apartments. It was the only residence in the area, snuggled amongst a bevy of offices and showrooms. The men had wandered up and down the street for most of the day, removing doors and cutting quiet holes in the windows of most stores.

"They're systematically checking each building," Steve said, after staring out the window for fifteen minutes.

Then they broke up. At first, Lauren thought they were going the other way—one of the men started north, but he was only retrieving something that had fallen in the grass. Three headed down Queen Street, while the other three walked towards the front of her building on the corner. They disappeared from sight.

"What do you think? Will they try to get in here?"

Steve furrowed his brow in thought. "Yeah. Probably." He peered back out the window, but the men had disappeared. "Is the view better from any of the other apartments?"

Lauren hurried away. "Come with me," she said to Alexander. He followed, and they squeezed out the door and entered the adjoining apartment. The men still weren't visible from their window, so they tried the following two residences, both without luck. "They'll have to break down the door downstairs," Lauren said, almost as an afterthought. "I locked it. If they bust it down though, the zombies will eventually find their way in, too."

She didn't think zombies would matter if the men found them. From what Alexander had described, they were ruthless and immoral. They were after him, mostly, and he was with them now. Did that put her and the others at risk? Harvey? A chill crept up her neck.

Where were the men? Had they entered the building yet? They needed to know; needed to get closer. Alexander reluctantly accepted her proposition to investigate.

Rather than returning to her apartment, they continued on towards the lift foyer, listening for loud noises from below. Alexander opened the stairwell door and let Lauren in first. She slipped in and closed it softly after he passed. They crept down the stairs, checking as far below as their line of sight would allow.

Alexander thought he heard something on level two. Lauren stood by the door listening, but the stairwell, and the levels below, remained silent. They pushed on, cautious, alert, poised to flee if they detected any sign of danger. The cautious voice in Lauren's head told her to return to the apartment, but she had to know if the men had entered the building. Otherwise, it would be a game of waiting. Hopefully they would reach the entrance and find the door locked, her concern unfounded.

Level one was silent. They climbed down the last flight of stairs in slow motion, as though with each step they expected to see the men approaching. Lauren's heart raced, not dissimilar to entering the shop the previous night. She caught sight of Alexander and didn't feel as inadequate, knowing he wasn't comfortable either. She realized they had no weapons—it had been an impromptu decision to investigate—not that weapons would help against men wielding machine guns, but if a zombie attacked, a knife would be useful.

Lauren reached the ground floor first, tuning her ears to the rush of wind and echoes in the concrete hallways. She heard a far off noise, but couldn't place it. As they rounded the stairs and walked on towards the foyer, a spear of terror struck her; the door had been smashed in. The glass panel lay shattered over the floor.

Alexander's expression was stiff with fear. She had faced a number of zombies trying to break the door, but the double-glazing had always held. The men had succeeded though. They might be anywhere now. Returning to the apartment would be risky. Suddenly Lauren felt a deep compulsion to hold her son, as though she wouldn't get the chance to do it again. *Don't think like that.*

"Any ideas?" she whispered.

"I was hoping you had one."

They had to climb. But once she and Alexander were in the stairwell, there was no real way out. She spied a fire extinguisher hanging off the wall. It wasn't the best weapon, but in a tight spot, it might help. Lauren tried to lift it from its place, but a thick cable secured it.

"What's the point of having it stuck to the wall like that if there's an emergency?"

"I think that's an aftermarket alteration," Alexander said. "I know one or two that have been stolen from apartment blocks like this." He scanned the foyer and hurried to the broken planes of glass on the floor. "This must be one of those older windows that don't shatter." He picked up a length about ten inches as though it were a snake and might bite him.

Using the sharp edge, he sawed at the cord and it began to tear, but the glass was difficult to handle. He applied more force, working it at different angles, until the cord gave way. The extinguisher fell and, as he reached out to grab it, the glass sliced his hand. He gave a sharp intake of breath.

"Did it cut you?" Kristy asked, juggling the equipment.

Alexander held his wrist. Dark blood splashed onto the concrete floor from a deep cut on the lower part of his index finger, above the webbing of the thumb. "Damn it."

"We need to wrap it."

"Tear a piece off my shirt," Alexander said. Lauren lowered the extinguisher and detached a jagged strip of black fabric from his Will. I. Am. t-shirt. She wrapped the length around his hand, covering the bloody gash.

"Keep the pressure on it until we get back to the apartment." His face was pale. "You good?"

"I'm not a fan of blood."

"Keep it tight. It will help stop the bleeding. I know that much from my first aid training. We'll be back soon." He nodded. She noticed the gold band on his wedding ring finger. "Were you married?"

He snatched his hand back. "It's nothing."

Lauren considered pursuing it, but he moved away and made his desire to end the conversation obvious. She lifted the fire equipment and led the way back up the stairs, hurrying past the platforms of each level in anticipation of meeting the men as they changed floors. As they approached level eight, Lauren thought about the open doorway in the foyer, and realized it was only a matter of time before zombies found the place, too.

FORTY-ONE

DYLAN AND Greg ran along the pavement in lengthy strides, pressing themselves against overturned cars, hiding behind open doors, anticipating the quickest and safest pathway through the mess. There was plenty of it with which to contend—zombies attacking each other, moving in random patterns, feeding, and dying for the second time. They were lucky most of the feeders were distracted with enough food to keep them occupied.

The first zombie came at them like a shaggy dog; a longhaired male that might once have been a rock musician, bumbling over the rubble. Greg squared the pistol and shot a neat hole through the front of its head. He didn't stop. Dylan watched him as he jogged on, gun ready, marvelling at how much the man had changed. His twisted ankle had completely healed, along with the ax wound on his shin and the subsequent infection. Greg had lost weight though. His face had thinned; the plumpness around his cheeks and neck had disappeared, their low calorie—sometimes no calorie—diet filching away excess fat. Dylan hadn't observed his own face for some time, but suspected a similar change had overcome him, too. Except for Greg, the rest of them had all been somewhat lean from the camping trip, but the current circumstances had exacerbated it.

They were still far away from their destination, a block and a half by Dylan's count. If they made it, he would find out if Lauren were dead, absent, or alive. They moved like men who had lived hard—fighting, spinning away from groping hands, dropping to one knee on the concrete curb, surprising their enemies with quick shots. Despite their lack of food, they were fast bundles of energy, motivated by life and death. Even the heat was secondary, and Dylan didn't even notice the sweat until it dripped into his eye. Blockades and barriers, rubble and rocks became their friends. They shot quick, dropped the empty magazines with lightning speed, and re-loaded sometimes with seconds remaining. They drew attention, but not enough to overwhelm. Elsewhere, shots cracked through the city, and another helicopter flew low across the sky, hidden by tall buildings. At one stage, they were back-to-back, firing with rapidity as bodies collapsed onto each other. The memory of Greg wanting him dead had faded into the back of Dylan's mind.

With the building in clear view and only a handful of derelict cars and straggling feeders in their way, Dylan thought they might actually make it. He took the lead and leapt a pile of rubbish spread over the pavement. Ahead on their left was an alleyway, and from it, Dylan saw a feeder emerge. He knew instantly it was a three. Its muscles bunched with each step, no jerky movements, dark eyes perusing the street. It halted when it saw them, and before either man could react, it sprang at them.

Dylan swung the gun around, firing in line with where it had been. Shots cracked. Its erratic movement caused him to miss, as though it knew where he was going to aim. He went again, and this time the bullet struck the top of its shoulder, spraying blood in a burst. It didn't stop the thing though. Greg fired twice, striking the zombie in the head. It hit an invisible wall and slumped forward onto its face, the echo of the shots rolling across the sky.

Dylan blew out air. "Close. I don't like those fuckers."

"Me neither."

They hurried along the footpath close to buildings Dylan remembered from his one and only visit to the place—a backpackers lodge, a taxation office, and the convenience store beneath the apartment block. He stopped outside and peered in, wondering whether Lauren had seconded items from the store for her survival. The front windows were broken in, and the remaining products had been strewn across the floor, mixed in with shelving and point of sale displays. Across the street sat the decayed remains of what was once the Queen Victoria market, where traders would come several times a week to sell meat, produce, and anything else of value.

At the entrance to the apartment building, Dylan skidded to a halt. The glass door had been smashed in, leaving shards all over the floor. They stood outside, peering into the shadows as Dylan reloaded.

The building was split between two law firms on the lower level and residential apartments on all those above. Just inside the entrance, a staircase led to the offices on the first floor, and a hallway to a foyer for the elevators to the residential apartments.

Before Dylan had chosen, though, the shadows further back moved, and from them a raggedy mess of feeders appeared, eager for their blood.

FORTY-TWO

THE TOYOTA four-wheel drive rolled on after the engine had given out. Callan summarized the situation from the passenger seat. Small Victorian-era houses sat nestled on their left all the way down the street. Ahead, a small intersection beckoned and beyond that, through the trees, there might have been a church, or an old bluestone building. A crowd of zombies milled around outside the structure, as if waiting for something. They were crossing the tracks too, drawn by the noise of the vehicle.

Momentum pushed them up a gentle slope towards the traffic lights. *Think.* If they could get over the rise, they might reach the intersection and have a shot at making the building.

"Grab what you can," Callan said, reloading the Remington. He stuffed two handfuls of shells into his pockets. "Stay with me, Blue." Kristy kept the compress against Jacob's ribs, and Bec still had both hands locked around the wheel, steering to avoid rubble.

They just made it over the peak, threatening to stop before the vehicle gathered speed on the downhill, passing through the intersection under Bec's guidance. The bluestone structure *was* a church, tall and solid, and Callan thought nothing would breach those walls. The roadway rose again and the four–wheel drive used the last of its motion, drawing to a stop.

Feeders attacked in a swarm, thumping on the windows and clawing at the door handles. Bec screamed. Blue Boy barked, fangs bared.

"Leave me if you have to," Jacob managed from the backseat.

267

"Shut the fuck up," Callan said. Fear energized him. He wanted to be out amongst them, cutting them down for his friends that had passed. "I need you both to carry him inside."

"What if nobody's there?" Kristy asked.

"Forget that," Callan snapped. "Just put the bags on your shoulders and carry him, okay?" Kristy nodded. "Don't stop. Just go for it."

There must have been twenty outside. He considered what would happen if the church was empty. He wished he had a way to call forward, ask them to open the doors. A thought struck him and he pressed the horn for several seconds, repeating twice more, hoping to alert potential occupants.

Jacob moaned. Bec wiped at her eyes. "Can you save him?"

"I can't say yet." Kristy lifted the padding. It was soaked in blood. "Once I clean the wound I'll know more."

"Let's do this," Callan said. He couldn't even get the door open. A large naked male had his hairy belly pressed against the door. Callan lay back across the passenger seat and got his legs behind it. The man went flying backwards and landed on the roadway.

Callan slipped out and fired into the mix of clumsy bodies. A knotty-haired woman lost half her head. He scampered around the other side, throwing elbows and jabbing the gun into their faces, allowing Kristy and Bec to get Jacob out. The zombies fell over, groping for his limbs. A wall greeted him at the trunk. He tried the poking trick again and one of the feeders grabbed hold of the gun. He stopped and yanked on it, but a firm grip resisted. Another—he couldn't tell if they were male or female—fell against him, fumbling for his arms. Blue darted at them, snapping his jaws at their legs, distracting them. Callan reluctantly released the gun and pushed the skinny feeder away. Beyond the growing wall of feeders, he heard one of the girls scream.

Gunshots boomed. Two zombies fell and he saw Kristy and Bec break free, carrying Jacob up the slope towards the church. Callan swivelled, perplexed, searching for the shooter. Another feeder clutched at him. Where was his gun? Callan threw the attacker away and swung a fist, connecting with gooey flesh. The thing went down, replaced by another. He spied the gun lying on the grass and reached for it, feeling the metal in his grip, bringing it around and blowing the face off a nameless man.

The others were halfway to the church. Blue ran after them, fighting off feeders with snapping and snarling. They seemed wary of him, diverting their course in an attempt to reach the others. Callan chased, shrugging off fans as they groped for his autograph in blood. With ten feet of spare space, he fumbled more rounds into the Remington. On the left, the two men holding rifles took aim and fired. Callan heard the thump of his pursuers falling behind him. He raised a hand and waved at them, having no idea who they were, only that they had probably saved their lives.

He reached the girls and Jacob. Blue scurried in and out of their legs. More zombies approached from either side. Callan ran in front and shot the first one in the neck and the second through the ear, sending a jet of blood and brain onto the grass. They had a clear path to the church now, and standing in the entrance holding the wooden doorway open was a man, waving them on and calling for them to hurry.

Callan ushered the others ahead and the man stepped back, allowing them through. Another gunshot cracked. Behind him, an imminent feeder fell dead. As he reached the doorway, he saw the two men. They had risen, completing their task to help. Callan waved them inside, but the lead man raised a hand and declined. They disappeared along the street.

He didn't know who they were, but he was grateful for their help and wished he could tell them so.

The girls carried Jacob through the hallway and laid him down at the base of the chancel. Blue hunkered on the wooden floor, panting, tongue rolling from his mouth. Callan scratched him on the head. Once again, the dog had proved his value, diverting attention where required.

Jacob was conscious, but the pain showed in the grimace on his face. Bec sat nearby in silence, watching with a concerned expression. Kristy had taken several candles from around the room and was hunched over Jacob, trying to examine the wound. She had performed a suture on Greg when he cut himself on the ax, but this was a gunshot wound, *and* her medical bag was still in the campervan.

"We have a gentleman who's been bitten by one of them," the man who waved them inside said. "Can you help him?"

"I'll go," Callan said. "Where is he?"

The man, whose name was Robert, led Callan back the way they had come through the narrow, twisting passageway. They branched off into a small room with a bed, on which the man lay. A woman, named Maria, and a little girl, Isabelle, sat beside him. There had been more of them, they said, but only the old minister had returned from their foray to get supplies.

What the hell was the old man doing out, Callan wondered. He appeared perky though, bright-eyed, his face full of color. The gash on his upper thigh told another story. They exchanged pleasantries—his name was Harlan, and he'd been minister at the church for twenty-seven years.

"I'm not leaving," he said. "Not dying yet, either." Callan immediately liked him.

"My sister is a doctor. She's treating another man for a gunshot wound. When she's done, she'll dress this as best she can with what we have." Callan studied the wound. "It's fresh. How long?"

"An hour or so." He glanced at the others and smiled. "Give us a moment, will you?" They left the room. He sat up with effort. "You've seen these bites before, haven't you?" Callan nodded. "How long have I got?"

In the soft candlelight, Callan bent to inspect the wound. It was of similar size to Johnny's. He thought about tempering the truth. What was the point? "Twenty-four, maybe forty-eight hours at best."

"Guess I'll get to meet the Lord a bit sooner than I would have hoped."

"Maybe not," Callan said. "We have medicine that can help. It's not a cure, but it can prevent the virus getting any worse."

"You have this with you?"

"Not with us. But another group we are traveling with does. If we can meet up with them again, we can treat you, too."

"I'd have to leave the church?" Callan nodded. Harlan considered this, and for a long moment, Callan thought he was going to tell him not to bother. Finally, he said, "Thank you."

"Do you have a first aid kit?"

"Yes, in the supplies room. Maria will show you where it is."

Callan returned to the nave with the kit. Kristy was still treating the wound. A bottle of alcohol stood on the floor beside him. "How goes it?"

Jacob stifled a cry. "Very lucky," Kristy said. "There's an exit wound. No bullet. Not too messed up inside. I need to close both wounds though."

"How you gonna do that?"

"I don't know yet." She sat up and cracked open the first aid kit, rifling through the contents. She selected several items and placed them on the floor beside Jacob. "No thread or needle. Can't stitch him up. And he'll need antibiotics if he makes it through." Callan wanted to ask what *if* meant, but let it drift.

Robert reappeared and Callan went to him. They had been there for almost five days, having abandoned their car after running out of fuel down the road. Harlan had found them out on one of his forays. They were reluctant to leave while there was still food. Others had come and gone—Harlan welcomed anybody who needed it—but it meant the supplies dwindled faster. People made contributions, but it never covered the losses. Harlan and two other men had been out scrounging for supplies in nearby houses when he was bitten. Robert asked how long before the government would be operational again. Callan didn't have the heart to tell him what he thought: that there would be no government for a very long time, if ever. They were on their own, but Robert appeared optimistic, and the world needed more of that.

Callan sat in the pews with Bec while Kristy patched Jacob up. Callan and Bec spoke about Campbelltown and their trek down. When Kristy was finally done, she joined them, removing her bloody, disposable gloves. She looked tired; dark shadows had formed around both eyes. Callan worried about her. She had toughened up beyond measure, but everyone had a limit.

"How is he?" Bec asked.

"I've cleaned both wounds and patched them up. It was a small calibre bullet, so the damage isn't too bad. He'll need to be stitched, but I don't have any thread or needles. If we can get back to the camper, it's all there."

"Thank you."

"He's not out of the woods yet. And I'm not sure we can move him today."

Callan said, "What?"

"He's been shot, Cal. Clean wound, but he's been messed up inside." She waved her hands around. "We're safe here. He's not moving. We go out there and come under any sort of attack and it might lead to more bleeding. It's too risky." Callan pressed his lips together. "I want to get back to the others more than anyone, but if we do that, we can't bring Jacob with us."

It was a good old catch twenty-two. He desperately wanted to get to Greg, Dylan, Evelyn and the others, but Jacob had been solid, and Callan wasn't about to start leaving injured people behind now.

Callan put a hand on Kristy's shoulder. "Okay then. How long before we can move?"

"I'll have to reassess every few hours. I wouldn't like to do anything before the morning."

"The old guy in there is bitten. Wound needs cleaning. I'll try and rustle up something to eat."

Hunger stirred. When was the last time he'd eaten a decent meal? Uncooked noodles, tinned pasta, crackers. It had all become their staple diet. He hoped Harlan had some decent food. In hindsight, his departure from the others had been thoughtless. Still, he had found Blue and Kristy and he would do the same thing again.

With Robert's guidance, Callan found cold pancakes and leftover bread in the kitchen. They ate quickly, savoring the taste, and afterwards there were two apples each from a tree on the property next door. Callan expressed their gratitude several times.

Kristy returned after evaluating Harlan. Her hopes were thin. He looked washed out, she said, the inflammation already working its way into his eyes and nasal passages.

Kristy suggested that condition—the age, physical size, fitness, and general health of a bitten subject—determined how quickly the virus moved through their system. Harlan scored poorly on all fronts. She estimated he had a day to get some serum before his deterioration escalated. That posed another problem. Did they risk taking him with them to find the others, or leave him behind?

They sat in the pews and tried to rest. Callan struggled with the nothingness of it all. He understood staying, but he kept thinking of the others and what they were doing. Were they all still alive? He was used to moving now, pushing on despite obstacles, towards their next destination. He wished they were back in the van. He missed the sound of the kids chatting, even the shouting and playing, which sometimes got on his nerves. He thought of Evelyn's smile, and the way she often looked at him. He felt odd thinking of such a thing. Sherry's death was still fresh, but the circumstances—the treachery and lies—had dampened his feelings for her. He couldn't just switch them off though. Still, there was something about Evelyn that appealed to him beyond the attraction. Her personality. She was kind and considerate in a way Sherry could never have been, and she had spirit too, although it wasn't misguided, like Sherry's. And there was Jake. He liked the kid, and he was pretty sure the kid liked him.

Still, he had no idea where that left him. Life was too crazy for a relationship now, and he wasn't emotionally ready to share intimacy with anyone. He would leave it to the Gods to decide how it played out.

FORTY-THREE

ALEXANDER REACHED the apartment first, fumbling at the handle with his good hand. He managed to open the door and, as Lauren followed him in, she glanced back along the hallway, expecting to find the men imminent. It was empty and silent, but what she discovered was almost as bad; intermittent drops of bright blood stretched along the corridor. *No.* How far back had that happened?

Claire took the door and held it open. "Where the fuck have you two been?" Lauren paused. "Hurry up. Get inside."

"Wait," Lauren said. "I have to check something."

Despite Claire's vocal protest, Lauren jogged back along the hallway, following the trail of blood. She rounded the corner and eventually reached the foyer outside the elevators. The marks continued all the way to the stairway door.

Lauren opened the door and located the first splatter of blood. It kept going down the stairs until it disappeared from sight. *Damn it.* How could she have been so careless? The cut was worse than she'd thought. It would need urgent medical attention. She listened for signs of the men, but the stairwell was silent.

She let the door close softly and hurried back to the apartment. The first aid kit was open on the table. Alexander was at the sink washing the blood from his hand. Lauren debated not telling them what she had found, but Alexander knew already.

"It dripped all the way here, didn't it?" She nodded. Steve cursed. "I'm sorry. I didn't put enough pressure on it. To be honest, I thought I was going to pass out a few times."

"It's okay," Lauren said. The group had all assembled in the living room. "We might have bigger problems. The men we saw on the street have broken down the door. One assumes they're searching the building. Alexander thinks they might be looking for him, although they might just be checking for supplies."

"Still, they don't know we're up here," Lorraine said.

"They might," Lauren said. "Alexander cut his hand on some glass and the blood has dripped all the way from the ground level."

"Can't we clean it up?" Steve asked. "At least the stuff near the door."

"Good idea."

Using a cloth and cleaning liquid from underneath the sink, Lauren started on the blood spots closest to the door, and worked her way along the passage until she reached the fourth apartment. Some disappeared easily; others required more intense scrubbing. Despite putting holes in one section of the cloth, she was unable to remove all traces though. It would come down to luck. If—

The crash of a door hitting the wall sounded from around the corner. Voices. Shouting. The men had reached their level. Lauren sprinted for her apartment, shaking cleaning liquid from the bottle as she ran. She slipped as she grabbed for the handle, but caught her footing and swung the door open. "They're coming," she said between gritted teeth. Alexander stood by the bench with Claire as she wrapped his hand in a swathe of bandage. "Hide in the bedroom cupboard," Lauren said to him.

Had she removed all traces of the blood? What if she'd left wet marks from the cloth? Her hands trembled and her throat was dry. Zombies were predictable, ruthless; dangerous men were not. She put a finger over her lips for silence and stood behind the bench. Lorraine sat on the couch. Steve stood near the table. "Stay with the baby, will you?" she asked Claire. Her friend disappeared into the bedroom. Lauren would not let anyone else face these men. She held onto the thin hope that she could talk them out of doing any harm.

They stood waiting. Further down the hallway, doors slammed open and gunfire chewed holes in plaster walls. Lauren jumped at this. Her heart beat faster. It was only a matter of time before they stormed her apartment. What could they do? Hide? Not all of them. She spotted the long-bladed knife she had taken down to the shop and swiped it from the sink. It wouldn't do much against guns, but provided some comfort. Still, she didn't want to force a confrontation. She would only use it if there were no other choice. The roof vibrated as they reached the neighboring apartment. No gunfire though. Silence followed. They waited, watching the door. Time drew out. Maybe they had—

The door shook as something on the outside stuck it. Lorraine screamed. Bullets chewed through the wood around the lock. The door swung open and crashed against the wall. Standing in the doorway was a man dressed in blue jeans and a singlet top, holding a machine gun. A second guerrilla stood behind him.

"Aha!" the first man said. He stepped through in heavy black boots. "Bingo."

"Please," Steve said, holding both palms up. "We're just—"

The gunman unleashed a spray of rapid fire. Steve danced backwards, holes opening in his chest. The noise stopped, and he fell onto the floor with a loud thump. Lorraine screeched, wailing as she ran to her husband's body and dived onto him, shrieking.

"Nobody says a fucking word," the man croaked, circling the tip of the machine gun. He had dark little eyes made of flint and the calloused skin from too much sun, or grog, or both. He reminded Lauren of a failed musician from a hard drinking '60s rock band. She couldn't breathe. She tried to conceal the knife behind her leg, certain that if he saw it, she'd wear a gutful of lead.

The first man honed in on Lauren as the other militia searched the apartment. "You got a kid with you? About seventeen, or eighteen. Wears a hoodie."

Lauren didn't take her eyes off the man. She tried to keep a poker face, fearful that even licking her lips would give the knowledge away. She didn't know whether she was allowed to talk or not. What if she responded and he shot her? So be it, she thought, standing straight. "No. This is all of us."

"Sure about that?" He peered at the other faces. Lorraine was inconsolable. Lauren prayed for Claire to keep the baby quiet, and that Alexander wouldn't get brave and surrender. Lauren had no doubt they would kill him.

The thump and crash of doors and cupboards sounded from another room. Harvey cried out. Lauren's chest tightened. The corner of the man's mouth curled up. His voice was rough and strident. "You've got five seconds to come out with that baby, or I shoot the brunette woman out here."

Lauren stopped breathing. Her logic went to jelly. She had to fight down a scream, to plead with the man not to hurt her son. She knew by his actions that he placed no value on life. Part of her wanted Claire to stay put.

Her friend appeared from the doorway holding Harvey. He looked happy. Tears. She closed her eyes as they spilled onto her cheeks.

"Oh, don't cry, princess."

The other man reappeared. Lauren let out silent thanks that he hadn't found Alexander. She hoped the kid was smart enough not to surrender.

"Nothing?" The second man shook his head. "Okay," he nodded. "We'll take you then." He reached out and grabbed Lauren by the back of the head. "Might have ourselves a fifteen-minute break in one of the other apartments."

The knife. As the man pulled her forward, Lauren's hand swung out from behind her right leg. She could stab him in the stomach. Jab the blade out and fill his guts. Part of her mind told her to do it. The other part told her not to be stupid, that even if she killed him, the other one would cut her throat after raping her. She fell to her knees and feigned struggle, allowing her to slide the knife under the bench with stealth. The man dragged Lauren to her feet by her hair, sending bolts of pain through her head, but she bit down a cry and stumbled after him out the door.

FORTY-FOUR

GREG WENT in first, but only because he had longer legs, Dylan thought. He beat Dylan through the doorway of the building with his 9mm pistol roaring its killing tune. Dylan snuck in behind him and they shot one, two, three; taking chunks out of their heads and necks until they had all crumpled on the floor. There were six in all, and it didn't take much longer than that to finish them off.

They stood in the aftermath of their handiwork amongst gun smoke and silence. It was momentary though. From somewhere higher up in the building the moans and cries of the infected floated to them. They passed an icy glance and checked their ammunition.

A little further and they discovered the trail of blood spots. They followed it to the elevator foyer and right up to the door of the fire escape stairs. Greg led them through, slow and steady, scoping out the ascent well in advance.

"What floor is she on?"

"I'm pretty sure it's eight. I hope this blood doesn't lead there."

On the second floor landing, they found a feeder face deep in a fleshy pile. Dylan couldn't tell if the body was human or one of its own. The zombie appeared to be male, with bulky shoulders and cropped hair, but it didn't even look up, as though the meal meant more to it than its life. Greg shot it through the top of the head.

The upper levels were stifling, and the stench grew worse. Their exposure had conditioned them, but it was almost intolerable. The screams and moans of the dead and dying drifted to them, and despite having heard it all before, goose pimples covered Dylan's arms. They had both killed hordes of feeders, but the prospect of facing more was always frightening and Greg's frown reflected the same. Blood on the floor meant someone had been alive. What if there were others—people they could save? *Lauren.* He still held faint hope of her survival. If she had holed up here for the last two weeks and been smart enough not to leave, maybe she had a chance.

The door on the fifth level slammed open, knocking Dylan backwards. A beefy zombie burst through, growling like a rabid mutt. Dylan lost balance and stumbled, falling to one knee as it came for him. Momentarily, he thought he might be in trouble, but the zombie went sprawling backwards under Greg's boot, hit the wall, and fell to the concrete. The big man raised his gun and shot the thing between its dead, soulless eyes.

Dylan lay there for a moment, thinking about what might have been. Why had he thought Greg wanted him dead? How many times would it take for Greg to save him before he abandoned the absurd notion? He stood, nodding his thanks, and stumbled, grabbing for the wall.

"You alright?" He took a deep breath. *No, I don't think I am.* He had pressed on and on amongst death and loss, thinking that if he kept moving, it would be all right. It had worked so far, but now he began to doubt. "You need to take a minute?" Greg asked.

Lauren. Finding her would keep him going. He imagined her in the building, needing their help. *Focus.* He pushed the thought of Kristy away, as he had done with his mother and father. "Nah. I'm good. Let's keep going." Greg watched him before moving on.

The trail of blood ended at the entrance to level eight. They stood there watching the splash on the concrete six inches from the bottom of the door, listening for sounds.

There was only silence. Maybe too silent, Dylan thought. There should have been zombies fighting and killing each other.

"You know the number?"

"815. But I've got a bad feeling the blood is going to end there."

Greg wrapped his fingers around the handle and pulled the door open. The smell was like a wave of sickness. They both screwed up their faces and entered, looking each way along the empty corridor. The blood spots continued on around the corner. Dylan read the room number signage and headed in that direction.

The rest of the hallway was clear. Dylan crouched and examined the floor. The blood stopped halfway along. He counted the doors and estimated Lauren's apartment number was beyond that. He stood and jogged towards it. As he passed another door, he thought he heard a noise from inside. He stopped, listened, and stared at the paint-flecked number hanging from the center. "You hear that?"

Greg joined him. "No. What was—"

A door opened down the hallway from the direction they had come. A tall man with a thick torso, ragged hair, and a long beard stepped out wielding a machine gun. His face transformed into a mask of rage; his teeth bared, eyes blazing. He twisted around, firing before he had lined up either man. Bullets punctured the wall, chewing plaster in thick chunks.

Time froze for Dylan. They'd come so far, fought their way here to find out whether his sister had survived, only to face a final, seemingly insurmountable hurdle. In that moment, Dylan understood one thing with greater clarity than all others: speed. He snatched the pistol up, firing in his mind's eye before it had happened, imagining the bullet striking the man in the forehead. His accuracy was instinct now—he'd shot endless rounds over the last few weeks, strengthening his self–belief with every hit. And much like Callan now, he rarely missed. The man's head rocked back and a neat red hole opened in the spot Dylan had imagined. The attacker fell, the gun hitting the carpet with a thud ahead of his burly body.

A second man of similar appearance stepped out of the doorway, firing in comparable random patterns. Both Dylan and Greg dropped, shooting simultaneously. Greg got the accurate shot this time, hitting the man in the shoulder first, and then the neck. He spun, circling bullets up the plaster, blood spurting from the neck in a mini-fountain. He fell back and crunched into the wall, still holding the gun as it fired its last round.

Silence. Dylan and Greg stayed low, waiting for more intruders. He didn't know if he had any rounds left. "You empty?"

"No. You?"

"Not sure. You got it covered while I check?"

"Yeah."

He made the change, dropping the magazine, which was empty, and slotting the last from his pocket into the pistol with the palm of his hand. Then he stood, gun aimed towards the dead men. Greg did the same. They looked at each other, as if unable to believe they were both still there.

"Shit man, you're bleeding," Greg said, reaching out for Dylan's right ear.

He twisted away. "Don't touch, mate. What if you get it?"

"Yeah. Right." Greg looked apologetic and timid.

Dylan touched fingers to the spot. They came away bloody. "Have I still got my ear?"

"Most of it." Greg smiled. Dylan did too.

He stood outside the door he thought was Lauren's apartment. Part of him didn't want to go inside, scared of what he might find. He didn't know how he would deal with it if Lauren were dead, or worse.

"Come on," Greg said, reaching out for the handle. "Waiting here isn't going to change anything."

He twisted the handle and the door swung open. Both men lifted their pistols, poised to shoot, and entered the apartment.

FORTY-FIVE

LAUREN COULDN'T breathe. The man had grabbed a fistful of dark hair and shoved her out the apartment door before she could think, before she could devise some way of remaining. It happened so fast, with so much force, and she was certain that if she tried anything, he would shoot her, the way he had gunned down Steve in cold blood.

Harvey. She would never see her darling baby again. Soon, both his parents would be dead. She hoped Claire would care for him. Claire loved her, and Harvey. It was all up to Claire now, her friend of three years, who had made a promise. That gave her some comfort.

The man pushed her down the hallway. She stumbled, thought she was going to fall on her face, but caught her balance at the last moment, twisting her ankle. *Kill me,* she thought. *Don't rape me. He's going to rape you. Him and the other man.* Lauren felt sick, not only for the potential violation, but because she had only given birth to Harvey six weeks ago. She hadn't even resumed sex with Todd. It was too soon; too much had gone on down there for her to get her head around it. The idea of *that* taking place filled her with a dread beyond comprehension. She would die before letting it happen.

At the third apartment, the man prodded her left, through the open doorway. He said something to the second man, and she heard the door close. Lauren spun, facing her attackers. Their grins pushed her panic to a new level. It was clear they were going to have some fun, as she had suspected. She had to fight back, even if they killed her. She searched the room for something to use. It was a chaotic mess. Furniture had been flipped and items were strewn across the floor; a lamp, broken plates, pots and pans, even the microwave had been tipped over. A knife.

"Get your kit off," the first man said. He motioned with the tip of his machine gun. "Take it off her, Goeby." The second man stepped over the rubble towards Lauren.

She backed away. "Leave me alone. That baby in there is mine. I've only just had him and I'm in no condition—"

"Shut the fuck up," the first man said. "You do this the easy way and you'll live. Make it hard and we'll kill you when we're done."

Goeby grabbed at her shirt, yanking on the sleeve. She pulled away and scurried backwards behind the kitchen bench. She couldn't do it; she couldn't stand there and let them take her like this. Lauren sought an escape path. Goeby closed in. The other man moved towards the other side of the bench, blocking her way.

From the floor, she took a long-handled metal spoon used for stirring stew or casserole. It had a little weight. She held it up, poised to strike. There was no deterring Goeby, though. He smiled, revealing stained teeth, and crept closer. Lauren waited, and as he groped at her shirt again, she whacked him on the head.

He screamed, "Bitch!" and threw a looping fist towards her face.

The first man rushed her. Lauren tried to smack Goeby again. The second man threw a knee into her right kidney. Pain filled her side and she fell onto her knees, spilling the metal spoon. Something struck the back of her head. She slumped to the floor, pressing her face into the linoleum, fighting back tears.

One of them tore her shirt, then grabbed the top of her expensive Calvin Klein jean shorts and tried to yank them down. Lauren screamed, swatting at them with a weak hand. A foot pressed down on the back of her neck. She tried to wriggle away, but the man applied more pressure, pinning her to the floor, and the pain, oh the pain in her neck was excruciating. A weight dropped onto her legs. She couldn't move. Tears filled her eyes. She began to hyperventilate.

They got her shorts off and ripped her knickers away, leaving her as bare-bummed as the day she was born. The men were laughing, taunting her, explaining what they were going to do in detail. Her consciousness threatened to tip, like the time she'd fainted taking a glucose test while pregnant and she hadn't been able to eat all morning. She imagined the force with which they would take her, the reckless contempt for body and person.

Gunfire sounded from the hallway. The men stopped. Pressure lifted from her legs. The second man, Goeby, started towards the door. "Wait," the other man hissed. "Don't go out there yet." Another round of shooting. The walls shook. Goeby sprang to the ready. Lauren held her breath. *Please, oh please, leave.* She had never wanted anything more in her life. Even the pain of Harvey's birth was bearable compared to this.

"What the fuck do we do?" Goeby asked. "Sounds like Sticks and Dicky are in a fight."

The first man considered this. "Go and have a look." Goeby left them. The first man stood and watched him leave. Lauren snuck a hand to her eyes and wiped away the tears. She had to come up with a plan, fast.

FORTY-SIX

A WOMAN holding a baby screamed. Dylan adjusted his aim. It wasn't just any woman; it was *Claire*, Lauren's best friend. And she had a baby?

"Dylan!" she screamed. "Oh my God, are we glad to see you." She hurried forward, cradling the baby. They embraced. Her thumping heartbeat touched his abdomen.

"Where's... Lauren? What happened here?" A man lay on the floor with a gunshot wound. Blood had pooled beneath him—too much for him to have survived, in Dylan's growing estimation. A woman sat at his side, her face bright red, eyes wet.

"Lauren's gone," she sobbed. "Two men just took her. You didn't see them?"

Terror seized Dylan's heart. "No. How long ago?"

"Two minutes."

"We just came up the hallway."

"They must be in another apartment."

Dylan let cold rage wash over him. "They took her?" Claire nodded. He glanced at Greg. "Let's go."

Dylan's hand tightened around the pistol. He tried not to think about what they might do to her. He would kill them; blow their heads off if they had touched her.

Greg led them back out into the hallway. It was silent and empty. "Which door?" he whispered.

"We'll have to try them all."

They opened the first two and scouted the empty space with their guns drawn and their fingers poised. Dylan itched to shoot someone or something. He kicked in several doors before realizing his efforts would not help their stealth. He roped his anger with thoughts of mistakes, fighting to control its disobedient manner.

The third apartment was the one. He felt it. They had stopped outside the door earlier. Why hadn't he tried it then? Dylan swore he had heard something. If it had been Lauren suffering, he would never forgive himself. He reached out and touched the handle, wondering what he would find inside.

"Want me to go first?" It was a brave offer, but Greg had already volunteered for the mission, which was probably more than Dylan deserved. Dylan shook his head. The door came open with a creak. He swung it in and stepped through, daring them to be there. They were, and somebody accepted the dare.

Pain struck his head. Dylan fell forward, fighting for balance but lost and toppled over, hitting the carpet. A scream sounded. His name. Yelling. A boot struck him in the ribs, knocking all the breath from him. "Ugghhh."

Gunfire. The thump of a body hitting the wall. He tried to swivel, sure it was Greg, sorry for all the bad thoughts he'd ever had about the man, wishing he had shown his gratitude every time Greg had saved his life. It wasn't his fight; none of it was. Dylan rolled as another boot chased him, connecting with his lower back, pain shooting up his spine. He gritted his teeth and tried not to cry out. Where was his gun? He climbed to his knees. When had he dropped—

The blunt metal handle of another firearm struck his chin. Bright spots filled his vision as he toppled over. Falling. Thump. Pain drove up through his spine. Once, he would have given up. He'd have lain on the ground and thought it was all too difficult. Now though, he crawled forward on his knees, pushed up, and reached for the couch. Greg was on his feet, wrestling a victory from one man while another headed for him.

"Dylan!" Lauren was lying on the kitchen floor. She was alive. It was one of the best feelings he'd ever experienced.

"Okay?" She nodded. He gave her a thumb up, climbing to his feet, and ran at them.

The second man swung wild blows at Greg as he grappled with the first, striking him in the back of the skull. Screaming, Dylan grabbed him around the neck and yanked him away. They fell backwards onto the floor. He wasn't much of a fighter; his fists never ended up where his mind wanted them to go. Instead, he tightened his forearm around the man's throat and held tight so the man was unable to move. Above them, Greg had pried himself free, facing off against his enemy with fists. The other man was shorter, with long curly hair and a goatee. Faded tattoos covered his wiry biceps. He looked tougher than an old piece of iron, but still Dylan would have bet on Greg.

They would settle it using their dukes like the old days. The man struck out his left fist, surprising Dylan with his speed. It clipped Greg on the cheek as Greg's meaty arm coiled.

Callan had once claimed that Greg would outbox every man in Albury. Dylan had never witnessed him in hand-to-hand combat, but Callan rarely overestimated people. It was the speed that surprised him; how could a big hand move that fast? It swung in an upward arc, striking the man flush on the cheek. The sound was like a snapping tree branch. The man's legs folded and he went down, eyes rolling back in his head. Dylan's prisoner, who had ceased moving, now squirmed like an eel, arms swinging wildly, and broke free, striking Dylan in the groin. Dylan let the man go. He spied his gun and rolled for it.

He took it in a firm, comfortable grip. Greg and the man faced off, the latter thrusting a knife at his friend. Dylan had an open shot. He wanted to kill these men badly for what they had put his sister through. He fired, striking the man in the shoulder. He fell to the floor with a cry, but he wasn't dead. Rage swept over Dylan as he wondered distantly if it was the virus or the serum or perhaps it was his losses. He imagined them attacking Lauren, holding her down, and... the gun roared again, knocking the man's head back. He fell back to the floor in a spray of blood. Dylan turned the gun on the other man and kept firing, lodging a shot in his chest, and another in the head.

The gun clicked; empty. Greg was yelling at him to stop. Dylan dropped it on the floor, chest heaving, hands shaking. He found Greg's stiff, anxious expression. "We got 'em," Greg said. "We got 'em."

Lauren ran to him and launched into his arms. He hugged her tight, warm tears on his cheeks. Despite telling himself there was a chance she'd be alive, he had never believed it; never for a moment. It was too implausible in this new world. She was the last person on earth to whom he had a blood connection. As children, they had shared Santa Claus and the Easter Bunny, lost their teeth, pulled each other's hair, suffered the wrath of both their parents for defying one rule or another through their teenage years. She was special and he would risk it all again to keep her safe.

"Are you alright?" he asked, pulling away. She nodded. "Did... they—" She shook her head. He hugged her again.

Lauren finished dressing and they returned to the apartment where the others were relieved to find she was safe, especially Claire, who cried as they hugged and wouldn't let her go.

The baby Claire was holding began to cry. Lauren took it, walked to Dylan, and offered it to him. "What? What do you want me to do with it?"

"Hold your nephew."

Dylan was dumbstruck. He couldn't think of anything to say. There was no humor in her expression, only a glassy-eyed appreciation that he was standing there. "Really? He's yours?" She nodded. Dylan folded his left arm so the elbow was point out as he had learned holding his older cousin's newborn. Lauren placed the baby's head in the nook of his left arm and laid the tiny body upon the inside of his forearm. "He's really yours?" Lauren nodded, tears spilling.

"Harvey, meet your Uncle Dylan."

FORTY-SEVEN

WITH THE numerous battles, Dylan had almost forgotten about the others in the campervan. He left Greg in the apartment to watch over Lauren and her group. The big man had argued for accompanying him, but Dylan wouldn't have it. They still required protection in case anything else wandered up onto level eight. Besides, Dylan explained, *he* had dragged them all along on the crusade and thus felt obligated to get them all to safety. He took one of Greg's spare magazines, which gave him about ten rounds, and headed down the hallway alone.

The plan was to reach the underground car park Lauren had told him about. She'd provided instructions about how to raise the door manually, but the real challenge was going to be finding the others and then steering the van back safely through the chaos.

Dylan followed the stairs all the way to the basement. The car park was sparse with vehicles. He supposed most had tried to flee the city with the rest of the population. He found the control box easily and tugged the panel with the switches in every position, but it wouldn't move. He considered returning to the apartment for Greg—he was an electrician and knew about these sorts of things—even if there was no power—until finally he saw the chain hiding in the corner and pulled on that.

The door clattered as it rolled up. He decided to leave it open enough to crawl under so when the others came back he could slide through and raise it again. The risk was that one of the feeders might find their way in, but he saw no alternative.

293

On hands and knees, Dylan crawled out into a laneway, and ran to the edge of the apartment building to take in the scene. Two zombies advanced from twenty yards. He put them both down with headshots and jogged on, hugging the buildings for cover. As he moved through the rubble though, something else unsettled him. Where were all the zombies? On their approach to the apartment block, it had been chaotic. Now, it was almost lifeless.

With his lungs burning, he reached the top of Franklin Street, observing some of the handiwork he and Greg had left behind. He stood on the corner and scanned the horizon for the campervan. No sign of it. He jogged on, pushing his aching legs up the hill. Near the apex, he passed a laneway full of nauseating smells and cool dimness. He glanced down its length and saw a large waste bin overflowing with dead bodies near the mouth. Beyond the entrance, in the shadows set by the high brick walls, something moved.

A noise from the road ahead drew his attention. It was the rumbling sound of an engine. *The campervan.* He checked the laneway again as he moved away, and spied it, materializing out of the dark brickwork beyond the waste bin.

A three. Its eyes were dark, almost empty, chilling his skin in a sweeping wave. Behind it, the shadows moved, and another emerged. He had the pistol out in seconds, firing at them from forty yards, but they were different than every other enemy he had faced. They had a cognizance that was scary, as though they anticipated his target before he had taken the shot. He pulled his aim left and right, missing shots he had earlier hit. With the final round, he struck the front feeder in the shoulder. It kept coming.

Dylan ran.

FORTY-EIGHT

EVELYN HAD run out of ideas. They had circled the north part of the city under the blaring heat until the fuel had almost run out. Gallagher had directed her into a clear space to refill the tank, wandering the length of the bus with a rifle poised to kill anything that came too close. That had bought them more time, but they couldn't keep driving around forever. Everybody was getting uptight. The kids were complaining. She had yelled at Jake for the first time in weeks. Gallagher continued pacing in the same irritating pattern. He didn't say much. She noticed he wasn't feeling well. She wished he would come up with an idea.

The threads of loneliness filled her for the first time since meeting the group. She had given up Kristy for dead, and that was heartbreaking. They hadn't known each other long, but she felt a sisterly connection with the woman. Callan had left the group. She'd probably never see him again, either. Evelyn didn't know if it hurt more that he had left them all without consideration, or because she missed him. The remaining comfort of having Dylan and Greg around had disappeared too. There was still Jake, of course, and Julie, but the others had all been in the same age bracket.

Part of what irritated Evelyn was that they weren't going anywhere. She had wanted to drive back towards the apartment building at the top of Franklin Street. Gallagher wouldn't have it, claiming it was too dangerous to take such a cumbersome vehicle into a tight location. How were the others going to get out? The same way they had gotten in, Gallagher said.

Evelyn didn't buy that though. She had been slowly working her way closer. They'd drive for a little while, and park in a clear space for a minute or two, then move on when the feeders approached. It was like playing cat and mouse. Every two or three turns she made, took them marginally closer to Franklin Street. She suspected Gallagher *suspected*, but he hadn't yet said anything.

They stopped in the center of the road on Victoria Parade, as close as they had been to the apartment building since dropping Dylan and Greg off. They were still too far away though.

Julie fell into the passenger seat and handed Evelyn a bottle of water. It was another thoughtful gesture, in a long list, from the older woman.

"How are you holding up, honey?" Evelyn looked grim. "Hang on. It won't be long now."

"I've been telling myself that for the last hour. What if it's not? What if it doesn't go the way we want it?"

Julie smiled. She put a hand on Evelyn's arm. "We don't, of course, but hope is all we have, if nothing else. Hope allows us to take another breath, another step forward."

"What if we've got no hope?"

"There's always hope. You might lose the things you love, the people you live for, but there's always more to be found if you look hard enough."

How could she argue with a woman who had just lost her whole life? "What do you hope for?"

Julie considered. "I hope we don't lose anybody else and I hope I survive long enough to enjoy the world again."

"I think you will."

"I think you're right." Evelyn reached out and squeezed her hand. Julie clasped hers over the top.

The enemy was on the movie again. Amongst the carcasses of a hundred vehicles, they stirred. A posse of type one feeders approached the van. They had about thirty seconds. "I'm going closer. I'm sick of this waiting. We said we'd get to the top of Queen Street. They might be expecting us."

"It's too risky," Gallagher said. "You take this thing in there and we might not get it—or us—out."

"That's what we said about the Army base in Canberra. We should *never* have gone in there, but we did, and now you're standing here because of it." Gallagher didn't blink. She had another response prepared, but in the end, he turned away. Evelyn took that as a non-objection. She pulled away from the curb, full of determination, grateful for another chance to help the people who had saved her and Jake.

It didn't take long. She spied Dylan sprinting up the slope from Franklin Street as the campervan approached the bend. He was still a hundred yards away, but ran like the devil was chasing him. He bounded over a body, around an orange Datsun with the hood raised, and glanced over his shoulder. "Come on," she whispered.

Gallagher stood between the seats. "Can you get closer?"

"Trying." Was he slowing down? *Yes*. His arms had begun to falter and his shoulders sagged forward.

Gallagher disappeared from her shoulder. Evelyn took the van up onto the curb and then right into a pile of debris, thinking there was a gap. She found a small two-door car blocking the way and had to jam on the brakes, searching the mirrors for a way out.

"Just push through it," Julie said. "There's a big enough gap."

Evelyn accelerated, striking the front of the vehicle with a shuddering crunch. Julie staggered forward, reaching for the seat. "Sorry!" But she got the tip through with an awful scrape of steel. *Don't stop*. She nudged it further, grimacing at the sound, and then they were through, racing away from the wreck.

Dylan approached. In the side mirror, she saw Gallagher swing the door open. She slowed the van, bringing it closer to the curb, and Dylan leapt for it, almost overstepping the mark. He thumped into the side of the doorway, crunching the frame. Gallagher grabbed him by the shoulder and pulled him inside, then slammed the door shut.

Evelyn drove on, swinging the camper through a pile of rubble in the center of the road. The zombies that had been chasing fell away.

"Go left, into Franklin," Dylan said, panting.

"Is it safe?" Gallagher asked.

"There's a car park underneath the apartment building."

"Did you find your sister?" Evelyn asked.

Dylan smiled, and there was a palpable relief in his expression. "Yeah. We did. She's... okay, now. Greg made it too."

Evelyn negotiated a pathway down Franklin Street, through the intersection with Russell. As they crossed the tramlines, she glanced left and saw masses of them wandering along the street towards the juncture. "Did you see that?"

"Yeah," Dylan said. "We gotta get inside, now."

He directed her to a tiny laneway further up the slope on their left. She drove for it and spotted the roller door for the car park, slowing the big camper as they approached. She saw the problem immediately. "It's not going to fit."

"She's right," Gallagher said. "We'll have to park outside." He pointed at the wall of another building. "There." Evelyn dragged the van to the side of the laneway and idled. It wasn't ideal, but she couldn't see an alternative.

Gallagher went to the entrance with a handgun. Evelyn shut off the engine. So it had come down to this, she thought with growing terror. She made sure the kids were up on the bunk, and took a rifle herself. A horde of slow, bumbling feeders with their rotting faces and long, stringy hair congregated at the entrance to the laneway.

"We'll hold them off," Gallagher said. "You load up on bags—the medicine and guns and as much food as you can carry."

Gallagher and Dylan went out side-by-side with bags of guns and ammo in one hand, their 9mm handguns in the other. They fired, dropping feeders, shooting holes in the enemies' chests, through their throats, and exploding their heads like watermelons. Evelyn followed, standing guard with the rifle booming as Julie guided the kids across the laneway, towards the door. In that moment, Evelyn felt profound gratitude towards the older woman for taking care of her son, knowing she would protect him with her life.

Zombies fell; a trail of bodies slumped over each other and blood splats covered the walls and road. It pooled in thick puddles beneath the corpses. The smell was horrendous and would be worse in a day or two, but there was no end to the count.

Julie guided the kids underneath the doorway, standing over them with a tight, determined expression. She swung her bags through and got down on one knee with a grimace. From there, she lay down and rolled through the gap as though she hadn't moved in such a way for many years.

Gallagher ushered Evelyn towards the gap. She removed her pack and swung it underneath. She got down on all fours, glancing back at the van they had called home for... how long had it been? A week? She couldn't recall. People had lived and died in that van; she'd gotten to know Callan and Kristy, saved lives, driven it across states, and spoken with Eric for the final time in it.

"Can't be helped," Gallagher said, reading her thoughts.

She rolled underneath and stood, clearing the way for the others. Julie and the children waited nearby. There was a long moment where neither Dylan nor Gallagher appeared, and Evelyn wondered if something had happened. She was poised to climb back underneath when Gallagher crawled through on his elbows. Dylan followed. He jumped up and hauled the chain, dropping the door as feet and hands clawed at the gap. The gate shuddered under the weight of the angry feeders. Evelyn wondered if it would hold.

FORTY-NINE

DYLAN SAT on the bed beside Lauren, watching his nephew. She unfolded a flat plastic sheet and placed it on the bed, then picked the baby up and laid him on it. "You wanna change him?"

"Nah. I'll watch this one."

She was overjoyed he could be there with them. Her frailty of the last few weeks had almost vanished now that her big brother had arrived. They had come all the way from Albury to find her, surviving more than imaginable. They had food and guns and *strength*. She knew Greg and his tough reputation from school in Albury. The others were brave and courageous too. She laid a hand on Dylan's arm, just to make sure of him. "I still can't believe you're here."

"*I* still can't believe you're a mother and I'm an uncle."

She scoffed. "Not a world that you'd want a baby growing up in, though."

Dylan gave Harvey his little finger and he clutched on with a tight grip.

"He's strong."

She had listened to the tale of her parents' deaths, insisting Dylan left no detail out, although he probably had. Lauren hadn't cried—in her mind, they had already died. She had prepared herself for that, weeks ago. Now, at least, she could put them to rest. Dylan stood and opened his arms. They hugged, long and gentle, a siblings' embrace. They had been closer when they were young; he had always looked out for her, despite his more passive nature.

"I'd like to get that prick Todd and wring his neck."

"I wouldn't let you waste your time." She tickled Harvey's chin. "We're better off without him, aren't we, bub? If I hadn't fallen pregnant, we'd have broken up." Lauren finished wrapping the nappy, then scooped up the baby, and dropped him on Dylan's lap. He sat frozen, peering at his uncle, whom he had only just met. Harvey reached out a tiny hand, and cooed.

"He likes you."

Dylan made soft noises. She wanted to ask more about Kristy. He'd touched on it; their relationship as it had developed, and his feelings, but again, she knew he had held back. Perhaps it was too raw. Perhaps he needed to talk about it.

"You wanna talk about Kristy?"

He continued making faces at the baby for a moment, and then his smile faded. "There's nothing to talk about." Lauren made a face. "I've dealt with it. Same as I dealt with Mom and Dad."

"You sure?" He nodded. "Okay." He looked tougher than when he'd last visited. What had he gone through to be there now? Had it hardened all the soft parts of him, the bits she loved, that made him different to the other guys she had known? He had always been kind and considerate and she worried it had been driven out of him. She supposed they had all changed though; must have, in order to have survived. "What about the virus? That really worries me." He had explained how the serum came about—the scientist who had developed it, but later died trying to find more.

"As long as I keep taking the serum I should be okay." But there was truth in his eyes that unsettled her. He didn't quite believe that. Maybe it was because he knew that at some point the serum would run out. Surely, Dylan had thought that far ahead.

"And Admiral Gallagher? He doesn't look so good."

"Klaus said it works differently with each person. Like the flu." He looked contemplative. "I don't know why it's not working for Gallagher, though. I wish we could do something for him." His mind disappeared in thought for a moment. "Hard to believe you survived all of this."

"When they evacuated the building, Claire and I chose to stay. Lots of people left though. That gave us access to food and water we otherwise wouldn't have had. Probably kept us alive longer."

"Well, I'm glad you did." He put a hand on her shoulder. "I need to speak to Gallagher."

Lauren wrapped Harvey and laid him in the cot, then returned to the kitchen where the heat was stifling. Julie and Claire had taken over, setting up what remained of their supplies into edible dishes. There were slices of potatoes and bowls of rice, both boiled on the gas cooker.

"I'll have to leave soon," Gallagher said, leaning against the kitchen bench with a bottle of cold water. "I need to find out what's at Station Pier. Whether there's anything that can take us across Bass Strait."

"Why? Why do you have to go now?" Evelyn asked. "Couldn't we wait it out here a couple of days? We've earned a rest. Maybe give the others a chance to catch up."

"I don't know how long this city will last. Something's brewing here. You heard what the man in Yass said. The threes are changing the type ones. I need to know what's at that dock."

Lauren studied the man. There was a hard edge to him; thick muscles under his shirt that flexed when he moved. He was average height, but stocky, and the cropped salt and pepper hair added to the toughness. But his eyes were bloodshot and rimmed in black shadow. He coughed regularly, interrupting his croaky voice.

"You can't go alone."

"I'll go," Greg said. Gallagher nodded thanks.

Dylan screwed the lid back onto his bottled water. "How well do you know the city layout?"

Greg's expression widened. "I don't, but what does that matter?"

"Where are you going?"

"Station Pier."

"Port Melbourne. Do you know even know where it is?"

"I can go," Alexander said. "It's about an hour from here by foot. That's if you don't run into any trouble."

Lauren frowned. "You can't go. Your hand's still a mess. It's not even stitched."

"Sarah can take a look at that," Dylan said. "She can stitch a wound now."

Greg was silent. He had no idea where the pier stood. Lauren didn't like where it was heading.

"I'll go," Dylan said. "I roughly know the way. I've driven down here a few times." Greg looked annoyed. Dylan frowned. "What? You've done more than your share of work." He turned to Gallagher. "You think we'll find anything?"

"I think it's our best chance to find a cruise ship or passenger ferry capable of crossing Bass Strait."

Lauren wanted to ask if Gallagher would even make it there. By her count from walking around the city during her lunch breaks for three years, an hour meant about four miles. "What about a car?"

"We'll assess as we proceed," Gallagher said. "Sure would make it easier, but we don't want to draw attention."

"What then? Even if there's a ship you can drive, we still have to all get down there."

"Can you check the campervan, Greg? I don't think it'll be any good now, and it's too risky to make it back from the underground lot. We'll have to find a couple of working cars down there," Dylan said. Greg nodded.

"We leave after dark," Gallagher said.

FIFTY

DYLAN AND GALLAGHER stepped out onto the street through the broken glass at the front entrance with their pistols loaded and their pockets full of ammunition. Part of Dylan couldn't believe they were actually leaving when they'd only just reached the refuge. He looked back at the dark silhouette of the apartment building, full of regret. It had to be done though. Gallagher was right. Night travel was safer than daylight. They could hide in the shadows and plod their way through the city. He hoped it would only take them a few hours and they would return before ten.

The heat of the day lingered, sticking to them like a second skin. Lauren had forced each person to peel off their clothes and wash them by hand in the laundry sink. Such things were long forgotten in Dylan's mind, but although the clothes were still a little damp, the feel of clean threads on his skin was pleasant.

Alexander and Lauren had given him a rundown of the streets to take and turns to make, drawing a map on the back of an old market flyer. Dylan had a vague idea of the direction—their parents had caught one of the big ferries to Tasmania and Dylan had driven them down to the pier. The darkness made it more challenging, but they had torches if they got stuck or needed to check the map. In the daylight, a smoky haze had covered the city, but at night, the orange flames from dozens of fires provided guidance.

"So it was follow Queen Street all the way to the bottom, turn right into Flinders, then right into Queen …"

Gallagher coughed. "Bridge. Queensbridge."

"That's it. Then follow that down to City Road and take City Road all the way down to Beach Street and turn right. It'll be up on the left."

"Sounds like you got it."

At the Clarendon Street junction, they spotted a group of men firing guns into the old McDonalds store. It was alight; twenty feet of orange and yellow flames illuminated the night. Dylan thought they'd have all the zombies in Melbourne attending soon. They watched the group for five minutes, ensuring there were no more wandering about, and then snuck down the opposite side of the street, using rubbish dumps and trashed cars as camouflage. Gallagher seemed grateful for the pause.

They walked on in comfortable silence for a time until Gallagher broke it with a question that surprised Dylan.

"You sorted things out with Greg yet?"

"How do you mean?"

"Greg told me something went down at the facility, after rescuing Klaus and me. He didn't say what, but he asked me how to win back a person's trust."

"What did you tell him?"

"I said you have to deliver for them, time and again, no questions. They have to know that you'll be there when it counts."

Dylan considered that. Technically, Greg had met the criteria. Dylan could recall countless times over the last week or two when Greg had delivered for him. "Greg has done that. He's been amazing."

"Then what's the problem?" Dylan explained what had transpired underneath the defense facility. "Then you have a choice to make, my friend, but let me tell you something. I was once in a similar predicament to you. I didn't trust a man, and he died because of me. I hesitated. The reasons now seem absurd. I still think about it from time to time, and I found out later I had no basis for my mistrust."

"I just can't get that moment out of my head. If he hadn't hesitated, would I have gotten bitten?"

Gallagher cleared his throat and launched into a coughing fit. "You'll never know. And does it matter? Even if he did hesitate—and I'm sure it wouldn't have been for any reason other than fear—it sounds like he's covered for you enough times to make up for it."

Gallagher's voice had become husky. Dylan couldn't recall him ever saying so much. All his points were valid though. He knew this. He just couldn't shake the feeling.

"We all have to make choices in our lives. Dwell on what might have been, or move on. Shit, I've had a ton of them, and none more significant than knowing I will soon die. I've spent the last few years drinking my time away. How much I missed I'll never know."

More truth. He wanted to trust Greg. The man was a legend and Dylan owed him his life for more than one rescue. If Greg died because Dylan hesitated, wondering whether to trust him, how would he feel? Easy answer. "You haven't been drinking lately."

"I had to move on. I didn't want what might be the last few weeks of my life to be empty and meaningless. I've had enough of that."

"Greg stopped drinking too."

Gallagher coughed into his fist. "That was another reason, too. Greg was a younger version of me. There are symptoms that alcoholics perceive in each other. Mine were obvious. He spoke to me about it early on. We chatted. I realized I had an opportunity to positively or negatively influence a young man. I thought that if I kept drinking, so would he. If I stopped …"

"You have no idea how grateful we are for that. Especially Callan. And Greg."

"Helped us both. Although nothing can help my other issue."

The virus. While Dylan was infected too, the last he knew, he was in a good place. Gallagher was struggling. Dylan wondered what it would be like dealing with that. "You think... it will kill you?"

"I know it will. I knew from the moment I was bitten that I would die. It's just a matter of how I dealt with it, and what I can do until then."

There was a depth to Gallagher they had all missed. To most of them, he was the quiet, ex-Navy tough guy in the corner who delivered fists and bullets when they needed him. It wasn't going to end well for the admiral, they all knew that, but the way he was conducting himself in the final week or two of his life was admirable. He didn't outwardly show it, but Gallagher had to be scared. Dylan thought it was true courage to be fearful of something, yet not show it—or more so, to battle onward when you were frightened, knowing a fatal outcome awaited.

The message about trust and forgiveness stuck with Dylan, too. Maybe it was time he forgave Greg and started trusting him again. That one hesitation amongst countless acts of selflessness to save all of them could surely be forgiven. Maybe he did need to make a choice and move on.

They reached the pier without further trouble. Dylan guessed it had taken them an hour, even at a slower pace to allow for Gallagher's dwindling health. They saw only a handful of zombies, and it wasn't until they got down near the sea where the salty smell of the water hit them, removing part of the stench from all the dead bodies.

"Good idea to come after dark," Dylan said.

"It was too easy." Gallagher coughed again. Dylan had administered a shot of serum to the admiral before leaving, although Gallagher didn't think it mattered for him, either way. "There should have been more of them." The admiral hobbled over to a nearby bench. He had struggled for most of the journey. A man of his age shouldn't have had such trouble. It was the virus, Dylan knew. It was changing him, despite the serum. He didn't know if Gallagher would even make a journey across Bass Strait. And what awaited Gallagher once he got there even if he did? He didn't like the thought of how it might end. "There's something more. Something…" He put both hands to his temples, as though he had a headache he couldn't shake. "I can feel them. The threes. They're in the city. A lot of them. They're…" He strained again. "Ready to go. Ready to make a final attack."

Jesus, Dylan thought. "That's sounds ominous."

"It is. We need to get on that boat as soon as possible."

They stood at the entrance to the pier where cars had once parked and visitors had taken in a restaurant or the ice cream shop while looking at the latest boat that had docked. The inky sea lay on either side, the silhouette of the pier building straight ahead. On the left, the outline of a boat was visible.

"Is that a ship?" Dylan asked.

"Looks like it. Probably the Spirit of Tasmania."

"That'll get us over there right? I mean, you can drive that?"

Gallagher nodded. "Most likely."

Dylan stood looking at it. Was it worth hoping? Worth thinking that maybe they might get there? "That is a damn good sight. We were lucky."

"A little. A boat runs every afternoon from here.

Dylan wished his father could have been there. He had planted the thought in Dylan's mind from the beginning.

310

Would anybody have considered it, had he not pushed the idea all along? His father had always been a man of vision, looking well ahead of the pack, anticipating their needs. Dylan supposed that was part of the reason for his business success. He tried to bury the ache and focus on the present. "What now?"

"This is where we part company," Gallagher said.

"What?"

"Go back to your sister."

"What about—"

"I have to prepare the ship. Make sure it's fit for a twelve-hour journey across that body of water, which can be treacherous at the best of times." He coughed, clearing his throat. "There are hundreds of checks to do before we can leave. If we come back in the morning it'll be two hours before we can depart."

"The morning?"

Gallagher rubbed his head again, grimacing as a wave of pain passed through. "We can't wait. They're moving. Something major is going to happen; I can feel it. Tomorrow might be too late."

If what Gallagher said was right, preparing the boat now made sense. Still, Dylan didn't like it. He didn't mind the part about returning to the apartment alone, but leaving Gallagher at the pier on his own to carry out all those checks and balances was worrisome. What if he was attacked or died? "I don't think it's a good idea. I'll stay with you and help out while you get it ready."

Gallagher shook his head. "Listen to me." All the sickness disappeared from his voice. Now it was strong, calm, and comforting. It spoke of a leadership Dylan couldn't yet comprehend, but he understood how people would follow this man. "This is the sensible solution. I prepare the ship, you prepare the people. You want to carry out your father's plans, don't you?" He let the thought linger. "I will help you do that. I'll get you and the rest of the group to Tasmania, that's a promise. You go back and rest up for the night, get the others ready, and in the morning you get down here at first light. That will be challenge enough. We'll leave the mainland behind and hope Tassie is in a better state and you can find out if your old man was right."

It was impossible to argue. He walked Gallagher up to the ship and watched as the admiral made his way through the building and up several flights of stairs until he reached the gangplank. He used the flashlight to signal down that he had made it.

Dylan started back, retracing the steps they had taken using the tall buildings against the sky as markers. He made good time.

He jogged down the middle of the road with the flashlight low to the ground, trying to avoid drawing too much attention. It was impossible to walk the trashed streets without it. They had not used it often on the way down to the pier, but he had relied on Gallagher and his inbuilt sonar to lead the way. That got him thinking about the admiral and their conversation.

They're coming. The words had spooked Dylan. What did it mean? How did Gallagher know? *The virus.* Just like the man from Yass, the admiral's infection was getting worse, and with it came some kind of mental connection. He understood things, perhaps even had an insight into their minds. Maybe they could look into his mind, too. Maybe they knew the group was planning to leave. Dylan didn't feel such a connection. Maybe the virus wasn't advanced enough in him.

He had made it three-quarters of the way back when he sensed something or someone watching from the shadows. He increased his pace, glancing back over his shoulder often, listening amongst the sounds of a dying city. He crossed at an intersection, hoping to catch a glimpse of whoever or whatever it was. He even walked backwards for a time, biting down on his desperation to use the flashlight, but knew that if he started poking a yellow beam about, it would attract the unwanted.

He carried the 9mm handgun in his right hand, fully loaded, his finger hovering over the trigger. He took aim at the darkness, pretending to shoot, practicing for what he considered the inevitable: something was coming for him.

He tried to focus on Lauren and Harvey waiting for him back at the apartment. That was really all he had left in the world now. His sister and his nephew. They were worth fighting for. He wondered what would have happened if he hadn't persevered with the search. He knew that answer, and it scared him more than what might lie in the shadows he passed. He pushed the thought away. She was safe; they both were. Dylan just had to make it back, and beyond that, get them safely to the ship. *That* was his focus now. The ship and safe passage to a new land.

Despite the necessary vigilance, tiredness filled him and his wits dulled. He ran for a block, forcing himself to be more alert. His heart rate rose and his senses intensified. When was the last time he'd slept? The church. He'd managed a few hours on the hard floor. It had been the same for weeks now; he hadn't had a trouble-free sleep since the lake.

A fresh fire blinked at him in the distance. It guided him for a time, but he decided to change his route and avoid it, in case men were in the vicinity. He had planned to go right at the next intersection, but as he rounded the corner, a noise sounded in the gloom ahead. Dylan stopped, eyeing the darkness, and stuck the gun out. "I'm ready," he said in a low voice. He waited. The shadows were still. Nothing happened. He contemplated resuming his original direction, but decided he was being a pussy, and that the noise had been a conjuring of his tired mind. What would the admiral do? He wouldn't have even stopped, Dylan thought.

The next bit happened with unnatural speed. It was as though he'd been walking in a daze, unaware of what was happening around him.

He heard footsteps, like a long line of people moving along the street towards him. He slowed, contemplating returning the way he'd come. Gunfire exploded, lighting up the road ahead with flashes on both sides of the street. A scream sounded over the gunfire unlike anything Dylan had ever heard. More movement. The distant sound of a car engine and squealing tires. He began to backtrack. It was ahead, whatever it might be, and Dylan knew that way was no longer an option. He turned and sprinted, poking the torch into the darkness, searching for a way out. The intersection was still too far ahead. Heavy footsteps, shouting, followed by rapid gunfire. He heard noises all around, like a stampede. He'd inadvertently walked into some chaos.

And then it was on him, a car or truck, maybe more than one, the noise crashing in like a wave through the darkness, screeching from around the corner, tires fighting for grip on the road, the gunfire all round. He swung the torch but lost it in his panic. He tried to get out of the way, but then it was too late and the last thing he remembered was spinning as something struck him from behind.

FIFTY-ONE

DYLAN WOKE in the blue light of pre-dawn. His skin was cold and his head ached. It took him half a dozen seconds to realize where he was and what had happened. He climbed to his feet through a blanket of rubbish, knocking a garbage bin over as he staggered for balance. Where was the torch? His gun? He dropped to his knees and searched the ground. The gun was snuggled under a plastic bag, and the torch had rolled past the bin.

How long had he been out? Hours at least. Dawn was coming. He wondered how Gallagher was doing, and if Lauren and the others back at the apartment were safe. He walked along the street, keeping close to the buildings, using them for cover. He had to get back to Queen Street. He checked the next sign and found he was on William. What had Julie said about the way the streets were named? King, William, Queen, Elizabeth. That meant Queen should be the next one parallel. He took a left onto Lonsdale, hurrying along the pavement as the early morning light pried away the darkness,

As he passed an odd-looking building, he glanced in through the dark windows and saw movement. Unconsciously, he slowed to a stop, feeling the pull of *something*, some unidentifiable darkness. *Run.* He heard the whisper of Gallagher's voice in his mind, telling him similar.

Dylan ran. He glanced back once as he approached the corner and saw shadows spilling out of the building. *Threes*, like black oil from a drum, pouring out over the streets. He didn't know what was going on there, but there were more of them than he had ever imagined.

By the time he made it onto Queen and sprinted the last two blocks to the apartment building, he was gasping for air. He raced in through the entrance, broken glass crunching under his feet. He threw the fire stairs door open and climbed with the torch beam bouncing in one hand and the 9mm in the other. On the second level, the shadows unfolded and a clumsy feeder came at him. Dylan shoved it backwards and shot it in the face. The noise stung his ears.

He slowed outside Lauren's apartment. Again, despite the risk, he'd somehow managed to avoid dying. *One day, your luck will run out.* He tried the door and found it locked. Good sign. He knocked three times and shortly heard the sound of footsteps. The door swung open and Lauren stood there.

"You asshole!" she yelled, pulling him to her with a heavy embrace.

"I'm okay," Dylan said. He stepped inside and shut the door. "We need to go now though."

Lauren said, "But we're not ready."

Greg put a hand on Dylan's shoulder. "Glad you made it back, mate."

Dylan thought of his conversation with Gallagher. *Make a choice.* "Thanks, mate."

"Where's Gallagher?"

"We found a ship. A big bastard. Gallagher stayed there to get it ready. He should have it going by now. But we have to move. Something is happening with the type threes. I saw them in large numbers coming out of a building. Like an army of them. I think they've started moving." His throat was parched and sore. "Water, please." Lauren handed him a fresh bottle of water and he drank, the back of his throat singing with delight at the coolness.

"I've found a couple of cars in the underground lot," Greg said. "A red Commodore and the white Toyota Ute— it's a quad cab."

"Great. We *have* to go now though. Let's move."

The others hurried about, drawing half-packed bags and baby items into a pile. Evelyn had packed two boxes of non-perishable food, and Dylan carried one to the door. Lauren returned from the bedroom with a bag in each arm.

"You got a pen and some paper?" Dylan asked.

"What for?"

"I want to leave a note for Callan telling him where we're going, just in case." Evelyn stopped at the sound of Callan's name. Dylan reached out and squeezed her hand. "Don't give up on him yet."

Greg said, "We've got nine people. That's two cars, plus space for luggage."

"Nine? What about Lorraine?"

"She won't leave Steve."

Dylan understood. "She'll die if she stays though."

"I don't think she cares."

Dylan slung one of the packs over his shoulder. He replaced the almost empty magazine in his gun and then stood before their assembly, feeling the weight of leadership rest uneasily on his shoulders. This had always been Callan's role, and more recently, Gallagher's. He peered around at their faces, full of fear, and expectation, with a shadow of hope: Julie holding Sarah's hand, Evelyn holding Jake's. Greg and Alexander had their guns, and Lauren cradled Harvey. Claire stood on the end.

"If one of the cars gets into trouble, the other one has to keep going. Just drive for Station Pier, understand?" They nodded. "We can't get sentimental about this. It's do or die now." He considered what to say next, losing focus in his desire to be away, but he found nothing inspirational. "Let's move out. Good luck, everyone." They began to disband. "Wait. Just… just don't give up, no matter what. Even if you think you're not going to make it." He looked at Greg and smiled. "One of us will have your back." Greg smiled and stuck out his hand. Dylan gripped it firmly and they shook.

They left the apartment in a line, Dylan leading the way, Greg bringing up the rear. On the ground floor level, Dylan jogged to the front entrance and secured the note to the doorway with electrician's tape he'd found in one of the other apartments. Even if Callan reached the building, it would be a minor miracle if the note were still attached.

The underground car park lay silent. Outside, beyond the concrete barriers and thick metal roller door, the sounds of the growing horde made Dylan uneasy. *You'll have to deal with that soon.* Greg led them to the two vehicles he had chosen for their escape.

"I checked almost every car," he said. "These were the only ones with a spare set of keys hidden inside."

"Any sign of zombies?" Dylan asked.

"Not that I saw. But be prepared."

Dylan led Lauren, Harvey, Claire, and Alexander to the red Commodore sedan. Evelyn, Jake, Julie, and Sarah followed Greg to the Toyota quad cab. They stopped at the tail as Greg scratched around in his pockets for the keys. Dylan heard the noise from the other car—a slobbery crunch that sounded like a dog eating its dinner.

"Back," Greg said, shifting his body in front of them. He moved slowly towards the front of the vehicle, gun pointed, searching the undercarriage.

Dylan drew his handgun and walked near them. "I thought you said you checked?"

A hissing woman with bloody jeans and gooey tendrils of long hair shuffled out from the other side of the vehicle and went for the closest person: Sarah. It was faster than they expected, as if accruing all its energy for the moment an unsuspecting victim wandered too close.

"Get back," Greg called out. He hurried along the opposite side, striking his hip on the mirror.

It's going to get her, Dylan thought. He and Alexander were too far away; too many people in between. It grabbed hold of Sarah's arm, slobbering and growling.

But there was Julie, the portly, middle-aged woman who had once been afraid to leave her house. She seized Sarah's other arm and yanked her away. The feeder lost its hold. Julie stepped around Sarah, protecting the younger girl with her girth, and swung the pack she was holding. "Get away from her!" The bag struck the zombie in the side of the head, knocking it off balance and onto the concrete. Julie pulled Sarah aside as Greg arrived and stuck the muzzle of the handgun in its ear. The thing mewled, bulging eyes rolling in their sockets. He blew away the side of its head and the thing slumped to the concrete in a bloody heap.

Greg circled both cars to ensure they were clear and then helped the others into the back of the quad cab. Evelyn would drive and Greg would shoot, where required. Alexander was the designated sniper from the back seat of the red Commodore; Dylan had allocated himself driving duties. Lauren sat in the front seat holding Harvey tightly.

Dylan started the engine, reversed out of the car park, and rolled slowly towards the door. Evelyn shadowed his trail. As he pulled within a car length of the exit, he braked and climbed out, listening for the slithering and groping outside. There was no option but to raise the roller door manually. He took hold of the chain and pulled, using his body weight. The gate began to rise. Bright sunlight shot under the gap. He expected to see legs scurrying toward the opening, but the roadway appeared to be clear. He raised the door high enough for both cars to pass through, and then hurried back to the driver's seat.

As he pulled the door closed, a type three strolled into the doorway.

FIFTY-TWO

DYLAN PUNCHED the accelerator and thrust the Commodore through the exit and into the zombie. It hit the windscreen with a crunch, rolled up over the car and bounced off the side, landing inside the car park. The red sedan screeched as it sped left into the laneway and disappeared.

"Go!" Greg screamed.

Evelyn floored the Toyota, felt the clunk and bump as she drove over the feeder, then passed under the roller door and out into bright sunshine. She spied the campervan on her right, tires flat and windows smashed. Useless. There was movement near it and then something crashed into the side of the vehicle with a heavy thud, rocking the car.

"Keep going!" She pulled on the wheel, hurting her wrist, glimpsing the end of the Commodore as it disappeared onto Franklin Street. "Follow him."

She did, the engine screaming. The vehicle raced down the laneway and leapt over the shallow cobblestone gutter with a thud. There were zombies everywhere: a plague, some quick, others sluggish, the crazy ones tossing the slow ones out of the way, racing after the car from all sides of the street. It was as though an army had been unleashed, an invasion from a conquering land.

"Greg?" Evelyn asked. She heard her voice tremble. She suddenly wanted to be back inside the apartment. Anywhere but here.

"I know. I don't know what the fuck's happening."

They raced up the slope to the intersection of Queen and Franklin. The Commodore disappeared around the left bend, knocking the attacking feeders to the side. That was the key,

Evelyn thought. Drive fast and the crazies couldn't get to them.

"Don't stop. Whatever you do, don't stop."

She had no intention of doing that. The sound of a chopper floated to them from overhead. Greg moved about in his seat trying to find it. "Where is it?" Evelyn asked.

"I'm not sure. Let me worry about that. You follow Dylan."

She glanced back and saw the same mask of terror on the faces of Julie, Sarah, and her beloved Jake. She hated putting him in such danger. He should have been somewhere safe, out of harm's way. She had failed in her duties as a mother to protect him time and again. She promised herself that if they made it through this, she would prioritize his welfare over everything else.

They pushed on down Queen Street, chasing the flashing brake lights of the Commodore as it flew beneath shadowy oak trees and alongside towering buildings. Evelyn surpassed her previous driving efforts, switching between brake and accelerator, rolling the steering wheel in both directions. *You can do this.* She glanced over at Greg, stiff-faced, hands holding on tight to the door handle.

Queen Street came to an end as the red Commodore skidded right, wheels smoking. Evelyn followed its line, passing an empty tram, and beyond the rail yards, where trains stood motionless. They raced along parallel to the Yarra River and made a sharp left, crossing the slow-moving body of brown water littered with a swathe of floating debris.

More cars, pile-ups, even a bus tipped onto its side. Dylan was driving like a genius maniac, swerving, braking, skidding, and speeding. Somehow she kept up, thankful for the Toyota's more powerful engine, but the next rear-view mirror look chilled her heart. "Oh, Jesus, Greg. What the hell is that?"

Greg rotated in his seat, as did Julie and the children. A crowd of zombies was chasing them in the distance—not the slow type ones, but type threes. Evelyn had no idea from where they had come, but there were more than she had ever seen in one place running along the street after them.

Dylan slowed so suddenly that Evelyn almost rammed into the red sedan. The tires screeched, the seatbelt pulling across her chest. She *was* going to hit them. To avoid it, she pulled the wheel right at the last moment and crashed into the dented side of another vehicle. Dylan and the others disappeared through a narrow gap between two towering piles of rubble.

"Hurry!" Greg screamed.

Evelyn yanked the gear stick into reverse, but when she put her foot down on the pedal, the engine groaned and the twisted squeal of metal on metal sounded. The car wouldn't budge. The bumper guard was caught on the other vehicle.

FIFTY-THREE

CALLAN'S GROUP had found luck the previous night when Harlan told them about the Toyota Camry tucked safely in the garage at the back of the church. Harlan had decided to go with them in hope that the serum would save him from the effects of the bite and prolong his already lengthy existence on God's once wonderful Earth. Callan was glad. He liked Harlan. He'd never met a religious leader with a sense of humor or who colored the world with such a unique perspective.

The tank was full of fuel, and although the vehicle didn't have the strength and durability of the old Toyota, it would be faster through the city. The problem now was space. With the four in the original group, plus Harlan, Blue Boy, and the other family, they were three seats short. Callan found Robert sitting with his wife and daughter talking quietly in the pews.

He called Robert over and stood on the chancel, giving him their plan to drive into the city, find the others, and catch a boat to Tasmania. It sounded outlandish, but Callan sold it hard. "You can come with us, if you like. I mean—you're welcome." Callan liked the idea of building numbers. They had enough weapons to arm more people, and volume was their best chance against the ever-growing enemy, both human and dead.

Robert shook his head. He was an unobtrusive, gentle man—hadn't engaged Callan or the others with more than a courteous hello, and walked with a primness that would struggle in the new world. "Thank you, but we're going to stay here."

That made no sense to Callan. He knew he should let it go; he would have to locate another vehicle if they accepted. "Are you sure? I mean, there's almost no food left here, and we don't have a great deal of weapons—we can leave you some, but…" Robert's wife, Maria, and daughter looked terrified. Callan understood their fear; they all felt it at times, but they couldn't hide forever. "I know it seems safe now, but in the longer term, you might regret it."

Robert's lips were tight, his brow creased deep in thought. "I know. But I won't risk my family out there again. I keep holding out hope that someone—*anyone*—will come along and save us. We've been through hell to get to here. I can't— no, *I won't* put them through it again."

"Good luck then. I hope help finds you soon."

The early morning sky was clear, the air warming up on its way to another scorcher, and the breeze brought familiar scents of death and decay. He wanted to leave at first light— they had just missed that, but could make it up if they hurried. In his experience, early mornings were the quietest time for the zombies. They would reach the central business district today and find out whether any of their friends were still alive. The thought left Callan feeling queasy.

He packed the last of their gear into the back of the Toyota—had even been able to salvage some of the supplies from the four-wheel drive, but it would be a tight fit. Jacob was a worry. Kristy had cleaned and disinfected the wound, patched it on both sides, but she needed to stitch it and keep checking for internal bleeding and infection. Purple bruising had colored the surrounding skin. Possible infection worried Callan. Greg had gone through hell from the cut on his leg. What would a bullet wound do? They had the antibiotics from the hospital in Canberra, but they were with the other supplies. Jacob was talking though, and had even started cursing, which Callan thought was a good sign.

Kristy had cleaned Harlan's wound, too, and he was perkier than when they'd arrived. He'd been moving around the church again since late the previous night. Callan thought that was just his attitude though. The serum offered him hope, but it wouldn't be long before the virus started affecting him, if Johnny was anything to go by. He was awake early, preparing for their departure like a kid going on an exciting holiday. Harlan had no idea what they were going into though.

They decided Jacob would sit in the front to avoid being bumped around. Harlan sat near the window, Kristy in the middle, and Bec on the other side, with Blue sitting on their laps. Callan rolled the car out of the brick garage and sought directions to the Queen Victoria market from Harlan.

Callan immediately enjoyed the advantages of the smaller vehicle, winding his way through broken pathways and the carcasses of a thousand cars crammed with the bodies of more. Sporadic zombies picked at the leftovers, ignoring them. He dared feel a sliver of optimism. They followed Hoddle Street in a meandering track, racing through the clearer sections. At Victoria Parade, Harlan told him to go right.

Twisted columns of vehicles—cars and trucks—sat for hundreds of yards ahead. Looking across the top of them as the street rose up a slight incline, he saw the air shimmered with heat. A gentle breeze blew their way and the smell hit them.

Bec gagged. "Oh my God. I can't take that."

"Breathe through your mouth," Kristy said.

They crawled their way through the mess of stalled traffic. The first tight spot brought the screeching sound of metal on metal as the Camry jagged the edge of some rust bucket left at the curb. Callan grimaced. Harlan just went on smiling. It got worse. Callan imagined long streaks down both sides of the vehicle, but he supposed it didn't matter. In all likelihood, the car would be discarded by the day's end—if they were still alive. They broke through and hit another clear patch and, for a time, they zipped along the grass of the median strip under the cover of hundred-year-old oak trees. For just a moment, as the leaves danced in the gentle breeze and the shadows cast relief from the heat, they might have been in a park somewhere, enjoying the summer's day.

Near the top of the slope though, Callan spotted movement from one of the buildings ahead. "Do you guys see that?"

Bec groaned. "Oh God. Yes. It's one of the scary ones that attacked us on the rail car."

"Where?" Jacob croaked.

"I don't see anything," Kristy said.

There wasn't just one, Callan realized. On the downward slope a hundred yards away, a number of feeders had marched out of a building.

"There! On the other side, too," Bec said.

Callan switched sides and saw another lot moving between the cars like a team of assassins. Jesus, they were heading right into their path. He checked his mirrors. Only way to go was forward. They'd come too far, squeezed through too many tight spots. They'd have to chance it.

"Down the hill further," Harlan said. "Left."

They raced for it as the threes spotted them, a blurry shadow of death converging as they ran through the tall trees on the grassy common separating both sides of the road.

"Faster, Callan!" Kristy screamed. Blue Boy barked frantically, slobbering against the window.

Callan yanked on the wheel, pulling the vehicle left to avoid a bus, then right, hard, as a slow feeder stumbled across their path. The engine groaned, the chassis squealing under the shift in weight. For a moment, he thought they weren't going to make it. He went further right and almost steered them into one of the thick oak trees sunk deep into the curb. Somehow, he managed to straighten up, pain shooting through his left arm. Several were almost upon them, gruesome sneers spread across their pallid, wretched faces.

The vehicle bounced and bumped as they hit the gutter. Jacob stifled a cry of pain. "Sorry." Something struck the trunk. Bec grabbed onto Blue. Kristy took off her belt.

Callan snatched a look at her. "What the fuck are you doing?"

Kristy lowered her window and poked out a handgun. Callan's eyes widened. Once, he might have told her to be careful, but there was no longer need. She was as tough as any of them; had proven herself time and again in these situations. He felt a deep admiration for her and how much she had changed from the person who had taken a six-week stress leave prior to the trip.

Several threes were still chasing, sprinting after them at a remarkable pace. *Don't stop.* Callan pushed the Camry harder, crashing through debris, tossing his passengers about. A bin smashed off the front corner, clattering across the pavement. Kristy wound down the window and maneuvered herself out.

"Grab onto something."

"Try and drive in a straight line."

But he couldn't; there was limited room to move between vehicles. He steered left. Kristy shrieked, grabbing at the seat belt anchor with her spare hand.

"Sorry!" He braked, trying to keep it straight and give her a clear shot.

Blue squirmed, desperate get out and fight. "Stay still, pup," Bec said. Jacob had his eyes closed.

The gun barked twice, but they were still coming. Callan slowed, drawing them closer, and Kristy fired again. One of the zombies fell from view.

"Good shot," Callan hissed.

They had passed the intersection. Callan didn't know how they were going to get back to it. There were no clear spaces in the traffic, only turns and short pockets for accelerating. Sooner or later, they would run into a dead end, and that would spell their doom. The zombies appeared to be in it for as long as it took.

Kristy fired again and another fell. Callan cheered, full of pride. He spied a narrow opening of one of Melbourne's many laneways and drove for it, climbing the curb with another jolt. The front end hit the wall of a building, metal screeching, sparks flying. He crunched the wheel and veered them into the cavity where they bolted down the narrow lane. Only two zombies were still following. Ahead, a large waste bin had rolled away from the back of a shop and onto the road. With limited room on either side, Callan only had one choice.

"Hold on! Kristy, get your ass back down."

They struck the bin, causing a deafening, metallic bang. It spun and crashed into the wall, creating another violent boom. They were all tossed around, restrained by their belts. Bec couldn't hold onto Blue and he ended up on the floor. He leapt back up onto her lap and she wrapped her arms around him, pressing her cheek to the top of his head.

Callan battled on, swerving from one side of the pass to the other, clipping junk and rubble. How long could they keep this up? They'd been lucky so far, and he knew that wouldn't last forever. He hung on though, fighting the wheel and pedals, switching his feet from one to the other like a dancer. Finally, as they reached the end, he braked and kept them in a straight line. He then snatched the wheel and steered the vehicle around a corner, tires screeching.

And then the mirror was empty. Callan waited for them to appear as he gunned the car through a clearer section. Bec and Harlan turned back around in unison. Jacob still lay back with his eyes closed. "They won't give up though," Callan said. Nothing was truer. "Harlan, how do we get to the markets from here? I think it's the top of Queen Street."

"I know the way."

He did, guiding them through more laneways and streets, avoiding sporadic type ones in various stages of wandering, picking, standing, and lying amongst the city trash. The sound of nearby gunshots drifted to them. Callan grew tense again, wondering from where it had originated. Until then, he had thought they would make it. They went right onto Queen Street and got the surprise of their lives.

Amongst the shady oak trees and towering buildings, the type three zombies were tearing the city apart. Several men dressed in Army gear shot automatic rifles as they crouched behind cars tipped on their sides. It was a battlefield. Callan's instincts told him to turn the Camry around and drive away from the city, back to the countryside where it was safer, and flee this hellish place. But he couldn't. They were close, so close to the apartment building. Were Greg, Dylan, and Evelyn waiting there? Was Jake? Or was it only Dylan's sister, to tell them that the others had never made it? Maybe they had found a boat and left for Tasmania. He wouldn't blame them. But he had to know what had happened to his friends, even if he died trying. He now understood Dylan's insatiable appetite to find out whether his sister had survived.

He spied a pathway beyond the clash. They crossed the median strip to the other side of the road as gunshots cracked around them. He pulled in close to the TED'S CAMERAS storefront, shaving a layer of paint off the doors of the Camry. He saw flashes of zombies everywhere—coming out of buildings, hiding behind cars; lines of type ones wandering the streets, drawn to the sound of gunfire and movement and the scent of human flesh. Two green tanks and a large Army truck sat in the middle of the road as soldiers scampered around. Where had the Army been all this time? Why weren't there more of them? Callan should have been swamped with relief at seeing them, but it didn't look like they could possibly win.

"That's it!" Harlan said. "That's the building there."

It stood a hundred yards up the road, just before the corner, a tall building eight or so stories high with dark glass windows all around. Callan thrust the car over rubble, smashing aside all manner of waste with the clang and clatter of metal lost beneath the gunfire and left the battle behind. He slowed the car, searching for a way through the mess, and made a circle, pulling it to the edge of the road on the opposite side of the street to the building.

Entrance was though a single door, now smashed in. A shadowy hallway beckoned beyond. Cars littered the road in between, smoky plumes rising from some, baby flames flickering in others. Callan spied something else near the doorway, too. He'd have to go the rest of the way on foot. He unclipped his belt.

"What are you doing?" Kristy asked.

"There's something there. Wait here. If anything happens to me, leave. Hold onto Blue."

Callan scanned the anarchy. He swung the door open and leapt out, eyes only for the flapping item, leaving Blue barking behind. He was certain the others had left something at the entrance. Sprinting, he leapt over the dead and undying, sidestepping bloody carcasses and unidentifiable messes. He slid over the hood of a car and landed on a dead body as he came down on the other side, feeling mush under his boots. Circling another smoking vehicle, he finally reached the door, skating over the grimy pavement, wondering if it were any of his friends' remains. He hit the doorway with a crunch and snatched the note from the last shard of glass.

FIFTY-FOUR

DYLAN'S WRISTS ached. He'd fought an epic battle with the steering wheel at every twist and curve, and it appeared they might now have made it. They had passed Crown and had almost reached the turn onto City Road—which would take them all the way to the sea—when someone said the others weren't following. Dylan didn't hear it at first. He was so focused on driving, watching for wayward type ones and the dark shadows of the threes he had spied gathering in the buildings.

"Dylan?" Alexander said. He was twisted around, looking out the back window.

Dylan emerged from his fog. "What?"

"The others. They're not behind us."

"Wha—" He checked the mirror. Broken cars and wandering type ones. How long since he'd seen them? "Fuck." What was the rule? *Drive on, even if we get separated.* It had been his rule, but had he ever mentioned it with the intention of following it? He thought of Evelyn, Greg, Julie, Jake, and Sarah. He imagined reaching the ship without them, traveling on to Tasmania with just Lauren, Harvey, Claire, and Alexander. He thought about the people they had lost: Kristy, Callan, his mother and father, Eric, Klaus, Johnny, Howard, and even Sherry. It wasn't the same without them. It would never be the same, and if the others didn't make it now, another piece of him would die with each of them.

Ahead, the median strip broke. "Hold on." He braked hard, momentum pushing them forward, and turned across the width of the road. A dark flash rushed from the shadows to meet them. *A three.* Alexander was fast. He wound the window down and poked the rifle out. The feeder hit the front left side of the Toyota with a crunch and bounced away.

"What did you think was gonna happen, fuckface?" Alexander said into the warm outside air.

Dylan yanked a hard right and gunned the engine. The feeder scrambled to its feet, chasing.

"Come on, baby," Alexander said, adjusting his aim. "Keep coming."

But the pathway was clear and the Commodore raced off, leaving the strident calls of the feeder behind. *Still,* he thought, *they would have to return this way soon.*

He sped on, in and out of unmoving traffic, catching a break for thirty or forty fifty yards here or there. He couldn't work out whether the abandoned cars had been coming into the city or leaving it, such was the random positioning of most.

He searched the battlefield ahead for the white Toyota. Problem was that there was so much white on the street it was difficult to differentiate. "Keep an eye out for them." He raised his foot off the accelerator at one point, thinking he'd spied it parked up on the curb facing the opposite direction. Same vehicle. Dark windows. He pulled up close, searching for an escape route just in case. As he reached the passenger door, a skinless face peered back at him. "Shit." He jumped in his seat and drove on.

They gathered speed and soon came upon the wreckage of another pile up and the narrow gap through which they'd passed earlier. Dylan edged the Commodore through the corridor and into a wide space. He scanned both sides of the road for the white Toyota.

"Turn around!" Lauren screamed.

It took a moment for Dylan to understand. Ahead up the slope, scattered throughout the battered cars and empty wreckages, were dozens of threes. This was the very thing for which they had always been petrified. Killing one or two was achievable, but a dozen… or two… Harvey began to cry.

Terror gripped Dylan, knocking him from his stupor. He turned in a tight circle, the wheels squealing. The white Toyota flashed into view. Greg was out of the car, head down, pushing against the hood. Smoke poured out from underneath the front wheels.

"They're stuck," Alexander said. He had the door open, ready to leap out.

What to do? Dylan wasn't so sure. There was no time for much. In thirty seconds, the first type three would reach them. He considered knocking into the car and trying to jolt it lose, but the risk of the rubble falling onto them was too high.

"We need to help," Alexander said. "If both of us push, we might get them loose."

That *might* work. It also meant stopping the car and both of them getting out, leaving Lauren, Harvey, and Claire alone. But if they didn't, he was sure the others would die. "All right. Let's do it."

He pulled wide and cut in beside the Toyota. He threw the door open and leapt out, snatching the handgun from Lauren. Alexander ran beside him, pumping the Remington. Dylan was grateful to the kid—he didn't know them, and couldn't have yet been out of his teens. So far, he'd done everything they had asked.

"It's stuck on the truck bumper," Greg shouted. "Won't budge."

"Kick the fucking thing!" Dylan yelled. They did, slamming the heels of their boots into the panel at the front of the Toyota.

The threes were closing. Beyond the next pile of debris, two of them led the others by a long distance, their bald heads and pale upper bodies gleaming in the sunlight. One of them had inky swirls over the top half of his body.

Greg sensed the imminent danger. He stepped away from the vehicle and scooped his rifle up off the road. In motion, he pumped a round into the chamber and took aim. The zombies roared their fury. If Greg missed, they were all dead. The rifle cracked. Once, twice, hitting their targets. Red streamers flew behind both as they hit the ground and slid along the blacktop.

Dylan thrust the heel of his boot down. *Crack*. He repeated the action in the same spot. Alexander did the same, breaking the guard free of the panel. Dylan and Greg went at it one after the other in a frenzy, and finally the steel bumper tore free.

"Go!" Greg screamed.

Evelyn skidded the car backwards away from the wreck. Dylan and Alexander were already running for the red Commodore. Greg slid into the car as the rest of the threes drew to within twenty yards. Evelyn took off, accelerating past the other car. Dylan landed in the driver's seat with a crunch and jabbed the gun into Lauren's leg. It got caught across the gearstick, and they lost critical time. He snatched it up and laid it across his lap, then burned away, watching the rear-view mirror. He screwed the wheel around, guiding the Commodore through the gap, clipping the edge with a bang.

There was a moment of terror when he thought they would get caught. The crunch and scrape of steel blared, the car bumping and shaking as he pushed the pedal to the floor. Lauren screamed, clutching Harvey to her chest. They slipped through the gap as the upper section of the rubbish pile collapsed, landing where they had been moments ago. The crash of metal and glass on the road was deafening. Dylan held tight, gunning the car forward. In the distance, he saw the brake lights of the other car and chased it.

FIFTY-FIVE

CALLAN STOOD outside the apartment building below the corner of Queen and Franklin Street. A gust of wind blew in, threatening to steal the note from his hand, but he held it tight, repeating the two key words. *Station Pier.* That had been the original plan. That's where the others had gone. Just how long ago Callan couldn't tell. They would have to be quick. He had no idea how to get there, but he had Harlan to direct them, and that would have to be good enough. Callan read Dylan's scribbled note with the sound of a chopper and gunfire violating the peaceful blue sky.

Callan,

If you're reading this note then you've made it. Keep going mate and tell me all about it over a beer. My shout. We're all still alive and we're going to Tasmania, just like my old man said. Gallagher has found a boat. He's going to float us there. Station Pier. I hope you can find the way. Hurry, I'll hold them up as long as I can.

Dylan.

His eyes swelled with tears. He wasn't sure why. Yes he was. They were all alive. Greg, Evelyn, Jake, Dylan, even Gallagher. He hadn't expected it; he had been preparing himself for the worst. This was relief. He supposed they were probably thinking the same thing.

Time was running out though. Perhaps it was the most difficult stage, too. The city was imploding. He sprinted back to the car and yanked the door open. The hinges squealed and creaked. "Station Pier. That's where they've gone. Going to Tasmania."

"What?" Kristy asked. "How?"

"Gallagher found a ship. I knew we went to that goddamn Army base for something." Jacob gave a pained smile. Blue barked once and shifted himself on Kristy's lap.

Harlan guided Callan again, pointing the way as he redirected them to avoid the chaos they had driven through along Queen Street. Kristy had her window down, the 9mm handgun ready if any ventured too close, and Blue stood as stiff as iron on Bec's lap, ready to attack. Cars were their biggest problem, spilling onto the curb, through shop windows, some reduced to black carcasses. Callan wondered where the people had gone. Had they escaped to another part of the world, died of the virus, or been changed into something more gruesome? Some vehicles still had bodies, but most were empty. He guessed what had happened to those who had fled.

More type threes appeared as they drove parallel to Queen Street. Beyond the buildings, they heard continuous gunfire. *The buildings,* Callan thought. *They were coming from inside the buildings.* They gathered behind the Camry as they edged their way through the streets. It struck Callan then. This was what the man at Yass was talking about. There was so few type ones left because they'd been changed into threes.

Callan had planned to go right at the next intersection and link up with the lower end of Queen Street, but it was a jam fest, and they couldn't get through. Half a dozen now windowless cars had met in the middle, spreading glass over the road. As he negotiated the gaps, Callan peered down the adjacent road.

"Oh Jesus, what is that?" Jacob asked. Callan stopped in the middle of the intersection.

Swarming up over the next hill through the traffic like a plague of mice were hundreds of type threes. It was the scariest thing Callan had ever seen.

"Drive," Kristy said, not taking her eyes from the sight. "Drive, please."

Callan did, scraping the sides of the vehicle as he forced his way through traffic. They passed the melee, screaming down the road between tall buildings on both sides of the street from which more type threes poured.

He would be astonished if they survived this. They had faced their share of danger, of nemesis, but a mass of pursuing type threes was more than anything they'd encountered before. If any luck remained, they would need every piece of it to make the pier.

The sound of a chopper floated to them. The same sound they'd heard the previous day, but this time it was much closer. A dark shape materialized from behind a skyscraper. It *was* a chopper—a green Army helicopter marked with the Australian Defence Force badge and flag. Instinctively, Callan flashed the headlights. "Yes!" Confirmation meant so many things. They still had an Army, maybe even a government somewhere, working to get the country back on its feet.

They'd made good pace as the chopper flew above them. Callan kept glancing at the mirrors, searching for the threes that had been moving along the other road. They reached another junction, this one clearer, with squat buildings on all corners. The chopper circled overhead, dropping in altitude as they passed through.

"I think it's going to land behind us," Bec said. Callan drove around the back end of an abandoned fuel truck and stopped on the other side of the juncture to watch.

Were they going to land? It was too risky with the threes running loose. But it dropped, the noise and gust mounting as heavily armed men squatted in the doorways, poised to leap out.

The first trickle of the threes reached the intersection, hanging back at the edge of the traffic jam as though preparing a covert attack. Could the chopper pilot see them? Callan saw a terrible situation unfolding.

"We need to leave," Kristy said.

"Wait."

The chopper touched down as the blades cleared the ground of loose debris. One of the Army men waved at Callan and the group, then signaled with a palm for them to stay put. The others located the hidden threes between the abandoned vehicles and began firing, the chatter of their fully automatic weapons heard over the helicopter blades. Two zombies fell out from the hiding spots with chunks of their torso and head missing. But others took their places and then several ran at the helicopter.

"Take off!" Callan screamed.

"We need to go," Kristy said.

He imagined the other threes racing up the slope. Did the Army people know about the horde? In moments, hundreds would be upon the chopper, and for the six or seven military personnel inside, no amount of weapons could stop them. Glancing around, the pilot sensed their predicament, signaling a take-off. The two men that had stepped out firing slid back onto the platform. On the other side, the first handful of threes reached the chopper and grabbed for the bottom rail. It tilted, and one of the men spilled out. Others arrived—five, then fifteen, twenty, leaping for the railing.

"Go!" Kristy screamed.

They had to leave. Callan took off, feeling helpless, watching the mirror as a swarm of threes reached the chopper and took hold of the rails. The men fired, cutting many apart, but fresh ones replaced the dead, angrier, and more intent on bringing it down. The chopper tilted sharply. Callan turned away. Moments later, the explosion shook the ground, shaking the coins in the ashtray.

They drove on.

FIFTY-SIX

DYLAN REMEMBERED the way to Station Pier and they made good time, leaving the bulk of the threes behind. They turned right onto City Road, following it through South Melbourne and into Bay Street, Port Melbourne, before hitting Beach Street and following the road into Waterfront Place. That took them up to the parking lot at Station Pier, surrounded by a precinct of cafés and restaurants where Lauren had brought them once on a trip down from Albury. The food had been spectacular.

Dylan spotted the ship from the roadway. He cut left onto the parking lot and tried to drive right onto the docks, but a mess of cars barred their way. They would have to walk the last bit.

"Let's keep moving. I've got a bad feeling there might be more of them on the way." Dylan hurried to the trunk and handed packs to Alexander, Claire, and Kristy. He hoped the ship had plenty of food because they hadn't brought much. The other car pulled up beside them—Greg, Evelyn, Jake, Sarah, and Julie. There should have been more. Out of all the people they had met, it should have been so many more.

"Thanks," Greg said. "We owe you... another one."

"It all evens out, believe me."

Deeper in the city, the growl of a thousand voices sounded. *God help anyone caught in that,* Dylan thought. Maybe their friends were in it, racing to meet them. He had given up on Callan and Blue Boy, though, and partly grieved for Kristy, as he had for their parents. Maybe one day when it all settled down, he would purge the rest and deal with the death of his loved ones, as most of them would need to do.

The others slung as much gear as possible onto their shoulders, and trudged onward. The walk was only a few hundred yards and, as they drew closer to the building, Dylan saw a plank leading from the upper level onto the ship. Gallagher stood at the edge of the vessel, signaling for them to go through the doorway. Dylan felt an overwhelming sense of relief that Gallagher was still alive, and they had made it.

They hurried in through a set of glass doors, past a reception area and counter, tables and chairs, beyond where people ate lunch and watched the docking ships. A set of stairs beckoned and they climbed, Greg leading the way, Dylan standing at the bottom as the others passed him.

The next level contained a series of desks and queues for incoming and outgoing passengers. The group walked through the rope barriers in silence, eager to reach the ship and be done with the mainland before the mainland was done with them. Outside, a platform led to the gangway, and on the other side, standing on the ship, was Gallagher.

The admiral looked beaten and bloody. He fought some off-screen battle and might not even last much longer. His eyes and nostrils were inflamed, scleras bloodshot, the lids and surrounding tissue, red. His nose was tender underneath, and as if to confirm it, he wiped it on the sleeve of his shirt. But he was still standing; Dylan had not been expecting that. The serum wasn't working and he might not be alive next week, but he had made a commitment to get them to Tasmania.

"We have to leave," Gallagher croaked.

"We can't yet," Dylan said. "We need to give the others more time."

Gallagher drew a pair of binoculars up to his eyes. "No time. If those bastards get here from the city and latch onto this ship, we're finished. I've already had to kill half a dozen of the crew. They'd locked themselves on the boat."

341

"Please. Give them five minutes?" There was a long, terrifying moment where Dylan thought he was going to ignore the question.

"The engines are primed. We're ready to move. I can't sit here for too long, it's wasting fuel. Five. That's it. Any more and we'll die too."

FIFTY-SEVEN

THEY REACHED the pier as the afternoon sun peaked, blazing down on the sea with blinding intensity. The heat cooked a million corpses and drove the sweat from the skin of those still alive as though they wept. There was no air conditioning, only the hot, fetid wind of a scorching summer blowing through the windows, permeating their hair and skin with a smell they might never wash free. Still, as they pulled into the Station Pier car park, Callan found before them a sight that was both amazing and horrific.

After leaving the site of the fallen chopper, Callan had demanded Harlan tell him another route. He was afraid the threes would chase them. Harlan had argued the direct course down Queen Street would be the fastest, but Callan had insisted. His gut instinct had served him effectively more than once, and he wasn't going to abandon it now. Reluctantly, Harlan revealed a number of alternates.

They fought on through the incessant traffic jam for more than a third of the way, along cluttered pavements outside battered shopfronts, across tram tracks, and even through a glass tram stop at one point. They smashed the headlights and indicator lights, cracked the windscreen driving too close to an overturned four-wheel drive with a pipe sticking out of the engine, and had lost both side mirrors before the third turn. Type ones stumbled into their path, slapped the windows when the Camry missed a gap or slowed for a sharp bend, and, in one case, dived off the top of a bus in front of them. But it was the threes who scared Callan shitless. They had the devil in their black eyes, the invisible fires of hell beyond the darkness. They watched from the windows of buildings, from the shadows of doorways, and in the bright sunlight, they moved with the super speed. He couldn't stop thinking about what the man in the supermarket at Yass had said: they talk with their minds. There were fewer of them on the alternate journey, but Callan knew that until they were sailing across Bass Strait on that damn boat, they weren't safe. And now, as their journey from Albury reached the final stage, they were coming. The question was whether they could outrun them.

That question had now been answered with a shattering response. The big boat was moving away from the pier. Callan strained his eyes to make sure. *They wouldn't.* Even from the distance though, he knew it was.

It didn't matter. He wasn't giving up. They would make it to the edge of the dock even if the ship had left without them, but they must hurry. Harlan was struck with the virus, but he could run. Jacob would have to risk it. If not, it wouldn't matter, he'd be dead soon. Callan drove forward, smashing through a blockage of cars, halting them with a loud scrape of metal.

He twisted around and peered through the back window. Shadows along the esplanade shifted and undulated, like a crowd at a rock show jumping to the beat.

"Out!" he screamed. The Camry would go no further; too many cars blocking the way. "We have to run for the pier. Grab what you can."

"The boat's gone!" Bec cried.

"NOW!"

They tumbled out of Harlan's tiny vehicle, Callan guiding Kristy and Bec to the front, helping Harlan and Jacob from the back. The older man went easier, shuffling his feet decked in brown loafers, but Jacob was another matter. He leaned across the seat and tried to swing his legs around, but they caught in the foot well. His tanned face strained, turning it a bronzy red. Finally, he got free and stumbled from the car.

Blue Boy ran towards the horde, barking and growling. "Blue! This way!" Callan screamed.

He wanted to scream a lot more. Bec was right; the boat was gone. They'd run out of time. What had they thought— that Callan and the others had died? That they'd given up? *Of course, you fool.* They didn't know Kristy was alive; didn't know that they had found more people. What if he ran for the dock and tried to signal them to stop? He wouldn't make it, and neither would the others.

He jogged ahead a short way, Kristy and Bec trying to keep up. He wanted them to move faster, but the heat and the pressure were too much. They ran through the far end of the car park, over lawns that would never again be mowed, and through an untamed garden beneath a row of three drab palm trees. Callan crossed a narrow road and then a short bridge over a causeway. Technically, he was on the pier, but the others weren't. He turned back, fighting the urge to scream for them to move faster. Blue Boy jogged past. Kristy reached him, panting, her beetroot face begging forgiveness. *Sorry, I've got nothing left.* Harlan was next, a way behind, suddenly looking sicker than Callan recalled in the Camry. Callan wanted to tell him it would be all right. He wanted to say they had the medicine and it would not make the disease any worse, but he couldn't, because the medicine was floating away with their friends and their hopes and dreams for a safer life. He had failed. And Callan knew that what was coming for them was a death beyond comprehension. Jacob was still a long way back. Bec ran at his side. He had given it everything, but the bullet wound and blood loss had zapped him of life.

Beyond Jacob was a sight worse than his nightmares. The zombie horde raced along the shoreline road towards them en masse. They ran in a pack like an army of ants he had once uncovered beneath a sheet of corrugated tin up in the dirt at the back of the property. Now, it was the same thing, only these monsters were once people that had become enraged with strength and psychosis and the insatiable need to eat human flesh.

Jacob and Bec staggered past him. Blue Boy rounded them up, like the cattle dog he was, filling Callan with an affection he couldn't put into words. Callan ran after them. "Come on. Not far." Bec smiled through tears. She knew what was going to happen. Jacob wore a perpetual mask of pain. "We might have to go for a swim."

Kristy stood where the boat had earlier been moored, ropes thicker than Callan's thighs hanging over the edge. She had discarded her supplies and begun loading a rifle. The others stopped at her side, dropped their bags, and peered out at the ship, now more than four hundred yards away. They were done. It was official: he had finally failed.

Jacob groaned and fell to the ground. Bec fell to her knees at his side. "Please don't die. *Please.*" His skin was grey and washed out. One arm fell off his stomach and onto the pier. Bec sobbed, pinching her eyes shut. Tears spilled down her cheeks. "You've still got to get that CD for me… the Beatles. *The White Album.* You owe me. You promised." Jacob lifted his arm and Bec took it, holding his palm to her chest. "Dad?" She wiped her eyes with the back of her hand. "Dad?" Callan had never heard her call him that. Jacob came awake. "You can call me Bec, okay? I want you to call me that from now on."

He smiled. "Okay." His voice was dry and cracked. "I'd like that… very much." He pulled Bec to the left side of his chest where she lay, sobbing.

Callan pulled the handgun from his waistband and dropped the empty cartridge onto the concrete with a clunk.

He slotted another into the pistol with a click and counted how many more in the pack. Ten. He spied a second handgun; removed it, and loaded that, heart racing, full of a primal urge to defend his people. He would take these motherfuckers head on and they would feel his wrath for all his friends that had died, and those who would soon join them.

The swarm reached the café and restaurant at the end of the pier, their burning eyes and hungry mouths screaming. It sounded like a train, the loudest thing Callan had ever heard. He moved away from the group standing at the edge of the dock: Jacob lying with Bec, Harlan on Kristy, Blue sitting patiently in waiting. They were sick, bloody, and beaten. He had been expecting this day; sooner or later, he had known it would come. He began walking down the pier towards them. Blue ran up to him and trotted by his side, looking up with those adoring eyes. They would face death together, he and his little mate, and Callan would have it no other way.

FIFTY-EIGHT

DYLAN HUNG over the edge of the railing at the port side of the boat as it drifted away from the pier. He watched the gap of water open up with the docks as the ship swung around, leaving Melbourne behind forever. Several columns of smoke rose in sooty plumes from the city. The wind picked up, and on it, he heard the distant howl of the breeze. There were no more choppers. No more Army. He wondered what had happened to it all—the government, the police, the military. He supposed it didn't matter anymore. What was done was done.

It was bittersweet, of course. He still had his sister, and they were on their way to Tasmania, a place that promised safety, and refuge, but they had lost so much—Kristy and Callan, and Blue too, along with almost everyone else. Whilst he hadn't expected Callan to show up at the last moment, part of him had hoped, and with the disappearance of that hope, a deep ache in the pit of his stomach remained. He tried to push it away, as he had done with his mother and father, but this was different. They had shared things beyond the realms of normality—life-changing moments, each saving the other countless times. He wished he had paid them back. He wished he had taken the opportunity to tell them that he loved them—Kristy again, and Callan, his brother for the first time.

He looked out at the horizon of the land, noting movement along the esplanade. His eyes seemed to have deteriorated over the last few weeks, probably from all the smoke and dirt he had peered through. He couldn't remember his last good wash. He squinted into the sun. Was that—*Yes*. Threes. A mass of them moving along the shoreline towards the pier. *Jesus*, they had been lucky to leave when they did.

Lauren came up beside him, holding the baby. The ship swung the other way, and they walked along the railing, bringing the pier back into view.

"How do you think Gallagher will go?"

Dylan tipped his head either way. "He was an admiral in the Navy once. Said he had commanded large ships, and had handled them in seas worse than this. We don't have much else."

"Is that someone on the pier?" Lauren asked.

"Huh? Where?" He strained hard, scanning the place she had indicated. He saw movement at the far end of the pier. The zombies had almost reached it. "The zombies? There's a shitload of them running along the—"

Lauren's voice was frantic. "No. This way. Closer. The small dots."

His eyes *were* crappy, but eventually he picked up a huddle of dots standing at the edge of the dock. Further on a lone figure walked towards the oncoming horde. He strained his eyes more and... a dog. *Blue Boy*. He tried to speak, but his parched throat failed. "Oh fuck... oh fuck... oh fuck."

"It's them!" Lauren screamed. "Oh Jesus, Dylan, we've left them behind."

Dylan stumbled backwards, not taking his eyes off the distant pier. He ran back towards the deck. They had to turn around. They had to go back for them. "GALLAGHER!" he screamed, grabbing hold of the metal rail of the stairs. "GALLAGHER! WE HAVE TO TURN AROUND!"

THE END

Authors Note

You made it. I hope it was worth the effort. I am grateful for your time, and interest, knowing how far you've come. I'm sorry about the cliffhanger, but I avoided them in the first two books so thought it was about time... I wrote at the end of book two about my plans to take the story away from this group of characters. More on that in a moment.

This book was a tale of two parts. I finished a short, haphazard first draft in record time. But there it sat for almost a month as I climbed Mount Daunting, knowing how much work I still had to do, how many plot holes, meaningless characters, and ridiculous scenes still existed. I wondered how the hell I was going to get the novel into an acceptable state to carry on the story. I realized around the third week of October that if I didn't get to work on a serious basis, I would miss my early December editing deadline and Christmas publishing date.

Thankfully, I got there. As challenging as it was, I had fun, and the more I read and reread the story, cutting, adding and polishing, the better I felt about it. I *could* take a shambling mess and turn it into something respectable.

Hopefully you're able to leave a review for this book on Amazon, and my thanks to those that have done so for the other books. It doesn't have to be a story, just a sentence or two about what you liked (or disliked). Right or wrong, people purchase based on the number of reviews a book has, so the more reviews, the greater chance of it getting into a new reader's hands. And for an Indi writer, that is everything, because we don't have the large money it takes to promote our work the way a publishing house does. Click here to leave a review for Escape.

Now, onto the fourth book ...

At the end of Survival I said I'd be switching to another location to follow a different "group" of survivors for the following three books. Hmmm... seems kind of mean given the cliffhanger for this book. I've got to think seriously about how I proceed here. At the very least I think I will tie up the fate of our intrepid group at the beginning of the next book.

I've also had another idea, which happens from time to time when I shake my head hard enough. *I* know what happens, but if anyone is interested, e-mail me about how you think the group will get out of the situation. Will the boat even turn around? Will anyone perish? What will happen in the next scene? Just a couple of lines about what might happen. The closest will receive a signed (or not, if you choose) paperback copy of the next book. I'll release the winner on my website after the new book comes out or maybe as a teaser beforehand.

For now, I need to finish a couple of books separate to this series, but I'll make an effort to get book four out as fast as possible.

If you haven't signed up to my mailing list, feel free to do so. It generally covers new book releases and every so often I do a giveaway of paperbacks from the series. **Click here to sign up.** Your e-mail address will never be shared and you can unsubscribe easily at any time.

Reader engagement is one of the best parts about writing books. As always, I'd love to hear what you thought about the story, good or bad, what else you're reading, or about any authors you're enjoying. I received lots of feedback via e-mail on the first two books and coming home from work to find reader comments in my inbox is always a pleasure. You can e-mail me at **owen.baillie@bigpond.com**.

Here are some of my links to social media; there are so many these days it's hard to keep up. I try to vary the content on each:

Facebook: **Owen Baillie Author** or **Owen Baillie**
Facebook: **Invasion of the Dead**

Website: **owenbaillie.com**

So before my author's note becomes a novel of its own, I'll wrap it up.

Thanks for reading,

Owen
Melbourne, Australia, December 2014.

OTHER AUTHORS UNDER THE SHIELD OF

DEAD ISLAND: Operation Zulu

Ten years after the world was nearly brought to its knees by a zombie Armageddon, there is a race for the antidote! On a remote Caribbean island, surrounded by a horde of hungry living dead, a team of American and Australian commandos must rescue the Antidotes' scientist. Filled with zombies, guns, Russian bad guys, shady government types, serial killers, and elevator muzak. Dead Island is an action packed blood soaked horror adventure.

Allen Gamboa

SIXTH CYCLE

Nuclear war has destroyed human civilization. Captain Jake Phillips wakes into a dangerous new world, where he finds the remaining fragments of the population living in a series of strongholds, connected across the country. Uneasy alliances have maintained their safety, but things are about to change. -- **Discovery leads to danger.** -- Skye Reed, a tracker from the Omega stronghold, uncovers a threat that could spell the end for their fragile society. With friends and enemies revealing truths about the past, she will need to decide who to trust. -- **Sixth Cycle** is a gritty post-apocalyptic story of survival and adventure.

Darren Wearmouth ~ Carl Sinclair

SPLINTER

For close to a thousand years they waited, waited for the old knowledge to fade away into the mists of myth. They waited for a re-birth of the time of legend for the time when demons ruled and man was the fodder upon which they fed.

They waited for the time when the old gods die and something new was anxious to take their place. **A young couple was all that stood between humanity and annihilation**. Ill equipped and shocked by the horrors thrust upon them they would fight in the only way they knew how, tooth and nail. Would they be enough to prevent the creation of the feasting hordes? Were they alone able to stand against evil banished from hell? **Would the horsemen ride when humanity failed?** The earth would rue the day a splinter group set up shop in Cold Spring.

H. J. Harry

WHISKEY TANGO FOXTROT SERIES

The world is at war with the Primal Virus. Military forces across the globe have been recalled to defend the homelands as the virus spreads and decimates populations. Out on patrol and assigned to a remote base in Afghanistan, Staff Sergeant Brad Thompson's unit was abandoned and left behind, alone and without contact. They survived and have built a refuge, but now they are forgotten. **No contact with their families or commands**. Brad makes a tough decision to leave the safety of his compound to try and make contact with the States, desperate to find rescue for his men. **What he finds is worse than he could have ever predicted**.

W. J. Lundy

Made in the USA
Coppell, TX
23 June 2020

29111304R00208